ETHAN KAILLE NOVELS BY D.B. JACKSON
FROM TOR BOOKS

Thieftaker

Thieves' Quarry

A Plunder of Souls (forthcoming)

THIEVES'
QUARRY

D. B. Jackson

TOR®
fantasy

A TOM DOHERTY ASSOCIATES BOOK
NEW YORK

This is a work of fiction. All of the characters, organizations, and events portrayed in this novel are either products of the author's imagination or are used fictitiously.

THIEVES' QUARRY

Copyright © 2013 by D. B. Jackson

All rights reserved.

Map reproduction courtesy of the Norman B. Leventhal Map Center at the Boston Public Library

Edited by James Frenkel

A Tor Book
Published by Tom Doherty Associates, LLC
175 Fifth Avenue
New York, NY 10010

www.tor-forge.com

Tor® is a registered trademark of Tom Doherty Associates, LLC.

ISBN 978-0-7653-6607-8

Tor books may be purchased for educational, business, or promotional use. For information on bulk purchases, please contact Macmillan Corporate and Premium Sales Department at 1-800-221-7945, extension 5442, or write specialmarkets@macmillan.com.

First Edition: July 2013
First Mass Market Edition: June 2014

Printed in the United States of America

0 9 8 7 6 5 4 3 2 1

For Lucienne Diver,
with deepest thanks for her advice,
encouragement, and friendship

A PLAN of
THE TOWN of BOSTON

all this Part is dry at Low Water

THE

South Battery

References to the Town.

A Dover Church
B Old North Meeting
C Anabaptists Meeting
D Funnel Hall
E Town Hall
F Old Meeting
G Prison & Court House
H Kings Chapel
I Work House
K Granary Publk
L Province House (Governor's lodge)
M Old South Meeting (the Riding House)
N Trinity Church
O Newsouth Meeting
P Hollis Meeting
Q West Meeting

Scale of Yards.

One or Half a Mile.

Dry at Low water, except to the Mid Channel

THIEVES' QUARRY

Boston, Province of Massachusetts Bay,
September 28, 1768

He heard the man's footsteps first, boot heels clicking on the cobblestone street leading toward Clarke's Shipyard. A moment later, Tanner came into view, a bulky shadow against the faint, distant glow of the comfortable homes of Boston's North End. He walked with purpose, his hands buried in his pockets. Every few strides, he glanced back over his shoulder.

Tanner passed Ethan Kaille without noticing him, though Ethan stood just off the lane, so close that he could have grabbed the man's arm as he hurried past. With the concealment spell Ethan had placed on himself a few minutes earlier he could have planted himself in the middle of the street and Tanner would have collided with him before realizing he was there. Still, Ethan breathed into the crook of his arm, so as not to give himself away with a puff of vapor in the cool autumn air.

He watched as the man walked onto the wharf and crept past the first of the shipyard warehouses. Tanner moved with more caution now, his steps on the gravel and dirt fill of the wharf nearly lost amid the sound of small waves as they slapped against ships' hulls and lapped at the timbers of the pier.

The moon, a night or two past full, hung low in the east, like some great, lidded red eye. Its reflection wavered on the smooth waters of Boston Harbor, casting just enough light for Ethan to mark Tanner's progress as the thief slipped from shadow to shadow.

Somewhere out on the wharf, amid the warehouses, Tanner had hidden a small package containing several gold watches that he had pinched from a watchmaker named Charles Short. All told, they probably were worth five times the ten pounds Short was paying Ethan to recover them. But Ethan tried not to think about that. A thieftaker's reputation depended not only on his cunning, not only on his prowess with a blade or his brawn, or, in Ethan's case, his skill as a conjurer, but also on his honesty.

Unless that thieftaker happened to be Sephira Pryce. But he tried not to think about her, either.

Ethan had been working this job for the better part of a month, watching the wharves, learning what he could of the men and women who unloaded trading ships when they arrived in Boston, even making inquiries with merchants and wharfmen about the captains of the various vessels. He had gone so far as to enlist the help of his old friend Diver—Devren Jervis—who worked the wharves when he wasn't involving himself in more questionable business opportunities in the city streets. Diver had been watching his fellow wharfmen on Ethan's behalf, looking for odd behavior or signs that one or more of them had come into some coin in recent days. It hadn't taken Diver long to settle on Tanner.

"He's not wearing jewels on his fingers, or anything like that," Diver had told Ethan two nights before as they sat in the Dowsing Rod, the tavern they frequented, which was located on Sudbury Street on the edge of New Boston, as the west end of the city was known. "But he's acting strangely just the same. Like he's hiding something. I think he's got those watches hidden away somewhere out there on one of the wharves. Or Clarke's

Shipyard. That's where he works, you know." He had paused then, sipping his ale and eyeing Ethan slyly over the rim of his cup. "So how much is Short paying you?"

Ethan had laughed. "Ten pounds. And if you're right about Tanner, four of them are yours."

It was more than he usually would have paid for such information, but he and Diver had known each other for a good many years, almost since the day, more than two decades before, when Ethan first arrived in Boston. Diver had only been a boy, but he had become Ethan's first friend in the city. He had known that Ethan was a conjurer—a speller, as his kind were called in the streets—for longer than anyone alive other than Ethan's sisters. And Ethan's work had gone well in recent months. He could afford to be generous.

After speaking with Diver, Ethan too had begun to watch Tanner, observing him from a distance as the man worked the shipyard, and following him through the narrow alleys of the South End to a small, run-down tavern where he spent most of his evenings. The thief was easy to spot: brawny and tall, mustached and fair-haired. He spoke with a faint Cornish accent, and he had a raucous laugh that frequently punctuated his own jokes.

It had taken Ethan only a couple of days to decide that Diver had to be right. Tanner was their man. The Cornishman had returned to the shipyard warehouses several nights running, each time arriving after midnight, skulking through shadows, and crawling on his hands and knees out near the end of the pier. He had also met with a number of men whom Ethan knew to be fences. But thus far, Ethan had yet to see Tanner exchange money or goods with any of them. And, on the one occasion when Ethan managed to get onto the wharf unseen and search for the watches himself, he found nothing.

That was why he had come tonight. He had guessed that Tanner would return to the shipyard yet again, and this time he intended to confront the thief while he had the watches on his person. As Tanner continued along the side of the warehouses, Ethan eased onto Ship Street and began to make his way toward the wharf, still concealed by the spell.

Out on Boston Harbor, in the distance and to the south of where Ethan walked, lights bobbed on the gentle swells: lanterns burning on a dozen or more British naval ships. Several of the vessels had been anchored within sight of the city for a week or more; eight others had sailed into view earlier this day. They were arrayed in a loose, broad arc, their reflections dancing and swirling like fireflies. They might have been beautiful had it not been for what they signified: more strife and fear for a city already beleaguered by its conflicts with the Crown.

But these were worries for another time. Tonight, Ethan had business with Christian Tanner.

He stole toward the wharf, placing his feet with the stealth of a housebreaker, peering into the shadows, trying to keep track of the thief. Before he had gotten far, however, he heard raised voices. A man cried out and was abruptly silenced. An instant later something—or someone—fell to the ground with a heavy thud. A torch was lit on the merchant ship nearest the end of the wharf, and then another.

Ethan started running toward the commotion, but halted at the sound of an all-too-familiar voice. It was that of a woman, low and gravelly, so she sounded as though she was purring as she spoke. Except that her words didn't match her alluring tone.

". . . Not very clever, Tanner," Sephira Pryce said. "Mister Short isn't pleased, and that means that I'm not pleased either. You're new here in Boston, but that doesn't excuse what you've done." She stood over the man, and even from a distance, even in the flickering light of the torches held by her toughs, Ethan could see that she looked lovely. Black curls cascaded down her back, shining with torchfire, and her breeches and the tight-fitting indigo waistcoat she wore accentuated the generous, perfect curves of her body. "When you come to a new city you should inquire of those who are familiar with its customs and its habits. You should find out who to avoid angering, and who to avoid altogether. Wouldn't you agree, Ethan?"

This last she pitched to carry.

Tanner, who was on his knees at her feet, bleeding from his mouth and nose and from a dark gash on his temple, looked around and licked his bloodied lips.

"Come now, Ethan," Sephira called, a smug smile on her perfect face. "Don't be shy."

Ethan rubbed a hand over his face and cursed under his breath. She had done this to him before, swooped in on one of his jobs at the last moment to rob him of the goods he hoped to recover, and thus of his payment. She knew the streets of Boston the way a merchant captain knew the Atlantic coastline. She had cultivated friendships with nearly every useful person in the province, from the king's commissioners on the Customs Board to Boston's most successful merchants, from the city's barkeeps and street peddlers to its most violent criminals. Most often, Ethan's jobs were too small to draw her notice. But on occasion, one of Boston's wealthier citizens hired him to recover something of value, arousing Sephira's interest in his work. It had happened three years before, when Ethan was hired to find the killer of Jennifer Berson, the daughter of Abner Berson, one of the city's most prosperous merchants, and again sixteen months ago, when Ethan was asked to recover goods stolen from one of the city's wealthier shopkeepers. And it seemed it had happened once more with this job.

Charles Short's wares might not have been the best in the city, but gold watches were enough to entice Sephira no matter who made them. Ethan had known this from the start; from the day Short hired him, he had expected her to be watching his every move, looking for some way to find the watches first. But he had been so careful; he had been sure that this time, at least, he had bested her.

"Show yourself, Kaille," she said, her voice hardening. "I want to see the look on your face."

On more than one occasion, Sephira and her men had come close to killing him. She was brilliant and deadly and her toughs were skilled street fighters, as good with blades as with pistols, and skilled with their fists as well. But as long as Ethan could conjure he could protect himself. He hesitated to answer her, but not out of fear: rather because he didn't care to be mocked.

"There's no sense in sulking. I've beaten you. Again. I would have thought you'd be used to it by now."

Cursing a second time, Ethan pulled his knife from its sheath on his belt, cut his forearm and whispered in Latin, "*Fini velamentum ex cruore evocatum.*" End concealment, conjured from blood.

Power coursed through his body and hummed in the ground beneath his feet, deep and resonant, like the tone of a pealing church bell. At the same time, a radiant figure appeared beside him: an old man, tall and lean, with a trim beard and the dark expression of a warrior. He wore ancient battle armor and the tabard of a medieval British soldier. He even carried a sword in a scabbard on his belt. He glowed with a deep russet hue, nearly a match for the color of the moon, except for his eyes, which burned bright like brands. This was Ethan's spectral guide, who allowed him to access the conjuring power that dwelt in the realm between the living world and the domain of the dead. Ethan had long suspected that his guide was also the wraith of one of his ancient ancestors, a link to his family's conjuring past. He called the ghost Uncle Reg, after his mother's oldest brother, a waspish, difficult man of whom the shade often reminded him.

The blood that had been flowing from the fresh wound on Ethan's arm vanished, and he felt the concealment spell begin to fade. Because Sephira wasn't a conjurer she wouldn't have felt the spell as Ethan did. But as soon as Ethan took another step on the wharf, she saw him. Her gaze settled on his face, and a broad predatory smile lit her features.

"There you are," she purred.

Her men, including a hulking, yellow-haired ruffian named Nigel, turned as one and started toward him. Nigel pulled a pistol from his coat pocket.

Ethan raised his knife to his forearm again. The toughs halted.

Ethan wasn't tall like Yellow-hair or broad in the shoulders and chest like Tanner. Those who had fought him in the past, as Sephira's men had, knew that he could handle a blade, either short or long, and that he could fight with his fists if he had to. But no one would have been afraid of him because of how he looked. His face bore a few scars, and his long hair had begun to gray at the temples. While serving time as a prisoner on a plantation in Barbados, he had lost three toes on his left foot to gangrene, and ever since, he had walked with a pronounced limp.

It was the threat of his spellmaking that made Yellow-hair and the others falter. They stared at his knife the way a child might gape at a rabid cur on an otherwise deserted lane. Even Tanner regarded him with alarm. Only Sephira appeared unconcerned. Actually, she looked bored.

"Leave him," she said in a low voice.

Nigel and his friends glanced back at her, all wearing frowns.

"We're not going to touch him," she said. "And he's not going to do anything to us. Isn't that right, Ethan?"

God knew he wanted to. He could cast a hundred spells, from simple illusions that would scare Yellow-hair into diving off the pier, to complicated, violent conjurings that would kill all of them. With a bit of blood and a few well-chosen words he could have snapped Sephira's neck or set her men on fire. But Sephira had powerful friends, and as much as he hated her, he wasn't willing to hang for her murder or return to the horrors of prison.

"I don't want to hurt anyone," Ethan said at last, forcing a grin onto his lips. "Just give me what's mine and I'll be on my way."

She laughed. He had to admit that it was a good laugh: throaty, unrestrained. Had it not been directed at him, he might have liked the sound of it.

"Nothing here is yours," she told him.

He pointed at the sack she held in her hand. "Those watches—"

"Are mine." She handed the watches to Nigel. "You can try to take them, but I think we both know how that will turn out."

Ethan's eyes flicked toward Yellow-hair, who smirked back at him. If he could have taken the watches from her with a conjuring he would have done so, but the power he wielded didn't work that way. He could hurt her, make her drop the package. He could make the wharf collapse beneath her. He could even grind the watches to dust, rendering them worthless—this last was quite tempting. But he couldn't make them leave her hand and appear in his own. If he wanted them, he would have to try to take them from her, and she was right: That might not work out well for him.

Ten pounds wasn't enough to justify risking his life or his freedom. Diver might have disagreed, but Diver was young, reckless. Ethan lowered his blade.

"Good boy," Sephira said, sounding like she was speaking to a wayward puppy.

"How did you know?" Ethan asked, his voice thick.

Her smile was luminous. "You know better than to ask me that."

She motioned for Nigel, and the big man returned to her side, as obedient as a hunting dog. Ethan raised his blade again, making sure both Sephira and Nigel understood that he was ready to conjure at the first sign of a threat.

Sephira leaned closer to her tough and whispered something that Ethan couldn't hear.

"How did you know, Sephira?" Ethan asked again.

"Ask your friend," she said, sparing him a quick glance. "Derrey is it?"

Derrey. Diver. He was known in the streets by both names. Ethan muttered a curse under his breath.

"We're leaving now, Ethan," Sephira said, turning away from Nigel to face him once more. "Good work on this one. You made it very easy for us."

She sauntered his way and then past him, hips swaying. Most of her men followed, including Gordon, a brute of a man, even brawnier than Nigel, and Nap, who was smaller than the others, though no less dangerous with a blade or gun. Ethan still held his knife over his arm, and he racked his brain for some spell that would stop her, allow him to reclaim the watches, and also enable him to make his escape.

But as Sephira walked away, Yellow-hair bent low over Tanner and in one quick motion slashed at the man's throat with a blade Ethan hadn't noticed before. Blood gushed from the wound. Tanner's eyes rolled back into his head and he toppled onto his side. Blood stained the wharf crimson and began to pool at its edge, seeping over the wooden boards to drip into the water below.

Ethan rushed forward, all thoughts of stopping Sephira fleeing his mind. He pushed past Yellow-hair, who merely chuckled. Reaching Tanner, he dropped to his knees.

"*Remedium!*" Ethan said, practically shouting the word. "*Ex cruore evocatum!*" Healing, conjured from blood! Usually a healing spell required that he mark the injured body part with blood. But in this case, blood was everywhere; the air reeked of it.

The wharf beneath him pulsed with power. Uncle Reg appeared again, though he hardly even glanced at Ethan or Tanner. Instead, the wraith stood with his back to them, staring after Sephira. And as the blood disappeared from the wood and dirt, and from Tanner's neck and shirt, the gaping wound began to close. Ethan couldn't tell if he had acted soon enough. Tanner had lost a great deal of blood in just those few seconds.

A part of him wasn't certain why he cared. Tanner meant nothing to him. But if Sephira wanted him dead, Ethan would do all he could to keep him alive.

At first, even after the gash had healed itself, Tanner didn't move. But leaning close to the man's face, Ethan felt a slight stirring of breath. He grabbed Tanner's wrist and felt for a pulse. Also faint, but unmistakable. Ethan sat back on his heels, and took a long breath. After what seemed like years, Tanner's eyes fluttered open.

Ethan cut himself once more and drew forth a bright light that hovered over them like a tiny sun.

"You're a . . . a conjurer!" Tanner said, trying to scramble away from him, although he was too weak to go far.

"Aye, I'm a conjurer. I just saved your life with a spell."

The man's hand strayed to his throat, his fingers probing the raw scar left by Nigel's blade. "Why?" he asked.

Ethan shrugged. "I don't know. Don't make me regret it."

With some effort, Tanner sat up. His arms trembled and his skin looked pasty. "Is she gone?"

"Aye," Ethan said. "But you need to leave Boston. If she sees you, she'll try to kill you again, and I might not be around to heal you."

"But—"

"Short—that's the man who owned those watches you stole—he wants you transported as far from these shores as possible. Failing that, he wants you dead. He made that clear when he hired me, and I'd wager every shilling I have that he told Sephira the same thing."

"So . . . so you were goin' to turn me over to the sheriff?"

Ethan made no answer. He didn't always turn in those he was hired to pursue, and he never killed any man unless left with no choice. He had lost too many years of his life to prison and forced labor to send men away for commission of petty crimes. And he had seen too many lives wasted in battles and in the harsh conditions he had endured in his plantation prison to kill for little cause. But he always insisted, under the threat of a painful spell-induced death, that those he captured leave Boston, never to return. The last thing he needed was for word to get around the city that he didn't punish the men he was hired to pursue. He would never be hired as a thieftaker again. He saw no reason to trust Tanner with this information.

"Aye, probably," he finally said. "And Sheriff Greenleaf would have dealt with you harshly. But Sephira took the watches and left me to heal you, so I suppose this is your lucky day."

Tanner's dark eyes narrowed. "Well, then—"

"Don't even think it," Ethan said. "Just leave Boston on the next ship that sails. If you don't, she'll kill you. And if she doesn't, I will."

Ethan climbed to his feet, let the light fade out, and started to limp back along the wharf to the city street. He needed an ale, and it seemed he also needed to have a conversation with Diver.

"I suppose I ought to thank you for savin' me," Tanner called after him.

"Don't bother," Ethan said over his shoulder. "I didn't do it for you."

Chapter TWO

Ethan followed Ship Street to Fish Street and continued along the edge of the North End, skirting the finer neighborhoods. He walked by warehouses and darkened storefronts, past Paul Revere's Silver Shop and the Hancock Wharf. The moon cast his shadow, long and haloed, across locked doors and clapboard façades. The air was cool and dry, laden with the smells of brine and fish, burning wood and ships' tar. After crossing over Mill Creek, he followed Ann Street as it turned away from the harbor and met Union.

Two men of the night watch stood at the far corner, speaking in low voices, one of them chuckling at some jest Ethan didn't hear. There was no established constabulary in Boston, and for now at least, there were no British regulars patrolling the streets. Men of the watch were expected to guard the citizens of Boston and their property from lawbreakers. And when they failed, which they did with some frequency, one of Boston's thieftakers—in most cases, Sephira Pryce or Ethan—was hired to recover the stolen items. The sheriff of Suffolk County, Stephen Greenleaf, bore some responsibility for keeping the peace as well, though he was but one man, with no soldiers or guards under his immediate authority.

The long and short of it was that even with several hundred British soldiers aboard ships in the waters off the city's shores, Boston remained a lawless city. Some of the men who served the watch were honest and competent; others were not. A few worked for Sephira Pryce, and took advantage of their time on the watch by robbing empty homes, so that Sephira could return the stolen items to their rightful owners, for a substantial fee, of course.

He didn't recognize either of these watchmen. This didn't mean necessarily that they worked for Sephira, but he would have felt better had he known at least one of the two. He kept his head down and his hands in his pockets as he walked past them.

"It's late to be abroad in the streets."

Ethan halted and turned. Both watchmen had stepped forward, their expressions hard. They were young men, one tall and spear-thin, the other shorter and brawnier. Ethan guessed that they both were armed, although they had yet to pull out either pistols or knives.

"Yes, it is," Ethan said. "I'm just on my way to the Dowsing Rod for an ale or two." His voice remained steady, and he met the taller man's gaze, unwilling to let them believe that he feared them.

"I'm less interested in where you're going than in where you've been."

"I'm a thieftaker," Ethan told him. "I was down at the wharves looking for a man who robbed a client."

The tall one continued to regard him like something a dog might drag in off the street, but Ethan could see from the easing of his stance, the slight droop of his shoulders, that this answer had satisfied him. "Find him?"

Ethan shook his head. "I'm afraid not."

"Well, better huntin' next time." The man was already turning away as he said this. The second man continued to watch Ethan, but he made no effort to stop him.

Ethan raised a hand in farewell and continued on toward the tavern, glad to get away with nothing more than a few questions. He cut through Wings Lane, a dark, narrow byway that connected Union and Hanover Streets and turned south toward Sudbury.

Before he reached the next corner, a gray and white dog bounded at him from the shadows between two shops. She ran a tight circle around him, her tongue hanging out, her tail waving wildly.

"Well met, Shelly," Ethan said, stopping to scratch the dog behind her ears.

She licked his hand and fell in stride beside him as he continued toward the Dowser.

Even here, closer to the center of the city, the streets were mostly deserted. On most nights as clear as this one, even this late, there would have been at least a few people walking the lanes, a chaise or two rattling past. But the arrival of the king's warships in Boston Harbor seemed to have brought a deeper chill to this autumn night.

Reaching the Dowsing Rod, Ethan gave Shelly one last scratching and a pat on the head. "Good night, Shelly," he said, and stepped inside.

The great room of the tavern shone with candles. The warm air was tinged with the pungent bitterness of spermaceti candles, the sweet scent of pipe smoke, the musty smell of ale, and the savory aroma of yet another of Kannice Lester's excellent fish chowders.

Kannice, the Dowser's owner, made the best food found in any of Boston's publick houses and she served good ales at a reasonable price. When Ethan first met her over six years before, she had already inherited the tavern from her husband, who died of smallpox during the outbreak of 1761. A young widow, whose beauty and sharp humor complemented a keen wit and savvy business sense, she had transformed the tavern from a dreary, broken-down haunt for rogues and miscreants into a reputable and profitable establishment. Her rules were simple: No whoring, gambling, or fighting. If you couldn't discuss politics or religion without getting into an argument, you were to take your differences out into the street. And if anything you said or did attracted the notice of the watch or the sheriff, chances were she didn't want you in her tavern.

She relied on her hulking barman, Kelf Fingarin, to keep order and to see to it that no one disobeyed. But Kelf rarely had to do more than serve ale and stew and, on occasion, toss a drunk out into the lane. Kannice was willowy and nearly a foot shorter than Kelf, but most of the time one of her tongue-lashings was enough to tame even the hardest man who set foot in her place.

Ethan stood just inside the door, scanning the tavern for her, but she was nowhere to be seen.

"Hiya Ethan," came a booming voice from behind the bar. Kelf raised a meaty hand in greeting. "You lookin' for Kannice?" he asked, his words coming out in one long quick jumble, as they always did.

"Hi, Kelf," Ethan said, grinning at the huge man and walking to the bar. "She in back?"

Kelf nodded. "Made the chowder tonight. Everyone's favorite. She can barely keep up. I can tell her you're here, though."

"No need. She'll see me soon enough." Ethan dug into his pocket and placed a shilling on the bar. "The Kent pale," he said. "And some chowder when it's ready."

"Right. Diver's in his usual spot." He nodded toward the back of the tavern. "If'n you're lookin' for him."

"My thanks."

The barman handed him a tankard of ale, and Ethan made his way back to Diver's table. The Dowser was crowded and loud this night. Some stood at the bar, eating oysters and drinking ales, while others sat at the tables drinking flips or Madeira wine and supping on Kannice's chowder. But whether at tables or at the bar, few of them greeted Ethan with even so much as a nod. He had been a prisoner, a convicted mutineer; he was known to most as a thieftaker and a rival to Sephira Pryce. A handful of those in the tavern might have known that he was also a conjurer. He had few admirers and fewer friends. Then again, those friends he did have, he trusted.

Diver sat alone, hunched over his ale. But seeing Ethan approach, he sat up, an eager look on his face.

"Well?" he said, as Ethan took a seat across from him.

"Well, what?"

Diver glanced around to make sure that no one would overhear. "Come on, Ethan," he said, lowering his voice. "You know. What happened with Tanner and the watches?"

"Sephira happened," Ethan said, trying hard to keep his tone free of accusation.

Diver's face fell. "What's she got to do with it?"

"She told me to ask you."

"*What?*" His surprise appeared genuine, and Diver wasn't that good a liar. Whatever he had done to tip off Sephira had been unintentional.

"Who have you told about this job?" Ethan asked.

"No one! I swear it!" His eyes were wide, even fearful. He knew better than to think that Ethan would try to exact a measure of revenge. But they had been friends for a long time; Diver looked up to Ethan the way he might to an older brother. The last thing he would have wanted was to fail him on a job, in particular if it meant losing money to Sephira Pryce.

"A girl, maybe?" Ethan asked.

"No." But Ethan could see the doubt in his friend's dark eyes. With Diver, there was always a girl—a different one from fortnight to fortnight, but he was rarely alone. He was tall and handsome, with curly black hair and a smile that could have charmed the queen consort herself.

"What's her name, Diver?"

"She wouldn't have told Sephira," he said, more to himself than to Ethan. "I know she wouldn't."

"Diver?" Ethan said, drawing the young man's gaze once more. "Her name?"

His friend sighed. "Katharine," he said. "Katharine

Chambers. I met her outside Faneuil Hall maybe a month ago. She wouldn't be working for Sephira. She's . . ." He shook his head, perhaps knowing better than to complete the thought aloud.

Ethan had never heard of the girl, but that didn't mean much. "Have you told anyone else about Tanner?" he asked.

Diver shook his head, his expression bleak. "No, no one." He looked Ethan in the eye. "You have my word."

Ethan nodded and took a long pull of ale. "Well," he said wiping his mouth with his hand, "there's nothing to be done about it now. I'd suggest you stay away from her, though."

"So, we don't get anything?" Diver asked.

"This is Sephira we're talking about. It's not like her to share with the other children."

The young man closed his eyes and rubbed his brow with his thumb and forefinger. "I needed that money."

Ethan didn't bother asking why. More often than not, when Diver said it that way he meant, *I've already spent that money.*

They sat in silence for some time. Ethan surveyed the tavern while Diver stared morosely into his empty tankard. Eventually Kannice came out of the kitchen, beckoned to Kelf, and vanished again. Soon after, the two of them reemerged bearing a huge tureen of creamy white stew. The tavern patrons roared their approval, and Kelf began to ladle the chowder into wooden bowls.

Kannice had spotted Ethan and she approached him now, her auburn hair shining in the lamplight, a few stray strands falling over her forehead. Reaching their table, she bent to kiss him lightly on the lips, her hair smelling of lavender, her breath tasting slightly of Irish whiskey.

She bobbed her head toward Diver. "He's been like an eager puppy all night, waiting for you to come in. I'd have thought he'd be happier now that you're finally here."

Ethan shrugged, and flashed a rueful grin. "Yes, well, things didn't go quite as we had hoped."

Diver glanced up at Kannice before looking away again. Kannice tolerated Diver because he was Ethan's friend, but she thought him a reckless fool who brought trouble on himself and on those around him. Ethan found it hard to defend Diver, because Kannice often was right. This night's misadventure was more typical than either Ethan or Diver would care to admit.

Kannice regarded Diver through narrowed eyes and started to say something, but Ethan took her hand and gave it a gentle squeeze. She clamped her mouth shut, and shook her head.

"I take it you're paying for his supper, then," she said, looking at Ethan again.

"I gave Kelf enough to cover both his and mine."

She chuckled, shaking her head a second time. "Fine. I'll leave you boys to work this out yourselves." She kissed the top of Ethan's head. "And I'll deal with you later."

This was Kannice's way of telling Ethan that she wanted him to stay the night with her. They had been lovers for the better part of five years, and though they didn't live together, and though Ethan had made it clear to Kannice that he wasn't the marrying kind, he would have faced down the king's army to keep her safe. Once, there had been another woman in his life: Elli—Marielle—to whom Ethan had been betrothed before his imprisonment. For many years, while serving his sentence on the sugar plantation, and even after his return to Boston, he had mourned the loss of his first love. But more recently that wound had healed. He and Elli remained on civil terms, but Ethan didn't long for her anymore. Today, Ethan was as devoted to Kannice as he had ever been to Elli.

Kannice walked back to where Kelf was ladling out the stew and said something that made the rest of her patrons laugh uproariously. She might have been un-

yielding when it came to her rules, but she could outdrink
a Scottish sea captain and she told jokes that would make
an old sailor blush.

"You're going to tell her what I did, aren't you?"
Diver said, once she was out of earshot.

Ethan took a quick sip of ale to hide his amusement.
"I'll tell her what happened. She'll work out the rest."

"Probably," Diver muttered. "I really am sorry."

"It cost you nearly as much as it did me."

"Aye, but I know how much you hate being bested by
Sephira."

Ethan looked away. Kelf was headed in their direction
carrying two bowls of steaming stew.

"There y'are," the big man said, placing the bowls in
front of them. "Another ale, Diver?"

Diver glanced at Ethan.

"We'll both take another," Ethan said before draining
his tankard and handing it to Kelf.

Once the barkeep had walked away, Diver turned to
Ethan again, a sheepish look on his face. "Ethan—"

"Leave it, Diver. Sephira's men didn't beat me. Sephira
didn't threaten you or Kannice or Elli and her kids. All
she did was take a bit of coin that I'd claimed for myself. It's not worth worrying about."

If anything, the younger man's shoulders drooped
even more after hearing this, but he muttered something
in agreement.

Kelf returned with their ales, and for some time neither man spoke. Ethan watched Kannice as she made
her way around the main room of the tavern, chatting
with her patrons, laughing at their jokes, chastising them
when they spilled their drinks. Now and again her eyes
found Ethan's and she smiled, but for the most part she
left him and Diver to themselves.

"I liked working with you," Diver said at length, pushing his empty bowl to the center of the table. "I liked
being a thieftaker, even if it was just for a little while."

Ethan eyed him. "Did you?"

"Aye," his friend said. "Was I any good at it?"

"You figured out that Tanner was our thief. That took some doing."

Diver beamed. "Does that mean I can help you with another job?"

"I don't know. Can you manage to take a girl to your bed without telling her my business?"

"Of course I can," Diver said, his color rising.

Ethan sat forward. "Are you sure? I'm asking you seriously. There are times when I'll want your help, but after this . . ." He shook his head. "If I'm going to rely on you, I have to know I can trust you."

The younger man held his gaze though Ethan could tell that the words stung. "You can."

Ethan regarded him for another moment. "If you tell me it's so, I believe you. Next time I need help, you'll be the man I turn to."

Diver grinned. "I'm grateful." He hesitated before asking, "What did Sephira do to him?"

"To Tanner, you mean?"

Diver nodded.

"She had one of her toughs cut his throat."

The blood drained from Diver's face. "They killed him?"

"No. She didn't want him dead," he said, knowing as he spoke the words that it was true. "She wanted to distract me. She figured I would save him. And I did, though only just." Ethan regarded his friend. "Do you still want to work with me?"

"Aye," Diver said, though his hand shook as he lifted his ale.

He said something else, but Ethan didn't hear what it was. A man had just entered the Dowser, one Ethan recognized, though at first he couldn't remember from where. His face was sallow and thin, his cheekbones high. He had a wispy beard and mustache, and his wheaten hair, straight and shoulder-length, tied back in a plait, looked almost golden in the dim light of the tavern. He was slight and short, and dressed as he was in a brown coat and matching waistcoat, tan breeches and what appeared to be a silk shirt, he looked like a merchant. But the man also wore silver-rimmed spectacles, and it was these that struck Ethan as familiar. After a few seconds, he realized why. This was one of the men who had met with Tanner, and who Ethan had assumed traded in pilfered goods. Tanner had met the stranger in a tavern in the North End, and the two of them had spoken for nearly an hour. Ethan recalled thinking at the time that this fence had to be new to the city. He felt even more certain of this now. He had never seen him before that day in the North End.

The fence stood near the doorway, surveying the crowd in the tavern, his brow creased, his gaze flitting from face to face. For just an instant the man glanced directly at Ethan, his lenses catching the lamplight so that they appeared opaque. In the next moment he looked away, having given no indication that he had recognized him. As he surveyed the rest of the tavern, though, the stranger's dark eyes widened in recognition. He didn't move right away, continuing instead to survey the room. But Ethan could tell that this was merely for show.

At last he crossed to the bar and slid a coin onto the polished wood. Kelf handed the man an ale, but said nothing to him, and the stranger turned away without a word. Again he made a show of searching for a place to sit, but when he left the bar he walked directly to where whomever he had seen was seated.

Ethan followed the man with his eyes, hoping that he would also catch a glimpse of the stranger's friend. This second person, though, was blocked from Ethan's view by a wooden post. Ethan shifted his chair as subtly as he could, but to no avail.

"Are you even listening to me?" Diver asked, leaning forward to force himself into Ethan's line of sight.

"No, I'm not. A man just walked in—don't turn! I saw him with Tanner about a week ago."

"What was he doing with Tanner?"

"Trying to buy watches, I think."

"Do you think he came here looking for you?"

Ethan shook his head. "No, I'm not sure he ever saw me. But I want to see who he's with." He drained his ale and stood. "Stay here. Don't do anything to draw attention to yourself."

"All right," Diver said.

Ethan walked to the bar, squeezing past a crowd of young wharfmen.

"I woulda brought you another ale," Kelf told him, taking his tankard and refilling it.

"I know. Thank you. I wanted to stretch my legs a bit."

The barman shrugged and handed him the ale.

Ethan took a sip and turned to lean back against the bar, doing his best to appear relaxed and uninterested. He could see the stranger now, though his back was to the room. Sitting across from him, his face shrouded in shadow, was a large man who looked very much like someone Sephira would hire for his brawn. Ethan didn't recognize him. He had dark, straggly hair and a broad, homely face. His nose was crooked and a dark scar ran from the corner of his mouth to his chin, so that his face seemed to wear a perpetual scowl.

The two men sat hunched over the table, their heads close together. The big man didn't seem to be saying much, but he nodded every so often.

After Ethan had watched them for several moments, his curiosity got the better of him. He bit down hard on the inside of his cheek, drawing blood.

Audiam, Ethan said to himself. *Ex cruore evocatum.* Listen, conjured from blood.

He felt the blood in his mouth vanish. Uncle Reg appeared beside him and power thrummed like a plucked string on a lute, making the air in the tavern come alive for the span of a heartbeat. No one standing near Ethan appeared to notice—only someone who conjured would. But the bespectacled man stiffened noticeably.

Ethan felt his blood run cold. The man had sensed his conjuring, and already was turning to look for its source. Biting down on his cheek a second time, he whispered a second spell. *Abi!* Go away! A second pulse made the tavern floor hum. The old ghost shot Ethan a filthy look, and vanished. An instant later the bespectacled man swiveled in his chair, his gaze passing over Ethan.

"What is it?" the big man asked, his voice now reaching Ethan's ears. "Did you hear—?"

But the stranger raised a hand, silencing him as he continued to search the tavern.

Ethan waited until the man had turned to look elsewhere, and made his way back to the table, his eyes fixed on Diver, the hand holding his ale steady. His mind was reeling, though. Whatever else this man was, he was also a speller, or at least someone who had been born to conjuring. Ethan hoped that he wasn't skilled enough with the craft to know what kind of spell Ethan had cast.

"It is nothing," he heard the man say at last, his voice low, the words tinged with a barely discernible accent that Ethan couldn't place at first.

"You was tellin' me about the ship," the big man said.

The bespectacled man didn't respond right away. Ethan assumed that he was still searching the tavern. If Ethan had sensed someone else casting spells near him, that's what he would have done. He regained the table and sat opposite Diver, though he kept his attention on the conversation now echoing in his head.

"Yes, the ship," the man said. Forced to guess, Ethan would have said he came from somewhere on the Iberian Peninsula; Portugal perhaps. "It arrived with the others. I do not know yet when it will dock—it does not matter really. What matters is that he does not find his way into the city."

"Which wharf do you think they'll dock at?"

"I do not believe that will matter either," the man said. "We are to keep him out of the city. The rest is of less importance, but it has been made clear to me that he must not reach Boston."

"Made clear?" the big man repeated. "You mean by Seph—?"

"Shh!" the bespectacled man said sharply. "Do not say anything more."

"Bu—"

"Nothing more. It was made clear to me. You know by who. We need not speak of it further."

The big man grunted and said, "All right then. And how're we supposed to keep him away?"

"That is my concern. You have other responsibilities, which I have already explained to you. See to them, and we will not have any surprises, even if the rest does not go as it is supposed to."

"You all right?"

Ethan looked over at Diver, who was eyeing him with concern. He held up a hand and shook his head.

"How much we gettin' for all of this anyways?" the big man asked.

"Ethan—"

"Quiet, Diver!" he whispered harshly. "I'm listening."

". . . pounds, divided the usual way."

"Aye, well that way still ain't right. You said last time it'd be changin'. Remember?"

"Listening to what?" Diver asked, obviously wounded by Ethan's tone.

Ethan glared at him.

". . . will change. Perhaps this time. But first we have to complete the task. After that we can talk about a new division of payment."

The big man grunted again, sounding unhappy.

The stranger and his friend fell into a brief silence. Then Ethan heard one of them put a tankard on the table. A chair scraped across the tavern's wooden floor.

"I am leaving now," the bespectacled man said. "I would suggest you leave this place as well. I am not sure it is as safe as we assumed."

"What's that mean?"

"Nothing," the stranger said, his voice low.

Ethan saw the bespectacled man emerge from their section of the tavern and make his way to the door. He watched out of the corner of his eye as once again the man surveyed the room, perhaps hoping that his unseen observer would reveal himself with another spell. Reaching the door, he glanced back one last time, his spectacles flashing in the lamplight. Then he slipped out into the night. Shortly after, the big man left as well, lumbering to the door without so much as a backward glance.

Still Ethan didn't release the spell, for fear that the stranger lurked outside the Dowser, waiting for him to do just that.

But he faced Diver again. "I'm sorry about that," he said. "I had cast a spell and was listening to their conversation."

"Whose conversation?" Diver demanded. Ethan could tell that he had pushed his friend to the limits of his patience.

"I didn't catch either of their names. I told you, I saw one of them with Tanner; the other I had never seen before. But he started to say something about Sephira. I'm sure of it. The other man cut him off before he could say more."

"What were they talking about?"

Ethan repeated their cryptic references to the ship.

"Do you think any of this is important?"

"I don't know," Ethan admitted. "But there was something else about the one who knows Tanner: He felt my conjuring."

Diver's brow furrowed. "You think he—" He stopped, his mouth dropping open and his eyes going wide. "You mean," he whispered, "you think he's a speller, too?"

"Aye. And if he is—and if he's working on something with Sephira—then this could be very important."

"So what do we do?"

Ethan managed not to laugh. "I'm not sure that 'we' do anything. I don't know that it's a good idea for you to help me with this."

"Why not?"

"Because it can be dangerous meddling in Sephira Pryce's affairs. And because you're not exactly the most reliable person I could choose as a partner."

Diver's cheeks colored. "I told you I wouldn't discuss your business with anyone else," he said, with an earnestness Ethan had never seen in him before. "And I meant it. I don't blame you for not trusting me. But I can help you with this."

Ethan felt his resolve weakening.

Diver grinned. "Come on. Give me another chance. I lost money tonight, too, and I wouldn't mind getting back at Sephira just a little bit."

"All right," Ethan said, knowing that if Kannice were listening, she would call him a fool and worse. "You're working the wharves tomorrow, right?"

"Aye, but I can skip it if you need me to."

"No, I need you there." Diver's face fell, but Ethan pressed on. "Where will you be?"

"Thornton's Shipyard," Diver said, his voice flat. "Or maybe Greenough's."

"Good. In that case you can be responsible for watching the North End wharves for Sephira or this friend of hers."

"How can I do that? You didn't even let me look at him!"

Ethan described the man and his companion. "Don't say anything to them. Don't even go near them. Just watch what they do and report back to me."

Diver frowned. Ethan could see that he was disappointed by his instructions. "All right. What are you going to do?"

"I'll be watching the wharves in the South End and Cornhill." He couldn't possibly watch all the wharves, of course. Boston's waterfront was as active as any in New England and was nearly a match for those in New York and Philadelphia, even with the hard times that had befallen the city in recent years. But he hoped that if he could stay near Long Wharf, the busiest in the city, he might learn something of value.

"Are you sure there isn't something else you want me to do?" Diver asked. "Maybe follow Spectacles, or his big friend?"

"I'm sure," Ethan said.

"Right." Diver drank the rest of his ale and stood. "Best be heading off then. I have an exciting day at the wharf ahead of me."

"Sleep well, my friend," Ethan said.

Diver nodded, but lingered by the table. "I really am sorry. It won't happen again."

"It can't happen again, Diver. It's not just my livelihood I'm risking by letting you help me. It's my life, and yours too."

"I understand."

Ethan smiled. "Good. Get some rest."

Diver left the tavern, raising a hand in farewell as he passed Kelf. Not long after, Kannice came to Ethan's table, as he had known she would.

She sat and took his hand. "Do you want to tell me what happened?" she asked.

Ethan chuckled. "Diver would prefer that I didn't."

"I thought as much. That's why I asked you."

"I won't bother you with the details, but the upshot is that Sephira learned of my work for Mister Short from a girl Diver knows, and it cost us a few pounds." He shrugged. "There's nothing to be done about it now."

"She could have killed you."

"Sephira has had ample opportunity to kill me, if that's what she wants," he said. But Kannice was right. It could have been far worse. For Tanner it nearly was.

He wondered if he had been too quick to let Diver work with him again.

"You know what I mean," Kannice said. "I understand that he's your friend, but you're best off leaving him to the wharves and doing your thieftaking on your own."

Sound advice. He would have been wise to take it.

"You're already letting him help you with something else, aren't you?"

She knew him as well as she did the wood grain of her tavern's bar, and she was as smart as anyone he had ever known. He would have been well served to have *her* work with him, but she was too clever for that.

"It's not a job," Ethan said, an admission in the words. "I saw something tonight, and I just want to make sure that Sephira isn't causing more trouble."

She glared at him, lamplight shining in her bright blue eyes. "And you thought it would be a good idea to let Derrey tag along as you meddle in Sephira Pryce's affairs."

Strange that it hadn't sounded half as foolish when he himself said much the same thing. He didn't like to admit that loyalty to a friend could be a fault, but perhaps he had been too quick to forgive Diver.

"Honestly, Ethan, sometimes I think his stupidity rubs off on you, like it's contagious or something."

She shook her head, got up, and started toward the bar. Halfway there, she stopped, heaved a sigh, and walked back to his table. Halting in front of him, she offered a contrite smile. "I didn't mean for that to come out the way it did. I just remember what's happened in the past when you've crossed her."

He remembered, too. Over the years, Sephira's men had beaten him to a bloody mess, stolen his money, and come close to killing him more times than he could count. "I'm not going out of my way to start a new fight with Sephira Pryce. I promise. But one of the men I saw in here tonight is a conjurer, and I think I overheard him and his friend talking about Sephira. I don't like the idea of her having access to spells."

"I can see that." She tilted her head to the side, a coy smile curving her lips. "Are you staying tonight?"

"I'd like to, if you don't mind having a man as foolish as me in your bed."

She grinned and draped the towel she was carrying over her shoulder. "It's never bothered me before," she said, and walked away.

Chapter

THREE

trange, dark dreams troubled his sleep. At first he was chasing Tanner through the narrow fog-shrouded byways of the South End. Soon, though, he was the one being pursued. He couldn't see who followed him, but he knew it had to be Sephira and her men, and he knew as well that they were intent on killing him.

Before long, though, he had stopped running. The be-spectacled man stood before him, a knife in his hand, blood on his forearm, and the words of a spell on his lips. Ethan grabbed for his own blade and fumbled with his sleeve, but he knew his own spell would come too late to block the fence's assault.

Which may have been why he felt so disoriented when he awoke suddenly to what felt like a mighty wave of conjuring power. It seemed to rise from the earth itself, like the deep rumble of thunder after a flash of lightning. The entire building trembled with it. Or did it? At first Ethan thought he was dreaming, and even after he opened his eyes to the faint morning light seeping into Kannice's bedroom around the edges of the shuttered window, he couldn't tell if what he had felt was real or imagined. His heart labored in his chest, and he took several long breaths, trying to calm himself.

Kannice stirred beside him. "Whassamatter?" she asked in a muffled, sleepy voice.

Ethan kissed her bare shoulder. "Nothing. Go back to sleep."

But he was already wide awake. He lay on his back, staring up at the ceiling, his body tense as he waited for another pulse of power. None came, and as the minutes dragged by he began to doubt that he had actually felt the first one. It would have taken a powerful conjurer to cast such a deep spell, and there weren't that many in Boston. At least, not among the people he knew.

His thoughts turned once more to the foreigner he had seen downstairs in the Dowser the night before. His awareness of Ethan's conjuring marked him as a speller. But Ethan had no reason to think that the bespectacled stranger was powerful or skilled enough to cast a spell as strong as the one he had just felt. Such an accomplished conjurer would have known what kind of casting Ethan had used the night before, and would have left the tavern rather than continue a conversation that, for good reason, he didn't want others to hear. A speller with such abilities might even have determined exactly who in the tavern had cast the listening spell.

But if Sephira's friend hadn't cast the spell this morning, who had? Tarijanna Windcatcher, a self-described "marriage smith," was a powerful speller and made no effort to hide the fact that she conjured. Janna, though, did most of her conjuring at night; the one time Ethan had gone by her place before midmorning, he had woken her with his knocking. Janna had been none too pleased.

Gavin Black, an old conjurer who lived on Hillier's Lane, gave up spells long ago, or so he claimed. From what he had told Ethan, it seemed he had done most of his conjuring as a younger man while sailing on merchant ships and captaining his own vessel. But he had

long since made his fortune, and though Ethan had spoken to him about conjuring, he had never known him to
cast a spell.

The other conjurers he knew of in Boston weren't
skilled enough to work such powerful castings.

If the spell had been real.

Ethan closed his eyes again, trying to remember what
he felt in the instant before he woke. At first all that
came to him was the physical sensation, the feeling that
the air around him, the bed beneath him, the walls of
the room, were all reverberating with a single tone, as if
God himself had struck some enormous bell. But sifting
through his memory of those first few sensations, he realized that he had awakened feeling vaguely uneasy,
though whether because of his dreams or something in-
herently dark in the casting, he couldn't say.

His pulse had slowed, but still Ethan knew that he
wouldn't get back to sleep. He swung himself out of bed
and began to pull on his clothes.

"Where are you going?" Kannice asked, her voice
husky with sleep. She smiled up at him. "It's early still."

"I can't sleep."

"I wasn't suggesting sleep."

He sat on the bed beside her. "I'm not sure I'm in the
mood for that, either."

Her expression grew serious. "What's the matter?"

"I thought I felt something. A spell. That's what woke
me."

"Nearby?"

He shook his head. "No. Maybe. It was so powerful it
was hard to tell. Somewhere here in Boston, but I can't
be sure of much beyond that. The truth is, I'm not even
sure it was real."

She frowned. "I don't understand."

"I might have dreamt it. It felt real enough, but I can't
think of anyone in this city with the strength or skill
needed to cast such a spell."

"You said last night that there was a man in the tavern. A conjurer."

"I don't think it was him," Ethan said. He stood again and reached for his shirt. "But I should go. Something about this isn't right." He wanted to know more about the bespectacled man, and eventually he would speak with Janna. She might not have been responsible for the spell that woke him, but at least she would be able to tell him whether or not he had imagined it.

He finished dressing and leaned over to kiss Kannice.

"A spell as big as what you felt," she whispered. "Could you have cast it?"

Ethan hesitated, nodded. "Aye. But only by taking a life."

She didn't blanch, or give any other indication that his answer had scared her. She merely said, "Watch yourself," and reached up to touch his cheek.

He wrapped his hand around hers for a moment. "Always."

He left her room, descended the stairs, and walked out of the Dowser into the street. The sun still hung low in the east, but the sky above was cloudless and a deep shade of azure. Vapor from his breath billowed into the morning air and was swept away by a cool breeze. A perfect autumn morning. No doubt October would bring gray skies and cold rains. But for today, at least, September maintained its gentle hold on the province.

Ethan set out toward Cornhill and the South End, where he leased a room from Henry Dall, a cooper. He had food there and he liked to check in with Henry periodically, just to let the old man know that he was well. Henry might have been his landlord, but he treated Ethan as he would a son. Knowing that Ethan was a thieftaker, he worried when he didn't hear from him for more than a day or two.

As Ethan walked toward his home, he considered again Kannice's question and his answer to it.

The spells cast by conjurers fell into three broad categories. Elemental spells were by far the simplest, and also the least powerful. Using one of the basic elements—air, water, earth, or fire—a conjurer could summon phantom sounds or visual illusions to confuse a foe or deceive the unsuspecting. When Ethan's mother first began to teach him and his sisters how to conjure, these were the spells she showed them.

Living spells were more potent and more difficult to cast. As the name implied, a living spell drew its power from some part of a living thing: blood or flesh, hair, feathers, or fish scales, grass, leaves, or tree bark . . . Such spellmaking went far beyond mere illusion. Using living spells, a conjurer could heal with blood, as Ethan had done the night before, or he could could kill with it. A powerful conjurer might raise a wind or a storm; he might conjure fire or draw water from the earth.

And yet, as powerful as living spells could be, they were nothing compared to killing spells. These conjurings required the taking of a life, and there were almost no limits to what they could do. A conjurer who was willing to kill for his spellmaking could reduce Boston to a pile of rubble or boil away the waters of Boston Harbor. He could rob others of their free will and force them to do his bidding, no matter how heinous.

In all his years, Ethan had cast only one killing spell, and though he'd had little choice at the time, he was still haunted by the memory. But he had encountered conjurers who had no qualms about taking lives in order to enhance their power. The spell he had felt this morning was almost certainly a killing spell. That would explain not only the potency of the casting, but also the unsettled feeling that had plagued him since he woke.

And once more, a voice in his head echoed, *If it was real.*

Breakfast could wait, and so could Henry. He needed to know more about this spell.

Under most circumstances he never would have gone

to Tarijanna so early in the morning. On the best of days she was difficult, even ill-tempered. She had few friends and though she tolerated Ethan because he was a speller and also because they shared a deep and abiding hatred of Sephira Pryce, she probably didn't like him any more than she did anyone else. But he had to know if he had dreamt that spell or truly felt it.

Making his way to Janna's home, Ethan passed the old Granary Burying Ground and King's Chapel, where his friend Trevor Pell served as a minister under the authority of the rector, the Reverend Henry Caner. Once beyond the chapel, Ethan cut south to Newbury Street, where homes and shops gave way to open pastures and wooded country estates. Sugar maples and white-barked birch trees lined the road and grew in clusters along the edges of fields and grazing tracts, their leaves, shading toward orange and bright yellow, rustling in the wind.

Tarijanna lived at the southern edge of Boston, near the town gate, on a narrow strip of land known as the Neck. She owned a run-down tavern called the Fat Spider, and lived in a small room on the second floor of the building. Most of those who frequented the Spider were themselves conjurers or people who came to Janna seeking her services as a spellmaker. She served food and drink in her tavern, just like the proprietor of any other publick house. But she also sold herbs, oils, and talismans. And she peddled her services as a conjurer. She specialized in love spells, which she used to find love matches for her clients. The sign outside her tavern read "T. Windcatcher, Marriage Smith. Love is magick." It might as well have said, "A speller lives here!"

Spellers were feared, even hated. Most people mistakenly equated conjuring with witchcraft, and though it had been the better part of a century since witch trials led to the execution of twenty men and women in nearby Salem, Massachusetts, suspected witches were still put to death throughout the province. Janna didn't seem to care.

Reaching the Fat Spider, Ethan knocked on the tavern door, expecting that he would have to rap on the gray, weathered wood for several minutes before hearing any response. He was wrong.

At the first knock, he heard a strong voice call out, "It's unlocked!"

Ethan pushed the door open and stepped into the dark tavern. As always, the air within smelled strongly of cinnamon, clove, roasting meat, and ale. Janna sat in a low chair by the fire, a cup in her hand, filled no doubt with watered Madeira wine.

Janna hailed from one of the Caribbean islands, though because she was orphaned at sea as a young girl, she didn't know which one. She also didn't know her exact age, or her family name—she chose Windcatcher because she liked the sound of it.

Her skin was a rich nut brown, and her hair, which she wore shorn almost to her scalp, was as white as bone. But though her thin, wrinkled face made her appear ancient, her dark eyes were as bright and alert as those of a child. If she had asked Ethan how old he thought she was, he wouldn't have known what to say.

"Kaille," she said upon seeing him, her mouth turned down in a scowl. "I shoulda known it was you. First person to come through that door, and you ain't gonna spend one pence. You like a bad omen comin' at this hour."

She said much the same thing whenever he came to her tavern. In fairness, she had a point. He rarely bought anything from her; he sought her counsel when he had questions about spells, because no one in the city knew more about conjuring than she did. The truth was, Ethan might well have been as close a friend as Janna had in Boston. He chose to believe that she greeted him this way because she liked him. Others she simply would have ignored.

"Nice to see you, too, Janna."

The scowl deepened. "What d'you want, anyway?"

He crossed to where she sat and pulled up a chair

next to hers. The fire in her hearth threw off a lot of heat, but still she had a shawl wrapped around her bony shoulders and a threadbare woolen blanket covering her legs. She often complained of the cold, even on the mildest days of spring and fall. For all the years she had lived in the city, it seemed to Ethan that she had never adjusted to leaving the islands.

"You're up early today," he said. "Earlier than usual."

She shrugged, her gaze sliding away. "Why would you care about when I sleep and when I don't?"

"You felt it too, didn't you?"

"I don't know what you're talkin' about."

"Look me in the eye, Janna."

Grudgingly, she faced him again.

"Did you feel something this morning?" he asked. "Did you feel a pulse of power? It came just after dawn, and it would have been strong enough to make it feel like the Spider was going to come down on top of you."

Janna glared back at him. "Yeah," she said at last. "I felt it."

Ethan sat back in his chair, feeling both relieved and alarmed. He hadn't imagined it. But then who could have cast such a spell?

"You weren't certain," Janna said.

He shook his head. "It woke me from a dream, and I didn't know if it was real or not."

She gave a low chuckle. "Oh, it was real. Like you said, I thought this old buildin' was gonna crumble it started shakin' so."

"Do you know what kind of spell it was?" Ethan asked.

"No," Janna said. "But it was dark, and strong as can be. If I had to guess, I'd say it was a killin' spell. But I couldn't tell what the magick was supposed to do."

"Neither could I. Do you know where it came from?"

"Somewhere in the city. But you knew that."

"There aren't too many of us who can conjure like that," Ethan said.

She shook her head. "You, me, Ole Black. We're the only ones I can think of." Her expression turned sly. "To be honest, Kaille, I figured it was you."

"It wasn't. And I don't think it was Gavin, either." He raised his eyebrows. "I assume it wasn't you."

"Woke me from a deep sleep," she said.

"So I figured, seeing as you're awake before noon." He smiled; she frowned. "I encountered a new conjurer last night, a friend of Sephira's, I believe. But I don't think he's powerful enough to have cast the spell we felt."

Janna's frown deepened. "You sure? A dark spell from a friend of Sephira sounds just about right to me."

"Most times I'd be inclined to agree. And maybe you're right. I intend to keep an eye on him. But right now, as far as I can tell, he's not strong enough."

"If you say so," Janna said, not sounding convinced.

"Is there anyone else new in town, Janna? Anyone who could cast a spell like this?"

"No one I can think of."

He had expected her to say as much. "All right," he said, standing. "My thanks." He crossed back to the tavern door and pulled it open. "If you hear anything about a new speller in Boston, someone capable of this kind of conjuring, you'll let me know, right?"

"There any gold in it?"

"I'm not working for anyone. I'm doing this for me."

"Yeah," she said, the scowl returning. "I thought so."

He smiled, stepped out onto the street, and started to pull the door closed.

"Kaille."

He poked his head back in the tavern.

"You were the first person I thought of; other minds might work the same way. You watch yourself."

Would she have given such a warning to someone she didn't like, at least a little? "I will. Again, thank you, Janna."

After leaving the Fat Spider, Ethan followed Orange

Street back north as far as Essex Street, and turned east
toward the harbor, making his way past the wharves
and stillhouses west of Windmill Point. The sun was
higher overhead, warming the air a little, but not enough
to drive off the autumn chill. Hundreds of gulls circled
over the shoreline, ghostly white against the deep blue
sky, their cries echoing through the city streets. A line of
cormorants, black as pitch, glided just above the surface
of the water.

Ethan could see a few merchant ships on the harbor.
Two or three white sails billowed in the distance, and
several ships closer to port were already on sweeps. But
the fourteen British naval vessels positioned near Castle
William, the fortification on Castle Island at the south
end of the harbor, dominated the waterways. Even at a
distance, Ethan could see red-uniformed soldiers on
their decks, and the black iron mouths of the ships' cannons gaping in the gun ports. Merchant ships piloted by
captains less bold than those who had passed the naval
vessels on their way to port might already have sailed to
Newport or one of the smaller ports in Newbury or Salem. If the Crown's show of force was intended to choke
off the flow of commerce into the city, it appeared to be
having the desired effect.

Ethan considered himself a loyalist. He had little patience with those who rioted in the streets, destroying
property as a sign of their dissatisfaction with British
colonial rule. Boston had seen too much of this in recent
years. Three summers before, when Parliament first an-
nounced its intent to impose a stamp duty on all official
documents, a mob ransacked the residence of Lieutenant Governor Thomas Hutchinson, as well as the houses
of several other Crown officials. And this past June,
when customs officers seized a ship belonging to John
Hancock and accused the merchant of smuggling, agitators in the city again took to the streets, this time threatening physical violence against Crown representatives.

Yet he knew as well that the king's men were far from

blameless. The seizure of Hancock's ship had been a vast overreaction to the merchant's failure to submit proper papers for a shipment of Madeira wine, and it had given Samuel Adams and his mischief-makers just the excuse they needed to riot. Throughout the summer, Governor Bernard had threatened—unnecessarily, to Ethan's mind—to post British army troops throughout the city, and as tension between loyalists and some of Boston's more outspoken Whigs rose, and rumors of the impending occupation spread, prominent men such as James Otis and Adams spoke with ever-increasing frequency of a looming confrontation.

As a loyal subject of His Majesty King George III, Ethan never had cause to fear any British soldier, at least not before this summer and fall. He had served in the British navy, fought in the Crimean War. He had more in common with the men on those ships than he did with the Adamses, Warrens, and Otises of the world. But he knew better than to think that the hundreds of soldiers waiting out on the harbor had come merely as a demonstration of the Crown's resolve. Boston was on the verge of becoming an occupied city, and Ethan couldn't help thinking that the landing of regulars at Boston's waterfront would lead to problems far worse than those that had brought loyalists and Whigs to this point.

Nevertheless, the city bustled as it would on any day other than the Sabbath. Though it was early still, both Essex Street and Purchase Street, which followed the South End shoreline northward toward the South Battery, were choked with people and carriages. Wharfmen and sailors made their way from warehouse to warehouse looking for a day's wage. Merchants in silk suits and peddlers in rags jostled one another, trying to find bargains before off-loaded goods reached the markets of Faneuil Hall.

Ethan scanned faces as he shouldered his way past people on the street, but he saw neither the bespectacled

man nor his brawny friend. To his relief, he also saw no
sign of Sephira or her toughs.

He limped on, his bad leg beginning to grow weary
and sore. He couldn't keep himself from glancing re-
peatedly at the warships. The lead ship appeared to be a
fifth-rate frigate, probably carrying forty-four guns. A
smaller frigate of perhaps thirty guns lay to the north of
her. He saw as well a post-ship, and several sloops-of-
war and armed schooners. It wasn't a fleet that would
have struck fear in the hearts of French naval captains,
but it was more than enough to pacify this city and its
harbor. All the ships had their sails struck; no doubt their
captains were awaiting orders. With just a glance Ethan
counted hundreds of men on the various vessels. And rumor had it that another wave of ships and soldiers was
on its way to the city from Halifax. The occupation
would begin soon enough, and it would be massive.

As he neared Long Wharf, which jutted out into the
waters of the harbor more than a third of a mile, Ethan
saw a group of men standing on the wharf, speaking
among themselves, their gestures animated. All of them
were well dressed in matching coats, breeches, and
waistcoats—ditto suits, as they were known. Several of
them wore tricorn hats and all wore powdered wigs.
These were men of means. Still, Ethan might not have
taken note of them had he not spotted a familiar face in
their midst.

Geoffrey Brower, the husband of his sister Bett, and to
hear her speak of him, a customs agent of some importance, stood among the men. He was taller and leaner
than the others, with a high forehead and a supercilious
expression on his lean face. Ethan didn't recognize any of
Geoffrey's companions, but given how similarly all of
them were dressed, he assumed that they were customs
men as well. He stopped where he was and watched them.

Every few seconds as they spoke, the men looked out
toward the British fleet, particularly those ships at its

north end. Looking that way himself, Ethan noticed that a pinnace holding several British regulars in their bright red coats and white breeches was approaching one of the ships, a sloop-of-war. The sloop had its sails struck, as did the other vessels, but Ethan could see no one on its decks. Not a soul.

Several more regulars in another rowboat made their way toward the sloop from the northern end of the island. And not long after, a second pinnace from one of the larger ships closest to the city's waterfront approached Long Wharf and the dock near where Geoffrey and his colleagues stood. The boat drew alongside the pier and two of the soldiers on board held her steady while Geoffrey and two other men stepped onto the vessel. Once the agents were settled, the oarsmen began to row the boat out into the harbor. Within a few minutes it became clear to Ethan that they too were headed toward the sloop.

Something had happened to the warship, something serious enough to worry the fleet's commanders as well as Crown officials here in the city. Still watching the rowboats, and glancing now and then toward the sloop-of-war, Ethan started toward the wharf. Three of Geoffrey's friends had remained behind, and he considered casting another concealment spell, like the one he had used the night before to follow Tanner, so that he could eavesdrop on their conversation.

He reached for his blade, only pausing long enough to look around and make certain he wasn't being watched.

His caution might have saved his life.

Perhaps twenty yards ahead of him, partially hidden in a narrow alley, stood none other than the bespectacled man and his companion. They hadn't yet noticed Ethan, although they would have had he spoken his spell. They were gazing out over the harbor, as he had been. Spectacles held a brass spyglass, which he raised now to his eye. It seemed to Ethan that he had it trained on the sloop.

Rather than halt again and thus draw attention to himself, Ethan kept his head down and walked past the men. But his pulse raced. Whatever had happened to the British sloop-of-war had drawn the attention of Sephira's conjurer friend.

Or perhaps the man had done something to the ship. Something that demanded a spell powerful enough to wake all of Boston's conjurers from their early-morning slumber.

*E*than went only far enough to find a spot much like the one where Spectacles and his friend were hiding—a narrow alley between a pair of old wooden warehouses—and watched the men from there. They were in the Cornhill section of the city, less than a block from the Bunch of Grapes Tavern. The streets of Cornhill were always busy, in particular at midmorning, and few of those making their way to and from the wharves would take notice of a lone man standing at a corner, much less pause to wonder what he did there.

Every few minutes, the brute standing with Spectacles scanned the street, and each time he did, Ethan managed to duck back out of sight before the man saw him. But Spectacles kept his gaze fixed on the British ships. Ethan had the sense that he too was waiting for some sort of signal or command.

They remained on the street for the better part of an hour, until at last the two men appeared to give up on spotting whatever it was they were looking for. They left the alley in which they had been standing and headed south, back the way Ethan had come. He waited, allowing the men to walk some distance ahead of him before following, but he already had an idea of where they were headed. As he anticipated, they soon cut away from the shoreline, crossed Water Street, and took Joliffe's Lane toward Bishop's Alley. They were walking toward Summer Street, where Sephira Pryce lived.

Convinced that he would be able to find the men there, Ethan retreated to his home on Cooper's Alley and cast a new concealment spell. He felt the thrum of power from the casting and knew that Spectacles would sense it also. But he hoped that the conjuring would be far enough away that it wouldn't unduly alarm the man. As Ethan spoke the spell Uncle Reg appeared, his eyes bright and eager in the dim light of Ethan's room.

"You can't come along," Ethan told the ghost. "Spectacles will see you, even if he can't see me. I can't take the risk."

Uncle Reg shook his head.

"I'm sorry. *Dimitto te.*" I release you.

The ghost glowered at him, even as he faded from view.

Sheathing his knife once more, Ethan left the room and descended the stairs, taking each step with care. He couldn't be seen, but he could still be heard, and he didn't want to frighten Henry, the cooper who rented him his room.

Shelly waited for him at the base of the stairway leading from his room down to the alley behind Henry's shop, her tail wagging. For some reason Ethan had never understood, dogs could see him even when he was concealed with a conjuring. He squatted down beside her, glancing around as he did to make certain that no one was watching.

"You have to stay here, Shelly," he whispered, scratching her head. "Or else you're likely to get me killed."

She licked his hand, but when he stood once more and walked away, she remained by Henry's cooperage.

Ethan followed Milk Street to Long Lane, stepping around people, placing his feet with care, and when possible using the rattle of passing carriages to mask his footsteps. Halfway along the lane Ethan cut between two houses and into d'Acosta's Pasture, an open expanse of grazing land sparsely occupied by cows and horses. After crossing the southern corner of the field and slipping between another pair of yards, he reached Summer Street and Sephira's house.

It was a large, white marble structure with a cobblestone path winding to the front door past tasteful well-kept gardens. It looked nothing like the house one might have expected Boston's most notorious thieftaker to own. Then again, Sephira had never been one to conform to expectations.

Nigel and Nap stood out front watching the street. They couldn't see Ethan, of course, but he took extra care to make certain that they wouldn't notice his footsteps. After passing the front entryway, he crept along the north side of the house to the first window. From previous visits to Sephira's home he felt reasonably sure that this window looked in on her sitting room, where he guessed she would be speaking to Spectacles.

Ethan knew better than to risk another listening spell. Still keeping to the shadows, he pressed himself against the marble exterior of the house and held his ear as close to the window as he dared. Closing his eyes, he tried to shut out all other sounds—the twitter of finches and sparrows, the whisper of the wind in the elms surrounding Sephira's home, the occasional whinnying of a distant horse—and he listened. After a moment, he began to catch snatches of the conversation taking place within.

He thought that the first voice he heard was that of the bespectacled man. ". . . Might not have been on any of them. Your information might have been wrong."

"It wasn't." Sephira's voice. "I pay a good deal for the information that comes my way, and that money buys reliability as well as discretion. He's out there. Or he's already in the city, and you've failed."

Silence. Ethan strained his ears, but heard nothing for several seconds.

"Come away from there," Sephira said eventually. "We have matters to discuss and I want your undivided attention."

"I told you, I felt a spell."

"Yes, I remember," she said, sounding impatient. "You also told me that it was some distance away. Back in Cornhill probably. And as I told you, that's where Kaille lives. I'm sure he conjures all the time. It had nothing to do with us."

"Well, what about the—?"

"That is enough, Afton," Spectacles said, cutting off the other man. Ethan wondered if Afton was the brute he had seen with the bespectacled man.

"What is he talking about?" Sephira asked.

"It is not important."

If Ethan needed confirmation that Spectacles hadn't known Sephira for long, this was it. He would realize soon enough that she couldn't be put off so easily.

"If you plan to remain in Boston for any length of time, Mariz, you'll need to learn that I tell you what's important, and what is not. Not the other way around."

"Of course, *Senhora*. Forgive me." Ethan heard little contrition in the man's voice. "But you and I have more urgent business. We both stand to lose a good deal if the man we seek escapes us. That is where we should concentrate our energies."

"Agreed," Sephira said. "But if you've lost him—"

"I do not believe we have. You say that your information is correct and that he was on one of the ships. I take you at your word. In which case, I expect that he remains out there on the water even now, and will wait until the soldiers disembark before making his attempt."

"You expect so, but you don't know it for certain."

"I know him," Spectacles said. "He is not always the smartest of men, but he is cautious. Waiting is the safest way, and so he will wait."

"There are hundreds of men on those ships," Sephira said.

"Yes. You see my point."

"He can hide among them, and escape when he's ready."

"Exactly. So rather than watching the ships, we should be looking for the items he has hidden. He will go to them eventually. He will not leave Boston without them. So if we can find them, we will find him."

"But we've been through this," Sephira said. "We don't know where to look and we don't know who else might be able to tell us. We have nothing."

"I cannot help you in that regard. I know him. I do not know this city."

"Right. So you should continue to watch the ships, and we will continue to search the city, just as I told you two days ago."

Spectacles didn't respond right away. Ethan thought he heard footsteps, and when next the man spoke, his voice seemed to come from right beside the window.

"Very well, *Senhora*. We will return to the waterfront."

"Good. First though, I still want to know what your friend here was going to say."

Another pause.

"I assure you, it was nothing. I felt a spell just a short time ago, as I told you. But I felt another pulse of conjuring power as well."

Ethan leaned closer to the window, thinking that perhaps the man might reveal something about the powerful casting he had felt early that morning. He should have known better.

"When?" Sephira asked.

"Last night. Afton and I were in a tavern at the other end of your city, and I felt a spell, right there in the room."

"What tavern?" Sephira demanded, biting off the words.

"I believe it was called the Dowsing Rod."

"The Dowser," Sephira said, her voice low. "You idiots! That's Kaille's tavern!"

"He owns it?"

"No, his woman does. But he's there all the time. That was his witchery you felt. Damn it!" A pause, and then she asked, "Did you see him?"

"I would not know him if I had."

"Well, he saw you. I'm sure of it. You felt witchcraft just a short while ago?"

"I have been telling you so."

"Damn it!" she said again. "Nigel! Nap! Get in here!"

Boots scraped on the stone outside the entrance to the house, and the door opened.

Ethan had heard enough. Sephira was too smart not to put it all together. He hurried back across Summer Street and into the pasture. His conjuring still kept Sephira and the others—even Spectacles—from being able to see him, but he didn't think he could rely on the spell for much longer.

He hadn't gone far when Sephira's voice reached him again. ". . . Him found!"

Ethan chanced a quick glance over his shoulder. Sephira stood at the entrance of her home, hands on her hips. Nigel, Nap, Gordon, Afton, and two other men had fanned out through her yard and the street in front of her house. Nap and Nigel carried pistols; the others held knives.

But Ethan was most interested in Spectacles. He stood with Sephira, but he had drawn his blade as well, and had it poised over his arm, looking like he was trying to decide what spell to cast. He would probably go with a finding spell first, followed by an attack of some sort. That was what Ethan would have done had he been in the other man's position.

Ethan had little choice. He couldn't make himself invisible to a finding spell—that level of craft was beyond him. Which meant that he needed to protect himself. Pulling his own knife from his belt, and still striding across the pasture, he cut his arm and whispered, *"Teqimen ex cruore evocatum."* Warding, conjured from blood.

The ground pulsed, as he had known it would. Uncle

Reg appeared beside him, ethereal in the bright sunlight. He had expected that, too. The thrum of the casting, and the shimmering appearance of Uncle Reg, would allow a conjurer to find him, even if he wasn't visible to the naked eye. So he wasn't at all surprised when he heard Spectacles—Mariz—shout, "There!"

The report of a pistol echoed across the pasture, and a bullet whistled overhead, a wild, blind shot.

Sephira shouted something that Ethan couldn't hear. She sounded angry, though whether because the shot had been fired or because it had missed, Ethan couldn't be sure.

He guessed that Nap had fired, although he didn't look back to make certain. Nigel would know better than to make the attempt. Sephira's toughs still couldn't see him, and Uncle Reg was invisible to anyone who wasn't a conjurer.

But an instant later, he felt power vibrate again in the ground, and he braced himself for Mariz's assault. It reached him in mere seconds, like a sudden wave rolling over calm waters. A powerful spell, though one he didn't recognize. It crashed into his legs, causing him to stumble momentarily. But his warding held; he felt the wave of power breaking, dissipating, retreating. Ethan kept his balance, and ran on.

Another conjuring rumbled through the earth. Ethan felt the spell approaching, and once more he tensed, wondering what Mariz had thrown at him this time. It caught up with him just a second or two later and fell over him like a cold mist. Once more he heard cries from behind him, not just from Spectacles, but from all of Sephira's men.

Looking down at his body and limbs, Ethan realized that Mariz had found a way to overcome his concealment spell. Or rather, to outwit it. It looked like someone had poured tar over him. In the time it took him to take but a single stride, he had gone from being invisible to the men searching for him to standing out like a red-coated British soldier in a crowd of clergymen.

Ethan spat a curse and tried to run faster, despite the agony in his bad leg. He dodged to the right and headed for a pair of country estates. Another shot rang out, but even the newest pistols of the day were too unreliable over great distances. Again the bullet soared past harmlessly.

By now though, Nap would have had enough time to reload, and the men could track him. Ethan still held his knife and he cut himself once more without slowing. He hesitated, wondering what spell might remove Mariz's conjuring.

"*Purga, ex cruore evocatum.*" Clean, conjured from blood. Power made the ground beneath his feet vibrate, but nothing else happened. He was still covered with whatever it was Mariz had thrown at him, an ebon figure amid the pale grasses.

He cut himself again. "*Aufer carmen ex cruore evocatum.*" Remove spell, conjured from blood.

It was a more powerful spell. It hummed in the ground and in the marble of the homes he had reached. Ethan knew immediately that it had worked. Too well, in fact.

He no longer looked like he was covered in pitch, but he also could feel that he had removed his own concealment spell. Anyone could see him.

Dashing between the estates, Ethan turned on to Long Lane and made his way back toward Milk Street.

At that next corner, though, instead of turning east toward Henry's cooperage, he went straight, again slipping between two houses into a small lot behind them. He soon reached Water Street. Here he turned west before heading north again onto Pudding Lane, where Diver lived. He was in the heart of Cornhill now, on a street crowded with working men, and people making their way from storefront to storefront. He slowed.

His leg screamed, and his breath came in great gasps,

but he seemed to have lost Nigel and the others, at least for the moment. He had cast enough spells that Spectacles wouldn't have much trouble locating him again; the man might not even have to resort to a finding spell.

Ethan had feared this day for years. Sephira Pryce had long been a formidable rival. Ruthless and clever, as deadly with her bare hands as she was with a blade or gun, she commanded a small army of men and had managed to ally herself with some of Boston's most powerful leaders. Ethan had but one weapon at his disposal that she couldn't match: spellmaking. The threat of a conjuring had stayed her hand in countless confrontations that might otherwise have ended in his death. And his ability to cast spells had allowed him to overcome her other advantages as they raced each other to find one stolen treasure or another. For so long, solely by dint of Ethan's skills as a conjurer, they had battled each other to a stalemate.

But now she had access to the same powers he did. With Mariz working for her, she might well be too strong for him.

Ethan didn't have much time to ponder this. The resonant pulse of another spell forced him into motion once more. He knew right away that this was a finding spell, and that it came from some distance, probably from back in d'Acosta's Pasture. Still, once Spectacles found him again, it wouldn't take Sephira's men long to surround him.

He managed a few steps before the conjuring reached him, flowing through the cobblestones beneath his feet and twining about his legs like a vine climbing a tree. The casting lingered on him for a few seconds before fading, but Ethan had cast finding spells of his own and so knew that this was more than enough. Mariz had figured out where he was.

Ethan still held his knife, but here in the middle of a lane, he couldn't cut himself and conjure, at least not without drawing far more attention to himself than he wanted. Instead, he bit down on the inside of his cheek, as he had the previous night in the Dowser. He hated drawing blood this way; it hurt far more than cutting his arm. But he needed to ward himself again, since he had likely removed his previous protection, along with Mariz's spell and his own concealment conjuring. "*Teqimen ex cruore evocatum,*" he whispered under his breath. Warding, conjured from blood.

The hum of the casting in the ground would allow Mariz to fix his location with that much more certainty, which meant that Ethan had to keep moving. But the warding made him feel safer.

Uncle Reg still walked with him stride for stride, his expression grim, his glowing eyes flicking Ethan's way every few seconds. They walked through the center of Cornhill and crossed through Dock Square past Faneuil Hall toward the North End. Ethan didn't have a destination in mind. He intended to stay away from Cooper's Alley and from the Dowsing Rod; those were the two places where Sephira knew to look for him.

Once past Faneuil Hall, he crossed over the Market Bridge and followed Mill Creek toward Ann Street. The lanes were less crowded here, and Ethan looked toward the ghost beside him.

"Is he more powerful than I am?" Ethan asked, knowing the shade would understand that he meant Spectacles.

Uncle Reg shook his head, but not before hesitating.

"But he's no less powerful either, isn't that right?"

The ghost nodded.

"Aye, I was afraid of that. The spell he tried to use on me, the one blocked by my warding, did you recognize it?"

Uncle Reg nodded again. He held out his hand and a flame appeared in the middle of his palm.

"A fire spell," Ethan said.

The ghost allowed the flame to die away.

"Was it strong enough to kill me?"

Reg shook his head once more.

Well, that was something at least. Maybe Sephira didn't want him dead . . . yet. Ethan slowed, finally halting altogether. If Sephira and her men were still tracking him, they knew by now that he was no longer in Cornhill. He waited for another finding spell, but none came. Had Sephira given up for the time being, knowing that with Mariz working for her she could find him anytime she wished? Had she gone to Henry's shop or Kannice's tavern? Or was she back at her home, drinking Madeira and laughing at Ethan, knowing that he still ran from her?

He almost gave in to the temptation to try a finding spell of his own. Knowing where Spectacles was might alert him to whatever Sephira planned to do next. But he didn't want to give away his location again, nor did he wish to give Sephira the satisfaction of knowing just how alarmed he was by this new ally of hers.

"I can't run from her forever," he said aloud.

Uncle Reg smirked and faded from view. Ethan often wondered where the ghost went when Ethan didn't need him. Reg often seemed eager to return there, and sometimes appeared to resent Ethan's summonses. There was much about the ghost Ethan didn't know, beginning with his name and his place on the Jerill side of Ethan's family tree. But in all important respects he trusted Reg as much as he did his closest friends, despite the shade's prickly personality.

Still protected by his warding, Ethan turned and started back toward Dall's cooperage and his room. He kept his knife out, and remained watchful, scanning the streets as he walked, and looking behind him every so often.

He saw no sign of Sephira or her toughs and by the time he reached Cooper's Alley he had allowed himself to relax. Still, he decided to stop into Henry's shop to check in on the old man and let him know that he was back.

Henry's shop was small and old. It had been built by the cooper's grandfather and had been passed to Henry's father, and then to Henry. Despite its age, though, it was sturdy. It had survived winds and storms and more than a few fires. Ethan's room was plain but comfortable. It wasn't the only place he had lived since his return from the plantation in Barbados on which he had labored as a prisoner, but it was the only one that had felt even remotely like a home.

Henry liked Ethan because he paid his rent on time. Ethan liked Henry because he didn't ask too many questions about Ethan's work as a thieftaker, and because he didn't know that Ethan was a conjurer. As far as the old cooper was concerned, Ethan was just like any other tenant, except with a somewhat more interesting profession.

A sign over Henry's door read "Dall's Barrels and Crates," and a second on the worn oak door said simply, "Open Entr." Ethan heard hammering as he approached the shop, and so knew before entering that the old cooper was all right. He sheathed his knife and stepped inside.

When he saw Ethan, Henry raised a hand in greeting, gave the hoop he was fitting over a barrel one last whack, and laid his cloth-covered hammer down on the workbench.

"Well met, Ethan!" the man said, his grin revealing a great gap where his front teeth should have been. Like his cooperage, Henry was small, but solid. His head barely came up to Ethan's chin, but his arms were thick and corded with muscle. His bald head shone with sweat and his grizzled face was ruddy with the exertions of his labor. He removed the leather apron that had been draped over his work shirt and sat down on a low stool, flexing his right hand, which had been injured long ago, and which still grew stiff on cold days. "Buthy today," he said with his usual lisp. He sounded weary.

"Busy is good, right?"

"I suppose. I could use a couple of days without busy."

Ethan grinned. "Well, I'll leave you alone. I just wanted to wish you a good morning."

"You had a visitor," Henry said, before Ethan could let himself out again.

Ethan felt the hairs on his arms and neck stand on end, and he had to resist the urge to reach for his blade. "When," he asked, his voice tight.

"Just a little while ago."

"One person, or several?"

"One. He went upstairs, stayed there for a minute or two, and then came back down. I saw him leave," the cooper added, anticipating Ethan's next question.

A few years ago, Sephira and her men had lain in wait for Ethan in his room, and Nigel and his friends had beaten Ethan to a bloody mess. Henry was in the shop at the time, and failed to notice their arrival. He had felt guilty about it ever since, and had gone out of his way to keep a closer eye on Ethan's room.

"Big guy?" Ethan asked.

The cooper bobbed his head.

Some of the tension drained out of Ethan's back and shoulders. At least it hadn't been Spectacles.

"All right. Thank you, Henry."

"You're welcome. Take care of yourself."

Ethan smiled and let himself out of the shop. He whistled for Shelly, who emerged from the shadows along the side of Henry's shop and trotted over to him, her tail wagging and her tongue lolling from her mouth.

"Come on, Shelly," he said. He drew his knife and walked around to the back of the shop.

The dog loped ahead of him, stopping at the base of the stairway and looking back at Ethan expectantly. She was hungry—no surprise there—but otherwise she gave no indication that she was alarmed. Ethan put the knife away again. If there had been someone in his room, Shelly would have known it.

"All right," he said, patting her head. "How about a piece of cheese?"

She licked his hand.

Ethan climbed the stairs, slowing as he turned at the

small landing halfway up and saw his door. A folded scrap of paper had been affixed to the doorframe with a small blade that jutted from the wood. He climbed the rest of the way, pried the knife out, and unfolded the paper.

The note, written in Sephira's neat hand, read, "Don't sleep. Don't even blink. —S."

Ethan exhaled slowly. It was a familiar warning, one that she had given him before. Unfortunately, Sephira's threats seldom turned out to be idle.

He let himself into the room, retrieved a small piece of hard cheese, and went back out onto the landing at the top of the wooden stairway.

"Here you go, Shelly," he said, and tossed the cheese down to her.

It landed on the cobblestones, bounced twice, and came to rest a couple of yards from where she stood. She bounded forward, sniffed the cheese, and was about to eat it when she suddenly stopped and looked back. She bared her teeth, her hackles rising, and turned, a deep growl rumbling in her throat.

Ethan grabbed his knife and pushed his sleeve up so that he could cut his forearm for a conjuring. But to his surprise, it wasn't Sephira or Nigel or even Mariz who had come for him. Instead, he saw Geoffrey Brower in his green silk suit, and with him a young man Ethan didn't recognize. This second man wore the dark blue and white uniform of a British naval officer.

"Ethan," Geoffrey said, eyeing Shelly and even taking a step back. "Call off the dog! Please! We require a word with you!"

*I*t's all right, Shelly," Ethan called, although he wasn't at all certain that he wanted anything to do with Geoffrey or his companion.

Shelly looked up at Ethan and gave a tentative wag of her tail. But then she eyed the two men and growled again. Her hackles were down though.

"She'll leave you alone," Ethan said. "You're free to come up." With that he stepped back into his room. He left the door open.

Moments later, he heard the two men ascending the stairs. He sat at the small table beside his bed, leaving a single chair for his visitors. Geoffrey and the other man soon reached the top of the stairway, but Geoffrey faltered at the door.

"Come in," Ethan said. "There isn't much room, but I don't imagine you'll be staying long."

The two men exchanged a quick look. Geoffrey appeared to brace himself, as he might when preparing to step into rank waters. Then he entered the room. The naval officer followed. Brower looked paler than usual; his overlarge forehead was furrowed. He looked like he had spent the entire day frowning.

The officer was about as tall as Geoffrey, but he stood

with his shoulders hunched. He was blandly handsome, with a square face and wide-set blue eyes, but he had a weak chin and had fixed an even weaker smile on his lips. He wore a powdered wig though he couldn't have been more than twenty-five or thirty years old. The wig was long and accentuated the length of his face. It also seemed that his uniform didn't fit him quite right, although Ethan couldn't have said if it looked too small or too big. It was overly tight across the man's middle, but it appeared too loose in the shoulders and chest.

"This is William Senhouse," Geoffrey said, breaking a brief silence. "He is third lieutenant aboard the *Launceston*, the lead frigate of the fleet currently anchored in the harbor." He indicated Ethan with an open hand, seeming to cringe at what he was about to say. "Lieutenant Senhouse, this is Ethan Kaille, my wife's brother, and a thieftaker of some renown here in Boston."

It might have been the nicest description of Ethan ever to pass Geoffrey's lips.

"I'm pleased to make your acquaintance, Mister Kaille," said Senhouse, stepping forward and proffering his hand.

Ethan half rose from his chair, shook the man's hand, and sat back down.

Geoffrey, noticeably uncomfortable, glanced around the room. "Ethan was in the royal navy for a time," he said, answering a question no one had asked. His gaze came to rest on Ethan again. "Weren't you?"

Ethan shifted in his seat. "That's right," he told Senhouse. "I served under Thomas Cooper at Toulon."

"Ah!" Senhouse said, nodding. "On the *Stirling Castle*. Very good. A bit before my time, but a fine ship."

Ethan said nothing. An awkward silence settled over the room once more.

"Forgive me for being rude, gentlemen," Ethan said. "But I've already had a long day. What brings you here?"

The men again exchanged glances.

"We need your help," Geoffrey finally said with another grimace.

Bett, Ethan's sister, had turned her back on spellmaking long ago, although she still possessed the ability to conjure. Like so many in New England she equated conjuring with witchcraft and believed that those who cast spells were servants of Satan. Preachers in New England's finest churches still railed against magicking and the dark arts in their sermons, and rather than admit that she came from a family of conjurers, Bett counted herself among the virtuous who fought such devilry.

Years ago, she had made it clear to Ethan that she wanted nothing to do with him or his spellmaking. Her marriage to Geoffrey had given her everything to which she had ever aspired. She lived in a large comfortable house, enjoying the society of Boston's finest Tory families, and she pretended that she had never been born a Kaille. For his part, Geoffrey seemed to share Bett's aversion to conjuring and her desire to pretend that she and Ethan were not related. As a customs official, he had much to lose from any association with Ethan and his scandalous past. Ethan could hardly imagine how difficult it had been for him to come here, much less ask Ethan for aid.

He sobered at the thought. It would have taken a true crisis to bring Geoffrey to his door.

"What's happened?" he asked.

To Ethan's surprise, Geoffrey deferred to Senhouse.

"I think it would be wisest if we were to show you," the officer said, his voice crisp.

Ethan narrowed his eyes, looking from Senhouse to Geoffrey. "Show me?"

"It would be easier that way," Geoffrey told him. "I . . . I don't want to speak of it here."

Still Ethan hesitated.

"I assure you, Mister Kaille," Senhouse said, "no harm will come to you. I give you my word as an officer in His Majesty's navy."

Ethan stood, eyeing both men again. "All right." He indicated the door with an open hand. "After you."

Geoffrey stepped out onto the landing, with Senhouse close behind. Ethan locked his door and followed them down the stairs.

"Tell me," he said, thinking once more of the scene he had witnessed at Long Wharf. "Does this have anything to do with one of the ships in your fleet? A sloop-of-war perhaps?"

Geoffrey spun around so abruptly he came within a hairsbreadth of tumbling down the stairway. The lieutenant regarded him as well, though with more grace.

"How did you know that?" Geoffrey asked in a whisper.

"I didn't know it for certain. I saw you at Long Wharf earlier today, Geoffrey. You were with several men who I assumed were also customs men. And then you rowed out toward the sloop."

"What were you doing at the wharf?" the lieutenant asked.

"I had business there," Ethan told him. "A matter that has nothing to do with the British fleet."

"I see," Senhouse said, though Ethan sensed that he wasn't entirely satisfied with this answer.

"So, is this about the sloop?"

All the color had drained from Geoffrey's cheeks, and a bead of sweat stood out on his upper lip. He nodded, his eyes wide, haunted. "Yes," he said. "I won't say more. Not here."

"Fair enough," Ethan said. "Lead on."

They walked the short distance from the cooperage to Long Wharf in silence. The people they passed in the road stared hard at Senhouse, some appearing impressed, others regarding the man with open hostility, and still others looking frightened. It wasn't every day that a British naval officer in full battle dress walked the streets of Boston, and with the royal fleet menacing the city's shores, Senhouse's presence seemed to draw even more notice than it might have under other circumstances.

Upon reaching the wharf, Geoffrey and the lieutenant escorted Ethan more than halfway out the length of the pier, past the warehouses to a small T-wharf that extended into the harbor. A pinnace waited for them there. Two regulars, clad in bright red coats and white breeches, stood on the wharf, and nine navy men—the cockswain and his oarsmen—waited in the boat. As Ethan and the others approached, the men in the boat stood, and all of the uniformed men saluted Senhouse. Several of them cast quick, wary looks Ethan's way, but they said nothing.

Senhouse paused at the end of the T-wharf and gestured toward the boat. "In you go, Mister Kaille."

Ethan stepped into the pinnace, taking care to keep his weight centered, and took a seat at the prow. Geoffrey joined him there; Senhouse and the two regulars took positions at the stern. The lieutenant spoke in low tones to the cockswain, who in turn barked a command at his men. Soon they were gliding away from the wharf. Ethan sat listening to the cockswain's rhythmic calls and the splash of the oars as they cut through the water. He watched Geoffrey out of the corner of his eye, waiting for the other man to explain what it was they needed Ethan to do, but Brower steadfastly avoided looking Ethan's way.

"Geoffrey—"

"Not yet," Brower said in a harsh whisper. "When we reach the ship." He glanced pointedly at the nearest of the navy men.

Ethan nodded once, and Geoffrey turned away again to stare out over the water. Ethan did the same.

As the pinnace skimmed past the *Launceston*, Ethan couldn't help but admire the ship. It wasn't as large as the *Stirling Castle*, the seventy-gun ship of the line on which Ethan had served during what was known to colonists as King George's War, and to the rest of the world as the War of the Austrian Succession. But it neverthe-less was an impressive vessel. He could see regulars on its decks; some marked the progress of the pinnace as it went by. And as he regarded the vessel, her cannons, the graceful curve of her hull, he couldn't help but think back to the days of his service in the British navy.

It had been years since Ethan last put to sea, but for a time he had been as comfortable on the deck of a ship as on dry land. Some of his earliest memories were of sail-ing jaunts taken with his father, who had been an officer in the British navy. As a boy he worked the wharves in his native Bristol and later, when he was old enough, Ethan followed his father's path into the navy.

His naval career didn't last long. The Battle of Toulon went so poorly for the British that the fleet commander, Admiral Thomas Matthews, was court-martialed along with most of his captains, including the captain of the *Stirling Castle*. Thomas Cooper, the vessel's captain, had done nothing wrong so far as Ethan was concerned. Ethan deeply resented the man's court-martial. Cooper was soon reinstated, but Ethan wanted nothing more to do with the navy. With his father's help Ethan was able to leave the service. He returned to Bristol and sailed for America aboard the first ship on which he could book passage. Once in Boston, he tried to make a living on land. But working the wharves was a poor substitute for sailing the seas. More to the point, within a month of his arrival in the New World, Ethan met and fell in love with Marielle Taylor, the daughter of one of Boston's wealthi-est shipbuilders. Soon they were betrothed and Ethan put to sea again, looking to make his fortune as second mate aboard a privateering vessel: the *Ruby Blade*.

His decision to take the posting aboard the *Blade* turned out to be the most fateful of his life. The captain of the ship, Rayne Selker, and his first mate, Allen Foster, were at odds from the moment their voyage began. When the ship's takings proved meager the mate began to chal-lenge the captain's commands. In private, Foster spoke of mutiny. By some stroke of ill luck—Ethan never found out how—the first mate had learned that Ethan was a conjurer. He convinced Ethan to use his powers on behalf of the mutineers and for a brief time they took control of the vessel.

Within just a day or two, Ethan came to regret the choice he had made. Foster was ill-suited to command; his treatment of the captain was brutal and cruel. When Selker's supporters launched an assault on the mutineers, Ethan aided their efforts and so helped them regain control of the *Blade*.

Ethan's involvement in the mutiny—and the spells he cast in support of the mutineers' cause—earned him a court-martial. His willingness to help the captain retake the ship saved his neck. He sailed aboard the *Silver Tassel*, which carried him from Charleston, South Carolina, where the *Blade* landed after the mutineers had been defeated, to London, where Ethan and the others were tried and convicted. Another ship—Ethan never learned her name and never spent more than a few precious moments every third or fourth day above decks—carried him back across the Atlantic to Barbados, where he served his sentence laboring on a sugar plantation under the scorching tropical sun.

The next time he boarded a ship, fourteen years later, the vessel carried him from the Caribbean back to the mainland—Charleston again—this time as a free man. It might have been the happiest of all the many voyages he had taken over the course of his life.

Looking at the *Launceston* and her sister ships, it occurred to Ethan that but for any one of a host of events—Cooper's court-martial, perhaps, or Ethan's subsequent decision to leave the royal navy—he might now be an officer in this small fleet menacing the city. Elli had once urged him to reenlist and no doubt his father would have leaped at the chance to smooth the way for him.

He found it surprisingly easy to imagine a different

life for himself—one in which he never set foot on the *Blade*, never allowed himself to be drawn into the mutineers' scheming, never lost years of his life to prison; one in which he was a British naval officer posted in Boston and married to Elli; one in which both of his legs were whole. He could see this other life dispassionately, without regret or longing. It was like standing in front of a shopwindow and imagining himself in clothes he could no longer afford.

A lone cloud passed in front of the sun, casting a dark shadow on the pinnace and rousing Ethan from his musings. Their small boat was drawing near the sloop-of-war. The cockswain's calls had hardly varied since their departure from Long Wharf, and the oarsmen had maintained a steady beat with their sweeps. But despite Geoffrey's efforts to hide from the men whatever had happened, these soldiers weren't fools. They knew something was wrong. Their expressions had turned grim as they approached the sloop, and the color had fled their cheeks. Ethan could almost smell their fear, like the faint scent of a coming storm in a freshening wind.

And as he eyed the sloop—HMS *Graystone* out of Bristol, according to the gilt lettering on the escutcheon—he felt his own apprehension growing. The sails had been struck the day before, when the ship entered the harbor, and the sloop's crew had long since dropped anchor. That the ship looked idle should have come as no surprise. But he saw no one on its decks; he heard no voices, no laughter, no sound whatsoever save for the slap of water against the ship's hull and the gentle rustle of gathered sailcloth in the breeze.

The oarsmen steered the boat to the sloop's rope ladder amidships. The two regulars who had been sitting with Senhouse stood, stepped to the center of the pinnace, and reached for the lowest ratline.

"We'll go up alone," Senhouse said, stopping the men.

They looked back at him, puzzlement on their young faces.

"But Lieutenant—" one of them said.

"Leave us here," the officer went on. "Go back to the *Launceston*. We'll signal you when we're ready to return."

The regulars still looked doubtful, but after a few seconds they remembered themselves and saluted.

"Yes, Lieutenant," the soldier said.

"Mister Kaille, Mister Brower." Senhouse gestured toward the ladder. "After you."

Ethan wanted to refuse, to demand an explanation before he followed any more of the lieutenant's instructions. But every man aboard the small boat was watching him, and he didn't think it wise to disobey a British navel officer in front of so many sailors.

He moved to the ladder, and while the oarsman on the ship side of the pinnace held the smaller vessel steady, he began to climb.

Years had passed since he last had been on a rope ladder, and his leg had grown worse in that time. But as he pulled himself up the ratlines, he felt the years slipping away. He reached the top of the ladder and swung himself over the gunwale and onto the sloop's deck.

Turning, he froze. What he saw made his breath catch in his throat.

From what little Geoffrey and Senhouse had said, and from all that they had refused to tell him, Ethan had assumed that some terrible tragedy had befallen the *Graystone*. Yet how could he possibly prepare himself for this?

The deck was littered with dead soldiers in the red and white of the British army. He spotted two naval officers in blue on the quarterdeck; they were also dead. There must have been thirty corpses above decks. They looked like toy figures strewn on the vessel and forgotten by some bored child. They weren't bloodied or bruised. Their bodies didn't appear to be broken; on the contrary, it appeared that they had dropped into a deep slumber just where they stood.

A small knot of crewmen lay at the sloop's stern,

dressed in loose-fitting breeches and tunics of brown and gray, pale blue and dingy white. He was too far from them to see much, but he could tell that again there was no blood, no sign of sickness or violence.

This was why they had brought him here. Geoffrey, at least, knew that Ethan was a speller. And these men had been killed by some sort of conjuring. That was the only explanation for what Ethan saw. No doubt Geoffrey hoped that he could tell them how the soldiers had died and who was responsible. Ethan wondered though how much Brower had said about his powers to Senhouse and others who served the Crown.

He heard a noise behind him and turned. Geoffrey was just stepping onto the ship. He straightened and surveyed the deck.

"You see now why I didn't wish to speak of this before?"

Ethan nodded.

Senhouse swung himself nimbly over the gunwale and joined them on the deck.

"When did this happen?" Ethan asked.

"We don't know," Geoffrey said, staring down at the nearest of the soldiers. "Last night perhaps. Or early this morning."

"Which one?"

As soon as the question crossed his lips, he knew that he had spoken with too much urgency. Geoffrey looked at him, as did Senhouse.

"We're not certain," the lieutenant said. "Why does it matter?"

Ethan hesitation lasted but an instant. "I don't know that it does. I just find it hard to believe that with so many British ships nearby you can't be more specific about the time."

Senhouse squinted up at the sun, seeming to gauge the current time. "There are men on the *Senegal*—that sloop there," he added, pointing to a ship just south of the *Graystone*, "who claim to have seen men moving about on this deck as late as first light this morning. But when pressed they weren't certain." He pointed to the vessel lying to the north. "No one on the *Bonetta* saw any movement after sundown last night. Hence our uncertainty." Senhouse paused, still watching Ethan. "Now, please answer my question. Why does it matter so much to you?"

"First answer a question for me," Ethan said. "Why have you brought me here?"

The lieutenant cast a look Geoffrey's way. Brower kept his eyes fixed on the dead soldiers.

"Mister Brower thought you might be able to help us determine what happened to these men," Senhouse told him. "He hasn't told me much about you. Just that you're a thieftaker, and that you have some experience with . . . well, I suppose with gruesome mysteries of this sort."

"He's right," Ethan said. "I do."

"Good. Perhaps you can tell us what happened here."

"May I look around? See the hold?"

"All you'll find below is more of the dead."

"Still," Ethan said, "I'd like to take a look."

Senhouse shrugged. "Of course. Take as much time as you need."

Ethan caught Geoffrey's eye and held his gaze for a moment. He and Brower had spent little time in each other's company, but the man appeared to understand the meaning behind Ethan's look. He said, "We'll wait for you up here."

"Thank you."

Ethan began by walking to the stern and examining the dead crewmen. Like the soldiers, they appeared to have died suddenly, without pain or warning. Their facial expressions were natural; their bodies looked relaxed. Once more, Ethan couldn't help thinking that they appeared to be sleeping. He bent and felt for a pulse on one of them, and then another. Nothing. There could be no doubt that they were dead.

Steeling himself, he walked to the ladder that led down into the hold, and lowered himself into the belly of the ship. The air belowdecks was warm and stale, and heavy with the stink of sweat and urine. A single oil lamp burned several paces from the hatch, but even in the dim light Ethan could see bodies scattered throughout the space. Most were soldiers, though here and there he saw a crewman. Two men lay on the floor, another was hunched over a table, and a fourth seemed to be dozing on a barrel, his head leaning back against a wooden beam. But the vast majority of the men were in hammocks, still lying much as they probably had before they died.

Ethan moved among the bodies, searching for anything that might tell him what kind of spell had killed the men, but the soldiers and crewmen below were as unmarked as those on the deck. Looking at them, he was reminded of Jennifer Berson, the young girl whose murder he had investigated three years before. She, too, had died without a mark on her, robbed of her life by a skilled and ruthless conjurer.

Had the powerful pulse of power he and Janna sensed that morning taken every life on this ship? All that Ethan saw, and much of what he had heard from Geoffrey and Senhouse, seemed to point to that conclusion. Why else would so many men still be abed?

He glanced back toward the hatch to make certain that he was still alone in the hold. Choosing the corpse of a young regular, he pulled out his knife and cut himself. He dabbed blood across the young man's forehead and traced a bloody line down from the bridge of his nose, over his lips and chin to his breastbone. Drawing on the blood that still welled from the wound on his arm, he cast his spell.

"*Revela potestatem ex cruore evocatam.*" Reveal power, conjured from blood.

Belowdecks, in such a closed space, it seemed to Ethan that he was surrounded by the puissance of his casting. It hummed in the wood of the ship, it seemed to make the dead air of the hold come alive, so that Ethan's nose and mouth tickled as he inhaled. Too late he remembered that conjurings at sea worked more powerfully than those directed at people or objects on land. It was something he had taken for granted during his time as a sailor, but had forgotten in the intervening years.

Ethan glanced at Uncle Reg, who had appeared beside him, before looking back at the regular.

A spot of light appeared on the young man's chest, dim at first, but growing brighter by the moment. It was vivid orange and it blossomed like the pleurisy root growing in the Common, spreading over the soldier's body. In fact, similar glows had suffused the bodies of several of the men lying nearby; Ethan's spell, amplified because he was out on the harbor, had spread to others.

Regardless, there could be no doubt. A spell had killed the lad and his companions. And though the conjurer who had cast it—who, Ethan assumed, had killed all these men—had to be both powerful and skilled, he or she hadn't known how to conceal the casting. Or hadn't bothered.

Ethan heard footsteps on the deck above him. Geoffrey and the lieutenant were walking toward the rear hatch.

"Ethan?" Geoffrey called. The two men started down the ladder.

He cut himself again.

"*Vela potestatem!*" he said, keeping his voice low. "*Ex cruore evocatam!*" Conceal power! Conjured from blood!

The spell pulsed like a war drum and began right away to take effect. But the orange glow on the men was bright, and this casting didn't work instantaneously.

Ethan strode back to the hatch. Hoping that he could keep Senhouse distracted until that orange glow faded.

"Yes!" he said, meeting the men at the base of the ladder.

"We called for you twice before you responded," Senhouse said, regarding Ethan through narrowed eyes.

"I'm sorry, sir. I didn't hear you."

"What exactly . . . ?" The lieutenant broke off, his eyes fixed on the part of the hold where lay the young regular, the glow on his chest and those of the others dimming like the dying embers of a fire. "What in the name of God?"

He started forward, Brower and Ethan following close behind.

"What is it, Lieutenant?" Geoffrey asked.

Senhouse said nothing, but continued to wind his way past bodies to the cluster of dead soldiers on whom Ethan's spell had acted. "Do you see that?"

Geoffrey glanced sidelong at Ethan, then peered over Senhouse's shoulder, trying to see what the officer was talking about.

The light from Ethan's revealing spell had nearly vanished; Ethan wasn't sure that he would have spotted it had he not known to look for it.

"See what?" Brower asked.

Senhouse stopped amid the soldiers and waved a hand. "These men. They're . . ." He narrowed his eyes again, looking from one corpse to the next. A frown had settled on his face. "Now that's damned peculiar. I don't see it anymore." He turned to look back at Brower and Ethan. "Did you . . . ?"

The question died on his lips when he saw Geoffrey's blank expression.

For a long time, neither man spoke. The lieutenant regarded the corpses again. Brower eyed Ethan, a sour look on his face.

"Mister Kaille, I'd like to know what you were doing down here," Senhouse said. "And I'd like to have an answer to the question I asked you earlier. Why you were so interested to know whether these men died last night or this morning?"

"Sir, I—"

Senhouse raised a hand, silencing him. He turned and looked Ethan in the eye. Despite the dim lighting in the hold, Ethan could see that the lieutenant's face had gone white save for a bright red spot high on each cheek. There was a hard look in his eyes. Ethan saw fear there as well, but the man was a British naval officer, and for the moment at least he seemed to have mastered his fright.

"There are nearly a hundred men on this ship," he said quietly, "and every one of them is dead. I see no blood, no bruises or cuts or injuries of any sort. I see no evidence that they took ill. They are dead, for no reason that I can see. I'm at a loss to comprehend what might have happened here. Yet I sense that you're not. You look and act and sound as though this is nothing new to you. You don't seem to find it at all unsettling."

"I assure you, Lieutenant, that's not the case."

Senhouse shook his head, his expression pained. "Forgive me. I intended no offense, nor did I mean to imply that you aren't troubled by what you see here. All but the foulest of demons would be. What I meant was, you don't seem . . . surprised that something like this could happen."

Ethan didn't like to tell anyone of his ability to conjure. The people who knew held his life in their hands. One word whispered to the wrong person, one loose remark uttered in casual conversation, one opening for Sephira Pryce or another enemy intent on doing him harm, and Ethan could be summarily tried and executed as a witch. But he sensed that Senhouse already knew, that he had reasoned it out for himself. He was waiting for Ethan to put words to his suspicions.

"I'm constantly surprised by the evil I see in my work," Ethan said, looking around the hold. "This is . . ." He shook his head. "Like you, I have trouble comprehending why someone would kill so many men, seemingly without cause." He took a breath. "But you're not asking me why, so much as how. And that I do understand."

"Perhaps we should go back above," Geoffrey said, his voice shaking.

"It's all right," Senhouse said. "Go on, Mister Kaille."

"What do you know of spellmaking, sir?"

He thought the man might laugh or scoff or even grow angry and accuse Ethan of mocking him. But Senhouse merely pondered the question before saying, "Very little, to be honest. I have heard of men and women being hanged or burned as witches. I've listened to preachers rail against those who would embrace Satan and his dark arts. But I've never encountered witchery myself, at least not that I know."

"I believe you have now, sir," Ethan said. "I've seen others who were killed by spells, and they look very much as these men do. They bear no wounds, they show no sign that anything ailed them before they died. To those who know nothing of conjuring it seems that one moment they were fine, and the next they were dead."

Again, Senhouse surprised Ethan with his equanimity. "That is an extraordinary theory," he said, his voice even. "A spell."

"Yes, sir."

"Is there any way to prove this? It's remarkable, of course, that so many should die in such a mysterious way. But can you offer me more than simply the lack of evidence for any other cause?"

Ethan wet his lips, knowing that their conversation was headed just where he didn't wish it to go. "There are ways to prove that a spell was used. But all of those methods would themselves require conjurings."

"I see," the lieutenant said. Ethan heard a note of skepticism in his voice, but at least the man hadn't yet rejected Ethan's suggestion out of hand. "You sound as though you know quite a bit about these matters. Why is that?"

"I've been a thieftaker for many years now," Ethan told him, refusing to flinch from the man's gaze. "I've seen many odd and disturbing things in the streets of Boston."

A small smile flitted across Senhouse's face and was gone. "Strangely, that's the first thing you've said to me that sounded like a half-truth."

Geoffrey cleared his throat, but Ethan remained intent on the lieutenant.

"Are you a witch yourself?" Senhouse asked him. "Is that why you understand all of this so well?" When Ethan didn't answer right away, he added, pointing to the dead soldiers lying around them, "I thought I saw a strange light on these men. A glow—deep yellow, or perhaps orange. Was that your doing?"

Ethan hesitated, searching for some way to steer their conversation in another direction. At last, seeing none, he sighed and said, "I'm a conjurer. That's what we call ourselves. For obvious reasons, most of us don't wish to be known as witches. I can cast spells myself, and sometimes I can sense when others have conjured. I felt a spell this morning. It woke me, in fact. It was as powerful a conjuring as I've ever felt. And I think that spell is what killed all the men on this ship."

"You felt it?" Senhouse said. "And you said nothing?"

"Until I boarded this ship, I had no idea what the spell I felt had done. When I sense a conjuring, I can't tell what kind of power is being used, or who is wielding it. Sometimes, if I'm close to the conjurer, I can tell where it has been cast, but in this case I didn't even know that much. Had you told me immediately what had happened, I might have hazarded a guess before we reached this ship, but as it was I had no idea."

Senhouse turned to Geoffrey. "This is why you suggested that we bring him here. Not because he's a thief-taker, but because he's a . . . a conjurer."

"Yes," Brower said. "I suspected witchcraft right off." His gaze slid toward Ethan. "To be perfectly honest, my first thought was that he might have done this."

Ethan gaped at him. "Thank you, Geoffrey," he said, with all the sarcasm he could muster.

"I no longer believe you're responsible. Truly, I don't," he added, clearly for Senhouse's benefit.

"What more can you tell me about this spell?" Senhouse asked, seeming to ignore Brower. "And what was that glow I saw earlier?"

"The glow came from a spell I cast," Ethan told him. "I wished to determine whether a conjuring had in fact killed these men. And my spell confirmed that this was the case."

"How?"

Ethan faltered. Explaining conjurings and the workings of power to people with no experience with them was a bit like trying to describe color to someone who had been born blind.

"The spell I cast reveals the residue of other conjurings. If there was none—if no other spell had been cast on these soldiers—nothing would have happened."

"But something did happen," Senhouse said.

"Yes. My spell revealed the orange glow that you saw. That is the color of the power wielded by whoever killed these men."

"The color?"

Ethan exhaled. "Every conjurer's castings have a distinct color."

"I see. And yours, I take it, isn't orange."

He had expected this. "No, Lieutenant, it's not. Let me show you."

Ethan pulled out his knife again and cut his arm. He felt self-conscious placing blood on the soldier in front of the other men, but he did not look away from the dead man, and he chose not to respond to the small whimpering sound Geoffrey made. Once more he spoke the reveal conjuring spell he had used earlier, taking care this time to control the flow of power. Uncle Reg appeared beside him, and his spell sang in the wood of the ship, but neither Senhouse nor Geoffrey gave any indication that they had noticed. As before, the orange glow of the killing spell spread from the man's chest over the rest of his body. But then the russet hue of Ethan's conjuring spread over the orange.

"Did you see that?" Ethan asked.

Senhouse nodded, staring at the corpse as if in a trance. "Yes, I did," he said, his voice hushed.

"The orange power is what killed him. That second color—the rust—is the residue of the first revealing spell I cast."

"I know nothing of this," Senhouse said, still sounding awed, still staring at the glowing corpse of the regular. "You could be misleading me, using a witch's tricks to dull my mind."

"Perhaps I could. But I'm not." He looked at Geoffrey, his expression hardening. "Mister Brower's suspicions notwithstanding, I have no reason to lie to you, and no reason to murder all these men. I'm a British subject, the son of a naval officer and once a sailor in His Majesty's fleet."

"As I understand it, you're also a convicted mutineer."

Ethan bristled. "Yes, sir, I am. And if you think that means I can't be trusted, take me back to the city, and I'll leave you to find on your own the conjurer who killed these men."

Senhouse rubbed his forehead, his eyes closed. "I apologize. That was a foolish thing for me to say." He looked Ethan in the eye. "We need your help. I'm sure I speak for Mister Brower when I say that without your . . . your expertise in this area, we're unlikely to find the person who did this."

"So, you're hiring me?"

"We're asking you to help us," Geoffrey answered. "And in return, I've been authorized to offer you ten pounds. Consider it a bounty on the head of the killer. Find him, and the money is yours."

Ten pounds was a considerable sum. Even Sephira Pryce might have killed for less.

"All right," Ethan said. He surveyed the ship once more, the bodies strewn about the hold. Aside from the color of the conjurer's power, he had little information with which to start. Except, of course, for the conversations he had overheard. Spectacles and Sephira were looking for someone who they believed was on one of the British ships. So, Ethan would look for this man as well.

"To start," he said, turning back to Senhouse, "I'll need the name of every man on this ship."

Chapter
SIX

For several seconds, neither Senhouse nor Geoffrey said a word.

The lieutenant narrowed his eyes, his brow creasing. "Whatever for, Mister Kaille? Surely you can't think that one of these men is responsible?"

Ethan wasn't about to voice his suspicions about Spectacles. Not yet, knowing so little. Sephira Pryce had too many friends among those who served the Crown. If she learned that Ethan suspected her associate of a crime of this magnitude, she wouldn't hesitate to kill him.

"Forgive me, Lieutenant," he said, "but you've asked me to inquire into the deaths of these men, and now you need to let me conduct my investigation."

Senhouse blinked once, obviously taken aback. To his credit, though, he recovered quickly. "Yes, of course. You're quite right. This way."

He led Ethan and Brower back to the ladder and up onto the ship's deck. After the darkness of the hold, the sunlight was blinding, and Ethan had to shield his eyes with an open hand. But he welcomed the cool touch of the autumn breeze and the clean, briny scent of the harbor air.

Senhouse strode to the stern and into the captain's

quarters. Ethan followed the lieutenant back as far as the doorway to the quarters, but faltered there. It had been more than twenty years since last he served on a ship, but still the old habits of a sailor remained deeply ingrained. A common seaman didn't simply walk uninvited into a captain's quarters.

Geoffrey, who as far as Ethan knew had never served in the navy, had no such reservations, and walked into Ethan from behind.

"Pardon me," Brower said, flustered.

Senhouse looked back at them and waved Ethan into the cabin. "It's all right, Mister Kaille," he said, with an understanding nod.

Ethan entered, though doing so still felt odd. The air was sour in here as it had been below, the faint hint of stale sweat and rancid food lingering beneath the bitter smell of spermaceti candles.

The man lying on the bed in the far corner of the cabin looked to be no older than Ethan. He had long brown hair that he wore in a plait. A powdered wig sat on a small writing desk bolted to the wall just beside the bed. Because the *Graystone* was too small to be a rated ship, her commander had not been a captain, but rather a lower-ranked naval officer—perhaps another lieutenant. Senhouse might well have been friends with the man.

"I'm sorry, Lieutenant," Ethan said, his voice sounding loud in the small space. "Who was he?"

Senhouse stared at the body. "His name was Jacob Waite. He was also a lieutenant. He received this posting only last month. You would have thought they had named him fleet commander, he was so pleased." After a few seconds more, he looked away and seemed to force himself into motion. Crossing to the desk he said, "The manifest should be in here somewhere."

He began to search the papers on the commander's desk. When he found nothing there, he knelt down to open the sea chest beside it. Finally he stood again, looking puzzled.

"That's strange," he said. "There should be a manifest here."

"Maybe the purser had it," Ethan suggested.

"Yes, maybe he did."

They left the captain's cabin and went back below to the wardroom, where the ship's other officers slept. The wardroom was somewhat larger than the captain's cabin, but more cramped. Six hammocks lined the walls, with small chests beneath each. Four of the hammocks held the bodies of dead sailors.

"That's Amos Porter," Senhouse said, pointing to one of the men. "He was first mate. Another lieutenant." Another friend. Senhouse didn't have to say this; Ethan heard it in his tone.

"And this was the purser," Senhouse said, turning to the hammock just to the left of the wardroom door. "Peter Logan." Senhouse stooped and picked up a sheaf of paper off the floor. "Here it is," he said.

"He had it out?" Ethan said, joining Senhouse beside the hammock.

"So it would seem." The lieutenant handed the manifest to Ethan.

Ethan glanced through its pages. In addition to the names and ranks of soldiers, crew, and naval officers, the manifest also listed items of cargo, noted the date and time of the *Graystone*'s departure from Halifax as well as where these men had previously been posted, and recorded every encounter with other vessels along the route from Acadia to Boston.

"May I take this with me?" Ethan asked.

Senhouse winced. "I don't have the authority to say you can. You're welcome to remain on board and look at it here, but I'd have to ask Captain Gell before I allow you to remove it from the *Graystone*."

"Gell?"

Senhouse walked out of the wardroom; Ethan and Geoffrey followed.

"He commands the *Launceston* and thus the fleet,"

Senhouse said, as they climbed back above decks. "I can speak to him on your behalf. I need to return to the ship anyway. And in the meantime, you're free to remain here and begin your investigation. I'm sure Mister Brower will be glad to stay with you and assist in any way he can."

Ethan had seen plenty of corpses in his day. He had witnessed killings and on more than one occasion he himself had killed. Still, the idea of remaining aboard the *Graystone*, its hold and decks crowded with the dead, didn't appeal to him at all. On the other hand, Geoffrey appeared terrified at the prospect, which made it a little easier for Ethan to bear.

"That will be fine," he said. "I'm sure Geoffrey will be most helpful."

Brower opened his mouth to protest, but closed it again without saying a word, seeming to understand that this was not a duty he had any chance of avoiding. "Yes, of course," he said at last.

"I can give you only so much time on the ship," Senhouse said. "Before long, we need to gather the dead. In this sun they're going to . . . well, they won't keep for long."

"Yes, of course," Ethan said, squinting against the glare as he surveyed the deck again. "What will you do with them all?"

The lieutenant shook his head. "I don't know. Usually we would give them burials at sea, but we can't dump them all in the harbor. And I can't imagine John—Captain Gell—will want to transport so many corpses into Boston."

"Castle William, then," Ethan said.

Senhouse considered this, gazing across the water toward the fortress. "Yes, perhaps. That's an excellent idea. I'll pass it along to the captain."

He moved to the port gunwale, pulled out a white handkerchief, and waved it over his head several times. Returning it to his pocket, he faced Ethan and Geoffrey once more.

"We can't keep you from speaking of what you've seen today. You've agreed to help us, and I have no doubt that before this is over you'll take your inquiry into the city. You'll have every opportunity to tell others what has happened. I beseech you not to tell anyone who doesn't absolutely need to know. Word of this . . . this massacre could spread panic through the populace. And it could embolden those who seek to undermine the authority of the Crown."

"I'm not sure that Ethan cares about that, Lieutenant."

Ethan bristled.

Senhouse's face fell. "Oh. I just assumed that since you . . ." He faced Ethan again. "Are you—?"

"Am I what?" Ethan asked, casting a dark look Geoffrey's way. For someone who had all but forced Ethan to involve himself in this matter, Brower seemed awfully quick to cast doubts on his trustworthiness. He had spent too much time listening to Ethan's sister cast aspersions on his character. "A rabble-rouser?" Ethan suggested. "A Son of Liberty?" He shook his head. "No, I'm not. But more importantly, for all intents and purposes, you've hired me, and that buys you not only my skills as a thief-taker, but also my discretion."

Senhouse's expression brightened. "Thank you."

No one spoke again until a faint cry of "Ahoy, the *Graystone*!" reached them.

Senhouse looked back over his shoulder. "Ahoy!" he called back. "My transport is coming," he told Ethan and Brower. "I'll climb down and meet them; fewer questions that way. Until later, gentlemen."

The lieutenant swung himself over the gunwale and began to climb back down the ratlines. When he had vanished from view, Ethan cast another glare at Geoffrey and started away, manifest in hand.

According to the papers, the *Graystone* left Halifax with a complement of fourteen crewmen, seventy-four regulars, and four army officers, plus the six naval officers and Lieutenant Waite. One regular had died, apparently of a fever, and had been buried at sea. That had left a total of ninety-eight men aboard the vessel.

Ethan paused and looked around once more. Two officers lay on the deck, and the other four were still in their quarters. The commander was accounted for.

"Geoffrey, would you mind counting the crew members?"

Geoffrey had settled himself on a barrel, his back against the foremast. "What? Count them? What for?"

"I would like to be able to account for every man who's supposed to be here."

Ethan felt certain that Geoffrey would refuse, but he heaved a sigh and stood. "Very well."

"Thank you. Just the crewmen. I'll count the regulars."

Geoffrey scowled, but walked across the deck to the cluster of dead crewmen at the stern.

Ethan began to count the regulars.

"There are six of them," Geoffrey called.

Ethan didn't bother looking back at him. "There should be more below."

"You want me to go back down there?"

At that Ethan did turn.

Geoffrey sighed again, sounding more like a spoiled boy than a customs agent. "All right," he said, and climbed down into the hold.

With Geoffrey gone, Ethan turned once more to the soldiers. He walked the length of the deck on the starboard side and back the other way on the port side. All told he counted twenty-four regulars and one army officer.

As he started toward the hatch leading down to the hold, Geoffrey emerged once more, looking pale, his face covered with a fine sheen of sweat.

"There were eight more down there. That makes fourteen total."

"That matches what's on the manifest," Ethan said.

"As I would have expected."

Ignoring the comment, Ethan went below. It didn't take him long to find the other three army officers in their hammocks. Satisfied that all the commissioned men were accounted for, he began to work his way through the hold, counting soldiers. But he knew that Geoffrey had been right: He was wasting his time. All the officers and crew were here on the ship. The regulars would be, too.

Except that they weren't.

There should have been forty-nine soldiers belowdecks. He counted forty-eight. He counted them twice more and reached the same total each time. At last he went back onto the deck and counted the men up there a second time. Twenty-four. He read through the manifest again, searching for any other notations of soldiers lost in transit to Boston. But there were none.

"How many regulars do you see up here?" Ethan asked.

Brower stood and turned a slow circle. "Twenty or so, I'd say."

"No, I need you to count them."

Geoffrey made no effort to hide his displeasure, but he walked a swift circle around the deck, halting by Ethan.

"Twenty-four."

"Please make a count below as well."

"Now, see here, Ethan—"

"Do it! Or would you rather I mentioned to Lieutenant Senhouse how unconcerned you seem with the loss of life on this ship? I don't imagine your friends at Customs would look kindly on such callousness on your part."

Brower glowered at him, and Ethan glared right back.

Geoffrey was the first to look away. He went back to the hatch, muttering to himself and sending a filthy look Ethan's way before vanishing from view.

While Geoffrey searched the hold, Ethan checked the wardroom and captain's cabin again, just in case the missing regular had died in either chamber. He found only the officers he had seen earlier.

Geoffrey was waiting for him on deck when he stepped out of Waite's cabin.

"Forty-eight," Geoffrey said, his tone bitter. "Would you care to tell me what this is about?"

"One of the regulars is missing."

Brower's eyes went wide. "What? That's impossible."

Ethan held out the manifest. "Have a look yourself. The *Graystone* left Halifax with seventy-four soldiers. One died on the way here. That should leave seventy-three, but we can only find seventy-two. This may be why the purser had the manifest out in the first place. A man is missing."

"Perhaps another man died and the commander and purser both neglected to make note of it."

Ethan shook his head. "I've been at sea, and I can tell you that no commander worth his salt would fail to note the death of a passenger or crewman. Besides, look at that manifest. It's as detailed as any I've seen. No, if another man had died before this morning, it would say so there."

"So, are you suggesting that the missing soldier killed all these men?"

"I'm not suggesting anything. I'm telling you that one of the regulars is missing."

Geoffrey looked down at the nearest of the dead regulars. "Damn," he muttered. "We have to tell Senhouse. And I expect he'll have to speak with Gell." He glanced Ethan's way again. "I think you've just assured yourself of a late night."

Ethan had no doubt that he was right.

Senhouse returned to the *Graystone* a short time later with a second naval officer and several crewmen. The naval officer, Dr. William Rickman, was the surgeon on board the *Launceston* and had been sent to certify the

deaths of those aboard the ship. The crew had been sent
to help Senhouse sail the *Graystone* to Castle William.
In all likelihood, Senhouse had prepared the men for
what awaited them on the ship because they managed in
short order to hoist anchor, unfurl the sails, and get the
ship under way. A few times, Ethan spotted one of them
staring at the dead, but for the most part they kept to
their work.

The doctor enlisted Ethan and Geoffrey's help in ar-
ranging the dead at the stern; grim work to be sure, but
neither of them complained.

After some time, though, Ethan excused himself and
approached the quarterdeck to speak with Senhouse of
the missing soldier.

The lieutenant managed to conceal his dismay at
Ethan's discovery although he did pull out his kerchief
and mop his brow. His hand appeared to tremble.

"Well, this certainly complicates matters," he said, his
voice low.

He paused to mark the ship's progress toward the island and to shout a command to the crewman at the
wheel. "I'll have to inform Captain Gell," he went on.
"But I expect he'll want us to to identify all of the dead
and compare their names with those on the manifest.
He'll want this other man found. Frankly, I want him
found, too, regardless of whether he's our killer."

"Yes, sir."

"Can you stay on with us at Castle William?"

"Stay on with you?" Ethan said.

"I'd like you to work with Doctor Rickman. I don't
know yet if it will be possible to identify these men
without making it known to every other soldier in their
regiment that they're dead. But I'm sure that the doctor
will need every bit of help he can get."

Ethan stared off toward Castle William, which loomed
large before them. The fortress dominated the island, rising from a mound of stone, austere and formidable. The
king's colors flew above it, the blue, red, and white

gleaming in the late-afternoon sun. Somehow, Ethan realized, as he watched the flag snapping in the wind, he had allowed himself to be drawn into a matter of the British navy, something he had vowed after Toulon never to do again. And yet ninety-eight men were dead—or at least ninety-seven were. How could he refuse Senhouse's request?

"If you can feed and house me for the night, I'll be happy to do what I can for the doctor."

Senhouse actually smiled, looking so relieved that Ethan had to smile as well. "Thank you, Mister Kaille."

A short time later, they docked at Castle Island. Soon Ethan, the soldiers, and even the officers were carrying bodies off the ship and up into the fortress. It was backbreaking, depressing work that grew ever more unsettling as the skies darkened overhead.

The fleet commander had ordered that the dead be kept as far from the barracks as possible, and so Ethan and the others carried the men from the island's wharf, past the smith's shop and garden sheds, to the underground vaults that were set aside for food and munitions storage in the unlikely event of a siege. By using the north entrance to the vaults they were able to avoid the barracks, which lay at the south end of the parade.

Stars had begun to appear in the sky when Ethan and Dr. Rickman carried the last of the bodies through the garden toward the vault. The air had turned cold, but still Ethan had sweated through his shirt and waistcoat. He and the doctor said little as they worked. Ethan could just make out faint strains of song in the distance, but he thought little of it until a sudden explosion overhead startled him so, he almost dropped the man he was helping Rickman carry.

"What in God's name was that?" he demanded.

Before the doctor could answer, another blast illuminated the fortress grounds and was met with cheers.

"They're celebrating the coming occupation," Rickman said.

"Who are?"

"The soldiers out on the harbor. Haven't you heard the singing?"

"I haven't paid much attention to it," Ethan said.

"Listen."

They halted, still holding the corpse. A third rocket went off above them, brightening the fortress like summer lightning and drawing more cheers. Even after the singing commenced once more, it took Ethan a moment to make out the tune. When he did, he shook his head and chuckled. The men were singing "Yankee Doodle," which British soldiers had been using to mock colonial militia since the Seven Years' War.

Ethan couldn't help thinking that the regulars seemed rather full of themselves. But he kept this to himself. He nodded once, signaling to Rickman that they should begin walking again. Rockets continued to burst overhead, and the singing and cheers drifted across the grounds from the harbor.

One last time they descended the steep stone stairs that led into the vaults, barely trusting their footing in the inconstant light of the torches that lined the stairway.

When at last they set down this last man, Ethan straightened and stretched the stiff muscles in his back and shoulders. The air belowground was even colder than it had been above. It was damp as well, but Ethan thought it likely that the bodies would keep longer in the vaults than anywhere else they might have been placed.

"I meant no offense," Rickman said.

Ethan looked at him. "I beg your pardon?"

The doctor was tall and hale with a kindly, round face and piercing dark eyes. His features were youthful, but his curly hair, which he wore far shorter than was the fashion in Boston, had already turned white.

"I didn't mean to anger you by pointing out what the men were singing," the doctor explained.

Ethan shook his head. "You didn't." He retrieved the

ship's manifest from a low stone ledge where he had placed it some time before and began to walk down the narrow corridor of the vault, looking over the bodies. He could hear more rockets going off, although down underground the explosions sounded muffled and dull. He couldn't hear the singing anymore. "Do you know many of these men?"

"Hardly any of them." The doctor spoke softly in an accent that marked him as a native of southern England, perhaps Southampton or Portsmouth. "Last I heard, Captain Gell intended to ask some of the officers from the Twenty-ninth Regiment to join us here and help identify them." He eyed Ethan in the torchlight. "Lieutenant Senhouse asked me to examine the men, but he still hasn't asked me what killed them. The crewmen did, but not William. Neither have you, for that matter. Why is that?"

"I've been carrying the dead for hours, Doctor. As grim a task as that was I didn't wish to make it worse. But you've raised the matter so why don't you tell me what you think killed them."

Rickman shook his head. "I have no idea. And what's more, I don't believe you. I think you do know, or at least can offer a theory. So before the officers arrive why don't we dispense with the games? Tell me what happened to these men."

Ethan didn't answer right away. He should have denied that he knew anything, but something in the doctor's manner stopped him. The man seethed with passion, with a righteousness that Ethan remembered from his own youth. In truth, Rickman reminded Ethan of another young man he knew—Trevor Pell, a minister at King's Chapel who had first helped him with his work several years before when Ethan was inquiring into the death of Jennifer Berson. He wondered if Rickman would accept that Ethan was a conjurer, as had Pell.

Before he could say anything, though, he heard boots scraping on the stone stairs leading into the vault. He looked back at the entrance, and Rickman turned as well.

Two men stepped into the vault, both wearing bright red uniforms. One of the men appeared to be in his early twenties—a young officer, who looked at the bodies arrayed before him with an expression of abject fear. His eyes twitched; it seemed that he was continually fighting the urge to close them and shut out the horror before him. His skin looked pasty, even in the warm light of the torches.

The other man couldn't have been more different. He was tall and broad in the shoulders. Some might have thought him handsome, though Ethan thought he looked more rough than refined, with a long nose, a strong chin, sunken cheeks, and widely spaced pale eyes. He wore his graying hair in a plait beneath his tricorn hat, a hat which he did not remove even here, in the presence of so many dead soldiers. His eyes swept over the bodies and came to rest at last on the doctor.

"Captain Gell sent me," he said, his voice thick with an Irish burr. "Perhaps you'd like to tell me why, Doctor."

"I'd suggest you look around you, Captain," Rickman answered, his tone icy. "These men are the reason why."

The officer's mouth twitched. "I can see that. But what is it you require of me?"

"Captain Preston, this is Ethan Kaille," the doctor said. "He is a thieftaker here in Boston, and is conducting an inquiry into the deaths of these men. All of them are from your regiment and one of them is missing. We need to match faces to names and see if we can determine which man escaped the fate of his comrades."

To this point, Preston had ignored Ethan, but he fixed his eyes upon him now, a faint smile on his lips. "A thief-taker?" he said. "You think these men were robbed?"

Ethan stared back at him. "Yes. Of their lives, at the very least."

The smile faded from the captain's face. "All right.

Let's get started, then. I want to get back to my soldiers. The rest of them . . ." he amended after a brief, awkward pause.

"By all means," Rickman muttered, just loud enough for Ethan to hear. "We wouldn't want to inconvenience the man."

Chapter
SEVEN

Captain Preston's manner might have been gruff, but he worked with swift efficiency, as did the young corporal he had brought with him. They moved down the line of dead soldiers, peering at their faces and, after a bit of deliberation, assigning a name to each one. Dr. Rickman held the manifest and checked off names as the officers worked. Ethan trailed behind them, feeling that with the bodies arrayed in the vaults his work here was complete.

Watching the other men, though, Ethan had an idea. He would have been best off waiting until he was alone with the dead soldiers, but he couldn't be certain that such an opportunity would present itself.

"*Veni ad me,*" he whispered as quietly as he could. Come to me.

His conjuring sang in the stone walls and the ground beneath his feet, and Uncle Reg winked into view at his side, his russet glow almost bloodlike in the dim space.

Preston glanced Ethan's way. "What did you say?" he asked. He gave no indication that he could see Reg or that he had felt Ethan's conjuring.

"It was . . . a prayer," Ethan said.

Reg grinned. The captain went back to examining the

dead, but Rickman eyed Ethan for another moment. As soon as the doctor turned his attention to the manifest once more, Ethan looked toward the glowing ghost.

I need to know if any of these men were conjurers, he said within his mind. *Do you understand me?*

Reg nodded and began to drift back along the corridor past the bodies that had already been identified. A short distance from the stairway, he halted, hovering beside the body of a regular. He stared back at Ethan, his eyes gleaming in the shadows. Ethan could hardly believe that the ghost had found someone. He had thought this a lark.

You're sure? he asked in his mind, as he approached the dead soldier.

Reg nodded to him and drifted off once more.

Stopping by the soldier Reg had indicated, Ethan looked down at the man. He was a large, young man with a broad fleshy face and long black hair.

"Can you tell me this man's name?" Ethan asked, still looking down at him.

"We've got him already," Preston said.

"Yes, I know. What was his name?"

The captain glowered at Ethan. Finally he shook his head in disgust. "Go," the captain told his corporal, his voice flat. "See who he's talking about."

The young officer joined Ethan by the dead soldier and looked down at the man. "That's Jonathan Sharpe," he said. "He was from York originally, but he fought over here against the French, and remained in Halifax with the regiment." The young man turned to Ethan. "Why? Is there something wrong?"

"No," Ethan said. "I thought I'd seen him before. Sorry to have troubled you." The lie came easily to him, though once again he caught the doctor eyeing him. He wondered if Senhouse or even Geoffrey had revealed to Rickman that Ethan was a speller.

Looking past the doctor, Ethan saw that Uncle Reg hadn't vanished again, as he thought the ghost might.

Rather, he had positioned himself by the dead soldiers whom Preston and his aide had yet to identify. As before, the ghost's glowing eyes were locked on Ethan's. Deliberately, he turned to gaze down upon one of the men and then looked up at Ethan again.

"Can I go back to the captain, sir?" the corporal asked.

Ethan barely heard him. "Another one?" he whispered.

Uncle Reg nodded.

"I'm sorry?" the corporal asked.

With a sharp shake of his head, Ethan looked away from the ghost.

"Aye, of course," Ethan told the man. "I'm sorry to have pulled you away from what you were doing."

The man edged away from him and rejoined Preston. Ethan followed him, forcing himself not to hurry, though his pulse was racing. Could there have been two conjurers among these men? The odds against such a thing were staggering. There were maybe fifteen conjurers among all of Boston's fifteen thousand residents, and yet it seemed that there had been two among these seventy-two soldiers.

He slipped past Rickman, Preston, and the corporal, walking until he reached Uncle Reg and the second conjurer the ghost had found. Ethan leaned back against the wall of the vault, and waited for the other men to reach this man.

You're certain? he asked Reg.

The ghost nodded.

Are there more, or just these two?

Reg held up two glowing fingers.

And you're really sure about both of them?

This time Reg scowled at him.

Right. Sorry.

Ethan watched Preston and his corporal. Seeing that they remained engrossed in what they were doing, Ethan turned his attention to the man Reg had indicated. He appeared to be somewhat older than the other soldiers; there were lines around his mouth and eyes, and his brown hair was flecked with silver. But he had a boyish face, with round cheeks and a smooth brow. Ethan guessed that he would have had a pleasant smile.

Before long, Rickman and the others reached the man.

"Do you know this one, Corporal?" Preston asked.

"Not well, sir, no. I think his last name might be Osborne." The young man looked back at the doctor. "Is there an Osborne on the manifest?"

Rickman searched the list. "Here he is. Caleb Osborne."

The corporal's expression brightened. "That's it! Caleb. Another who came to fight the French and stayed in these parts."

Ethan caught the ghost's eye and held Reg's gaze. Caleb Osborne and Jonathan Sharpe. He would learn what he could of them, as well as the man who turned out to be missing.

They reached the last of the dead a short time later, and once the corporal had identified this last man, Rickman thumbed through the pages of the manifest.

"That's most of them," he said, sounding weary. "But there are still nine who neither of you knew." He turned to Ethan. "I'm afraid we won't have a name for you tonight."

"The officers who spent the most time with these men died with them," Preston said. "They would have been able to identify all of them, obviously. But I'll go back to my ship. Maybe one of my sergeants will be able to help with these last few."

"Thank you, Captain," Ethan said.

"You didn't answer me before," Preston said. "At least not really. What is it you think the missing man did?"

Ethan shrugged, making an effort not to look at Uncle Reg. "I don't know. He might simply have deserted. Or he might have had something to do with the deaths of these others."

Preston turned to the doctor. "And how exactly did they die?"

Rickman was watching Ethan. "We don't know that, either."

"You must have some idea, Doctor. Nearly a hundred men are dead—the crew in addition to these regulars. Was it an illness of some kind? Could it be yellow fever so far north this time of year? Was it influenza? It couldn't have been smallpox—not from the looks of these men."

At last Rickman turned to face the captain. "We're still trying to determine what it was. There are several possibilities, but we don't know yet."

Preston frowned. "Well, you should inform us when you do."

"Of course, Captain."

The captain glanced once more at Ethan and left the vault. The corporal hurried after him.

Neither Ethan nor the doctor said a word until the sound of the officers' footsteps on the stone stairway had receded. Ethan heard no more rocket explosions, but he couldn't say for certain when they had ceased. Uncle Reg still lurked beside him in the corridor, and it occurred to Ethan that because he had summoned the ghost, Reg couldn't leave until he dismissed him. He wasn't sure he wanted to in front of Rickman.

"What do you think I should tell the captain, Mister Kaille?" the doctor asked after some time, looking over the corpses arrayed in front of them. "Shall I make up some tale about yellow fever or pleurisy?"

"I'm not a doctor," Ethan said, stepping past him and starting to make his way toward the stairway.

"I didn't say you were. But I knew a man once—you remind me of him."

Ethan halted, took a breath, turned.

"He was a wheelwright in Farnborough," Rickman went on. "He kept to himself, but he was well known in the city nevertheless. Strange things always seemed to happen when he was around. Inexplicable things. One winter he took ill, and I was called in to look at him. He had a tumor—it should have killed him. And yet by spring he was well again, and he lived to be an ill-tempered old man."

"What does this have to do with me?"

"There were whispers, rumors," the doctor said, walking toward Ethan. "People said that he cured himself with witchcraft, that in fact he had drawn upon the dark arts throughout his life. He never did anything too grand. I don't believe he wanted that kind of attention. But I do know that nothing short of witchery could have saved his life."

Ethan could no longer look Rickman in the eye. "Again, I have to ask you: What does this—?"

"I believe these men were killed by some sort of devilry," Rickman said. He stopped a few paces short of where Ethan stood. "What's more, I believe you know this already, and that you were asked to inquire into their deaths for that very reason."

"I see," Ethan said. "So you also suspect that I'm a conjurer myself."

"Yes, I do."

Ethan forced a thin smile. He was too weary to deny it, and he didn't think that Rickman would have believed him anyway. "Very good, Doctor. I hope you'll keep in mind that people like me are still hanged as witches. I'd prefer that others didn't know."

Rickman blinked once, his mouth open. For all the man's bluster and confidence, he seemed to have been quite unprepared for Ethan's admission.

"Yes," he said. "Yes, of course. I mean, no, I won't tell anyone. I just—" He regarded Ethan with wonder, his face like that of a child watching rockets go off for the first time. "You really are a witch?"

Maybe Ethan should have been amused, but having the truth wrung out of him for the second time this day had put him in a sour mood. "We prefer to be called conjurers or spellers," he said, his voice flat. "But yes, I am."

"Good Lord," the doctor said, breathless. "I have so many questions."

Ethan turned and walked to the stairs. "I'm sure. But it's late, and I have no desire to answer them."

He started to climb out of the vaults, and a moment later heard Rickman hurrying after him. Uncle Reg walked at Ethan's side, watching him expectantly.

"Sorry," Ethan whispered. "*Dimitto te.*" I release you.

"Perhaps we can speak tomorrow," the doctor said, the words echoing in the narrow stairway.

Ethan said nothing.

The air aboveground had grown as cool as that in the vaults, and a fine gray mist had settled over Castle William, partially obscuring the stars overhead. Ethan could still hear a few men singing on the ships, but the choruses of "Yankee Doodle" seemed to have stopped.

Rickman and Ethan walked to the officers' barracks, a short distance south of the vault, and found a pair of empty cots set just inside the door of the first building. Ethan was famished and would have liked to wash off the faint musty smell of the vaults. He thought he could also smell the stink of rot and death on his clothing, but he might have imagined it. He had spent too much of his day among the dead. Despite his hunger and his desire to bathe, he fell onto one of the cots and soon had drifted into a deep, dreamless slumber.

He awoke to find himself alone in the barracks. Daylight streamed in through the building's small windows, and a steady wind whistled in the stone. Officers shouted commands on the parade nearby, their calls a counterpoint to the rhythm of marching and the rattle of rifle drills.

Ethan climbed out of bed, ran a hand through his hair, and headed outside. The sky was covered with high, white clouds. Ethan shielded his eyes with an open hand and looked around for Rickman or any other familiar face. Seeing no one he knew, he walked back to the vaults and descended the stairs. Before he reached the corridor he heard voices and thought he could smell a hint of rot coming from all those bodies.

Stepping into the torchlight, he saw the doctor standing with the corporal from the previous night and a second British officer he didn't recognize.

"Ah, Mister Kaille," Rickman said. "Welcome. If you can bear with us for a minute or two, I think we'll have a name for you."

"All right."

The three men wasted little time moving down the line of dead. They bothered only with those men who hadn't been identified the night before. When they reached the last of the bodies, Rickman looked through the manifest once more and nodded, a satisfied grin on his face.

"Simon Gant," the doctor said, looking at Ethan.

"Gant," Ethan repeated. The name sounded familiar. He said it again and looked at the corporal he had met the night before. "Do you know him? Can you tell me anything about him?"

The young officer's jaw tightened. "Aye, I know him, the deserting bastard. I'd like to get my hands on him, too. Never liked him. Always thought he was hiding something, if you know what I mean. I should have known he'd come to this."

"Maybe I can find him for you," Ethan said. "Tell me what he looks like."

"He's a big man," the corporal said. "Tall, brawny. He has red hair and a ruddy face. I suppose some might say he's good-looking; he always seemed to have a lady with him when he was on leave."

An image had started to form in Ethan's mind. He had seen this man; he felt certain of it.

"His nose looks like it had been broken a couple of times, but the really odd thing about him is that his eyes—"

"Are different colors!" Ethan broke in.

"That's right!" said the man, sounding surprised. "One's blue and the other's green. You know him?"

"It seems that I do," Ethan said. "I needed the reminder. Thank you."

The corporal grinned.

Ethan knew Gant, all right. He had met the thief once, years ago, when he first returned to Boston from Barbados. But the memory of their encounter remained clear, because of all that had come after. As the corporal said, Gant was a brute of a man; tall, broad-shouldered, thick around the middle. He had stolen some coin and jewelry from a home in the North End, and the man he robbed, a shopkeeper of some limited means, was one of the first to hire Ethan as a thieftaker.

Ethan had little trouble tracking Gant down; the thief had been blessed with great physical strength but little intellect. But at that time Ethan wasn't as skilled with spells as he was now, and Gant managed to get away.

The next thing Ethan heard, Sephira Pryce had intervened, retrieving the goods from Gant and returning them to the shopkeeper. Initially, Ethan blamed poor luck for the loss of his commission. Only later did he come to realize that any time he took a job he risked losing money to Sephira and her toughs. But in the weeks and months that followed this first incident, Ethan began to hear stories about Gant and Sephira. Some said that he worked for her. Some said that she wanted him dead. Some said that their feud was all a ruse, that in fact they were partners.

And then, in the fall of 1761, Gant left Boston to fight the French, and that was the last Ethan heard of him. Until today.

The corporal and his friend still stood in the vaults watching Ethan and the doctor. Ethan sensed that they expected—or at least hoped—to be assigned some new task.

For his part, Ethan needed time alone with the dead—or if not alone, at least not in the company of the soldiers. Apparently Rickman sensed this.

"Thank you, gentlemen," the doctor said to the officers. "Your help has been invaluable. We'll be certain to convey as much to your superiors."

The corporal's face fell. "There's nothing more you need?" It seemed that working in the vaults, even with scores of dead men arrayed before them, was preferable to laboring on the ships.

"Thank you, no," said the doctor.

The two men exchanged a look and offered a reluctant salute to Rickman. The corporal nodded once to Ethan and led his companion back up the stairs.

"My thanks, Doctor," Ethan said, walking to the body of Jonathan Sharpe, the first of the dead men Uncle Reg had indicated the night before.

There were active conjurers—men and women like Ethan who cast spells with some frequency. And there were others, like Ethan's sister Bett, who out of fear, or ignorance of their family history, or some odd sense of righteousness, never conjured. Ethan wanted to know which best described the two dead conjurers in the corridor.

He lifted the first man's arm and pushed up his sleeve.

"What are you doing?" Rickman asked.

Ethan paused over the dead man. Admitting to the doctor that he was a conjurer was one thing; he wasn't prepared to explain Uncle Reg to the man. He didn't know how Rickman would react to the notion of a ghost joining them down here in the vaults. "I have reason to believe that this man and one other down at the end of the corridor were both conjurers. I want to see if they were active spellers or if they merely had speller blood in their veins." He went back to working the sleeve up the dead man's arm.

"How can you tell?"

"From that," Ethan said, pointing to the dead man's forearm. It was scored with a lattice of white scars, which had been made even more stark than usual as the man's arm had started to grow bloated.

"The scars?"

"That's right." He pulled Sharpe's sleeve back in place, laid the man's arm back down, and pushed up his own sleeve to reveal similar marks. "You see?"

"But why—?"

"Blood," Ethan said. "Conjurings need a source, usually a living source for more powerful spells. Blood is the most easily available, as well as the most effective." He pushed his sleeve back down and walked to the second conjurer, Caleb Osborne, the older man with silver-flecked hair.

Osborne had no scars on his forearm. At least not his left forearm. But when Ethan looked at the corpse's right forearm, he found that it was thick with scarring. Osborne must have been left-handed. Ethan looked more closely at the man's hands and found that the left was more heavily callused than the right.

"He's scarred, too," Rickman said.

"Yes. They were both active conjurers. I wonder if each knew that the other was a speller."

"I had no idea that there were so many of your kind," the doctor said, his voice low.

"There aren't. I was rather surprised to find even one among these men. To have found two is . . . most odd."

"And yet you knew to look." Rickman's tone was mild enough, but he watched Ethan, perhaps expecting him to flee at any moment. Or to attack.

"A conjuring killed these men. That much is clear to me. And so it struck me as logical that there might be conjurers aboard the ship."

"And you think that whoever is responsible might have been directing his attack at one or both of these . . . these conjurers."

"I believe that's one possibility."

"Are there other possibilities?"

"Of course," Ethan said, thinking of Spectacles and of Sephira Pryce.

Torches flickered and spluttered in the ensuing silence.

Aboveground, commanders continued to exhort their men.

"There's nothing more that I can do here," Ethan said, his gaze sweeping over the dead one last time. "And I'd like to return home."

Rickman took a long breath. "Yes, of course. Let's get out of here. I'll see to it that you're rowed back to Long Wharf immediately."

They left the vaults, climbing back up into the light of day, like reprieved souls rising from the devil's realm. As much as he had tried to inure himself to moving among the dead, Ethan was deeply relieved to know he wouldn't have to go back down there again.

It took some time for Rickman to find someone who could get a message to Lieutenant Senhouse on the *Launceston*, and still a while longer for Senhouse to dispatch a pinnace to the island. But eventually, late in the morning, the small boat that would take Ethan back to Boston reached the fortress.

Rickman accompanied Ethan onto the wharf. "Thank you for your help," he said, extending a hand. "I found our time together most educational."

Ethan grinned. "I was glad to be of service. As my inquiry continues, I may need your expertise. Will I be able to reach you aboard the *Launceston*?"

Rickman's expression sobered, and he leaned closer, still gripping Ethan's hand. "For a while longer, yes," he said, speaking softly. "But the fleet is only here to transport the British army. Once they're settled on land, our presence here is no longer necessary. Do you understand what I'm saying?"

"The occupation will begin soon. Today? Tomorrow?"

Rickman straightened without answering and released Ethan's hand. "Take care of yourself, Mister Kaille."

"And you, Doctor."

Ethan stepped into the boat. Once he had settled

himself, the oarsmen pushed off from the dock and started back across the harbor to Long Wharf.

With the tide heading out, and a strong breeze roughening the waters, the journey back to the city took the better part of an hour. Ethan spent much of the time wondering whether it was happenstance that had put Jonathan Sharpe and Caleb Osborne together in the Twenty-ninth Regiment, or if the two men might have known each other and planned to wind up in the same company. What, if anything, did they have to do with Simon Gant? And what role, if any, had they played in the spell that killed them and ninety-five of their comrades? There were too many coincidences and too many questions hanging over this one ship.

Upon landing at Long Wharf, Ethan made his way back toward Henry's cooperage. It had been the better part of a day since last he had eaten a decent meal, and he could smell the staleness in his clothes.

But as he approached his home, he felt an unexpected brush of power. It wasn't a pulse, as it would have been if someone had spoken a conjuring. Rather, it felt as if he had walked through a spell, a conjured spiderweb, minute fibers of power stretching and breaking across his face and limbs.

A pulse of power followed an instant later. Ethan grabbed for his knife, knowing that he had too little time, that he had been careless, and fearing that his foolishness would cost him his life.

He felt the spell rushing toward him; he could almost hear it humming in the cobblestones. It hit him full in the chest, knocking him off his feet, stealing his breath. He hit the ground hard, tried to get to his feet.

But he could feel darkness taking him, and there was nothing he could do to stop it.

Chapter

EIGHT

A splatter of cold water to the face woke Ethan up. He opened his eyes, felt the world heave and spin, and squeezed them shut again. The last time he felt this way, he had spent the previous night celebrating his release from Barbados by drinking two flasks of Madeira wine all by himself.

"More water."

He recognized that voice, but before he could open his eyes again, or tell them that the first splash of water had been enough, he was doused a second time.

"Time to wake up, Ethan," Sephira said.

Someone snickered. Yellow-hair probably, or maybe Nap.

Ethan opened his eyes again, and though the world around him still spun, he managed to force himself up onto an elbow. He was lying on grass, and his first thought was that they had taken him to the Common again, as they had once before when intending to kill him. In the next instant he realized that if Sephira had wanted him dead, he would never have awakened. Surveying his surroundings, Ethan saw that he was on a lawn behind Sephira's house. Yellow-hair, Nap, and

Gordon stood nearby. Yellow-hair—Nigel—had a bucket in his hand and a mocking grin on his face.

Mariz stood apart from them. He had his sleeve rolled up and he had already cut himself. A small trickle of blood ran down his forearm toward his wrist. It was like having a loaded pistol pointed at Ethan's head. Feeling the way he did, there was no way Ethan could conjure quickly enough to best the man.

"Those were good spells," Ethan said, rubbing the back of his neck. "Detection?"

Mariz smiled and nodded, his spectacles flashing white for an instant as they reflected the glare.

"And a sleep spell?"

"Basically," he said, his accent thickening the word.

"I have access to witchcraft now," Sephira purred, looking far too pleased with herself. Her hair was down, black curls shining. She wore her usual clothes: black breeches, a matching waistcoat fitted snugly around her curves, a silk shirt cut low. As always, she looked stunning. "And I have my men as well. There's nothing you can do to hurt me, and no way you can leave here without my consent. So you're going to answer some questions for me, and after we're done I'll decide whether or not to kill you."

Ethan answered with a short, breathless laugh. "That sounds fair. But can we do this over supper? I haven't eaten all day."

Sephira stared at him, then gave a laugh of her own. "All right." She turned on her heel and started toward the house. "Bring him."

The three toughs closed on him, but to Ethan's surprise, Nap offered a hand and pulled him to his feet. They arrayed themselves around him, with Mariz following a few paces behind, and escorted him into the house.

Sephira had seated herself at the head of a long table in her dining room. Not for the first time, Ethan admired the tasteful artwork and tapestries that adorned her walls. She indicated with an open hand the seat to her right.

"Sit," she said. "The food will be out momentarily."

Ethan took his seat. The others remained standing nearby.

"You were eavesdropping yesterday."

He saw no sense in denying it. "Aye. Rude of me, I know."

"Why?" she asked, ignoring him. "What did you hope to learn?"

"I wanted to know more about Spectacles here," he said, lifting his chin toward Mariz. "I overheard him in the Dowsing Rod the night before, and I saw that he sensed my spell."

"It seems that too often you listen to other people's conversations," Mariz said. "This could get you killed."

"Why did you eavesdrop on him in the tavern?" Sephira asked, drawing Ethan's gaze again. "What is it you're after?"

"I'm not after anything. I recognized Spectacles when he walked in. I'd seen him with Tanner, and since you had just robbed me of my earnings from that job, I was interested in hearing what he had to say."

Before Sephira could ask him more, a servant entered the room carrying a platter of cheeses, fresh bread, apples, and pears. The man laid the food before them and retreated into the kitchen.

"Help yourself," Sephira said.

Normally, Ethan would have hesitated to eat any food Sephira offered him that she didn't eat herself. He didn't think she was above poisoning a rival. But on this day he was so hungry that he didn't even hesitate. He took cheese and bread and began to gorge himself. Sephira watched him, appearing amused. After a few moments she stood, retrieved two glasses and a flask of wine, and returned to the table. She poured a glass for Ethan and put it in front of him.

"Drink this, before you choke yourself," she said.

Ethan swallowed what was in his mouth and took a long sip of wine.

"Thank you."

"Where have you been that you haven't eaten?" she asked.

"Who says I've been anywhere?"

"I do," Mariz answered. "The detection spell by your home was not the only one. I placed one around that tavern as well. You did not go to either location until this midday."

"Where were you, Ethan?" Sephira asked again.

Sometimes Ethan refused to answer Sephira's questions simply on principle. Too often she treated him like he was another one of her lackeys. He resented it, and went out of his way to defy her. But on this occasion it occurred to him that he might learn something of value by telling her at least part of the truth.

"I was at Castle William."

Her eyebrows went up. "Castle William," she repeated. "Why?"

"Representatives of the Crown requested that I inquire into an assault on one of their ships. The *Graystone*."

He paused, allowing the vessel's name to sink in. Sephira's expression remained unchanged, but Mariz cast a quick look in her direction, and Nigel and Nap, who were leaning against the far wall of the dining room, exchanged glances.

"It seems someone used a conjuring against the ship," Ethan went on. "Every man on board was killed."

Even Sephira couldn't mask her response to that.

"Every man?" she repeated, leaning forward. Her eyes flicked in Mariz's direction before fixing on Ethan again. "You're sure of this?"

"I'm sure. Every man on the ship was killed. Nearly a hundred in all." He turned to look at Spectacles. "Whoever cast a spell that powerful would have had to take a life for the conjuring, don't you agree?"

Mariz didn't flinch from Ethan's gaze. "*Sim, eu concordo*. I agree."

"I noticed the other day that you and your friend—Afton, I believe—were keeping a close eye on the British fleet. Was it the *Graystone* you were watching?"

"You are what my people would call an *intrometido*," Spectacles said, his voice low and menacing. "You meddle in the affairs of others when you should not."

"Yes, Ethan has always been too inquisitive for his own good," Sephira said, sounding far less concerned about his transgression than had Mariz. "I'll admit, it's not one of his more endearing traits." She sipped her wine. "Our interest in the fleet is no different from that of any other person in the city. This business of the impending occupation has all of us on edge."

"So, Mariz here is just another concerned citizen," Ethan said.

A dazzling smile lit her face. "Exactly."

Ethan considered bringing up Simon Gant, but there were limits to what Sephira would tolerate, and he wasn't sure he was ready to reveal just how much he knew. Keeping silent, he reached for an apple and bit into it.

"What is it these representatives of the Crown have asked you to do?" Sephira asked.

Ethan swallowed before answering. "They want me to find the conjurer who killed their men." He eyed Mariz again. "What were you doing just after dawn yesterday morning?"

"Sleeping."

"Alone?"

Mariz laughed. "Sadly, yes."

"Do you think that Mariz here is the one who killed those soldiers?" Sephira asked. She laughed as well. "Is that what all this is about? Is that why you've been following him and listening to our conversations?"

The only thing worse than being intimidated and beaten

by Sephira and her men was being ridiculed by her. Ethan knew this, because she ridiculed him a lot.

"There aren't many conjurers in Boston capable of casting a spell that powerful," Ethan said. "And since Mariz is new to the city, I thought it a possibility."

Sephira shook her head, still chuckling. "Go home. There's nothing more for you to learn here. It wasn't Mariz. I assure you it wasn't."

"Pardon me for saying so, Sephira, but your assurances don't carry much weight with me."

The smile vanished from her face, leaving her expression stony. "Well, they should. And you ought to watch yourself. I've said you can go. I'd suggest you leave now, before I change my mind."

Ethan took another bite of his apple and looked around the room. Nap and Nigel had straightened and were regarding Ethan the way hunting dogs would a fox. At a word from their master, they would attack. Mariz held his knife loosely in his right hand; his left sleeve was still pushed up.

Ethan stood and nodded to Sephira. "My thanks for the food."

He backed out of the room, watching her men, expecting Sephira to sic them on him.

"How much are they paying you?" Sephira called after him.

"Enough to keep my interest," Ethan said. "But probably not enough to draw yours."

She laughed at that and raised her cup of wine in salute.

Ethan let himself out of the house, stepping past Gordon, who stood guard outside the front entrance. The big man didn't try to stop him, but he did enter the house, no doubt to make certain that Ethan had left with Sephira's permission. Ethan took one last bite of his apple and tossed what remained onto Sephira's lawn.

He was confident that he had bought himself some time, but he knew that it came at great risk. Without lying to Sephira and the others, he had given them the impression that Simon Gant was dead, murdered with every other man aboard the *Graystone*. He knew Sephira well enough to understand that she wouldn't leave anything to chance; if she had been intent on finding Gant, she would now be just as intent on confirming his death. And eventually, when she learned that he had gotten away before the spell that killed his shipmates was cast, she would be furious with Ethan. It wouldn't make any difference to her that he hadn't actually lied. But Ethan would deal with her when the time came. In the meantime, he assumed that he had a day or two in which to find Gant and figure out why Sephira was so interested in his return to Boston.

Ethan headed back to Henry's shop, still intent on washing up and putting on a change of clothes. Mariz's sleep spell had left him unsure of the time, and with the sky still clouded over, he couldn't fix the position of the sun. But as he neared the streets that lay closest to Boston's southern wharves, he saw that there were still plenty of people abroad in the city. It couldn't have been too late in the afternoon.

He cut through the heart of the South End and soon turned the corner onto Cooper's Alley. As he did, he spotted a lone figure lurking in the byway next to Dall's cooperage. Even from a distance, Ethan recognized the man. He was slight and young, with the face of a lad half his age, but he wore the long black vestments and stiff white cravat of a minister. Trevor Pell.

Ethan slowed, looking around for Henry Caner, the rector of King's Chapel, or perhaps Sheriff Greenleaf. Pell had proven himself a friend on more than one occasion, but he would have come to Ethan's home only in the most dire of circumstances.

"I'm alone," Pell said. "Except for this girl." He squatted down and Shelly emerged from the byway, her tail wagging. "She's been keeping an eye on me. She working for you?"

"Aye, she works for me," Ethan said, grinning as he walked to where the minister waited for him. "Unless someone else gives her food. Then she'll work for him."

"Ah." Pell gave the dog's head one last scratch before standing. "Sounds like a thieftaker to me."

Ethan grinned. "I suppose it does." He looked around again. An old woman hobbled toward them carrying a basket of bread, and Shelly trotted off after her. "Are you just out for a walk?" Ethan asked. "Or did you come for a reason?"

"As it happens," Pell said, his voice dropping, "I came looking for you yesterday, but couldn't find you. I . . . I need to ask you some questions."

Ethan nodded, understanding far more than Pell knew. "Aye, but not here on the street. Come upstairs."

They went up to Ethan's room. Once they were inside, Ethan retrieved a small pouch of mullein from the table by his bed. Mullein was one of the most powerful of all conjuring herbs, and it worked especially well for warding spells. After barely surviving the attacks of a powerful conjurer several summers before, he had made sure that he always had a supply on hand. Taking three leaves from the pouch, he said, "*Tegimen ex verbasco evocatum.*" Warding, conjured from mullein.

Pell jumped at the pulse of power, and started a second time when he spotted Uncle Reg leering at him from the corner of the room. The minister was not a conjurer; he had never learned to cast spells. But he had conjuring blood in his veins, and so could feel spells when they were cast, and could see spectral guides like Reg. And yet, for all the times he had been present when Ethan cast, he never seemed to get used to the thrum of power or the appearance of Ethan's ghost.

"What kind of conjuring was that?" the minister asked, in a tremulous voice, still eyeing Reg.

"A warding spell. There's a new conjurer in the city, and he works for Sephira Pryce."

Pell faced Ethan. "Well, that may be the answer to the question I came here to ask. Yesterday—"

"You woke to the pulse of a powerful spell."

"Yes," the minister said. "You felt it, too."

"I expect every conjurer in Boston felt it."

"My first thought was that you had cast it," Pell told him. "But the more I thought about it, the more I realized that it felt too . . ." The minister trailed off, shaking his head.

"Strong?" Ethan suggested

Pell looked up. "Dark."

"You have good instincts," Ethan said. He told Pell what had happened to the *Graystone* and about his time at Castle William. Senhouse had asked for his discretion, and yet having been back in Boston for but a short while, he had already told Sephira and Pell of the *Graystone*'s fate. But he knew that Sephira would keep his secret out of her own self-interest, and Pell would keep it because he was naturally discreet.

"Dear God," the minister said, his face ashen. "Every one of them. How powerful would a conjurer have to be to do that?" He faltered, but then added, "Could you do it?"

Ethan pondered the question. "I don't think the casting itself would have been that difficult," he said, choosing his words with care. "But whoever cast it would have had to source the conjuring in a life."

"You mean the sorcerer killed someone when he conjured? Like with the Jennifer Berson murder a few years ago?"

"Yes," Ethan answered, although he was thinking not of the Berson girl, but of a kindly dog: Pitch, Shelly's constant companion. Ethan had cast a spell sourced in the life of the poor creature in order to fight off the conjurer who murdered Jennifer Berson and thus save his own life. The memory of that casting had haunted him ever since. Aside from Kannice, he had told no one of what he had done that night. "He would have killed someone, or something," he said. "It could have been an animal rather than a person and it still would have been a powerful casting."

"But dark."

"Aye. Very dark."

"Do you think that this new conjurer did it?"

"I think it's possible. He and Sephira have seemed unusually interested in the fleet, and it turns out that a former associate of Sephira's came to Boston aboard the *Graystone*, but managed to get off before the spell was cast."

"I see," Pell said. "Well, tell me how I can help."

Ethan kept his amusement to himself. Between Diver and Pell one might have thought that Ethan was putting together his own thieftaking empire, one to rival Sephira's. He understood, of course. Both men were young and saw in Ethan's work the excitement and adventure that they couldn't find working the wharves or tending to the souls of the King's Chapel congregation. As it happened, though, there was something Pell could do for him.

"I'm glad you asked, Mister Pell," he told the young minister, drawing an eager smile from the man. "Within the next day or two, officers of the fleet or the occupying army will have to deal with the dead, and when they do they'll need to inform the families of those soldiers who live here in Boston. I'd like you to get the names of any men whose families belong to your congregation."

Pell's face fell. "That's all?"

Ethan considered this. "Well, if you think you can get the names of men who attended .other churches that would be very helpful."

"But even that . . ." He shook head, frowning once more. "Surely there's something more that I can do. I mean, yes, of course I'll do as you ask. But . . . Where are you going now?"

"First, I'm going to wash off and change into clothes that don't smell of sweat and dead men. After that . . .

well, I believe Henry Caner would say it's best that you don't know. He still thinks that my conjurings will lead you to Satan."

"Ethan—"

"How many times has Mister Caner threatened to have me arrested, tried, and hanged as a witch?"

Pell looked down at the floor. "Several," he muttered.

"And do you wish to see him follow through on that threat?"

"Sometimes. It depends on the day."

Ethan chuckled. A reluctant smile crept across the minister's face.

Pell crossed to the door. "I'll leave you to wash," he said. "If I may offer some advice, use plenty of soap."

"Very funny."

"Perfumed soap, if you have any."

Ethan scowled. "Get out."

"I'll let you know what I can learn about the dead soldiers."

"Thank you," Ethan said. He watched the young minister leave.

Once Pell was gone, Ethan retrieved a pitcher from the basin in his room, took it down to the street and filled it with water from the pump near Henry's shop. He didn't wish to take the time necessary to heat it in his hearth, nor did he wish to invite more attention from Mariz and Sephira by casting. So upon returning to his room he stripped off his stale clothes and washed himself with water so cold it made his skin tingle. After drying himself, he put on clean breeches and a fresh shirt, waistcoat, and coat. He strapped on his blade, and as an afterthought tucked the pouch of mullein in his pocket. Satisfied that he was prepared for Mariz or whoever else he might meet, he left his room.

Upon walking around to the front of Henry's shop, however, he found the old cooper standing in the street speaking with another man, who towered over him. This second man, imposing, with a bold hook nose and small pale eyes, Ethan recognized at once: Sheriff Stephen Greenleaf. Spotting Ethan, Henry pointed his way. Greenleaf turned, said something more to the cooper, and strode toward Ethan.

"How can I help you, Sheriff?" Ethan asked, halting where he was and resisting the urge to reach for his blade.

"You could do some of your witchery for me, so that I might put a noose around your neck and rid this city of you for good."

"And failing that?" Ethan said.

"Hutchinson wants a word with you."

The sheriff started walking northward toward the center of the city. Ethan had little choice but to follow.

Lieutenant Governor Thomas Hutchinson, chief justice of the province, was the one man in Boston with whom Ethan was even less eager to speak than Greenleaf. Their previous encounters, especially those that occurred back when Ethan was inquiring into the death of Abner Berson's daughter, had been unpleasant to say the least. Hutchinson was a difficult man tasked with an onerous job: administrating a city and province whose citizens had grown increasingly resentful of their colonial masters.

"Do you know what he wants?" Ethan asked at length, as they made their way through Cornhill.

Greenleaf regarded him briefly but didn't reply.

The Town House, where Hutchinson and other provincial officials had their offices, was one of the most impressive structures in the city. Constructed of red brick, it had a graceful steeple, fine statues of a lion and unicorn on either side of its gable, and elaborately carved facings around its famous clock. It had long been one of Ethan's favorite buildings, despite the fact that most every time he entered it and ascended its marble stairway to the second floor, he found himself in some sort of trouble.

Greenleaf led him to the door of Hutchinson's courtroom and knocked once. At a summons from within they both entered.

Ethan had first met Thomas Hutchinson three years

earlier, also in this chamber. The night before their initial encounter, Hutchinson's home had been destroyed by a mob of Stamp Act agitators. Hutchinson, a tall, slight man, who sat with his back straight and his shoulders thrust back, had not changed much in the intervening years. There were a few more lines on his high forehead and at the corners of his mouth, but otherwise he hadn't conceded much to age. He had a long, prominent nose, and he wore a powdered wig of curls that framed his face, giving him a slightly feminine aspect. He was dressed in a black suit and white silk shirt and cravat, as he had been the last time they met in these chambers. That summer morning in 1765 it had been clear that the previous night had taken its toll on him. His large dark eyes had been bloodshot, his skin blotchy. He didn't appear to be in much better spirits on this day.

"Mister Kaille," he said. "It's been some time." He turned his gaze to Greenleaf. "Thank you, Sheriff."

Greenleaf left them.

"Do you know why I've summoned you here?" the lieutenant governor asked.

"I have some idea, yes," Ethan said. "I would imagine you wish to speak with me of the *Graystone* and her men."

Hutchinson regarded him, his lips pursed a bit. "Yes, that's right," he said at last. "To be honest, I wish that we might have found some other manner in which to investigate this devilry. But I can see why Mister Brower recommended that we involve you, and I know as well why Governor Bernard agreed, despite his misgivings."

"Yes, sir."

"I don't understand much of what Brower told me about you. But I gather that you're a witch, and that it was witchcraft that killed General Gage's men aboard the *Graystone*."

Ethan could have throttled Brower for telling Hutchinson that he was a conjurer.

"You have nothing to say?" the lieutenant governor asked.

"No, sir. I can help you find this killer; I may be the one person in Boston who is best equipped to do so. I don't believe anything else matters."

Hutchinson's smile was as thin as a blade. "I admire your confidence, misplaced though it may be. You seem to have misunderstood me, however. Some of the others seem to think as you do. But I find myself agreeing with Sheriff Greenleaf. He believes that far from being the best person to solve these murders, you're much more likely to be the person who committed them."

"That's ridiculous," Ethan said, his stomach tightening. It didn't surprise him to learn that the sheriff thought him guilty of such a crime, but having Greenleaf believe this was one thing. Having the lieutenant governor and chief justice of the province believe it was quite another. "Why would I have killed those men? And why after doing so would I agree to help investigate their murders?"

"Fine questions. I have no answer for you. And to be honest, I have no time to deal with such puzzles now. In case you hadn't noticed, Boston is about to welcome over a thousand new residents—all in uniform—with several thousand more on the way."

"All the more reason to leave the investigation to me, Your Honor, just as Mister Brower and Lieutenant Senhouse intended."

"Yes," Hutchinson said. The word itself seemed to taste bitter on his tongue. "It shouldn't surprise you to hear that I have a different solution in mind."

He was almost afraid to ask. "What solution is that?"

"You have to understand, I have nothing against you personally. And I have no desire to return to the barbarities of the last century. But it seems to me that those who governed this colony before Governor Bernard and myself were so horrified by events in Salem and Ipswich, and even here in Boston, that they grew complacent over the years. I believe that they—that all of us—have become too tolerant of your kind."

"Tolerant," Ethan repeated. "You believe people in Boston are tolerant of conjurers?"

"You're alive, Mister Kaille. And apparently a number of people know what you are and have known for some time. As I understand it, there are others like you. An African woman who lives on the Neck. An older man on Hillier's Lane. And others."

Janna. And old Gavin Black. Ethan wasn't sure what others Hutchinson meant, but he was as certain as he could be that most if not all of them had no more to do with the killing of the *Graystone*'s soldiers than had Janna or Black.

"You see my point," Hutchinson said. "There are so many of you now, and any one of you could be responsible for these atrocities."

"I had nothing to do with the attack on the *Graystone*. Neither did Janna or Gavin."

"So you say. But nearly one hundred of His Majesty's men are dead, and I haven't the luxury of your certainty. I can't take the time to find the one witch among you who did this. And since you're all abominations in the eyes of God, I feel that I would be perfectly justified in purging all of you from the city. I don't relish the idea of public hangings or burnings, but I'd be a fool if I didn't also acknowledge that such a display might prove useful as the occupation proceeds."

"You truly are considering this," Ethan said.

"Of course I am. This occupation will begin in a matter of days, and I don't want this inquiry of yours hanging over us indefinitely."

"I don't want that either, Your Honor. I assure you it won't take that long. Give me ten days and I will have your murderer. I swear it."

Hutchinson shook his head. "Ten days? That's out of the question. I can give you five."

"That may not be enough time," Ethan said.

"Then perhaps I should have the sheriff arrest you and your witch friends straightaway."

Ethan glared at him. "You do understand that limiting my inquiry in this way makes it more likely to fail."

"I disagree," Hutchinson said, the thin smile returning. "I have been a leader of men for a long time, and I've learned that demanding results tends to produce results. I have every confidence that if I were to give you a fortnight, you would take a fortnight. I've chosen instead to give you five days, and I'm certain that you'll avail yourself of that time. And if in the end I'm proved wrong . . ." He shrugged his narrow shoulders. "Well, we still have my solution, don't we?"

Hutchinson picked up a piece of parchment from his desk and began to read what was written there. "That is all, Mister Kaille."

"Yes, sir," Ethan said, making no effort to mask the bitterness in his tone. He let himself out of the courtroom, closing the door smartly behind him.

Greenleaf still waited for him in the corridor.

"What did he say?" the sheriff asked, his smile telling Ethan that he already had some notion of how the conversation had gone.

"He gave me five days," Ethan said, striding past him.

Greenleaf's face fell, making Ethan wonder if he had expected Hutchinson to deal with him even more harshly. It took the sheriff little time to recover, though.

"Well, I suppose you had better get busy then," he called, his words echoing in the Town House stairway.

Ethan didn't bother to answer.

than seethed as he left the Town House and set out for the North End.

Hutchinson's time limit was troubling enough. Ethan hoped that he could find Gant within five days, but he was far from certain of it. More disturbing by far, though, was the lieutenant governor's apparent eagerness to purge Boston of all its conjurers. With his superstition and his fear of conjurers, he threatened to take Boston, indeed the entire Province of Massachusetts Bay, down a path that had been trodden before, with tragic results. It didn't matter whether one called Ethan's kind witches or conjurers; tied to a stake or standing on a hangman's gallows, they were all mortal souls. Suddenly Ethan was the only man in Boston who could prevent what would amount to a massacre.

He thought about running back to the Fat Spider to warn Janna, and making his way to Hillier's Lane to tell Gavin Black. Perhaps they could leave Boston, find a safe place to stay until this matter was settled. But what of the other conjurers Hutchinson had mentioned, the ones Ethan didn't know offhand? Was it fair to warn Janna and Old Black and leave the others to fend for themselves? Better, he decided, to conduct his inquiry as quickly and effectively as possible, and save their lives that way.

The place he had been heading before meeting up with Sheriff Greenleaf—the place he hadn't been willing to take Mr. Pell—was a run-down tavern in the North End called the Crow's Nest. It sat just past Mill Creek, at the south end of Paddy's Alley, near the waterfront.

Kannice made a point of keeping the Dowsing Rod as reputable as possible. She didn't allow whoring or fighting or any other activities that might attract the notice of the sheriff. The Crow's Nest, on the other hand, might not have existed had it not been for whores, fights, and the trafficking of stolen and smuggled items. Ethan felt certain that Sheriff Greenleaf knew quite well what went on within its begrimed walls, but that a steady flow of coin convinced the good sheriff to look the other way.

The Nest had been in business since well before Ethan returned to Boston from the Indies, but over the years it had been run by a parade of ill-fated proprietors. One had been killed during a tavern brawl, at least three had been transported to the Caribbean for crimes ranging from theft to battery to murder, and another had disappeared under circumstances that to this day remained a mystery.

The current owner was a small, understandably skittish man named Joseph Duncan. Dunc spoke with a faint Scottish brogue and often rushed his words, making him difficult to understand under the best of circumstances. To make matters worse, he often had a lit pipe clenched between his teeth. He had taken ill during the smallpox epidemic of 1764, which proved even more deadly than the 1761 outbreak, and many assumed that he would meet a fate similar to that of other Crow's Nest proprietors. But to everyone's surprise, Dunc survived. His face, though, was ravaged by the disease, leaving his skin pitted and scarred.

When Ethan walked in, Dunc was standing at the bar,

perusing a newspaper. He glanced up from the paper, but quickly went back to reading. An instant later, he looked up a second time and pulled the pipe from his mouth.

"You're not welcome here!" he said, leveling a bony finger at Ethan. "I've told you that before."

Ethan walked to the bar and tossed a half shilling onto the wood. "An ale," he said to the bartender, a lanky man with large eyes and a crooked nose.

The bartender looked to Dunc, who was still eyeing Ethan.

"I'll leave when I've finished my ale, Dunc," Ethan said. "Not before. So you might as well tell him to serve me."

Dunc glared at Ethan for another few seconds before replacing his pipe with a click of his yellow teeth on clay. "Fine," he said, picking up his newspaper again. "One ale."

The barkeep took Ethan's coin and filled a tankard for him.

Ethan sipped his ale and leaned against the bar, eyeing the Scotsman. "I didn't think you were the kind of man to hold a grudge for so long."

Dunc continued to read, saying nothing.

"It looks like the repairs went well," Ethan went on, surveying the tavern. "This place looks as shabby as ever."

Dunc cast a dark look his way, but promptly turned to the paper once more. He was reading the *Gazette*, the foremost Whig newspaper in the city.

"You know, it really wasn't my fault."

Dunc threw the paper down on the bar. "Wasn't your fault?" he repeated, spittle flying from the side of his mouth as he tried to talk around the pipe. "You come in here and call Sephira Pryce a liar and a cheat in front of all my patrons! And when her men go after you, you nearly burn the whole place down with what I can only assume was witch—"

Ethan raised a finger just in front of the man's face, silencing him. "Keep your voice down!"

Dunc continued to glower at him, but for several moments he said nothing more. He puffed hard on his pipe, making the leaf in its bowl glow brightly in the dim tavern, and blew a cloud of sweet smoke from the corner of his mouth.

"What do you want, anyway?" he asked. "I thought you only drank in that tavern your woman owns."

"I have some questions for you."

The Scot's laugh was high and harsh. "Are you fool enough to think I'd help you?" He leaned closer, and when he spoke again it was in a whisper. "Do you have any idea what Miss Pryce would do to me if she found out?"

"I have a fair notion, yes. Especially because this concerns her as well." Ethan leaned toward the man and dropped his voice. "But do you have any idea what I'll do to you if you *don't* help me?"

Dunc stared back at him.

"She won't find out," Ethan said, his voice still low. "You have my word. And despite everything between us, you know what that's worth."

The Scot hesitated, nodded.

"Do you want to talk in back?"

Dunc shook his head. "People will see us go back there and they'll know for sure that I helped you. Better we stay out here. Make it quick."

"All right. What have you heard from Simon Gant lately?"

Dunc took a step back from him, nearly losing his footing as he did. "Gant? How do you—?" He clamped his mouth shut around the stem of his pipe, the bowl gleaming again. "No!" he said with a hard shake of his head. "I won't speak of him!"

"Be reasonable, Dunc. You wouldn't want me to leave here angry."

"I'll take my chances with you, Kaille. Better you than—" He shut his mouth again.

"Just tell me when you last saw him."

Dunc shook his head and reached for his newspaper. Ethan slapped his hand down on the paper, making the smaller man flinch.

"Was it recently, within the last day or two?"

The Scotsman regarded him with wide, fearful eyes. But after a brief pause he nodded almost imperceptibly.

"Do you think he's still in the city? Is that why you're so scared?"

"Wouldn't you be?"

"Do you know why Sephira might be looking for him?"

"No," he whispered. "I swear I don't. But . . ." He licked his lips. "They didn't part on the best of terms."

That much Ethan had gathered for himself.

"Do you have any idea where he—?"

"No more, Ethan. Please."

Ethan considered pushing him for one last answer, but in the next moment thought better of it. Dunc wasn't a bad sort, and Ethan had no desire to see him beaten or killed. "All right. But know this. I'll be watching the Nest. If Gant comes here—whether it's to meet with someone or sell goods—I'll learn of it. And if I have to tear this place apart to get at him, that's what I'll do. So you should ask yourself whether you're better off protecting him or helping me."

Dunc kept his eyes on Ethan, but he reached for the paper once more. This time Ethan let him have it. He drained his ale and left the tavern. He could threaten the man all he wanted; he knew that it wouldn't change Dunc's mind. Ethan couldn't blame him. Had he been in the Scot's position, he too would have been more afraid of Gant than of himself.

Ethan intended to go to the Dowser next. There had been no time for him to speak with Kannice before leaving the city the previous day, and she would be wondering why she hadn't seen him last night.

But as he stepped out onto Centre Street he noticed that people were walking toward the shores of the harbor, and

that a crowd had gathered down at the water's edge. He
thought he knew already what had drawn the interest of
so many, but he followed Centre Street onto Lee's Wharf
to make certain. From the wharf, he had a clear view of
the harbor and was able to confirm his suspicions.

The British fleet was on the move. The vessels were still
arrayed around Castle William, but several had sweeps
out. Others were already far enough from the fortress to
have raised sails, and were now cutting across the harbor
toward the city. Rickman had been right: The occupation would begin within the next day, perhaps this very
night.

At least a hundred men and women were standing
with Ethan on the wharf, and another dozen or two had
gathered on the street behind them. Yet they were all so
still, so utterly silent, that Ethan could have closed his
eyes and convinced himself that he was alone.

"Won't be long now," one man finally murmured,
breaking the silence. Others nodded their agreement.

"Let them come!" one young man cried.

People looked at him, but no one responded.

Ethan turned and started back up from the wharf. He
hadn't gone far, though, when he felt power hum in the
cobblestone. It wasn't a strong spell and it seemed to have
been cast from a distance, but he sensed the conjuring
spreading through the city like a ripple in the surface of
a pond.

He was still too close to the crowd watching the ships
to pull out his knife and cut himself. Fortunately, he had
the mullein. He took out the pouch, removed three leaves,
and spoke a warding spell under his breath.

His conjuring whispered in the street, an answer to
that distant spell, and Reg stared at him, insubstantial in
the late-afternoon light.

A few seconds later, the other conjurer's spell reached
him, coiling around his legs. Another finding spell. It felt
much like the conjuring Mariz had used to locate him
earlier, and Ethan wondered if Sephira had already

learned that Gant was still alive. He didn't expect that
he would have to wait long to find out.

He strode away from the crowded wharf, following
Ann Street back toward Union, but halted before he
reached the busy intersection. He preferred to face
Mariz and Sephira where he could use his knife to con-
jure. And he had no intention of luring them closer to
Kannice and the Dowser.

As he expected, Mariz reached him a short time later,
though surprisingly the conjurer was alone.

Mariz stopped a few paces from Ethan and glanced
around, a sour look on his thin face.

"It was you?" the man asked, sounding genuinely disappointed.

"Who else would it have been?"

"What are you doing here?"

Ethan smiled thinly. "I don't answer to you, Mariz.
Or to your boss."

Spectacles looked like he might argue, but instead he
shook his head and turned to leave again, back the way
he had come.

"Who were you looking for?" Ethan called after him.
"That finding spell would only have worked on a conjurer. Who did you think you would find here?"

"Stay out of my way, Kaille," Mariz said over his
shoulder. "This is none of your concern, and I see no need
to involve you. But if I have to, I will kill you."

"I think you'll find that more difficult than you
imagine."

Mariz flashed a quick grin and continued away.

Ethan watched him go before making his way to the
Dowser. Who had Mariz been looking for? Had another
conjurer come to Boston? And if so, what did he or she
have to do with Gant?

Ethan faltered in midstride.

Was Gant the conjurer? Sephira and Mariz had been
interested in the *Graystone*, and Ethan felt certain that
they were looking for Gant, just as he was. But it had

never occurred to Ethan that Gant might be a conjurer, too. Ethan had used spells during his one encounter with the man, but his conjuring had been too inept and too weak to have much effect. Gant was able to escape without resorting to spells of his own. At the time, Ethan assumed that Gant didn't possess any spellmaking abilities. But what if he had been mistaken?

He wondered for the first time if there had been not two but three conjurers on the *Graystone*. He could dismiss as mere coincidence the presence of two spellers on the ship, but not three. Maybe Sephira hadn't brought Mariz to Boston because she wanted to match the man's power against Ethan's. Maybe she faced a more significant danger.

By the time he reached the Dowsing Rod, the sky had begun to shade to a dark, brooding gray, and Beacon Hill and the spire of West Church were dark silhouettes against the clouds. Ethan entered the tavern and was embraced by the warm scent of baking bread and some sort of savory stew. There were few people inside—it was early yet—and he spotted Diver right away.

Ethan crossed to the bar, tossed a half shilling to Kelf, and made his way back to where Diver was sitting, sipping an ale and reading the *Gazette*.

Seeing Ethan, his friend set the paper aside.

"Where have you been? Kannice was asking after you last night and I didn't know what to tell her."

"I spent the night at Castle William," Ethan said, knowing that this would leave his friend speechless.

He wasn't disappointed. Diver's mouth fell open, but he couldn't manage a word.

Kelf came to the table bearing a cup of ale, a bowl of beef stew, and a round of bread. "Hereyago, Ethan," the barkeep said, running the words together as always. "Anythin' for you, Diver?"

"Another ale," Diver said, still staring at Ethan.

Once Kelf was gone, Diver leaned forward. "What were you doing out there?"

"It's a long story," Ethan said. "And I'm not sure how much I can tell you right now." The tavern was filling up, and Ethan didn't want to be overheard. Besides, trusting in Diver's discretion was never the best idea, as he had been reminded two nights before. "It's enough to say that I'll be working on behalf of the Crown for the next few days."

"The Crown?" Diver said, admiration in his voice. He nodded, his lips pursed. Ethan hadn't seen Diver this impressed in some years, probably since he had worked for Abner Berson.

Ethan picked up his spoon and began to eat.

"Well, I'm sorry to say that I can't tell you much," Diver said. "I've looked for Spectacles the past two days, but I haven't seen him. I'm not even sure he's in Boston anymore."

"His name is Mariz," Ethan said between mouthfuls. "I think he's from Portugal. I know he's working for Sephira. I saw him right before I came here."

Diver blinked. "Oh."

Ethan grinned. He would have walked through fire to save Diver's life, and Diver would have done the same for him. But that didn't mean he couldn't occasionally enjoy a laugh at his friend's expense.

"He found me, Diver," Ethan said. "He managed to use a sleep spell on me, and the next thing I knew I was at Sephira's house."

"Busy day."

"Very." Ethan sipped his ale. "Tell me this: Have you heard anything about Simon Gant coming back to Boston?"

"Gant?" Diver said, with a shake of his head. "Don't even joke about something like that."

"I'm not joking."

Diver frowned. "I thought Gant was dead."

"He's not, although it seems possible that someone went to a good deal of trouble to try to kill him. I'm almost certain that he's somewhere in the city, and that Sephira is looking for him."

"Oh, I'm sure she is," Diver said.

"Why?"

He shrugged. "You heard the same things I did. They had some kind of falling-out. And Sephira isn't the sort to forgive and forget. If he's alive, he'd be smart to get as far from here as he can."

Ethan took one last spoonful of stew and set his bowl aside. Leaning in, he asked in a low voice, "Did you ever hear anything about Gant being a conjurer?"

Diver considered this. "Not that I recall. But didn't you have dealings with him?"

"I did, but that happened a long time ago. He didn't use any spells against me. He didn't need to."

Ethan sat back again and reached for his ale.

"There you are," he heard from behind him.

He turned in his chair and smiled. Kannice was making her way to their table, a dishrag slung over her shoulder, candlelight shining in her auburn hair.

Reaching Ethan, she stooped and kissed his cheek. "I missed you last night," she whispered in his ear.

"I missed you, too."

Kannice straightened and cast a cold look Diver's way. "So are you going to tell me where you were?" she asked, turning her gaze back to Ethan. "Or are you going to make me guess?"

"Diver didn't believe me when I told him. I'm not sure you will either. I spent the night as a guest of the British army at Castle William."

"You were arrested?" she asked, her voice rising.

Ethan frowned. "I was employed. But thank you for showing such faith in me."

Diver grinned; Kannice merely scowled.

"You're working for the Crown?" she said, arching an eyebrow.

Kannice had always shown far more sympathy than Ethan for those who opposed Parliament and His Majesty the King on everything from the Stamp Tax to the Townshend Duties. During the Quartering Act crisis in

New York a couple of years before, Kannice had cheered efforts by the colonial assembly to deny troops access to publick houses and other private property. Now, with occupation imminent here in Boston, she feared that she and other tavern owners would be forced to provide housing and food for countless regulars.

She knew that Ethan had served in the royal navy, and she tolerated his Tory leanings, just as he did her Whiggish sympathies. Apparently, though, supporting the Crown was one thing; working for the king's men was quite another.

"Aye," Ethan answered, careful to keep his tone neutral. "And if I could tell you why, you'd understand."

"I see." She crossed her arms over her chest, her expression growing remote.

Kannice was as kind and generous a woman as Ethan had ever known, and she loved him deeply—more than he deserved, he sometimes felt. But when she wanted she could be as cold and hard as a New England winter.

"You're going to have to trust me, Kannice," he told her. "This isn't about politics."

"All right," she said, sounding skeptical. "You boys enjoy your ale. I have work to do." She turned on her heel and walked away.

Ethan glanced at Diver, who had the good sense to keep his eyes trained on his tankard.

After a few moments, Diver said, "Tell me more about Spectacles."

He was probably more interested in breaking the silence than in hearing anything Ethan could tell him, but still Ethan was grateful for the distraction.

"Mariz? He's an accomplished conjurer," Ethan said, and drained his ale.

He raised a hand and caught Kelf's eye. The barkeep nodded and began to fill another tankard.

"And," Ethan added, "he's not afraid to use his craft. He set up detection spells around Henry's shop, so that he would know when I went home. He attacked me with that sleep spell. And just before I came here, he used a finding spell."

"What did he want with you this time?"

Ethan tapped a finger to his lips, thinking. "That's just it. I don't think he was looking for me at all. He was disappointed when he realized that his casting had found me. He wouldn't tell me who he had been trying to find, but I think it was Gant."

"So," Diver said, speaking softly, and looking around to be sure that no one was listening. "Do you think that Gant and this guy Mariz are fighting it out to see who gets to be Sephira's speller?"

"No," Ethan said, shaking his head. "There's more going on here than that."

"Well, did one of them have some connection with whatever it is you're doing for the Crown?"

"I think so. But I don't know—"

Ethan stopped and stared at Diver, his mind racing. How had this not occurred to him earlier?

Kelf brought him his ale and set it on the table with the usual "Thereyago, Ethan." Ethan didn't say a word.

Once the barman had left them, Diver asked, "Are you all right?"

"I'm an idiot."

"Why? What's happened?"

Ethan looked around, trying to decide how best to make up for his foolishness. A cheer went up from the men at the front of the tavern, and Kannice and Kelf came out of the kitchen bearing another tureen of steaming hot stew, which they placed on the bar.

"I'll be back," Ethan said, standing and stepping away from the table.

"Ethan, what's going on?" Diver called after him.

Ethan didn't answer. He needed someplace private, someplace where no one would see him, where he didn't even have to worry about a chance encounter. He strode across the tavern, grabbed Kannice by the hand and started to drag her toward the stairway leading up to the second floor of the Dowser.

"What are you doing?" she demanded.

"Just come with me. Please."

Her expression darkened, and she began to resist. "Ethan—"

"I need your help, Kannice," he said, his voice low and tight. "And it can't wait."

Some of the men at the bar were laughing now.

"He's a bold one, isn't he?" one man said in a loud voice, drawing more guffaws from the others.

Ethan looked back at her and held her gaze for a moment. Seeing that he was in earnest, her expression softened and she followed him to the stairs.

When they reached the second-floor corridor, she asked in a whisper, "What is this—?"

He stopped her with a raised finger and shook his head. He pulled her on down a second hallway that led to the door to her private chamber, only stopping when they reached her threshold.

She regarded him for the span of a heartbeat, concern in her cornflower blue eyes. Drawing the key from within her bodice, she slipped past him and unlocked the door. He followed her inside and closed the door behind him.

Kannice had turned to face him. "Now, what's this about?"

Ethan pushed up his sleeve and pulled his blade from the sheath on his belt.

"I need to cast a spell. I couldn't chance doing it out on the street and I couldn't wait until later." He gave a quick shake of his head. "I mean, I could have, but it's important and—"

"It's all right," she said. She took a step toward him and took his free hand in hers. "Tell me."

"That spell I felt yesterday morning—do you remember?"

"The one that woke you," she said.

"Yes. It was . . . it killed every man aboard one of the British ships out in the harbor. Ninety-seven in all. Soldiers, sailors, officers. Every one of them."

"God save us. That's why you're working for the Crown."

"Yes."

"I'm sorry. I didn't—"

"It's all right. The point is, I saw the color of the power that killed them. And all this time I've been thinking that the spell was cast by a man who's now working for Sephira."

Kannice's eyes went icy. "That sounds about right for her."

"Perhaps," Ethan said. "I'm not sure. But earlier today, he used a spell on me. It put me to sleep. And it's only just occurred to me that I should be able to see the residue of that conjuring on me. I should be able to say for certain if he's the killer."

He laid the edge of the knife on his forearm and dragged the blade across his skin. Kannice winced and looked away. He marked himself with blood much as he had the dead soldier aboard the *Graystone*—a streak across his brow, and a second tracing the contour of his face and neck from the bridge of his nose to his breastbone.

"*Revela potestatem ex cruore evocatam,*" he said, as blood continued to well from the cut. Reveal power, conjured from blood.

Ethan felt the blood on his face vanish, like sweat evaporating in a summer breeze, and he sensed the spell as well. He knew that Gant and Spectacles would know that he had conjured, but this once he didn't care. Nor did he spare a glance for Uncle Reg, though he sensed the ghost beside him.

He looked down at his chest, where Mariz's spell had hit him earlier in the day, and also at his legs, where the finding spell had touched him. In both places, the residue of power looked the same. It glowed bright in the dim bedchamber.

"Is that it?" Kannice asked, pointing at his chest. "Is that from his spell?"

Ethan nodded, but said nothing.

The conjuring that had killed those soldiers had been a bright fiery orange. He could close his eyes and picture it perfectly.

The power glowing on his chest looked nothing like it. It was a pale, warm beige, the color of dead grasses on a late-summer afternoon.

"Is it the same as what killed the men on that ship?"

"No," he said, raising his gaze to meet hers. "It's not even close. Sephira's man didn't cast that spell."

"Then who did?"

He shook his head, looking down again at the pale glow of Mariz's conjuring. "I'm not sure," he told her. "But I think it's time I found Simon Gant. He might be able to tell me."

than cut himself again and cast a second spell to make the glow from Spectacles's spell vanish. He waited until the pale light had disappeared and turned toward the door.

"Wait," Kannice said. She sat on her bed and beckoned him over.

He walked to the bed and sat beside her.

"How did you get caught up in this? Why would representatives of the Crown come to you?"

"Geoffrey," he said.

It took her a few seconds. "Your sister's husband?"

"He works for the Customs Board. And, of course, he knows I'm a conjurer."

"And who is Simon Gant?"

"Another of Sephira's playmates. Word is that he betrayed her several years back. I thought that Mariz—the man who used those spells on me—that he might have been trying to kill Gant. I now know that's not the case. But if Gant is a conjurer—"

"Why would Sephira care about the British fleet?" Kannice asked.

That stopped Ethan cold. "I don't know."

"You said that ninety-seven men died. Even Sephira Pryce isn't so brazen as to think that she can take on the British Empire."

He weighed this, saw the logic in it. "Go on," he said at last.

"The occupation is about to begin and there are plenty of people who are unhappy about it. Some of them would stop at nothing to see that those regulars never set foot in this city."

"I thought you were one of them," Ethan said, smiling to soften the words.

She smiled back at him. "Aye, well, I can't conjure, can I?" Her grin faded. "You do see where I'm going with this."

"You think that the Sons of Liberty have declared war on King George's army."

"It's not as foolish as you're making it sound," she said.

"You're right, it's not. But even if Samuel Adams and his friends suddenly had access to such power why would they attack a single ship? And why choose the *Graystone* as opposed to the *Launceston* or one of the other rated ships?"

"I don't know," Kannice said. "Maybe their spell didn't work the way they intended. Maybe they were aiming for all the ships and the spell only worked against one of them. But if you ask me it's much more likely that this was the work of Adams and the rest than it is that Sephira would be willing to take on General Gage."

She had a point.

"All right," Ethan said. "Thank you. I'll give that some thought."

He started to stand, but Kannice grabbed his arm.

"Where do you think you're going?"

Ethan grinned again. "Back downstairs."

She shook her head and kissed him deeply on the lips. "I don't think so. There's a roomful of men down there who think you brought me up here for something other than a bit of conjuring. We wouldn't want to disappoint them."

They kissed again, and Kannice began to unbutton his waistcoat and shirt.

"I thought you were angry with me for working on behalf of the Crown."

She smiled and whispered, "I've forgiven you for that."

They went back down to the tavern's great room some time later. The Dowser was far more crowded now—most of those drinking ale and eating Kannice's stew hadn't been in the tavern when Ethan and Kannice went up to her chamber. But that didn't stop them all from whistling and applauding when the two of them reappeared. Ethan blushed to the tips of his ears, but Kannice didn't seem at all embarrassed.

"Don't applaud too much boys," she said, her voice carrying over the din. "Or else we might go back up for an encore and you won't have any more stew until morning."

As the men started laughing anew, she winked at Ethan and hurried off into the kitchen to prepare more stew. Ethan returned to the table and was surprised to find that Diver was still there. His friend cast a hurt look his way, but said nothing.

"It wasn't what it seems," Ethan said.

"No? Then why is your face as red as a regular's coat?"

Ethan smiled, feeling sheepish. "All right, it was what it seems, but it was more as well." He looked around, much as Diver had earlier in the evening, making sure that they wouldn't be overheard. But with so many now in the tavern no one could hear what he said and no one was paying them much heed. Keeping his voice down, he told Diver about the *Graystone* and the spell he had cast in Kannice's room.

"Why didn't you tell me earlier?" Diver asked when Ethan had finished. He still sulked, refusing to look up from his ale. Sometimes Diver was more boy than man.

It was part of his charm and also the reason Kannice thought him a wastrel.

"Because I didn't know if I could trust you to keep it quiet."

He did look up then. "That's not fair!"

"Isn't it? I can't have you talking about this all over the city. Especially now. I don't know what happened to the men on that ship, and until I do the fewer that hear of it the better. Do you understand?"

Diver nodded sullenly. "Aye, I do. And I know that I cost us both by talking about Tanner when I was with Katharine. But when are you going to start trusting me again?"

"I think I just did."

A small smile stole across Diver's face. "Aye, all right." He finished his ale and stood. "I should be going. I suppose you don't need me looking for Spectacles anymore."

"No," Ethan said. "But you can start looking for Gant. Don't go near him if you see him and don't let him see you if you can help it. But if you find him, I want to know about it."

Diver's smile broadened. "I'll keep my eyes open." He winked. "And my mouth shut."

After he left the bar, Ethan sat alone for a while longer, sipping his ale and, when it was gone, watching Kannice and thinking about what she had said upstairs. At one point, Kelf caught his eye and held up a tankard, asking Ethan if he wanted another ale. Ethan shook his head.

Ethan had had some dealings with Samuel Adams and his fellow Sons of Liberty a few years before when investigating the Berson killing. One of the so-called patriots had turned out to be a conjurer and an agent of the Crown. Ethan and Adams exchanged some harsh words during the course of Ethan's inquiry, but in the end Adams saved his life and Ethan managed to defeat the conjurer who had betrayed Adams's cause. He and the tax collector had not spoken since, but Ethan was certain Adams would remember him. He was less sure of how the man would respond to his questions about the *Graystone* and her fate.

Eventually, the tavern crowd thinned. Kelf and Kannice cleaned up and Kannice led Ethan upstairs to bed and sleep. Ethan slept poorly, though. He had odd, disturbing dreams of the dead on Castle William and he woke often. Several times, he drove himself from slumber after sensing conjurings, or at least thinking he did. He couldn't tell if he imagined the spells or if they were real.

When at last he woke to morning light, he felt no more rested than he had the previous night.

Kannice offered to make him breakfast, but he refused.

"Where are you rushing off to?" she asked, watching from the bed as he dressed.

"I'm going just where you told me to go." He grinned at the confused look on her face. "I'm going to speak with Samuel Adams. As you said, maybe he can shed some light on all of this."

"You could breakfast with me first."

Ethan shook his head, his grin fading. "The fleet was on the move yesterday evening. I'm convinced that the occupation will begin today, and I doubt that Adams will sit idly by while the regulars land. If I want to find him at his home, I have to go now."

He didn't add that he had only so much time before Hutchinson would begin rounding up Boston's conjurers and hanging them as witches; he didn't wish to alarm her. But already he felt the pressure of the lieutenant governor's ultimatum.

Kannice sat up, sobered by what he had said about the occupation. "Do you know yet where the men will be billeted?" she asked.

"No. If I hear anything I'll let you know."

He walked to the bed, kissed her lightly on the lips, and left.

The clouds that had covered the sky the day before

had passed, and the sun shone on Sudbury Street and Beacon Hill. This being the Sabbath, the streets were empty save for a few horse-drawn chaises and a number of children in ragged clothes who appeared to be playing tips.

The Adams estate, which had been owned by Samuel's father before it came to the son, was one of the more famous homes in the South End. It was a fine dwelling that overlooked the waterfront, one of the most impressive houses in its neighborhood, but it didn't rival the ornate estates of men like John Hancock and Thomas Hutchinson. Its fame derived not from its appearance, but rather from its tangled legal history and, of course, the fame, or infamy, of its current owner. Ten years ago, before Ethan returned to Boston from his imprisonment, Sheriff Greenleaf had attempted to auction off the Adams property. Samuel was newly widowed and in debt and the family property had been embroiled in a decades-old land-bank scandal. But Samuel challenged the sheriff's authority and prevailed on the provincial authorities to let him keep the house. Ever since, the property had been a site of public curiosity.

It was located on Purchase Street, not too far from where Ethan lived. Upon reaching the house, Ethan paused to admire the grand observatory on its roof and the quaint gardens leading to its entrance. He approached the door and knocked. He didn't have to wait long before the door opened, revealing an attractive young woman who smiled at him despite the quizzical look on her oval face.

"May I help you?"

"Please forgive the intrusion, Missus Adams. I'm looking for your husband."

"Of course," she said. "And you are . . . ?"

"My name is Ethan Kaille. Mister Adams and I met several years ago."

"Who is it, Betsy?" came a voice from within the house. Adams stepped into view. He wore dark breeches and a white shirt with a red waistcoat and matching cloak. His gray hair was tied back from his face and he carried a black tricorn hat. Seeing Ethan he halted, staring hard, his eyes narrowed. He held up a finger, which trembled slightly, asking Ethan to keep silent for a moment.

"Kaille," he said at last. "Ethan Kaille. Isn't that right?"

"Yes, it is, sir. I'm flattered that you remember."

"Well," he said, walking to the doorway and glancing sidelong at his young wife. "Ours was a most . . . unusual meeting; not one I'm likely to forget."

"Yes, sir. I'm wondering if I might have a word with you."

Adams frowned, his head shaking visibly with the palsy that Ethan recalled from their previous encounters. "I'm afraid you've chosen a bad day to come, Mister Kaille. I'm going to have to put you off for now. Perhaps in another few days—"

"It's about the occupation, sir."

For several moments Adams said nothing. "Very well. You'll walk with me?"

"Yes, sir. That would be fine."

Adams turned to his wife. "I'll be gone much of the day."

"I expected as much," Mrs. Adams said cheerfully.

"You'll be all right?"

"Of course."

Adams kissed her cheek, placed the tricorn hat on his head, and motioned for Ethan to follow him as he set off down the garden path to the street. Ethan thanked Mrs. Adams and hurried after her husband.

"I remember our conversations," Adams said as Ethan caught up with him. "Even after you saw what Peter Darrow and men like him were willing to do in order to hinder the cause of liberty, you remained opposed to us."

Ethan smiled reflexively. "What I remember, sir, is that I opposed your tactics: riots, destruction of property, disregard for the rule of law. What some call a cause others might see as mindless incitement."

"When the law is unjust men of good conscience must

sometimes step outside its bounds. Not to do harm, mind you, but to expose that injustice for all to see." Adams gestured toward the harbor with an open hand. "But I believe we're entering a new stage in our fight for liberty. By bringing their soldiers to our shores, Parliament and the king undermine any claim to legitimacy they might once have had. Don't you agree?"

Ethan started to respond, but stopped himself. "I didn't come to discuss politics, sir. I need your help."

Adams regarded him, his pale eyes ice blue in the morning sun. "You said that you came to speak of the occupation."

"Aye, but not—"

"Then it's politics, Mister Kaille. That is the reality of the age in which we live."

"All right," Ethan said, relenting with a sigh. "Have it your way."

"My wife will tell you that I usually do," Adams said, grinning. "Now, what can I do for you? You're a thief-taker, aren't you?"

"Aye, sir, I am. And I come to you in that capacity." Ethan hesitated, unsure of how to proceed. "There's only so much I can tell you, though I should inform you that I'm currently in the employ of the Crown—or more accurately servants of the Crown here in Boston."

Adams straightened. "Has something been stolen? That's what thieftakers usually do, isn't it? Recover stolen goods?"

"It is, but no, nothing has been stolen. At least not precisely."

Adams halted and turned to face Ethan. "In that case, I must ask if you have been employed to spy on my allies and me."

"No, sir. I swear that I haven't. I wouldn't take such a job even if it was offered to me."

They stood that way for several seconds, Adams holding Ethan's gaze. At length he nodded and started walking again.

"Then what?" he asked.

"You recall that I'm a conjurer as well as a thieftaker. That's why the king's men came to me. There has been . . . an incident. An attack of a sort on the British fleet. And I need to know if you or the men who work with you were involved in any way."

"This attack—it involved witchery?"

"I have your word that you'll speak of this with no one?" Ethan asked.

"You do."

"Yes, it involved a conjuring."

"Was anyone hurt?"

Ethan faltered, unsure once more of how much he could say. Geoffrey wouldn't have been pleased to know that he was talking to Adams about any of this. Neither, he assumed, would Senhouse. He was less certain about Rickman. But as much as he disapproved of Adams's tactics he realized in that instant that he trusted the man.

"Men died, sir. Dozens of them."

Adams looked at him, a pained expression on his face. "I'm very sorry to hear that." He shook his head, facing forward again. "No, my colleagues and I didn't do this. We would have had no part in such an attack. You may not have approved of our tactics in combatting the Stamp Tax back in sixty-five, but if you know anything about the Sons of Liberty you know that we have pursued our goals through legal means whenever possible."

Ethan didn't point out that street riots and destruction of personal property were not, strictly speaking, "legal means." He and Adams had long disagreed on where one might locate the line between civil action and criminality. Instead he asked, "Are there members of the Sons of Liberty who are conjurers? That you know of, that is."

"No," Adams said. "I'm not sure that I would know if there were, but I've neither seen nor heard anything that would give me reason to suspect . . . As I recall, you don't like it to be called witchcraft."

"No, sir. We refer to it as spellmaking, or conjuring, or casting."

"Well, I've not seen any sign of those things."

They had come to the South Battery, which offered a clear view of the harbor and Long Wharf. The entirety of the British fleet, save for the *Graystone*, had been positioned around the pier, broadsides facing the city and soldiers manning their cannons. A battle ship—a sixth-rate ship of the line—had joined the fleet overnight, making the royal presence that much more formidable.

"Look at that," Adams said, gazing out at the vessels and looking stricken. "This is how Parliament responds to legal petitions and reasonable pleas for relief." He shook his head once more. "No, we would not resort to violence. We'll meet this challenge with more boycotts, more petitions. Either they'll listen or . . . or they won't. Regardless of what they do we as a people will need to decide what our next recourse might be."

"Last time," Ethan said gently, "it wasn't you who resorted to violence, but an agent of the Crown. Could that have happened again? Is there someone new in your circle, someone who might have betrayed you?"

That of all things made Adams smile. "Not this time, no. In fact, right now we have an ally in the king's own military of whom agents of the Crown are completely unaware, not because he lies in hiding, but because while in plain view he wears the face of a loyal British officer."

"You have a spy?" Ethan asked, not quite believing him.

"Not a spy, no. He's a naval officer who serves aboard one of the ships. But he sympathizes with our struggle against tyranny. Before all is said and done I expect he will join our cause."

"A naval officer," Ethan repeated, recalling a conversation from the previous day. "A surgeon perhaps?"

Adams couldn't have looked more surprised if Ethan

had declared himself sovereign of all Britain. "Yes. How did you know?"

"Doctor Rickman?"

The man glanced around, genuine fear in his eyes. One might have thought he saw representatives of the King and Parliament lurking at every street corner. "Mister Kaille, I must insist that you tell me how you've come to know this!"

"It was a guess, sir. That's all. You have my word. I met Rickman at Castle William, and he warned me that the occupation would begin shortly. He struck me as . . . well, as someone who didn't approve of Parliament's tactics. I assure you, I haven't mentioned to anyone the conversation I had with him."

Adams stared hard at Ethan, fresh appraisal in his eyes. "I believe you must be a very good thieftaker."

"Thank you, sir."

They began walking again. Ethan sensed that Adams was on his way to Long Wharf, perhaps to lead yet another mob in defiance of the coming occupation.

"So what do you think of this?" Adams asked, indicating the ships in the harbor with a vague wave of his hand. "You've made it clear that you disapproved of our actions in the past, and you've noted that the good doctor disapproves of what Parliament is doing now. But how do you feel about this occupation?"

Ethan almost said something clever about how men like Adams and Otis had brought the occupation on themselves; a small part of him still believed that this was so. But seeing the fleet arrayed around the city's waterfront disturbed him far more than he had thought possible. Boston hadn't been his home for long—not when one factored in the years he had spent as a prisoner in Barbados. Yet, it felt more like home than any other place he had ever lived. He feared that with the arrival of regulars the city would never be the same.

"I feel sad, sir," he answered after some time. "I know that's not really what you were asking, but it's the truth."

Adams regarded him. "It's a fine answer," he said, his voice subdued.

They walked in silence, passing close to Cooper's Alley and turning down Mackerel Lane toward the wharf. Reaching the edge of the pier, Adams halted and once more looked out over the water. A few others had gathered around the wharf to watch the ships. Some stood together in small clusters, speaking among themselves; others stared out at the fleet, their expressions grim.

"I would have thought the landing would have begun by now," Adams said.

"So would I," Ethan said, keeping his voice down. "It will before long."

"I agree." Adams turned to him. "I have to be on my way, Mister Kaille. I have men to see in the Bunch of Grapes." He pointed at the tavern, which sat just across from the wharf. "And also at the Green Dragon."

"Yes, sir, of course. Thank you for your time."

"I hope you find whoever it is you're looking for. Military force is the last refuge of despots and tyrants. Those men don't belong in our city. By attacking them we only justify their brutality."

"Yes, sir."

Adams tipped his cap and strolled toward the Bunch of Grapes.

As he passed one group of onlookers, a woman called out, "God bless Samuel Adams and the Sons of Liberty!"

Adams smiled and waved to the woman before entering the tavern.

Ethan started up King Street, thinking that he would go to King's Chapel to see if Pell had any information for him yet. He hadn't gone far, though, when he heard someone calling to him from behind. Turning, he saw Geoffrey striding toward him, a deep scowl making his forehead look even steeper than usual.

"Good morning, Geoffrey," Ethan said, with false brightness.

"Was that Samuel Adams I just saw you with?" Brower demanded.

"Aye, it was."

"Lord help me," he said, shaking his head. "What can you be thinking? Speaking to that man—being seen in his company in the middle of Boston—when you're working on behalf of Parliament and the king!"

Ethan started walking again, forcing Geoffrey to follow. It was all he could do not to pummel the man for speaking to him so. When at last his rage had subsided enough that he could speak again, he said in a taut, low voice, "I was thinking that if those who oppose the occupation had anything to do with what happened to the *Graystone*, Mister Adams might know of it. And if you don't approve of the manner in which I'm conducting my inquiry I'd suggest that you find another thieftaker who can conjure."

"Did you tell Adams what happened to those men?"

"I told him that a conjuring had been used against a ship, and that some men had died. I didn't get any more specific than that."

"Didn't get—" Geoffrey shook his head. "Good God, Ethan! What happened to the discretion you bragged about the other day?"

Ethan walked a few more paces in silence before halting again. Though loath to admit it, Ethan had to admit that Geoffrey was right. Adams had sworn that he would keep their conversation to himself, but Ethan doubted that Brower or any of his colleagues would place much stock in the word of Samuel Adams. And Ethan had promised William Senhouse that he would be circumspect in pursuing the matter. Already he had told too many people.

"You're right," he said. "I apologize. I'll be more careful in the future."

Brower seemed surprised by his apology. "Thank you." He hesitated, and when next he spoke it was with a note of surrender in his voice. "Did Adams tell you anything?"

"No. He claimed to know nothing about the *Graystone* and her fate. And," he added, anticipating Geoffrey's next question, "I believe him."

"So, what have you learned, other than that Samuel Adams claims to know nothing of the attack?"

Before Ethan could answer, he felt power pulse in the street. By now he recognized the conjuring: It was another finding spell, probably cast by Mariz. It had originated nearby, perhaps at Sephira's home. Ethan felt the spell flow past him, like ocean water running up a beach and over his feet and legs. But it passed him by. It seemed that Mariz was tired of finding Ethan. He was looking for someone else.

"Ethan!" Geoffrey said, his voice stern. "I asked you a question."

"Aye, you did," Ethan said, striding away once more. "I've learned plenty, but not enough. I'll be in touch when I have more to tell you."

Geoffrey was still calling after him when Ethan turned the corner onto Cornhill and headed toward the North End.

Chapter
ELEVEN

Ethan wasn't sure where he was headed. Mariz had been searching the North End yesterday, and it stood to reason that he would be looking there again. But beyond that Ethan had no sense of where to begin his search; he was working on instinct, nothing more.

He crossed over Mill Creek into the North End and ducked into a small alleyway. There, hidden from view, he pulled out the pouch of mullein and removed three more leaves for a warding. After a moment's indecision, he put them back, thinking better of the spell. If Mariz was looking for Gant, the casting would alert both men to Ethan's approach. Better to eschew conjurings for now.

He followed the winding lane that fronted the harbor and led eventually to the dock for the Charlestown ferry. The name of the street changed every few blocks—Ann, Fish, Ship, Lynn, and finally Ferry Way. No matter what it was called, though, most days, it would be crowded with wharfmen, merchants, and travelers to and from Charlestown. But today, even here, the streets were quiet, no doubt because of the impending occupation. He kept to the edges of the lane, moving from shadow to shadow, knowing how easy it would have been for Mariz or Gant to spot him, had they been there.

By the time he reached Gee's Shipyard at the end of Ferry Way, he had started to wonder if he had been too quick to assume that the men were in the North End. He could search the streets in the center of this part of Boston, closer to the Old North Church. But those were finer neighborhoods; a man as rough in manners and appearance as Simon Gant would be conspicuous there.

He turned south on Princes Street, intending to head back south. But he had taken only a few steps when he felt a new burst of power, followed but a second later by another.

This second conjuring was by far the stronger of the two. It was so powerful in fact, so startling, that Ethan didn't realize he had drawn his knife until he found himself pushing up his sleeve to cast. Like the spells he had sensed earlier, neither of these conjurings had been directed at him. But he also felt sure that at least the second conjuring had been no mere finding spell. He didn't know what it was; only that it was strong, and had come from the west.

He hesitated, unsure of where he ought to go. He didn't know the northern lanes as well as he did the streets of Cornhill and the South End nearer to his home. He could smell the Charles River, though, and the Mill Pond as well. *The dam.*

He sprinted to the causeway that ran between river and pond, and followed it toward New Boston. Unlike most of Boston's avenues, the Mill Dam was still unpaved, consisting of compacted dirt and gravel. His leg was aching before he was halfway across, but he could see the ancient windmill in the distance, and to its south the wooden spire of the West Church. Keeping his eyes fixed on the church, he hobbled on. By the time he reached the end of the dam and the shipyard there, he was breathing hard and starting to sweat through his waistcoat.

He paused, bent over, and rested his hands on his knees, trying to catch his breath. Sephira would have laughed at him and called him an old man. He could hardly have blamed her.

"Where now?" he muttered, his gaze sweeping over New Boston and Beacon Hill. This part of the city was far more sparsely populated than either the North or South Ends, but Ethan couldn't decide if this made it easier or harder to find someone.

He hadn't felt any spells since those two conjurings, and while he still didn't wish to give his position away, he also had no desire to confront Gant or Mariz defenseless, without a warding in place. Making his decision, he cut his forearm.

"*Tegimen ex cruore evocatum,*" he said. Warding, conjured from blood.

His own spell pulsed in the street. He glanced at Uncle Reg, who had appeared at his elbow.

"Do you know where those spells were cast?" he asked the ghost.

Reg shook his head.

Once more, Ethan surveyed the lanes and occasional low roofs sprawled across the hill and fields before him. Making his decision, he struck out toward West Church. The chapel stood at the center of New Boston, near one of the few lanes in this part of the city as busy as the lanes of the North and South Ends. He didn't know if he was any more likely to find Mariz and Gant there than in the streets that lay closer to the Charles River. Again, he was acting on instinct.

He walked down the deserted lane, wary, his blade held ready, his sleeve still pushed up. If Mariz and Gant appeared before him in that moment, dueling with spells, Ethan didn't know what he would do, or which man he would help. It seemed he was leaving that to instinct, too. If it turned out that the two men were working together, and they simultaneously cast spells against him, he would be in trouble, even with the warding he had conjured.

He reached Lynde Street and the church, but still saw no sign of either conjurer. Continuing past, he circled the block and cut south and east around the small cluster of houses on Staniford Street and Green Lane. Still nothing.

It had been more than a quarter of an hour now since he had felt any spells other than his own, and neither conjurer had come looking for him after he cast the warding spell.

"I'm going to try a finding spell," he said.

Reg offered no response. He just stared back at Ethan, his bright gaze unblinking.

Ethan picked three mullein leaves from the pouch he carried and held them in the palm of his hand.

"*Locus magi ex verbasco evocatus.*" Location of conjurer, conjured from mullein.

Once more the cobblestones thrummed with his casting. The leaves vanished from his hand and he felt tendrils of power spreading out in all directions from where he stood, questing for another conjurer, like shoots on a vine looking for the next tree or trellis to climb. At first he sensed no one, and he began to wonder if both men had escaped New Boston without his knowledge.

He soon realized, though, that in fact his spell had found someone. The power emanating from whoever it was felt so weak that he hadn't noticed at first. The conjurer was close by, just a short distance to the north and west.

Ethan quickened his pace, passing the church once more and turning onto Chambers Street. There he slowed, searching the overgrown fields on either side of the lane.

When at last he spotted the man, he couldn't have been more surprised. He had expected an ambush of some sort. But the conjurer Ethan found wasn't waiting for him, skulking in the grasses, a bloodied knife held ready. Far from it.

Ethan recognized Mariz at once, though the spectacles were missing from his face. He lay sprawled by the edge of the lane in a thick patch of grass and weeds, his legs bent, one arm twisted beneath him at an awkward angle, the other limp on his chest. His wheaten hair and wispy mustache and beard shone in the sun. A thin trickle of blood ran from his nose, and another stained the corner of his mouth.

Ethan hurried to the man's side and leaned over him, resting his hand on Mariz's wrist. He felt a pulse, but it was weak and too fast. Mariz's lips and skin had a bluish tinge and the man's breath came in shallow gasps. Ethan caught a glimpse of something glinting in the grass nearby—Mariz's glasses. He picked them up and slipped them into his pocket. Raising his head, Ethan looked around. He was all alone on the lane; there wasn't another person in sight. He didn't think he could carry Mariz all the way to Sephira's home, and even if he could, he wasn't sure it was a good idea to move the man so roughly.

After weighing his options, he tore some grass from the ground and cast an illusion spell. Such spells were usually among the easiest to conjure; they were called elemental because they didn't require blood or mullein, or even grass. They could be conjured from water or fire. But this illusion had to appear to others on the far side of the city, and Ethan needed to speak through it, something he had learned to do only a few years before.

"*Videre et audire per mea imagine ex gramine evocatum,*" he said. Sight and hearing, through my illusion, conjured from grass.

He felt the conjuring in the ground, watched as the grass in his hand disappeared. Then he closed his eyes.

Imagining the inside of Sephira's house was easy. Locating her, if she was even there, was more difficult.

The illusion—an image of himself—materialized in Sephira's dining room, the part of her house Ethan knew best. Seeing the chamber through the illusion's eyes, Ethan realized that no one was there.

"Sephira!" he made the image say. "Sephira Pryce!"

Through the illusion, Ethan heard footsteps behind

him. He made the image turn and saw Nigel step into the room.

"Kaille!" he said, pulling out a knife. "What the hell are you . . . ?" He trailed off, the angry sneer on his horselike face sagging into puzzlement as he saw how insubstantial this image of Ethan looked. "What the hell?" he said again, breathing the words this time. He took a step back from the illusion.

"I'm doing it with a spell, Nigel," Ethan said through the image. "It's an illusion, an image of myself. I'm in New Boston. Get Sephira for me. It's important."

"I don't take orders from you."

"Please," Ethan said. "You know I wouldn't do this if I thought I had any choice."

Yellow-hair's expression soured. He didn't lower the knife, but after another moment he nodded and strode from the room.

Ethan waited in the grass on Chambers Street, his eyes closed against the sunlight. This conjuring was harder than a simple illusion spell, but not so taxing that he couldn't maintain the image of himself.

After a few minutes, Nigel returned to the dining room leading Sephira. Nap and Gordon were with them.

"What is this, Ethan?" Sephira asked, her hands on her hips. "You think that you can use your witchcraft to—?"

"Mariz is hurt."

She blinked. "What?"

"Mariz is hurt. He's here in New Boston, on Chambers Street between Cambridge and Green. He's unconscious, and I'm afraid that if I try to move him on my own I'll make matters worse. You need to send a carriage."

Sephira considered him for what seemed an eternity.

"Why are you doing this?" she asked. "Why are you trying to help him?"

"Because I'm beginning to understand that there's someone out here who's more dangerous than Mariz. You're wasting time, Sephira, and I'm not sure how long he has."

Still she hesitated. The mistrust between them ran deep, and had for too long. It had become a habit, as hard to give up as liquor. At last she turned to Nigel and the others and said simply, "Go." Yellow-hair sheathed his knife and led Nap and Gordon from the room.

Facing the image of Ethan again, Sephira asked, "Can you heal him?"

"I don't know. I'll try."

"Do you know who did this to him?"

"I think we both know, don't we?"

"I have no idea what you're talking about."

She managed to say it without averting her eyes, without blushing, without any change in her expression or the tone of her voice. Ethan supposed that there was something admirable in the ease with which she could lie, even as one of her men lay dying in the street. He wasn't above admitting that there were times when he wished he could do something equally cold-blooded. But it served to remind him of the obvious: that despite his willingness to help Mariz and thus help her, he and she remained mortal enemies.

"Fine, Sephira. I'll see you soon."

"Ethan!" she said, before he could release the illusion spell. She stared at his image, then shook her head. "Never mind."

He let the spell end, opening his eyes and squinting against the glare of the midday sun.

Mariz hadn't moved, but he still appeared to be breathing, though with difficulty. Ethan leaned over the man and felt his limbs, his touch light, gentle. None of the bones seemed to be broken. Looking more closely at the one arm that had been pinned beneath Mariz, Ethan saw that while the bone remained whole, the elbow had been dislocated. He had seen similar injuries on the plantation in Barbados and knew how to mend it without resorting to a conjuring. He gripped the man's upper arm firmly in one hand and the lower arm in the other, thinking that Mariz was lucky to be unconscious for this. With a sharp motion he snapped the joint back into its normal position. Feeling the bones grind against one another, he winced in sympathy.

When Ethan was done, he sat back on his heels and exhaled heavily. After several seconds, he turned his attention to the conjurer's ribs, which were fractured in a number of places.

Before he could try a healing spell, however, Ethan heard voices approaching. Several children and two women were walking toward him, dressed in their church finery. Ethan was still bent low in the grass, which may have been why they hadn't seen him yet. He cut himself and whispered, "*Velamentum nobis ambobus, ex cruore evocatum.*" Concealment, both of us, conjured from blood.

In the last hour, he had cast enough spells to draw the attention of every conjurer in Boston. Gant could have shown up at any moment, and he would have seen Uncle Reg's glowing form, even if he couldn't spot Ethan. But the women and children felt and saw nothing. They strolled past without so much as a glance toward Ethan and Spectacles, the children laughing and running, the women chatting amiably.

Ethan saw that others were heading in his direction as well. Sabbath services were over. The road would be more crowded now. But Mariz continued to labor with every breath. While the next group of churchgoers was still some distance off, Ethan cut himself and gently rubbed blood onto Mariz's side. He then spoke another spell in the softest of whispers, his bloodied hands covering the spot where Mariz's ribs had broken.

"*Remedium ex cruore evocatum.*" Healing, conjured from blood.

This was more complicated spellmaking, and harder to maintain. He held his hands steady, and allowed the power of his conjuring to course through his fingers into Mariz's bones. Sweat beaded on his brow, but he didn't pause, knowing that healing spells worked best when the power flowed uninterrupted into flesh and bone.

The second cluster of people walked past him—three couples this time, one with a small child—and yet another appeared on the lane in the distance.

All the while, Ethan could feel Mariz's ribs gradually knitting back together beneath his hands. The man didn't stir, but his breathing grew deeper, more rhythmic. When at last Ethan allowed his spell to dissipate, he felt reasonably sure that he had mended the broken bones.

He heard a distant rattle. Looking southward, he saw a black carriage led by a large bay turn onto Chambers Street from Cambridge.

Ethan cut his arm again. "*Fini velamentum ex cruore evocatum.*" End concealment, conjured from blood.

He felt the pulse of power in his knees and legs where they rested in the grass. Glancing at Uncle Reg, he saw that the ghost was watching him, a disapproving scowl on his lean, glowing face.

"I take it you think I should have left him here to die," Ethan said.

The ghost stared at him for another second before looking away, his mouth twitching beneath his mustache. Ethan suppressed a grin. Usually Reg made him feel foolish for one lapse or another; it felt good to return the favor.

He stood to face the oncoming carriage. Nigel sat atop the box, steering; Nap and Gordon rode within the carriage, leaning out the doors and eyeing Ethan. Yellow-hair eased back on the reins so that the bay halted just beside Ethan. At first, none of Sephira's men moved. They simply watched him.

"Mariz is here," he said, pointing at the wounded man, but keeping his gaze on Nigel.

Yellow-hair glanced down at Mariz before looking at Ethan again. "How do we know that you didn't do tha' to him?"

"You'll just have to take my word for it." When that didn't appear to convince the man, Ethan added, "If I had attacked him, why would I stay here and call for all of you?"

Nigel's mouth twisted in doubt, but he reached back and tapped twice on the door closest to Nap. Nap and Gordon hopped out of the carriage and made their way over to Spectacles.

"Be careful with him," Ethan said. "Four of his ribs were broken. I think that at least one of them pierced his lung. And I don't know what kind of head injuries he has, but he hasn't moved or made a sound since I found him."

Nap nodded once, and he and Gordon lifted the man and carried him to the carriage. They placed him on the long seat opposite where they had been riding and climbed back in themselves.

"Miss Pryce wants you to come back with us," Nigel said.

Ethan had been prepared for this. There was no more room within the carriage, and so he climbed onto the box beside Nigel, and gripped it hard as the big man flicked the reins and the carriage pitched forward.

Ethan and Yellow-hair said nothing to each other the entire distance back to Sephira's house. They passed right by the Dowsing Rod and, a short time later, King's Chapel. Ethan wondered what Kannice or Pell would have thought had they seen him riding a carriage with Sephira Pryce's toughs. He grinned at the idea, drawing an odd look from Nigel.

When they reached the Pryce estate, Nigel drove up a dirt path that led to the back of the house and stopped the carriage near a side door. Afton, Mariz's friend from the Dowser, was waiting by the door and lumbered over to the cart as soon as it had halted.

"What happened to him?" the man asked, staring hard at Ethan.

"He was attacked by a conjurer," Ethan said. "I didn't see it, so I don't know who it was. He had broken ribs, a dislocated elbow, and I'd guess a blow to the head as well."

Afton helped Nap and Gordon take Mariz into the house. He paused at the doorway, though, and looked back at Nigel, who had remained with Ethan.

"Miss Pryce is in the study," Afton said, his eyes flicking in Ethan's direction. He disappeared into the house.

"You heard him," Nigel said.

Ethan let the tough lead him inside, through a small chamber, the kitchen, and the dining room until at last they came to the study. As he had during previous visits to Sephira's mansion, Ethan deemed that "study" was not the proper word for the room. He imagined that men like Samuel Adams and James Otis had studies filled with books and papers from the colonies and England, perhaps even from France and Spain. Only a woman like Sephira could have filled a chamber with wood and glass cases containing every imaginable variety of firearm and blade, and called it a "study."

Sephira sat in a plush chair in the far corner of the room, a half-empty glass of Madeira next to her on a small but elegant wooden table. Her legs were crossed, her arms resting on the arms of the chair. Her long black curls snaked around her neck and draped over her shoulder.

Ethan had a feeling that she had been waiting for him. She pointed at a chair that was identical to hers and said, "Sit." To Nigel, she said, "Get the door," a dismissal in the words.

Ethan did as she instructed. For once, Nigel had forgotten to take Ethan's weapons from him. He had a knife on his belt and that pouch of mullein in his coat pocket. If he wanted to, he could destroy her.

"Tell me again what happened," Sephira said.

Ethan explained to her how he had felt the initial spell and had followed the pulse of power to the North End, only to be drawn to New Boston by two more conjurings. He told her about finding Mariz, and listed the man's injuries and what he had done to heal him.

"He still needs a doctor," Ethan told her.

"I've already called for one. But it sounds . . ." She looked down at the rings on her fingers, twisted one into place. "I believe we owe you a word of thanks."

"You can show your appreciation by answering some questions for me."

Her laugh was dry—not the usual throaty laugh that he liked so much in spite of himself. "I don't think so," she said.

"Was he looking for Gant?"

Her gaze lingered on Ethan as she reached for her wine and took a long sip.

"If he can do this to Mariz," Ethan said, "and if he knows that you're after him, he might come looking for you."

She smiled. "Ethan, you're worried about me. I'm touched."

"I want to find Gant."

Her smile hardened. "And you thought you could frighten me into helping you? You believe I'm afraid of Simon Gant?"

"Why was Mariz looking for him? What is it you want with him?"

"I'm grateful to you," she said. "And when Mariz wakes up—if he wakes up—I'll tell him what you did. That seems the least I can do." She stood. "You can go now."

Ethan remained in his chair. "No, I can't," he said.

She stared down at him and narrowed her eyes. "What do you mean, you can't?"

"There's a spell I need to cast first. There's nothing any of you can do to stop me from casting it, but I was hoping you would give me your permission."

"What kind of spell?"

"One that might tell me who cast the spell that hurt him."

Sephira didn't say anything at first. But Ethan could see her mind working as she calculated the costs, the risks, the possible benefits of letting him proceed.

"All right," she said after some time. "I'll let you cast your spell." A thin smile touched her lips. "Since I can't do anything to stop you."

"Thank you." Ethan stood. "Where is he?"

"I had him taken upstairs. Come."

She led him back through the common room to a broad stairway with dark wooden steps and a carved banister to match. The stairs reached a landing halfway up, and continued both to the right and left, reaching an open balcony that looked down on the stairway. On the wall above the landing hung a portrait of Sephira that very nearly did justice to her beauty. The artist had rendered her in her usual street dress: breeches, waistcoat, a white shirt open at the neck. She was posed sitting in her study in a high-backed chair that bore more than a passing resemblance to a throne. Ethan passed the portrait without comment.

Sephira's men had put Mariz in a cramped bedroom at the far end of the upstairs corridor. Aside from the small bed and a bureau of drawers near the single window, the room was unfurnished and quite plain compared to the rest of the house. There were a few personal items on top of the bureau—a cotton kerchief, a hairbrush, a pair of simple sewing scissors—leading Ethan to guess that this was the quarters of one of Sephira's servants.

A man who Ethan assumed was a doctor stood beside the bed, bending over Mariz, who lay on top of the covers.

Afton hovered on the other side of the bed, glaring at Ethan.

"Has he moved or made any sound?" Ethan asked.

The doctor looked up from his patient and shook his head. "He's having some difficulty breathing, but I can't see why. And there's a welt on the back of his head. I'm afraid there's not much I can do for him. He needs rest, and time."

"Very well," Sephira said. "Thank you, Doctor."

"Of course, Miss Pryce. I'll come back tomorrow if you like."

"Yes, fine."

The man closed up his medical case, glanced at Ethan again, and left the room.

"Leave us," Sephira said to Afton.

The big man looked like he might argue, but seemed to think better of it. He cast one final warning glance at Ethan and left as well.

Once Ethan and Sephira were alone, she crossed her arms over her chest and leaned against the wall that was farthest from the bed. "Go ahead."

He had cast spells against her and her men many times, but Ethan had never conjured while Sephira watched him. He had to admit that it made him uncomfortable, though he couldn't say why.

He pushed up his sleeve again and pulled the knife from his belt.

"You've had that the entire time?" Sephira asked.

Ethan grinned, knowing that Nigel would have some explaining to do.

He cut his arm, dabbed blood on Mariz's face and neck, and drawing on the blood that continued to flow from his arm said, "*Revela potestatem ex cruore evocatam.*" Reveal power, conjured from blood.

His spell rang through the floors and walls of the house. Uncle Reg winked into view and bared his teeth at Sephira. She, of course, was oblivious of all of it. But a moment later, she gave a small gasp.

Light had blossomed on Mariz's chest and spread like a bruise over most of his torso. Orange light, just like the glow Ethan had seen on the dead soldier aboard the *Graystone*.

"What is that?" Sephira asked, her voice hushed.

"Power," Ethan said. "The residue of the spell that struck him in New Boston."

"But that color. Does all witchcraft look like that?"

"Every conjurer's power looks different. And this color I've seen before."

She looked up from Mariz, her eyes meeting Ethan's. "Where?"

"On a dead soldier aboard the *Graystone*. I believe the spell that hit Mariz was cast by Simon Gant."

TWELVE

*E*than left Sephira's house a short time later. He had wondered if she might try to keep him there, to force him to tell her more of what he knew. But the idea that Simon Gant had come so close to killing Mariz seemed to have frightened her. Perhaps he should have enjoyed her discomfort, but the truth was it unnerved him.

As he neared the heart of the South End, he saw that the streets were far more crowded than they had been earlier and that almost everyone was heading toward the waterfront. Ethan cut through the smaller lanes, avoiding the mobs, and soon reached Battery March, which afforded him a clear view of the harbor and Long Wharf.

Hundreds of British regulars had already mustered on the wharf. They stood in strict rows, resplendent in red and white, rifles at their sides. Longboats were converging on the wharf from the naval vessels still anchored in a broad arc around the city's wharves and shipyards. Each of the boats carried additional soldiers, and even from a distance Ethan could see that still more men waited for transport aboard many of the navy ships. The occupation had begun, and by the look of it Ethan guessed that this first wave would bring more than a thousand men into Boston's streets, more than he had thought, more than Kannice, Kelf, and others had spoken of since the ships appeared in the harbor. This for a city of fifteen thousand people.

There was nothing anyone could do to prevent the regulars from coming ashore. Had there been, Ethan was certain Samuel Adams would have thought of it by now. Rather than watch the soldiers gather on the wharf, Ethan left the South End and made his way up to King's Chapel.

The chapel was one of Boston's older churches. It might also have been one of its least attractive. It had been rebuilt several years before, and its refined wooden exterior now was concealed within an austere stone façade. In a city with a history of devastating fires, the new exterior made sense, but it gave King's Chapel a forbidding, ponderous look. Worse, the chapel remained unfinished, with no spire or bell tower to offset the heavy look of the sanctuary.

Still, Pell seemed to enjoy serving the King's Chapel congregation, and he always expressed great admiration for the Reverend Henry Caner, the chapel's rector, a sentiment Ethan did not share.

Within, the chapel was far more welcoming. Graceful columns, painted in shades of tan and brown and crowned with intricate carvings, supported the high ceiling. Sunlight streamed through the windows, two stories high, that lined the main sanctuary, lighting boxed pews of natural wood. A portly man in black robes and a white cravat stood at the raised pulpit beside the altar at the far end of the church. Caner.

He turned at the sound of Ethan's footsteps, peering across the distance and squinting.

"Who is that?" he asked. He had a deep voice, a homely but friendly face, and a genteel manner; Ethan could see why others liked him.

"It's Ethan Kaille, Mister Caner."

Caner straightened, his bushy eyebrows knitting. "What do you want? You're looking for Trevor, aren't you?"

"Yes, sir. He told me—"

"He's not here."

"All right. If you can just tell me where to find him, I'll leave your church."

"I don't believe I will tell you, Mister Kaille. But I'll thank you to leave just the same."

Theirs was an old feud, and Pell, unfortunately, was their battleground. In fact, their hostility for one another grew out of their shared affection for the young minister. Caner, Ethan knew, wished only to protect Pell from what he believed to be Ethan's corrupting influence. And though Ethan believed that the rector's concerns were misplaced, a part of him admired the man's devotion to Pell.

"I'll wait for him," Ethan said, slipping into the nearest pew and sitting.

The rector glowered at him, perhaps thinking that he could cow Ethan into leaving. When he realized that this tactic wouldn't work, he went back to reading in the enormous Bible perched before him.

After several minutes of this, Caner sighed, the sound echoing in the sanctuary. He descended the curving stairway from the pulpit and walked down the aisle to where Ethan sat.

"You're holding him back," the man said. "Don't you understand that?"

"Holding him back in what way?"

"He's been with us for several years now. Too many years. He's been reading for orders. He should have sailed back to England by now for his ordination. He should be out in the countryside, leading a congregation of his own. But as long as you involve him in your intrigues, as long as you convince him that Boston is too exciting to leave, he will never follow his calling."

At least the rector no longer thought that Ethan was leading Pell to Satan, as once he had. Caner knew that

Ethan was a conjurer—although he often called him a witch—but he had come to accept that Ethan usually used his powers for noble purposes. Still, Ethan wasn't willing to take responsibility for Pell's career path.

"Mister Pell makes his own choices."

"No, he doesn't!" Caner said. "He stays here for you, for the adventure you offer him. For years now I've begged you to keep away from him. And still—"

"And still you don't accept that you do so in vain."

Ethan and Caner both turned toward the back of the chapel, where Pell was emerging from the stairway leading down to the crypts.

Ethan glanced sidelong at Caner. "I thought you said he wasn't here."

Pell's mouth fell open. "Mister Caner! You lied?"

Caner lifted his chin. "I dissembled." When neither Ethan nor Pell said anything, he added, "Well, he wasn't here in the sanctuary."

"Do you have the names yet," Ethan asked Pell.

"Yes, I wrote them out for you."

"What names?" Caner asked.

"The dead from the *Graystone*," Pell said.

Caner's gaze flicked from one of them to the other. "You know about that?" he asked Ethan.

"Yes, sir. Geoffrey Brower asked for my assistance with the inquiry."

"Ah, yes, Brower," Caner said. "He's married to your sister, isn't he?"

"Yes, sir."

The rector started to say more, but couldn't seem to get the words out. His bow-shaped mouth was frozen in a small "o," and Ethan could see that the realization had come to him at last. "Do you mean to tell me that . . . that this was some form of . . . that witchcraft killed these men?"

"A conjuring," Ethan said. "Witchcraft is the stuff of children's nightmares and preachers' sermons. And yes, that's precisely what we're telling you." He turned back to Pell. "You have the list with you?"

The minister pulled a rolled piece of parchment from within his robes and handed it to Ethan. Ethan opened it and scanned the list, which was not very long—eight names. His eye was drawn to the name about halfway down the page.

"All of these men were from Boston?" he asked.

"Yes, why?"

"There's a name on here—Caleb Osborne—" He trailed off, shaking his head. It was possible that Osborne still had family here in the city. If so, they might not want it known among Boston's clergymen that Caleb was a conjurer.

"You know him?" Pell asked.

"I've heard others speak of him. Is this his address beside the name?" Ethan asked, trying to read Pell's scrawl. "Fourteen Wood Lane?"

Pell looked over Ethan's shoulder. "Yes, that's right."

Ethan read through the rest of the list, but he didn't recognize any other names. "All right." He stood. "Thank you, Mister Pell, Mister Caner."

"Have you learned anything yet?" Pell called, as Ethan walked back toward the chapel entrance.

"Yes," Ethan said. "But I don't understand any of it."

Wood Lane was back in the North End, near the waterfront and North Square. Number fourteen was a wheelwright's shop, not a home, but a worn and rickety stairway along the side of the building led to a weathered gray doorway. Ethan climbed the stairs and knocked once.

He heard quick footsteps and the click of the lock. The door opened a crack, and a woman peered out at him. She was pale and slight, with dark eyes, and brown hair that she wore in a tight bun.

"Yes?" she said, sounding both suspicious and frightened.

"Missus Osborne?"

"Who are you?" the woman asked.

"My name is Ethan Kaille. I'm a thieftaker, and I'm conducting an inquiry for the Customs Board. I wonder if I might speak with you. I won't take but a few moments of your time."

"What do you want to talk about?"

"Your husband."

She laughed, though the sound was as brittle as dried kindling. "I have no husband."

"Isn't this the home of Caleb Osborne?"

"Let him in, Molly," a second woman said from behind the first.

The first woman looked back over her shoulder. Another moment passed before she opened the door wide and waved Ethan inside.

The room was as small and simple as Ethan's own. A pair of beds stood near a window that looked out over the narrow yard behind the wheelwright's shop, and a fire burned in a woodstove near the door. The floors were worn, as was the paint on the walls. A table stood on uneven legs, flanked by two chairs that looked as old as everything else, save for the brightly colored cushions resting on each one.

The second woman stood beside one of these chairs, her hands clasped in front of her. Her eyes were hazel rather than brown, and she wore her hair in a plait rather than a bun. But she resembled in both complexion and stature the woman who had answered the door.

"Did you say your name was Kaille?" this second woman asked.

"That's right."

"My name is Hester Osborne," she said, her tone grave. She indicated the other woman with an open hand. "This is my younger sister, Molly. Caleb Osborne is our father."

A small, strangled sound escaped Molly, but she looked

more frightened than sorrowful. Hester crossed to her sister and took her hand.

"My pardon," she said. "I meant to say *was* our father. This has been a difficult day."

"Yes, ma'am," Ethan said. "Both of you have my deepest condolences."

"Why would the Customs Board be interested in him?"

"They're interested in learning what happened to his ship."

"I don't understand," the older woman said, still holding her sister's hand.

As before, Ethan wasn't certain how much to reveal. "Your father's death wasn't the only casualty on board the *Graystone*. I'm wondering if either of you ever heard your father speak of a man named Simon Gant."

Molly flinched at the name and sidled closer to her sister. Hester put her arm around the woman.

"That should answer your question," Hester said.

"What can you tell me about him?"

"Not very much, I'm afraid. He and my father worked together for many years before going off to fight the French. Father didn't tell any of us—my mother included—what kind of work they did, but I gather that it involved smuggling or thievery or some other kind of mischief. He and my mother fought about it sometimes."

"Is your mother—?"

"She died some years ago."

"I'm sorry," Ethan said. After a pause he asked, "Have you seen Simon Gant in the last few days?"

Molly stared at the floor, wringing her hands.

The older sister shook her head. "No, and to be honest I hope I never see him again."

Ethan couldn't help thinking that this was a common sentiment where Gant was concerned.

"Well, thank you," he said. "Again, my deepest sympathies to you both."

"Thank you, Mister Kaille."

Ethan turned to leave the room, but didn't move. Facing the women again, he said, "You told me that Gant and your father worked together. Do you know if they had dealings with Sephira Pryce?"

"Miss Pryce?" Hester said. "No, I would have remembered that. Father never mentioned her."

A frown creased Ethan's brow. Each time he thought he had found some useful information he learned something else that left him even more confused than he had been before.

"I see," he said. "Well again, thank you."

He let himself out of the room, descended the stairs, and walked out onto Gallop's Wharf with his hands buried in his pockets. Long Wharf lay to the south, bathed in the warm glow of the late-afternoon sun. The water sparkled, and gulls wheeled overhead. Regulars were still massed on the pier, arrayed in neat columns. Ethan saw no more longboats in the water. A train of artillery had been brought ashore as well, adding to the show of force.

An officer stood near the men barking orders, his voice at this distance mingling with the strident cries of the gulls. Several other officers waited at the base of the wharf; Ethan wondered if the captain he had met at Castle William was among them. As the regulars began to march off the pier, officers took command of smaller units and led them into the streets of Boston.

Ethan started back toward the South End, staying close to the waterfront so that he could mark the progress of the troops. For so large a force, they vacated Long Wharf rapidly. By the time Ethan had crossed back into the South End and was nearing King Street, the last of the regulars were marching through the city. They carried muskets fixed with bayonets, and they marched to the steady rhythm of several drums and the high sweet notes of a corps of fife players. Young men bore flags at the van, and behind the soldiers horses pulled the artillery pieces.

Men, women, and children lined the streets to watch the procession. Most were grim-faced, although a few men near the Town House made their approval obvious, nodding ostentatiously, emboldened in their support of the Crown by the arrival of the troops. But what struck Ethan was the silence of the crowd. Few people spoke; he heard no cheers or jeers. Still, many in the throng followed the men. Ethan did the same, driven by his curiosity.

The regulars marched to Boston Common, and while a group broke off from the main column and headed north toward Treamount Street, most entered the Common and there continued to march, seeming to perform for the benefit of those citizens who had accompanied them. Watching this, Ethan couldn't help but think of Kannice. He wondered where all of these men would be quartered. Governor Bernard and the Massachusetts Council had been arguing the point for weeks, the governor threatening to seize control of publick houses and inns—like the Dowsing Rod—the council claiming that the regulars ought to be billeted at Castle William. So far there had been no resolution, and many feared that lodging the men among Boston's citizens would lead inevitably to bloodshed. Ethan didn't fear this might happen; he knew with cold certainty that it would.

He continued to watch the regulars from a distance, aware that he should have been working but unable to ignore what was happening to his city. For so long he had counted himself a loyalist. To the extent that he subscribed to any political persuasion, he had been a Tory. The arrival of these men, though, changed everything. It was one thing to contemplate an occupation. Seeing it begin was another matter entirely. Yes, this was a colony, a holding of the British Empire. But these soldiers didn't belong here. That was the thought that went through his mind over and over. *This isn't right. This shouldn't be happening. They should not be doing this in Boston.* Samuel Adams would have been amused, or perhaps encouraged. Kannice might have been proud of him.

These thoughts consumed him so that he gave little thought to the tingle of power he felt in the soles of his feet, or to the lad who had appeared beside him. That is, until the boy spoke.

"You're Kaille."

It was an odd voice, and Ethan knew why as soon as he looked at the boy. He was perhaps ten, with golden hair and ragged clothes, and eyes that glowed like those of Uncle Reg.

Ethan looked around, trying to spot the conjurer who had cast this illusion spell.

"You're Kaille, right?"

This wasn't the first time a conjurer had used the image of a child to communicate with him. Memories of those earlier encounters, with a cruel, waiflike creature named Anna, still haunted him.

"Yes, I'm Kaille."

"Good. Come to Darby's Wharf."

"Why?"

"Now, Kaille. We have to talk."

"Who—?"

The boy vanished before Ethan could finish the sentence. There were few people anywhere near him, and none seemed to have noticed the sudden appearance and disappearance of the lad.

"Damn," he muttered. Then, "*Veni ad me.*" Come to me.

Uncle Reg appeared, his stance alert. Ethan half expected the ghost to reach for his sword.

"Is my warding still in place?" Ethan asked.

Reg nodded.

"Good. Come with me."

Ethan left the Common and strode back toward the waterfront with Reg beside him. Darby's Wharf was close by, which made Ethan wonder if this conjurer might not have been powerful enough to send an illusion spell as far as Ethan himself had sent his illusion earlier in the day, when he alerted Sephira to the attack on Mariz.

When Ethan reached the wharf he found it deserted. Warehouses cast elongated shadows across the pier, chilling the salty air. Small swells from the harbor sloshed against the sides of the wharf, and the ropes tying a single moored ship to a pair of wooden bollards creaked faintly as the vessel shifted.

He slipped his knife from its sheath and stepped onto the wharf, sweeping his gaze over shadowed corners.

A radiant figure stood by a warehouse wall, perhaps twenty yards away. Glancing around one last time, Ethan started toward the image.

It was a man, tall, brawny, thick in the middle. He had a roguish look—a handsome face with a crooked nose and square chin. His hair might have been red, his face ruddy. It was hard to say with the image glowing so. But even though the figure's eyes gleamed brightly, Ethan could see that one appeared darker in color than the other. The figure glowed as white as the moon, rather than with the true color of Gant's power. It seemed the thief wished to conceal that from Ethan.

"Gant," Ethan said as he neared the image. He looked around again, trying to find the conjurer.

"Kaille," the image said.

"Why are we talking like this?" Ethan asked. "Show yourself."

The illusion shook its head. "I don't think so. You've been looking for me. Why?"

"Who told you I've been looking for you?"

"Why?" Gant asked again.

"You were supposed to be aboard the *Graystone*. You deserted. A good many people are looking for you. It's not just me."

"Aye, well, we both know what would have happened if I'd been on the *Graystone*."

"Do we?" Ethan asked. "It seems to me that if you

had been aboard the ship nothing would have happened."

"What?" The illusion stood stock-still for a few seconds, as if Gant had fallen asleep on his feet. Just as abruptly, it jerked into motion again. "Are you saying you think I killed all those men?"

"Why don't you tell me who you think did it? Maybe we can figure this out together."

"Stay away from me, Kaille," the image said, the voice hardening. "Stop looking for me. Stop asking people about me."

"Like I said, I'm not the only one. Do you think you can keep Sephira Pryce from finding you? The British army doesn't like it when soldiers desert. Do you think you can warn them away, too?"

As he spoke, Ethan reached into his pocket for the pouch of mullein, hoping that Gant might not notice. But apparently Gant could see through the eyes of his illusion just as Ethan could through his.

"Stop what you're doing!" the image said.

Ethan froze, but he didn't remove his hand from his pocket. He had the pouch in hand, and thought that he could conjure without pulling out individual leaves. He might use more mullein than he intended, but he could buy additional leaves from Janna.

"Let me see your hands!" Gant said.

Ethan had had enough of this. He needed to know where Gant was, and so began to whisper a finding spell under his breath. But he only managed to get out the first word or two when he heard a footfall behind him. Directly behind him.

Ethan spun, desperately trying to yank his hand from his pocket. He caught a glimpse of Gant's face—one blue eye, one green eye. He didn't see more except for the mammoth fist that connected high on his cheek. The blow seemed to lift Ethan off of his feet. Tiny points of white light erupted behind his eyes. The next thing he knew, he was lying on his back. Although not for long.

Hands grabbed him by the lapels of his coat, hauled him off the ground. Gant dug a fist into Ethan's gut, doubling him over and stealing his breath. Even as Ethan retched, yet another blow to his jaw sent him sprawling onto his back once more.

Addled, unable to see for the white light, unable to catch his breath, he heard Gant take a step toward him again. Forcing his eyes open he saw a blade glint in the fading daylight.

"You should have listened," Gant said.

He tasted blood and cast the first spell that came to mind.

"*Ignis ex cruore evocatus.*" Fire, conjured from blood.

Ethan couldn't direct the spell with any precision—he felt as though the entire wharf were spinning—but he did manage to set Gant's sleeve ablaze.

Gant swore, slapped at the flames with an open hand, his knife clattering on the ground.

Blood still flowed from the cuts in his mouth, and Ethan cast again. "*Pugnus ex cruore evocatus!*" Fist, conjured from blood.

Gant staggered the way he would have if Ethan had landed a physical blow on the side of his head. By now, the brute had extinguished the flames, but rather than casting a spell of his own, or renewing his assault, he fled. He didn't even bother to retrieve his blade.

Ethan made no attempt to chase him. He lay on his back, his eyes closed, trying to control the sensation that he was spinning. When at last he opened his eyes again, Uncle Reg stood over him, grinning.

"You find this amusing, don't you?"

The ghost nodded and started to fade from view.

"No, you're staying with me," Ethan said.

Reg frowned, but grew brighter once more.

Ethan staggered to his feet and gingerly touched his fingers to his jaw and cheekbone. Gant's blows hadn't broken anything, but if left untended his bruises would look terrible come morning.

He walked back along the wharf to the street, weaving a bit at first, but soon finding his stride. Reg watched him, but Ethan ignored the ghost, pondering what Gant had just done. Why would a conjurer use an illusion spell to call him to the wharf, use another to speak with him, but not use his spellmaking powers to attack? Gant must have known as well as Ethan did that he was strong enough to beat Ethan to within an inch of his life without resorting to conjuring. But he hadn't even warded himself against Ethan's attack spells. It made no sense.

Still turning these questions over in his mind, Ethan returned to his room. Upon reaching it, he used two mullein leaves to place a warding spell on his door. Then he lay down and took a long breath.

"*Dimitto te*," he murmured. I release you. He felt a small pulse of power and knew that Reg was gone.

Some time later, he awoke with a start. His room was completely dark, but beyond that he had no idea of the time. He sat up with some effort, and allowed a wave of dizziness to pass. His bruises felt swollen and fevered and the inside of his mouth felt like he had been chewing on glass.

Without bothering to light a candle or look in a mirror, he cut himself, marked his injuries with the welling blood, and cast a healing spell. The pulse of power still thrummed in the walls when the throbbing pain in his jaw began to abate. He couldn't keep himself from bruising a little, but he could keep the injuries from bothering him as much as they might if he did nothing.

When he had finished, he opened his door and stood still, listening. Strains of laughter reached him from the south. Closer by, two men were singing an off-key version of "Vain Is Ev'ry Fond Endeavor," sounding forlorn and very drunk. Ethan assumed that it was late, but not overly so. He left the room and walked to the Dowser, his stomach rumbling.

As he neared Treamount Street, he saw in the distance a cluster of regulars, and heard shouted arguments and raucous laughter coming from a crowd of men who had gathered not far from the soldiers. Rather than pass too close to what appeared to be a dangerous encounter between troops and the citizenry, he circled around through Cornhill and along Brattle Street and approached Kannice's tavern from the north.

He had expected to find the mood in the Dowser subdued. Most of those who enjoyed Kannice's ales and chowders also tended to share her political leanings. This should have been a sad day for them all. But upon opening the tavern door, Ethan was buffeted by sounds of celebration. The great room was packed with men and more than a couple of women, all of whom were laughing uproariously and singing "Jolly Mortals Fill Your Glasses." As Ethan stood in the doorway, Tom Langer, one of Kannice's usual crowd, climbed onto a table and straightened with some great effort. He raised his tankard, spilling ale on his shoes, and shouted, "God bless Elisha Brown!"

"Elisha Brown!" came the answering cry, followed by more cheers and renewed singing.

Kannice stepped out from behind the bar and put her fists on her hips. "Tom, get down from there before you fall and dent my floor with your skull!" But even she was grinning.

Tom looked at her sheepishly and climbed back down.

Kannice turned and spotted Ethan in the doorway. She canted her head to the side, grimacing and shaking her head. She walked over to him and reached up to his swollen jaw, wincing.

"What have you done now?" she asked.

Ethan shrugged. "I found a man I'd been looking for."

"Well, aren't you the clever one," she said archly. She smiled to soften the words. "Come on, I'll get you some food and a maybe a raw steak for that face."

"The food will be enough, thank you," Ethan said, letting her lead him to the bar. "What's all this about Elisha Brown?"

Kannice's eyes danced. "He and a bunch of others are living in the Manufactory on Treamount. When the British commander ordered him and his friends to give up the building for the regulars, he refused. Barricaded himself inside. He's in there still."

"And the regulars?"

She waved a hand. "Oh, some are on the Common, others are in Faneuil Hall and the Town House. A few are back down at the wharves." Her grin returned. "But they're not in the Manufactory."

"That's a dangerous game to be playing with the British army," Ethan said.

She sobered. "I know," she said, so that only he could hear. "But it's given people here in town something to celebrate."

Kelf placed a bowl of chowder and an ale in front of Ethan. "You've looked better," the big man said.

"My thanks, Kelf."

"Who was this man you found?" Kannice asked as Kelf moved down the bar to serve some ales.

"Simon Gant, the one I mentioned to you last night."

"What did he want with you?"

"He wants me to stop looking for him," Ethan said. "But I still think he might have murdered every man on the *Graystone*, and he very nearly killed the conjurer Sephira has working for her now."

She frowned. "Wait. You mean he's a speller, and he beat you with his fists?"

"Strange, isn't it?"

"Frightening is more like it," Kannice said. "If he can kill every man on that ship, what's to keep him from killing you any time he pleases?"

Ethan had no answer.

Chapter

THIRTEEN

*K*annice's question occupied his thoughts throughout the night. He slept poorly again, his dreams darkened once more by what he assumed were imagined bursts of power that seemed to reverberate through every bone in his body.

He woke to the first gray light of dawn, feeling more exhausted than he had when he lay down the night before, but knowing that he wouldn't get back to sleep. The five days Hutchinson had given him were slipping away; he needed to find Simon Gant. After lying awake for several moments, he rolled out of bed, dressed silently, and managed to leave the room without waking Kannice.

His face still hurt from the beating Gant had given him and the skin over his bruises felt tight and tender. The muscles in his back and legs and arms ached. Hard though it was to credit, he knew that he would have felt even worse if he hadn't cast his healing spell the night before. Not for the first time, he wondered if he was getting too old for thieftaking. Worse, he wondered how he would make a living if ever he decided that in fact he was.

Clouds covered the sky again, heavier than they had been two days before. A stubborn wind blew over the city from the west, carrying the scent of rain and the promise of a cold, dreary day. Ethan made his way back to the Common, where canvas tents blanketed the rolling terrain. The soldiers were up and milling about, and thin tendrils of gray-blue smoke from a hundred cooking fires drifted across the camp.

As Ethan drew near the first of the tents, a regular armed with a musket and bayonet blocked his way, demanding to know what business he had with the king's soldiers. Ethan told him he had come to see Lieutenant Senhouse, but the man didn't know the name. When Ethan explained that Senhouse served on the *Launceston*, the man regarded him with contempt. He might as well have said that Senhouse was with the French army.

"Ya mean he's a navy man?" the soldier said, his voice high, his words just barely comprehensible through his Irish brogue.

"Didn't any of the naval officers come ashore yesterday?"

"Look around ya, man. This here's an army camp. Th' navy boys are on their ships, an' good riddance t' them."

"What about William Rickman. He's a doctor, also with the *Launceston*. But—"

"Ya'd have t' ask someone else," the man said.

Ethan stared at the ground, trying to recall the names of the officers he had met at Castle William.

"Preston," he said, looking up again. "Thomas Preston."

The soldier's expression darkened. "Ya mean *Captain* Preston."

"Aye, forgive me. Captain Preston. I'd like to speak with him. Please."

Ethan thought the soldier might refuse. But after staring at him for another few seconds, he turned and started off toward the center of the camp. Ethan followed.

Ethan had remembered the captain's name, but until

he spotted the man standing with several of his regulars, he hadn't been sure that he would recognize him. Preston was the tall, gaunt-cheeked soldier whose rough manner Ethan had found so off-putting at the fort.

The young soldier marched Ethan right up to the officer.

"Yar pardon, Captain, but this man says he knows ya an' needs a word."

Preston looked Ethan up and down, his small eyes narrowed. "You were at Castle William," he said, just as Ethan was starting to wonder if the man would remember him.

"Yes, sir."

The captain's expression soured. "All right. The rest of you go off and . . . and do somethin'. We need a moment alone."

The regulars regarded Ethan with unconcealed curiosity, but moved off as Preston had instructed.

"What was your name again?" Preston asked.

"Ethan Kaille, sir."

"Right. Kaille. You're the thieftaker the customs boys brought in to find out what happened to the *Graystone*."

"That's right."

"Do you know yet?"

Ethan almost said something about knowing who was responsible for the deaths aboard the ship, but again he heard Gant's denial, spoken through the illusion he had conjured. More, he saw the way Gant's illusion had stopped moving. Gant, he realized, had been too shocked by the accusation to maintain his conjuring. Could he have been unaware of what his spell had done?

"I'm making progress," Ethan told the captain at last. "But I need a bit of help from you."

"Those bruises on your face—I don' remember those from before."

"No, sir. I got them from a man named Simon Gant."

Preston's eyes narrowed again. But before he could say anything, another young regular approached him and saluted.

"Yes, what is it?"

"Lieutenant Colonel Dalrymple requests your presence, sir."

Preston frowned. "Aye, I'm sure he does," he said under his breath. Then, so the soldier could hear, he said, "Tell him I'll be along presently."

"Yes, sir." The man saluted, turned smartly, and left them.

"Walk with me, Kaille."

Ethan fell in step with the man.

"That name," Preston said, as they wound their way past regulars and small fires. "Gant—it's familiar to me."

"Yes, sir," Ethan said. "He was one of yours. He's the man from the *Graystone* who deserted before the ship was—before the men died."

"I see. And you want us to help you find him. Perhaps exact a bit of revenge for the beating he gave you."

Ethan bristled, but swallowed the first denial that leapt to mind. "This isn't about revenge," he said, after composing himself. "I believe he had something to do with what happened to the *Graystone*. That's why he beat me."

Preston halted and faced him. "Are you a military man, Kaille?"

"I served on the *Stirling Castle* at Toulon, under Captain Cooper. My father was an officer."

"Then you might have some small idea of what it is we're trying to do here." He made a sweeping gesture with an open hand. "Look around you. I'm still trying to billet my men, and in the meantime we're having to make do with a camp that's barely secure, in a city that's only nominally under control."

Ethan wasn't sure that he would have described Boston in such terms. He knew, though, that the Crown and Parliament had been shaken by the summer's riots and the continued agitation led by Adams, Otis, and Boston's other Whigs.

"You're worried about finding one deserter," Preston went on. "I'm trying to house these men and thus prevent a hundred more desertions. I can't be searching the city for a single man."

Ethan glared. "Even if that man might have had a hand in killing dozens of your regulars?"

"Even so," Preston said. "We're not here to wet-nurse the colonies. This is an occupation. You're the thieftaker. You find him. Now, if you'll excuse me." He tipped his hat, and started away again.

Ethan let him go, but he didn't leave the camp. Preston was right in one thing: He was a thieftaker. Some of these men had served with Gant; perhaps a few of them knew something of his past.

He started to pick his way through the clusters of tents and fire circles, asking, "Has anyone seen Simon Gant?"

At first, his question was met with blank stares or wary head shakes. A few men claimed—sincerely, it seemed—to have seen Gant within the last day, and they tried to direct Ethan to a different part of the camp.

The response of one older man, however, drew Ethan's interest. Ethan had just mentioned Gant to a group of regulars standing around a dying fire. None of these men knew anything about him. But Ethan happened to catch a glimpse of a soldier with a weathered, lined face, who overheard Ethan's inquiry and after casting a sharp look in Ethan's direction, deliberately averted his gaze and began to walk away.

Ethan thanked the young soldiers and hurried after the older man.

"You there!" he called, but the man didn't slow his pace or look back.

"I have questions for you!"

No response.

"Helping a deserter is a court-martial offense, isn't that right? Do I need to find an officer?"

A few nearby regulars heard this and looked from Ethan to the man he pursued. The older soldier stopped at last. His shoulders dropped a bit and he turned to face Ethan.

"I didn' help him," he said, glancing at the other regulars.

"In that case, you have nothing to fear from me."

The soldier scratched his stubbly chin, his eyes fixed on Ethan. "What do you want t' know?"

"Anything you can tell me."

A taunting smile curved the man's lips. "Simon do that t' you?" he asked, pointing to Ethan's bruises.

"Would that surprise you?"

"Not in the least."

"What's your name?" Ethan asked.

"Corporal Jonathan Fowler," the man answered with some reluctance.

"I'm Ethan Kaille. I'm a thieftaker here in Boston."

"That figures," Fowler said.

"What do you mean?"

The soldier shook his head. "It doesn't matter."

"Let me decide that," Ethan said. "Why does it figure that I'm a thieftaker?"

Fowler's mouth twisted to the side, and he stared off over the camp. "Simon's a friend. I wouldn't tell ya nothin' if he was here still. But desertin' . . ." He shook his head. "The man's an idiot."

Ethan waited for the corporal to say more.

"All the time I knew him—and that's been a while now, since we fought the French—he would talk about this bit of treasure he had put away. That's what he called it. Treasure. Like he was some privateer sailin' the Barbary Coast."

"Did he tell you where it came from?"

"He tried to be all mysterious about it. But eventually he got around to tellin' me that he stole it from someone he worked with. You, probably."

"Me?" Ethan said, frowning.

"Well, at some point he mentioned a thieftaker. So I just assumed . . ."

"Did he ever give you a name. Pryce, maybe? Sephira Pryce?"

"Sephira? A woman?" A dry laugh escaped the man, like a grunt. "Well, that explains a lot."

"What does it explain?"

Fowler shook his head, the faint smile lingering on his face. "The bastard. The bloody, cowardly bastard." He scratched his chin again and let out another laugh. "Aye, it could have been this woman. I seem t' remember the name Pryce coming up once or twice. But he never gave a Christian name, and he definitely never let on that it was a woman. He always talked about how dangerous this person was, how he'd risked his bloody neck stealin' this treasure of his." He shook his head once more. "And now I find out it was from a woman."

Ethan almost told him that Sephira was no one to be trifled with, and that he himself always kept a wary eye on the streets to make certain that Sephira and her men weren't coming for him. But for now he was content to let Fowler think the worst of Simon Gant. It seemed the best way to keep him talking.

"What else did he tell you about this treasure of his?" he asked. "Do you know what it is, or where he's got it hidden?"

Fowler didn't answer right away. Ethan could see him working out the math in his head, figuring the possible value of whatever information he possessed.

"Well, that's the rub, isn't it? The where and the what, as it were. Without that, you've got nothin', do ya?"

"What do you want?" Ethan asked.

Fowler grinned. "Half."

"How do I know what you have to tell me is worth half?"

"Ya don't. But without me you've got nothin'. So no matter what it is, you're better off splittin' it than not."

"I don't think so," Ethan said. "If you knew enough, you would have already found his riches for yourself. But you don't know much of importance. Or maybe you know all too well how risky it would be to try to steal Gant's treasure out from under him. Either way, half is too much. I'll give you a quarter."

Fowler shook his head, an exaggerated frown on his face. "No, that's—"

"All right," Ethan said, turning and starting away. "Thank you for your time."

"Now wait a minute!"

Ethan walked without looking back.

Before long he heard the man hurrying after him. Fowler caught up with him and grabbed his arm.

"Hold on!"

Ethan stopped and faced him once more.

"A third," the man said.

"A quarter. And if you don't let go of my arm, I'm going to break your nose in front of all your friends."

Fowler straightened, but he released his grip on Ethan's arm. "Fine. A quarter."

Ethan nodded. "Done. What and where?"

"I'm not exactly too sure of the where. But the what is more than enough t' make up for that." He leaned in closer, his breath stinking of the previous night's whiskey. "Pearls!" he whispered. "Gobs of them!"

"Pearls," Ethan repeated to himself.

"That's right. Enough that you'd never have t' work again. Even if ya gave me a third."

"A quarter," Ethan said absently. He remembered hearing, back when he first returned to Boston from the Caribbean, of a stolen shipment of pearls. Much of what he heard came from whispers in the street or the back of a tavern, because the pearls were taken not from a merchant or gem trader, but from a smuggler who had no recourse with the customs commissioners or the sheriff. He didn't recall anyone linking the theft to Sephira, but that meant nothing. Even then, she was skilled at taking credit when she wanted it and avoiding blame when she didn't.

Pearls were valuable enough to draw Sephira's interest. They were surely dear enough to drive a man like Gant to kill.

"What else do you know?" Ethan asked.

"What else do ya need?"

"He never told you anything about where he hid them?"

Fowler shook his head. "I don't think he trusted me that much. Or anyone else, for that matter."

"That I believe," Ethan said. "Very well. If I find the pearls, and I can sell them or get a reward for returning them, you'll get a quarter." It was an easy bargain to make, since Ethan had little interest in finding the pearls. Fowler didn't need to know that, though.

The soldier's grin returned. "Don't try t' cross me, Kaille. I'm paid t' carry a musket, and I don't think much trouble would come of usin' it on a man like you."

"Probably not," Ethan said. Before Fowler could walk away, Ethan asked, "Did you ever see Gant with Caleb Osborne or Jonathan Sharpe?"

The man narrowed his eyes. "How do you know them?"

"Answer the question."

"Aye," Fowler said. "Now that ya mention it, they was thick as thieves, those three."

"My thanks," Ethan said.

He left Fowler there and headed back to the Crow's Nest. He needed to have another talk with Dunc. When he reached the run-down tavern, though, the door was locked. Ethan rapped hard on the faded wood and waited. After a few minutes he knocked a second time.

"Open up, Dunc!" he called. "You wouldn't want me to do anything to damage the place."

Seconds later, he heard a bolt thrown and the door opened just enough for the Scotsman to stare out with one eye.

"Go away, Kaille," Dunc said, his voice thick. "We're closed. It's Sunday."

"You're never closed. Not even on Sundays."

"Well, we are today."

He tried to push the door shut again, but Ethan jammed his hand against the wood, stopping it. "What's with you today, Dunc?"

With a heavy sigh, Dunc pulled the door open all the way. Dark purple bruises covered much of his face. His other eye was completely closed and badly swollen, and his left arm hung in a sling.

"You look worse than I do," Ethan said, chancing a grin.

Dunc's smile was thin and fleeting.

"Was this because of me? Because of the questions I asked you the other night?"

The Scotsman shook his head. "No." But he didn't look Ethan in the eye as he said it.

"It wasn't because of me, but it was related to what I asked you."

"Let it go, Ethan."

"Gant, or Sephira's boys?"

"It doesn't—"

"Gant, or Sephira's boys?" Ethan asked again, his voice rising.

Dunc, stepped back from the doorway, walked to the bar and sat. Ethan entered the tavern and after closing the door once more joined Dunc at the bar.

"Do you want an ale?" Dunc asked.

"No, thank you. Was this about the pearls?"

Dunc gaped at him. "How . . . ?" He shook his head. "I don't even want to know."

"Was it?"

"Gant came in here looking for them," he said, the words muddied by the swelling of his jaw and lips and cheeks. "Thought I had them. I don't," he added quickly, correctly guessing what Ethan's next question would be.

"Why would he think you did?"

The way Dunc looked at Ethan one might have thought that he had asked the most foolish question ever. And maybe he had. Just about every smuggler who came to Boston wound up here. It would have been the most obvious place to hide the pearls. Except . . .

"But I thought Gant had the pearls," Ethan said. "How could he not know where they were?"

"Maybe he had a partner."

Ethan tapped a finger against his lips, considering this. For the first time since Geoffrey and Senhouse had shown up at his door, he thought he might have an idea of what all this was about. "Gant did have a partner," he said. "Caleb Osborne."

"You know Osborne, too?" Dunc said. "Oh, right, of course. I bet you spellers all know each other."

"No, I never knew Osborne. And now he's dead."

"Aw, come on, Ethan. I didn't want to know that."

"Has Sephira been in here looking for the pearls, too?" Ethan asked.

"Nigel and Nap have. Not long after Gant. They were more gentle about it than he was, but they threatened worse." He wiped a trickle of spittle from the corner of his mouth. "I wouldn't want to be there when Gant and Nigel meet up."

"Really? I would." Ethan straightened and patted Dunc's good shoulder. "Take care of yourself, Dunc. Stay out of trouble."

"I try. It seems to find me anyway."

As Ethan reached the door he paused and looked back at the Scotsman. "You don't happen to know where Gant lives, do you?"

"I doubt he has a place now, but I've heard people say that he used to live near here. On Hull Street, I think, behind a coppersmith's shop. I forget the name."

"That's all right. I'll find it. Hull Street was where he lived before he left to join the war?"

"Aye," Dunc said. "Word was he had a brother who lived there after he did. The brother left soon enough; went back to England. I think the place has been deserted ever since."

"All right. My thanks."

"Kaille," Dunc called to him, as Ethan opened the door. "Could you . . . You can heal, right? With witchery, I mean?"

Ethan smiled. "Aye, I can heal." He closed the door again and went back to the bar. He pulled out his knife, pushed up his sleeve, and said, "Why don't we start with the arm?"

After easing the pain in Dunc's shoulder and healing the worst of his bruises, Ethan left the Crow's Nest for Hull Street. He soon found the coppersmith's shop and, making sure that he wasn't seen, walked around the side of the building to the yard in back. The moment he stepped into the overgrown grass, he felt the cool brush of a conjuring on his face. Another detection spell. Had Mariz left this one, too, hoping that he would find Gant returning for the pearls? Or had this one been left by Gant, to warn him of intruders? Ethan reached for his knife again, and stood still, waiting for the first pulse of an attack spell. None came, leading him to think it must have been Mariz's detection conjuring. It seemed that Sephira's conjurer still hadn't recovered from Gant's assault.

A small shack, its wood weathered and gray, stood before him. It had a single window along its side, though the shutters had been broken. The door in front stood ajar, its hinges rusted. Beyond the house sat an old cart, its wood bleached as well and one of its wheels broken, so that it leaned heavily to one side. Ethan was certain that the house and yard had been deserted for months, at the very least. Stepping up onto the small porch at the front of the structure, he pulled the door open with some effort. The wood scraped the porch wood and the hinges creaked.

The house looked as bad within as it did from outside. A table rested on two legs and one of its sides; the other two legs lay in the middle of the room beside two broken chairs. A bed stood in the corner, its ropes so slack that they drooped to the floor. The floor itself was covered with straw and rat droppings. But Ethan could see as well signs left by a recent visitor: streaks of warm color where the broken furniture had been moved, scraping the ancient planks and clearing away the dust and dirt. At least one floorboard had been ripped up.

He scanned the rest of the house, including a second, smaller room off the back of the first, but there was little more to see. He could have torn up the rest of the floor, but if Gant hadn't—and he assumed that it was Gant who had come most recently—he saw little use in doing so himself. This had been a waste of time, something he didn't have in abundance.

As he crossed back to the door he heard voices. He considered another concealment spell, but this space was too small. If the men were coming to search the house, it wouldn't take them long to find him. Instead, Ethan stepped outside, his knife poised over his arm.

Nigel, Nap, and Gordon halted at the sight of him. Nigel reached into his coat pocket, but appeared to think better of pulling whatever weapon he had hidden there.

"Kaille," he said. "What are you doin' here?"

"Same thing you are. Looking for Gant. He isn't home."

"Was this Gant's place?" Yellow-hair asked, with what Ethan assumed was an attempt at feigned innocence.

Ethan didn't bother to answer.

"Miss Pryce won't be happy that you were here," Nigel said. "She don't like it when you stick your nose in where it don't belong."

"Aye, well, when I start caring about Sephira's likes and dislikes, I'll be sure to let you know." He started past the men, although he never turned his back to them, and he kept the blade edge poised over his forearm the entire time. "Gant isn't here," he said again. "There's nothing to see."

"We'll be the judge of what's worth lookin' at," Nap told him.

Ethan had hoped they would say as much. He would have wagered the ten pounds Geoffrey had promised him that they were looking not for Gant, but for the pearls.

"Suit yourselves."

They watched him go, but didn't follow, and once Ethan was beyond their sight, he hastened toward Wood Lane. He and Sephira after the same man. And for now at least, he was half a step ahead of her.

than approached Number Fourteen Wood Lane warily, making sure that he wasn't seen and searching the street and the nearby alleys for Simon Gant or more of Sephira's toughs. Seeing no one who struck him as suspicious, Ethan climbed the ramshackle stairway again and knocked at the door of Caleb Osborne's daughters.

He heard footsteps within the room and a woman's voice called, "Who's there?"

"It's Ethan Kaille, Miss Osborne. I wonder if I might ask you and your sister a few more questions."

A long silence met his request.

"Miss Osborne?"

"Hester isn't here right now."

"Well, perhaps you can tell me what I need to know."

Again, she didn't respond.

"Miss Osborne? Molly?"

At last she pulled the door open and gazed out at him. If anything, she looked paler than she had the last time he saw her. She was dressed the same, her hair up once more, her dark eyes wide and alert. She glanced past him, even rising up onto her toes to look down the stairway and into the alley.

"Hester isn't here," she said again.

"That's all right. You can answer a few questions, can't you?"

"I suppose I can." She peered down the stairs again and retreated into the room. Ethan followed and started to close the door.

"Leave it open," the woman said.

"All right."

She sat and picked up some sewing that had been left on the floor beside her chair. The fabric with which she was working bore a floral pattern that was as bright and cheerful as the rest of the room was gloomy.

"What are you making?" Ethan asked.

Her smile transformed her face. She was quite pretty when she didn't appear to be terrified. "More cushions," she said, pointing at the one on the chair nearest her own. "We sell them to some of the shops here in the North End."

"You do good work."

She beamed. "Thank you."

"The last time I was here, I asked you if your father had ever worked with Sephira Pryce."

"Yes, I remember. And we told you that he hadn't, at least not as far as we knew."

"Hester also mentioned that your father and Simon Gant had been involved in smuggling."

Molly stared back at him, defiant. "That's right. Our mother didn't like it at all. They fought all the time. When he went off to war it was . . . well, it was a blessing."

"I understand. But I wonder, did your father or Gant ever bring their smuggled goods into your home?"

A single line creased her forehead. "I don't know."

"Did your father ever mention what sorts of things he was smuggling?"

"Don't answer that."

Ethan turned. Hester Osborne stood in the doorway, bearing a small canvas sack. Ethan could see that it held a loaf of bread and some vegetables.

"Good day, Miss Osborne," he said.

She glared at him before stepping past him and kneeling beside her sister.

"Are you all right?" she asked, sounding so concerned one might have thought Ethan had brutalized the girl.

"Yes, I'm fine. He's been asking more questions about Father."

The older sister looked back at him over her shoulder, her expression still stern. "Yes, I gathered as much." She stood and faced Ethan. "I think you should state your business, Mister Kaille. And then you should go."

"All right. I came to ask if either of you knew anything about a parcel filled with pearls that your father and Simon Gant might have stolen some years ago, before they left to fight the French."

"Mama talked about pearls."

"Hush, Molly!"

The younger woman flinched.

"What did she say about them?" Ethan asked.

"What is your interest in this?" Hester asked him. "Do you want these pearls for yourself? Or is there some reward that you hope to claim as your own?"

"If you must know, neither." Corporal Fowler would have been disappointed to hear Ethan say this, but it was the truth.

Hester's laugh, however, was harsh, disbelieving.

"I'm trying to find out what happened to your father and the ship he was on," Ethan said. "That's what I've been hired to do. I believe that the pearls have something to do with his death, and I believe that Gant and Sephira Pryce's men are out there right now, searching for them." He looked at Molly before meeting Hester's gaze again. "And I'm afraid that eventually their search is going to bring them here."

Molly gave a little gasp. Hester laid a hand on her shoulder, but didn't look away from Ethan.

"You're trying to scare us," she said.

"Perhaps," Ethan admitted. "But that doesn't make it any less true."

They stood in silence for several moments. A dog barked in the distance and a gust of wind rattled the open door and stirred the loose strands of hair that had fallen over Hester's brow.

"I remember Mother speaking of pearls," the older woman said at last. "It was during another of their fights. I don't recall anything specific. But I do think that Father had them in the house, at least for a short time. Mother got very angry with him whenever he brought any of his . . . she called it his 'sinner's bounty.'" She grimaced at the memory. "Anyway, she grew angry whenever he brought it home."

Ethan looked around the small room. "Was there a particular place where he kept his goods?"

This time, both women laughed.

"Did I say something funny?"

"This was in our old house, Mister Kaille," Hester told him. "Molly and I moved to this room after Mother died. Father had debts and once Mother was gone, we couldn't pay them off and keep the house. So we sold it and moved here."

"And where was the old house?"

"In New Boston, on Green Lane. Our mother is buried there."

Ethan felt himself sag. Of course. He should have anticipated this. Sephira wasn't half a step behind him; she was days ahead.

"Near West Church?" he asked, unable to keep the weariness from his voice.

"Not too far from it. Why?"

He shook his head. "It doesn't matter. Can you tell me the number?"

"Twenty-eight. But the house burned to the ground two years ago. It's since been rebuilt, but anything that might have been ours has likely been lost."

He should have expected that, too. "I see." He turned to leave. "Thank you both for your time. I'm sorry to have disturbed you."

He descended the stairs in a daze, feeling as though he hadn't slept in weeks. This was why Mariz had been in New Boston, and Gant as well. Ethan doubted that either of them had found the pearls there—otherwise, why would Sephira's men have been at the shack on Hull Street, and why would Gant have beaten Dunc? But he also doubted that he would find anything at the site of the old Osborne house. Both Gant and Mariz would have searched there.

He had wandered down a blind alley, and he had no idea where to go next.

He made his way out to Fish Street, and began the long walk back to the South End, his thoughts roiled and chaotic. Already it was the second day of October; it had been three days since he had gone out to the *Graystone* and two since his conversation with Thomas Hutchinson, and still he knew little more than he had when he began his inquiry. Each time he thought he was close to finding Gant, or at least being able to tell the customs agents how they might find him, something happened to throw him off the path. At this rate, not only would he lose the offered reward to Sephira, as he did too many other rewards he tried to collect, but he would doom every conjurer in Boston to the hangman's gallows.

And yet, even as he contemplated the unthinkable, the kernel of an idea began to form in his head. It carried risks, and not just for himself. But as far as he could tell, it was the best option he had left. As he crossed over Mill Creek, he turned toward upper Cornhill rather than heading toward his room.

Nearing Dock Square, though, Ethan halted in his tracks. There were regulars posted at the corners of Union and Cornhill Streets, all of them dressed in full uniform, the red seeming to glow even in the dull light of an overcast day. Their muskets were fixed with bayonets, and though they stood at ease, speaking among themselves or chuckling at a comrade's joke, their mere presence chilled Ethan's blood. He shouldn't have been surprised to see them. They hadn't occupied the city so that they could hide from view. This was what the king and Parliament and General Gage had had in mind. Still, knowing this and actually seeing armed soldiers in the streets were two different things.

He continued past the men, but began to look for others. And doing so, he saw them everywhere. They stood at other corners, they walked the streets in small groups and patrolled near the waterfront. There were dozens of them outside Faneuil Hall and the Town House, where Kannice had told him they were to be garrisoned.

Ethan tried to tell himself that he had nothing to fear from them. He had never allied himself with Adams, Otis, and the others. But he didn't like that the men were there.

He buried his hands in his pockets, lowered his head, and walked, trying to avoid making eye contact with any of the soldiers he passed. And with his shoulders hunched, he made his way to Diver's room.

His friend lived on Pudding Lane—which was now called Devonshire, though Ethan still thought of it by its old name—in a room much like Ethan's own. It sat above a bakery, and the woman who owned the property had taken a shine to Diver. She was old enough to be his grandmother, and doted on him as if she were. She gave him loaves of bread almost daily, and occasionally left more expensive treats for him. It was one more way in which Diver was the most fortunate wastrel Ethan had ever known.

The building itself was newer and sturdier than Henry's cooperage. The old building had been completely destroyed by the great Cornhill fire of 1760 and rebuilt of brick, as mandated by city law. Diver's room was located at the back of the building. It was simple and small, but warmer in the cold months and cooler during the summer than Ethan's. Still, they paid about the same in rent.

On most mornings this close to midday, Diver would have been at the wharves already. But this was Sunday, and the shipyards at which Diver labored tended to work their men on Saturdays and give them Sundays off. Reaching Diver's door, Ethan knocked, waited, and after some time knocked again.

"Diver!" he called. "Are you in there?"

"Aye, hold on," came Diver's voice from inside. The door opened, revealing Ethan's friend, shirtless and barefoot in a pair of breeches. His dark curls were tousled and he squinted against the daylight.

"What time is it?" he asked, frowning at Ethan.

"Almost midday." Looking past Diver into the room, Ethan saw the bare back and long red hair of a woman in Diver's bed. "Late night?"

That coaxed a grin from him. "What do you want, Ethan?"

"I have a business proposition for you. I need help, and I think you're the only one who I can trust with this."

His eyes went wide like those of a boy who had just been given his first musket. The look was half joy, half amazement. "You're serious," he said.

"Aye. But we need to get started now. And," Ethan added, looking past him to the woman, "we can't discuss it in front of anyone."

Diver nodded. "She'll be dressed and out of here in five minutes." He started to close the door.

"Is that Katharine?" Ethan asked, stopping him.

"What?" Diver's face went red. "Oh. No, it's not. I told her I never wanted to see her again. This is Deborah. I'll introduce you before she leaves."

Ethan didn't think there was any need. Chances were Diver would be with someone new by week's end, and he would never see Deborah with him again. But he kept that to himself and waited patiently outside the room while the two of them dressed. True to his word, Diver introduced Ethan to the girl as she was leaving, presenting Ethan in a manner befitting someone of great celebrity. Deborah smiled at Ethan, kissed Diver's cheek, and left, hips swaying as she descended the stairs. Diver stared after her in a way that made Ethan wonder if he was wrong to dismiss the girl as he had.

"You like this one, eh?"

"Aye, I do."

"Good for you, Diver. It's about time."

Diver looked at him. "What is?"

"Nothing. Forget I said it."

His friend looked down at the girl one last time as she stepped out onto Devonshire. Once she was out of sight, he turned to Ethan again. "So what's this all about?"

"Inside," Ethan said.

Once they were in the room, with the door closed and a pot of water warming on the stove, Ethan began to relate to Diver all that he had learned about the pearls and Gant's role in their theft.

When he finished, Diver let out a low whistle. "Well, I never liked Simon Gant. I was scared to death of him, if you want to know the truth. But going up against Sephira . . ." He shook his head. "You've got to admire him for that. I wouldn't have the nutmegs."

"I prefer to think that you're too smart," Ethan told him. "But we'll leave that discussion for another day." He had been sitting back in an old wooden chair, but now he leaned forward, the chair creaking as he rested his elbows on his knees. "When was the last time you dealt with smugglers?"

Diver hesitated. Under most circumstances, Ethan knew, he would have claimed to have given up such activities, knowing that Ethan wouldn't approve. But he seemed to understand that on this day Ethan needed to hear the truth. "It's been a while now. Since last winter at least."

"You still know people, though, right? If you needed to find something, or sell something?"

"Of course," the younger man said. "What is it you want me to do?"

"If you had pearls to sell, and you didn't know where they had come from, or if you knew but didn't want to answer any questions about them, where would you go to sell them?"

"The Crow's Nest," Diver said right off. "That's still the best spot."

Ethan shook his head. "They're not there. And at this point I'd wager that Dunc wants nothing to do with them. Where else?"

Diver ran a hand through his curls, his brow furrowed. "That's hard to say. I might have to think about it, and get back to you."

"No time for that," Ethan said. "I'll trust you to find the right place."

"You'll trust me . . . ? I don't follow."

"I need you to find a buyer for those pearls."

"But I thought you didn't have them."

Ethan grinned. "Well, that's where this gets a little dangerous. I *don't* have them. Neither will you. So you're going to have to use some caution when you speak of them. Maybe say that you have a friend who's trying to sell the pearls. If you want to imply that it's me, go ahead. Just don't use my name, or anyone else's for that matter."

"The men who are likely to show interest in these pearls are going to want to know more about them than I'm guessing you want me to tell."

"I'm sure," Ethan said. "But I'm not as interested in attracting potential buyers as I am in drawing the attention of Simon Gant. So here's what you'll say: You don't know much about where these pearls came from. Only that they've been here in the city for several years, and that they had been lost for a while, but recently turned up somewhere in New Boston. If anyone asks for more information than that, tell them you don't know."

"Several years in the city, found in New Boston." Diver nodded. "That's easy enough. What else?"

Ethan closed his eyes and rubbed a hand over his face, brow to chin. "It's not easy at all, Diver. Understand what it is I'm asking of you, what it is I'm getting you into. If

I'm right, Gant has already killed a shipful of men simply to protect his stake in this shipment. He nearly killed Mariz with a conjuring. He beat me senseless and did the same to Dunc, all because of these pearls. He's going to hear what you're trying to sell, and he's going to come looking for you. And because he stole these from Sephira, we're going to be drawing her attention, too. She's been hunting the man all through Boston, and she won't stop until Gant is dead or she has the pearls."

Diver stared at him, puzzlement furrowing his brow. "Well, now it sounds like you don't want me to help you."

"I do. I can't think of any other way to lure Gant out from wherever he's been hiding. But I want you to understand the danger in what I'm asking you to do. Once you start this, you can't stay here. Chances are Gant and Sephira's toughs will come here to search your place, and they won't be gentle about it. If you're here, they'll hurt you. Or worse."

"So, I won't be here."

"Is there somewhere else you can stay? With Deborah maybe?"

Diver's cheeks reddened again. "Aye, maybe. I'll find a place. Don't worry about it, Ethan. I can do this."

Ethan laid a hand on Diver's shoulder. "I know you can. But just the same, I'll be keeping an eye on you, and on them. If anyone contacts you, tries to set up a meeting, you let me know, and I'll be there with you. I won't let anything happen to you."

"Can't you find Gant on your own? Your way, I mean."

"I can," Ethan said. "But he'll feel a finding spell. He'll know someone's looking for him. He might even guess that it's me. I don't want to give him that kind of warning. I'm sure that he's looking for these pearls, and I'm sure that he'll want to find them as quickly as he can and then get as far from Boston and Sephira as possible. I'm hoping that we can make him a little careless."

"What if this doesn't fool him?" Diver asked. "What

if it doesn't fool Sephira, either? What if one of them already has the pearls, and they know that I'm making it all up?"

"They don't," Ethan said. "I'm not sure of much, but I do know that if the pearls had been found Gant would be long gone and Sephira would be hunting him down instead of sending Nigel and his buddies all around the North End."

Diver weighed this. "Then it sounds like I should get started right away."

Ethan stood, patted Diver on the shoulder. "My thanks. I'd like to tell you that there's a hundred pounds sterling waiting for you at the end of this if it works, but there's not. I'm getting paid ten pounds. I'll give you four, but that's about all I can offer."

"That's more than enough. I still owe you from what happened with Tanner. And you've spent at least that much on my ales and stew in the Dowser."

"Nevertheless, I'm in your debt," Ethan said. "Let's plan to meet at the tavern each night until this is over. I want to know everything that happens."

He let himself out of Diver's room and descended the stairs to the street, feeling considerably better than he had just an hour before. Sephira always managed to outthink him, but he couldn't imagine that she would anticipate this gambit.

Chapter
FIFTEEN

*H*e had intended to head home after leaving Diver's place, but as he stepped back out onto the street, he saw people streaming through the city lanes toward the First Church. At least, that was where he thought they were going. As he followed, however, driven by curiosity and something else he couldn't name, Ethan saw that those leading the throng had passed the church and Town House, and were continuing west toward the Court House.

This, too, they passed. As Ethan caught snatches of conversation and repeated mention of certain words—"lobsterbacks," "barracks," and, most often "Brown"—he realized that they were leading him to the Manufactory House. Thus far today he had heard nothing new about Elisha Brown, but he assumed that he and his comrades were still holding out in the building. Listening more closely, looking around at the expressions of those walking with him, he sensed the crowd's trepidation as well as its excitement. It seemed that the people heading toward Treamount didn't know whether to expect another moral victory for the colonists or a bloodbath.

Reaching the broad avenue and following the onlookers to the great brick structure, Ethan saw a host of regulars and an officer, powerfully built and resplendent in his red uniform, standing at the fore of their column. He was looking up at the building, speaking with someone. Following the direction of his gaze, Ethan saw a man with dark hair and a ruddy face leaning out of a second-story window, and shouting back at the officer. Elisha Brown, no doubt.

The regulars carried muskets, but as of yet they hadn't aimed them at the building. Ethan wondered how long that would last. To his relief, he saw no sign of the British cavalry or of heavier guns.

Scanning the larger horde that had gathered around the building to watch whatever unfolded, Ethan caught sight of a familiar shock of gray hair. After a moment's hesitation, he pressed through the mass of people until he had reached Samuel Adams's side.

"Good afternoon, sir."

Adams glanced his way, looked a second time. His face brightened. "Mister Kaille!" he said. "What brings you here? Are you ready at last to join our cause?"

"I was drawn here by curiosity, nothing more. I saw the crowd gathering and I followed."

"I see," Adams said, a tinge of disappointment in his voice. He turned back to the scene before them, his head moving ever so slightly with his palsy, concern creasing his brow.

"Brown and his friends are taking a great chance," Ethan said. "You should get him out of there."

"I should?" Adams said, rounding on him. "I have nothing to do with this. Contrary to what you and some others might choose to believe, James Otis and I are not responsible for every act of defiance by the citizens of Boston. Brown didn't take direction from me or anyone else. He did this because he believes this occupation to be wrong, and because he doesn't wish to give up his residence, however temporary it might be, in order to make a few of King George's men more comfortable."

Ethan said nothing, and Adams turned away once more, a touch of red shading his cheeks.

"Forgive me, Mister Kaille. These past few days have been difficult for all of us. I'm not insensitive to the danger. But Elisha has chosen his own path, and like you I can only watch to see what happens next." He shrugged, a small, guarded gesture. "I don't believe that Dalrymple and his men want this confrontation. They don't wish to be humiliated, of course, and therein lies the true peril. But word is that General Gage has more men on the way—a few thousand more—and Dalrymple wouldn't be so foolish as to resort to violence before his reinforcements arrive."

"I hope you're right."

A wan smile flickered on the man's face, although he didn't look away from the building. "Yes, so do I."

They both fell silent and watched. Much of the crowd had quieted as well, perhaps trying to hear what Brown and the British officer said to each other. Ethan could make out little of it, and none of what he heard was of much interest to him. Lieutenant Colonel Dalrymple wanted the building for his men and claimed authority to take it. Brown refused to acknowledge that authority and claimed to have no intention of leaving any time soon. The rest of what they said was of little importance.

After a few minutes of this, those who had come expecting to see something more dramatic began to lose interest. The silence that had descended on the mass of people gave way to murmured conversations, and to catcalls, most of them directed at the regulars and their leaders, but a few aimed at Brown and his friends.

Ethan scanned the crowd, more out of habit than any expectation that he might recognize someone. The one person he knew who might have been drawn to this sort of encounter was Diver, and Ethan had left him back on Pudding Street. But as he continued to survey the street, a lone figure drew his attention. At first he took little notice of the man, who was skulking at the edge of the crowd, his great shoulders hunched, his hands deep in his pockets.

Ethan soon realized that while the man appeared to be pacing, every pass brought him closer to the Manufactory. And he realized as well that he had seen the hulking frame and red hair before. Simon Gant.

"Your pardon, sir," Ethan said, starting away from Adams and taking care to keep his gaze fixed on Gant.

"Yes, of course, Mister Kaille," Adams called to him. "Good day to you."

Ethan raised a hand in farewell, but all of his attention was on the big man. Skirting the densest part of the gathering, he made his way toward him. He moved with great care, and tried to conceal himself behind others. But he never let Gant out of his sight, and he reached for his knife as he walked. He hid the blade within his sleeve, so as not to alarm those around him, or cut anyone as he squeezed past.

Gant watched the building—Ethan wondered what interest he had in Elisha Brown and his confrontation with the regulars—and paid little attention to those around him. Ethan might have made it all the way to the man without being spotted had it not been for an older woman who objected to his attempts to step past her.

"You'll just have to wait there, mister!" she said, glaring at him with small blue eyes. "We all want to see better, and I have a friend inside! So you just stand there with the rest of us and stop pushing me!"

Ethan raised his hands to indicate that he meant her no harm, and glanced toward Gant, to make certain that the man hadn't seen him yet. He hadn't.

But that hardly mattered, because in putting up his hands, he had forgotten that he held the knife. The old woman let out a little gasp, pointed a bony finger at Ethan and shouted "He has a knife!" in a shrill voice that must have carried halfway to Newport.

Everyone in the vicinity turned to look at him. So did Gant.

Ethan stared back at him and the big man's eyes widened with recognition. He bolted down Treamount, shoving one woman to the ground and lowering his shoulder so that he barreled over an unsuspecting man. Ethan threaded his way through the mob, trying to be more gentle than Gant, but also doing his best not to let the thief get too far ahead of him. He jostled several people, earning glares and shouted insults, and at least one kick to the shin. But soon enough he was clear of the crowd and running after Gant.

The red-haired man turned down Queen Street. Ethan followed, pushing at his sleeve, and wondering what kind of spell he might use to slow Gant down. Gant cut off of Queen at the Court House, sprinting through the square that the old building shared with the prison and Old Meeting House. Ethan's bad leg slowed him, and he could feel the man pulling away from him.

When he lost sight of Gant, he despaired, thinking that he had lost him. But he didn't slow. Not yet. And as he reached Water Street, he saw Gant again.

The man had stopped. He stood with his arm braced against the brick side of a building, a pistol aimed at Ethan's head.

Ethan stopped and threw himself to the side, taking cover between two shops and waiting for the report of Gant's weapon. It never came. When Ethan finally leaned out to look again, Gant was gone. Swearing, Ethan leaped to his feet and started after him again, hoping that he had continued down Water Street.

The lane was empty save for two carriages that were ahead of him and heading in the same direction he was. No one could see him. He cut himself and said "*Locus magi ex cruore evocatus.*" Location of conjurer, conjured from blood. Reg fell in step beside him, seeming to run without effort, which was disconcerting since the ghost was at least four hundred years older than Ethan.

The conjuring flowed from him down into the street, and rebounded an instant later. Gant was ahead of him, still on Water Street. He would have felt Ethan's finding spell, and should have warded himself against any conjured attack.

But Ethan felt no pulse of power. Maybe Gant didn't wish to give Ethan any better sense of where he was. Or maybe he was content to rely on his gun and his strength.

On that thought, Ethan slowed, peering into every alley, expecting with each turn of his head to find himself staring down the steel gray barrel of the thief's pistol.

"Where are you, Gant?" Ethan called, halting. "There's no sense in hiding. I can find you with another spell. You know I can."

He cut himself again and cast a second finding spell. Gant was ahead of him still, but close. It seemed that he had stopped running, too. By halting, Ethan had probably saved himself. He looked at Reg, who was staring ahead, his gaze avid, hawklike.

"Should I put him to sleep?" Ethan asked, his voice low.

The old ghost grinned at him.

Ethan laid the blade of his knife against his arm.

"Don't do it."

Gant stepped from the shadows, his pistol trained on Ethan's chest.

"You won't hit me from there," Ethan said.

"You don't know that."

"Where are the pearls, Gant? Is that what you were looking for at the Manufactory?"

Gant cursed and took a step toward him, looking very much like a man who wanted to put a bullet through Ethan's heart. "Leave it alone, Kaille! This is none o' your concern!"

"Why are you using a gun, Gant?" Ethan asked. "You're a conjurer, just like I am. We both know it."

The man shook his head, looking for all his brawn like a little boy. "I don't like that magicking stuff." He held up the pistol, but quickly aimed it at Ethan again. "I prefer this. Now those pearls—"

"Are Sephira's. And she's not going to be happy when she finds out that you're still in the city looking for them."

"You leave Sephira t' me."

Ethan laughed. "Well, now I get it. You're not stupid, you're insane."

"You watch what you say t' me, Kaille," Gant said, growling the warning. "You're a pest, nothin' more. But that don't mean I won't track you down and kill you."

Ethan had heard enough. He cut a quick short gash in his forearm and as blood began to well from the wound he said, "*Ambure ex cruore—*"

It would have been a scalding spell, one that he had used in the past to great effect. But before he could get all the Latin out, he saw Gant's pistol hand move fractionally.

He dove to his left, pushing off with his good leg, just as he saw white flame leap from the gun and heard the report echo off the buildings around him. The bullet whistled past, but Ethan landed awkwardly on his elbow and knee.

"*Ambure ex cruore evocatum!*" he said through gritted teeth, even as he heard Gant running again. Scald conjured from blood!

Gant howled with pain, but he was already a good distance away. Ethan knew that he would keep running. It would take him too long to reload his pistol, and he had made it clear that he didn't wish to engage Ethan in a battle of spells.

Ethan sat up, flexed his elbow, and tried to straighten his leg. The elbow hurt, but seemed to be merely bruised. His knee was another matter. He didn't think he had broken anything, but the kneepan felt as though it was in the wrong position, and every movement of his leg sent barbs of white-hot pain up his leg. He dragged himself out of the middle of the lane, and once he was on the safe side of the iron posts lining the street, cut himself once more, cursing the raw aching of his forearm.

Rubbing blood on his knee, he said, "*Remedium ex*

cruore evocatum." Healing, conjured from blood. The spell sang in the cobblestones and flowed from his hands into his leg. At first, as the kneepan shifted back into its normal position, the pain worsened. For an instant Ethan thought he might pass out, and he had to bite back the bile rising in his throat. He squeezed his eyes shut, and concentrated on his conjuring, doing his best to keep the flow of power steady. After some time, the agony passed, and the pain in his leg began to subside. He cut himself once more, and repeated the spell.

When he could bend his leg without grinding his teeth in agony, he climbed to his feet and began to limp back home. He thought about trying another finding spell, just to make certain that Gant hadn't decided to come back and try to shoot him again. But his arm hurt, and he was weary from the spells he had cast. He wanted only to go home and sleep.

He should have known better than to think that was even possible. When Ethan turned onto Cooper's Alley, he spotted Yellow-hair standing by the door to Henry's shop. He held a pistol in his hand. When had everyone started carrying firearms? Seeing Ethan, he grinned.

Ethan had stopped, and now he grasped his knife and started to back away. All concerns about his raw forearm had fled his mind. He didn't think he could run far, but with a spell he might be able to escape. Nigel seemed to read his thoughts.

"You don't want to do that," the big man said with a shake of his head.

"Why not?"

Nigel indicated Henry's shop with the barrel of his pistol. "She's in there, waitin' for you."

Henry.

"If she's hurt him, if she's so much as disturbed a hair on his head, I'll kill her. And I'll kill you, too."

The man's grin returned. "Get inside."

Ethan knew he had no choice. He walked to the door and reached for the handle.

"Hold on," Nigel said, walking toward him, his hand outstretched. "Give me your knife."

Ethan cut his arm. "Try to take it from me," he said.

Yellow-hair stopped in midstride. Ethan opened the shop door and stepped inside.

Henry was seated by his workbench, grinning broadly, the gap in his teeth making him look like a small child. Sephira sat next to him, a disarming smile on her flawless, deceitful face. Nap stood near the door.

"Ethan!" Sephira said as he walked in. Her gaze flicked to the cut on his arm, and her smile tightened. "How nice to see you. I was just telling your charming friend here that you and I have been rivals—friendly rivals, of course—for near to eight years now. I can't believe so much time has gone by."

"Are you all right, Henry?" Ethan asked, though upon reflection he realized that he had never seen the cooper look happier. Sephira was famous and beautiful and she had come to his shop. Henry had no idea of how much danger he was in, and probably wouldn't have believed it if Ethan had tried to tell him.

"I'm fine." He looked at the bleeding cut on Ethan's arm and his face fell. "What happened to your arm?"

"It's nothing."

Henry seemed more than happy to accept this. "Mith Prythe—" His cheeks colored and he cast a sheepish glance her way. "I mean Thephira," he went on, his lisp even more pronounced than usual. "She knows a guy—in France no less—who might want my barrels for his wine!"

Ethan looked at Sephira, who returned his gaze steadily, without any sign that she felt ashamed for lying to the old man. "That's very exciting."

"I've always wanted to go to France. But if I can't go, at least my barrels can."

"That's right," Ethan said. "Listen, Henry. Sephira and I have some business to discuss. So we're going to let you get back to work now, all right?"

"There's no need for that." Sephira purred the words. "We can talk about it right here. And I'm sure we're not disturbing Henry. Are we?" She flashed a dazzling smile.

Henry just shook his head. Ethan glanced over at Nap, who had turned away to hide the smirk on his face.

"All right," he said, looking at Sephira again. "What are you doing here?"

"Nigel mentioned that he saw you a short time ago," Sephira said. "And that you were somewhere you didn't belong. I wanted to impress upon you how important it is that you not go there—or anywhere like it—again."

She might as well have been holding a blade to Henry's throat.

Even Henry seemed to understand. The joy Ethan had seen on his face upon entering the shop was gone now, and he was looking back and forth between Ethan and Sephira.

"I've tried asking you for information," Ethan said. "That hasn't worked, and so I've had to look into things on my own. If you care to answer my questions, I'll be more than happy to stay out of your way."

"The things you want to know don't concern you. You're interfering in matters that you don't understand. People could get hurt."

People. Henry. Kannice. Ethan knew that she wouldn't hesitate to harm or kill anyone who meant anything to him. His arm itched where the blood from his cut had begun to dry. He would have loved an excuse to set her hair on fire with a conjuring, but Henry didn't know that he was a speller, and Ethan wasn't willing to cast in front of the old cooper unless he had no choice.

"Simon Gant just told me much the same thing," Ethan said. "None of you seem to understand that I've been hired to look into these matters. That makes them my concern. And you should take your own warnings to heart. People *could* get hurt. Remember that."

"You saw Gant?" she asked, trying too hard to sound uninterested.

"Yes."

"Where? When?"

Ethan said nothing.

She sat watching him for another moment, a smile frozen on her lips. There was no amusement at all in her eyes, though, and when she stood and moved toward the door, her movements were taut, as if it was all she could do to leave the shop without lashing out.

"You're a fool, Ethan," she said, not bothering to look back at him. "After all these years, it shouldn't surprise me. But it always does."

She let herself out, with Nap close behind. They left the door open.

"She didn't even say good-bye," Henry whispered, staring after her.

"I'm sorry, Henry."

The old man shook his head. "No, I am. I should have remembered the stuff she's done to you. She didn't come for me; she came for you." He turned to Ethan. "She was threatening to hurt me, wasn't she?"

Ethan grimaced. "Aye, she was."

Henry looked out the door again. "Well, don't worry about me. Do what you have to do, whatever it is."

He gripped the man's shoulder. "I will. Thank you." He hobbled to the doorway, intending to go up to his room.

"You hurt your leg?" Henry asked.

"It's nothing."

"Well, you should do something about that arm," Henry called after him. "You shouldn't just let it bleed like that."

Chapter

SIXTEEN

*H*e wanted to tear Sephira's home apart stone by stone. He wanted to find Simon Gant and cast a spell that would shatter every bone in the man's body. He wanted to wring Geoffrey Brower's neck for getting him involved in this matter in the first place.

Instead, he paced the floors of his tiny room, despite the ache in his bad leg and knee. He felt useless and sensed the hours ticking away. Worst of all, he had the feeling that he was missing something obvious. He knew that Osborne had helped Gant steal the pearls seven years back. And now he knew for certain that Sephira was after the smuggled goods, too, not that there had ever been any doubt.

He had let Gant get away, but he had Diver working on luring the man back out into the open. Thinking of this, he sighed. As tired as he was, he needed to conjure again so that he could tell Diver that the pearls might not be in New Boston after all. This time, at least, he didn't have to cut himself. Using the water in his washbasin, he cast an illusion spell, and sent an image of himself back to Diver's room. But when he looked at the room through the eyes of his conjuring, he found that Diver was already gone.

Vowing to try again later in the day, he let the conjuring end and resumed his pacing.

An idea came to him and he halted once more. He knew that neither Gant nor Sephira would help him. But what about Osborne? Ethan wasn't sure that it was even possible. But perhaps there was someone who could help him find out.

"*Veni ad me.*" Come to me.

Power thrummed. Uncle Reg appeared before him, glowing like a newly risen moon, his eyes gleaming in the dim room.

"You were a conjurer," Ethan said. "And when you died you took this form. Is that right?"

The old ghost nodded.

"Is that what happens to all conjurers when they die? Do they all go to wherever it is you are?"

Reg nodded again, more slowly this time.

"And can they be summoned? I can call for you; we both know that. But can I summon any ghost if I know his name?"

The ghost's expression darkened, his thick eyebrows bunching, his nostrils flaring. He crossed his arms over his chest, his fists clenched, and he shook his head.

"No?" Ethan stared back at him, gauging what he saw on the man's face. "You're telling me that it shouldn't be done," he said at length. "Not that it can't. Isn't that so?"

Reg didn't move.

"This is important. Osborne should know where the pearls are, and he might know a good deal else that will help me get to Gant."

Ethan reached first for his knife, but reconsidered and chose to use mullein instead. He couldn't say why. Most of the time he conjured with whatever was at hand, without giving much thought to how the source for his spells matched the casting itself; it might have been one of the reasons why he was not yet as accomplished a conjurer as Janna. On occasion, though, he gave more careful consideration to his selection of a source. And sometimes, as now, he went on instinct. He was about to summon an unknown and potentially hostile ghost. Somehow using blood for this struck him as risky. Mullein had protective properties; it seemed the wiser choice.

He pulled out nine leaves. It was a lot for any spell, but this was more complicated spellmaking than Ethan usually did.

Turning back to Reg, he found the ghost still glaring at him in that same defiant stance.

"I know you don't like this. I'm sorry. Truly. But I'm going to do it, and I need you to help me speak with him."

Reg didn't shake his head in refusal; Ethan probably couldn't expect any more acquiescence than that.

"*Provoco te, Caleb Osborne, ex regno mortuorum ex verbasco.*" I summon thee, Caleb Osborne, from the realm of the dead, conjured from mullein.

Even having chosen to use so many leaves, even knowing that this was a deeper casting than he had attempted in years, Ethan was startled by the might of his conjuring. He felt the pulse in his bones; the entire building seemed to shake. Power hummed in the walls and the floor; it reverberated within his mind until he felt that he would never again hear any other sound. Every conjurer in Boston would know that a potent spell had been cast, but he couldn't help that.

And yet, nothing else happened. No ghost appeared. Ethan glanced toward Reg, but the old man wasn't looking at him. Rather, he was turning his head from side to side, perhaps searching for Osborne's shade. He appeared troubled, even frightened. Ethan had never seen him like this.

"What's happening?" Ethan asked.

Reg held up a hand to silence him, though he continued to search. At last he faced Ethan again and shook his head.

"It didn't work?" Ethan asked, incredulous. "But I felt the conjuring. That was one of the most powerful spells I've ever cast."

Reg shook his head again.

"So a ghost can refuse a summons from a conjurer if he isn't linked the way we are."

The ghost shrugged, appearing as confused as Ethan felt.

Ethan nearly gave up then. That was what Reg wanted him to do. But another thought came to him. There had been a third conjurer on the *Graystone*. Jonathan Sharpe had been younger than both Gant and Osborne. Maybe he had been less skilled as a conjurer and thus would be less able to resist Ethan's summons.

He took more mullein from his pouch, leaving him with enough for only one more minor spell. He would have have to buy more from Janna, and soon.

"There was one other conjurer on the ship," he told Reg. "I'm going to try summoning him."

Reg scowled.

"*Provoco te, Jonathan Sharpe, ex regno mortuorum ex verbasco.*" I summon thee, Jonathan Sharpe, from the realm of the dead, conjured from mullein.

This spell echoed through the building as powerfully as had the first. The old ghost began to look around again, but almost immediately looked back to Ethan, his gleaming eyes as wide as moons.

And at the same time, a second glowing figure took form beside him: a young man, both familiar and strange. Ethan recognized the long hair and fleshy, thick features from the corpse he had seen on Castle William. But that wasn't the same as knowing a man in this ghostly form. The shade of Jonathan Sharpe towered over Reg, and over Ethan as well. His eyes were similar to those of the old ghost, but his body glowed with an aqua hue. He wore the uniform of a British regular, but as far as Ethan could see, he didn't carry a weapon. Which was fortunate, because he regarded Ethan with manifest hostility and even took a menacing step toward him. Ethan re-sisted the urge to back away, knowing—or at least hoping—that the ghost couldn't harm him.

"My name is Ethan Kaille," he said. "I summoned you because I'm trying to find the cause of your death and that of every other man on the *Graystone*. Can you help me?"

The ghost seemed not to hear him. He turned toward Reg and advanced on the old man. Reg fell back and drew his broadsword, something Ethan had never seen him do.

Sharpe's ghost faltered.

"Sharpe!" Ethan said. "Look at me!"

The shade faced him once more.

"Did you know Caleb Osborne and Simon Gant?"

Sharpe eyed him, looking confused. Finally, he nod-ded.

"And you knew about the pearls?"

The ghost's expression turned guarded. He offered no response. "I think they're the reason you were killed. I think that Gant attacked the ship with that spell so that he wouldn't have to share them with Osborne."

Sharpe shook his head, an expression of contempt on his face. Even in death, he remained loyal to his friends. Ethan couldn't help thinking there was something noble in that.

"They're hidden somewhere in the city, aren't they?"

No answer.

"Do you know what kind of conjuring killed you, what kind of spell it was?"

The ghost dragged a finger across his throat, a grim smile on his lips.

"A killing spell. Yes, that's very helpful."

Sharpe's smile melted away, leaving him looking ter-ribly young. His eyes fixed on Ethan's, he placed his hand over his heart and then made a fist.

Ethan nodded. The spell had attacked their hearts, squeezing them so that they stopped beating. That was

why the orange glow from Ethan's *revela potestatem*
spell had spread outward from the chests of the soldiers
on which it worked. "I understand," he said. "I'm sorry."

The young man looked away. Reg stepped forward,
and though he still held his sword, he placed a hand on
Sharpe's shoulder, and stared hard at Ethan.

"All right," Ethan said. He sensed that he could have
learned more from the dead man, but he also understood that he should have listened to Reg. This was
wrong.

"*Dimitto vos ambos.*" I release you both.

As soon as the words crossed his lips he felt another
surge of power. He watched as the two ghosts vanished.

Alone in the darkened room, Ethan muttered a curse.
He opened his door, just to let in some light and cool air.
But after having a small bit of cheese and smoked meat,
he left again, this time heading back to the North End.
Spellmaking, it seemed, could help him only so much,
and he couldn't afford to wait for his next chance encounter with Gant. He needed to know where the man
was hiding.

Geoffrey Brower and Ethan's sister Bett lived in a large
stone house near North Square in one of the city's finer
neighborhoods. Ethan had been inside once, when he first
returned from Barbados and Bett was moved by some
uncharacteristically charitable impulse to have him to
dinner and introduce him to his nieces and nephew. She
hadn't invited him to the house since.

Reaching the path that led to Bett's door, Ethan faltered, wondering if coming here had been a mistake. For
years Ethan had convinced himself that Bett turned her
back on spellmaking because she had no aptitude for it,
because the conjurings hadn't come to her as easily as
they did to Ethan and the youngest child in the Kaille
household, Susannah. The truth, he had come to realize,
was far more complicated, and far less convenient for
him. When he and Bett first entered their teen years and
began to learn spellmaking from their mother, he had no

more skill as a conjurer than she. If anything, her attention to detail made her castings more effective than his.

But she never enjoyed it. Even at that tender age, she seemed to believe that conjuring was wrong in some way. Perhaps she shared their father's devotion to the Church and more godly pursuits. Or maybe she preferred Ellis's company to Sarah's, just as Ethan had felt more comfortable with their mother. Whatever the reason, by the time Susannah began to conjure, Bett had already started to turn away from spellmaking, and from Ethan. Ethan and Susannah were inseparable until Ethan left home to join the navy. Bett always seemed aloof. Only much later did it occur to Ethan to wonder if she had been lonely. And by then, the bond between them had been so badly frayed that he no longer knew how to mend it.

He was ashamed to admit that he often wished Susannah could have settled here in Boston, rather than Bett. But his beloved youngest sister lived an ocean away, in the Scottish Isles, and Bett lived in this grand house before him, with its marble columns and fine gardens.

Taking a long breath, Ethan walked up the broad walkway to their portico and rapped on the door with the brass knocker.

Ethan had thought that a servant would answer his knock—when last he visited, dinner had been served by an African slave. But when the door opened, a young man of perhaps sixteen years stood before him, well-dressed, and looking like he had never labored a day in his life. He was tall and gangly, with a high forehead and narrow nose like his father's. Poor lad.

"You're George, aren't you?" Ethan asked.

The boy looked both pleased and surprised. Perhaps Ethan had been too quick to judge. The smile was entirely Bett's, and with it he was quite handsome. "I'm afraid you have me at a disadvantage, sir."

Ethan extended a hand. "Ethan Kaille. I'm your uncle."

He half expected the lad to recoil; he was his mother's

son, after all. But he gripped Ethan's hand fairly beaming. "Of course! I remember you now, Uncle. You came once, when I was just a boy."

"Aye, I did. It's good to see you again."

"George?" came Bett's voice from within the house. "Who's there?"

"It's Uncle Ethan, Mother," he called back to her.

Bett entered the hallway and joined her son at the door. She didn't look happy to see Ethan, but she managed to hide this from George and said, "Good day, Ethan," in a passably civil tone.

"Good afternoon, Bett."

"I take it you're here to see Geoffrey."

"Yes."

"George, go fetch your father."

Ethan could see that the lad didn't want to leave. But he said, "Yes, Mother," and flashed another smile Ethan's way. "It's good to see you again, Uncle."

"And you, George."

The boy went off to find Geoffrey, leaving Ethan with Bett. He knew better than to think that she would invite him into the house.

"He seems a fine lad."

"Thank you. He is. He doesn't know you're a conjurer."

"Or, I assume, that spellmaking runs in our family."

Bett lifted her chin. "That's right. He's a God-fearing young man, and I intend for him to remain so."

"And so he thinks the reason he never sees me is that you and I dislike each other?"

"He knows you're a thieftaker, and that we don't wish to bring that element into our home."

"Ah," Ethan said. After all their years of feuding, he had thought that Bett couldn't hurt him anymore. But this stung.

"I'd thank you to keep away from him, Ethan. He's young still. I'm sure he finds the idea of what you do exciting, even enticing. I don't want—"

"I understand, Bett. Rest assured, I'll do nothing to corrupt him."

Mercifully, Geoffrey arrived a moment later.

"I didn't expect to see you here, Ethan," Brower said, joining Bett in the doorway and extending a hand.

Ethan shook it. "No, I don't suppose you did. I won't keep you long."

Brower smiled bracingly, the way he might if he were about to embark on a long and unpleasant journey. "Very well. Let's walk."

"Thank you, Bett," Ethan said, glancing at her one last time.

"Are those bruises on your face?" she asked, as Ethan started to turn away.

He raised a hand to his jaw, having forgotten his injuries. The pain from Gant's blows the other night had abated, but it seemed the marks remained.

"It's nothing," he said. "Just part of my exciting life."

He started down the path toward the cobblestone lane. Geoffrey caught up with him as he reached Middle Street. They followed the thoroughfare to Princes, and Princes around the base of Copp's Hill up toward the Charlestown ferry, walking into the teeth of a cold wind.

"You have news?" Brower asked at last.

"You should have the sheriff look for a man named Simon Gant," Ethan said. "He's a conjurer, and so he's dangerous. He's also a former associate of Sephira Pryce."

"Gant," Geoffrey said. "That name is very familiar."

"He's the soldier who was missing from the *Graystone*. You would have already been told that he's a deserter."

"Yes, that's it. Unfortunately, the sheriff is busy with the rabble occupying the Manufactory. Aren't officers in the army already looking for this man, Gant?"

"You would think they would be," Ethan said, unable to keep the disdain out of his voice. "But they give no indication that they're interested in finding him. That's why I thought that if you could convince Sheriff Green-leaf to join our effort, we might have a better chance of apprehending him."

"I see," Geoffrey said. "And you're certain now that he's the one who killed all those men?"

"As certain as I can be."

"Why did he do it?"

"I'm still trying to figure that out. It may have had something to do with a lost parcel of smuggled pearls. Sephira Pryce is looking for him, too. Or more precisely, she's after the pearls."

"I take it he's also the one who beat you."

Ethan glanced Geoffrey's way, expecting to see a mocking grin on the man's face. But he appeared to be in earnest.

"Yes, he is."

"Is that common in your line of work? Being assaulted?"

"Are you contemplating a change in profession, Geoffrey?"

Brower's laugh was high-pitched and very loud. Ethan was certain he had never heard it before.

"Hardly," the man said. "I was merely . . . curious." Ethan noticed with some surprise that his cheeks had turned crimson. "I find what you do intriguing."

"Bett's worried that George will follow my example and become a thieftaker. Maybe she should be more concerned about you."

"I'm not sure I'd go that far," Geoffrey said with a bit more of his usual stiffness. He halted. "Is that all you wanted to tell me? That I should enlist the sheriff's aid in finding Gant?"

They hadn't yet reached the ferry, but Ethan was ready to turn around, and Brower seemed to be, too. The wind still blew a gale and the clouds overhead were darkening with every gust.

"Aye," Ethan said.

They started back the way they had come, falling into

an uneasy silence. After walking some distance, Geoffrey cleared his throat and glanced Ethan's way.

"Have you been to the Common to speak with the commanders there? Are you sure they know of Gant?"

"Oh, they know of him," Ethan said. "I was on the Common this morning, trying to interest Gant's captain, a man named Preston, in the matter. But he's more concerned with keeping the men he has than with pursuing one who's already deserted."

"To be honest, I cannot blame him," Geoffrey said. "Desertion has been a problem among the regulars in the other colonies. Now that they're here it will be for us as well. I've heard that Dalrymple has already lost soldiers in the one day they've been in the city. The army doesn't pay their men very well, and this occupation is a good deal more than most regulars signed on for." Again, they walked a distance in silence. Their moment of mirth had passed, and it seemed that once more Brower didn't know what to say to him. When at last they came within sight of Geoffrey's home, he stopped again and extended a hand. "Well, thank you, Ethan. I'll see to it that the sheriff is told of this man. And if we find him, I'll also see to it that you receive the ten pounds' reward I mentioned the other day."

"Thank you, Geoffrey."

Geoffrey hurried off to his house, and Ethan walked toward the Dowsing Rod, his collar turned up against the wind. Before he was halfway to Kannice's tavern, large cold raindrops began to pelt down on him. He kept his head down and cursed himself for not wearing a heavier coat. By the time he reached the Dowser he was soaked and bone-cold.

Just as he stepped through the door, he felt power surge through the stone under his feet. He spun, half expecting to see Gant standing behind him, a bloodied blade in his hand. But the street was empty, and the casting, powerful though it was, had passed him by. Too many spells, too much power. He wasn't used to sensing so many conjurings. Most spells in Boston came from him or from Janna. But with Mariz and now Gant walking the streets and conjuring every day, he felt vulnerable. He wondered if this was how other conjurers in the city felt when he cast.

He thought of going back out into the rain to see if he could find whomever it was who had cast that spell. But Kannice had spotted him, and she hastened to the door and tugged him inside. Seeing how wet he was, she ordered him up to her room for a dry pair of breeches and a shirt. When he came back down, she hung his coat and waistcoat, as well as the damp breeches and shirt, over chairs that she positioned by the bright fire burning in her hearth. She sat him at a table and brought him a bowl of the previous night's stew that she had heated on the cooking fire in her kitchen.

He ate two bowls and though he still wondered about the spell he had felt, he also had to admit that it was better to be inside by the fire than out in the rain and wind. He shifted his chair closer to the hearth and sipped a glass of Madeira that Kelf had poured for him. Kannice had given him the chowder, as she so often did, but Ethan insisted on paying for his wine. He rarely allowed himself such luxuries, but the drink warmed him, calmed his head.

Having spoken with Geoffrey, he felt for the first time in days as though he had the advantage on Simon Gant. He might not have been able to find the man again on his own, but soon Brower would have the sheriff looking for Gant as well. During their few encounters, Gant had not exactly distinguished himself with his intelligence; he wouldn't be able to evade capture for long. Ethan had to hope that the Crown's men found the smuggler before Sephira did.

But this new spell gave him pause. Perhaps he had been wrong to get Diver involved in his affairs. Sephira was dangerous enough. But sending Diver out to do business with a conjurer had been damned stupid, even if that conjurer felt more comfortable with a pistol in his hand than with blood on his arm. He would tell Diver so tonight, as soon as his friend came in from the wharves.

As he sipped the wine and stared at the flames, he heard the tavern door open behind him. He glanced back and saw a British officer shaking the rain off his cloak and hat. Turning once more to the fire, he settled back into his chair and stretched his legs out before him.

It was only when he heard the officer speaking to Kannice, and asking for him, that Ethan turned again.

"Mister Kaille!" the man said.

Ethan stood. "Doctor Rickman."

The surgeon crossed the great room in three long strides and shook Ethan's hand.

"I hadn't thought to see you again," Ethan said. He pulled a chair away from the nearest table and set it opposite his own. "Can I buy you a glass of wine?"

"No, thank you," the doctor said, lowering himself into the chair. "You're a most difficult man to find. I've been to your home, and was sent here by the cooper."

"Well, I'm glad you found me." He allowed a conspiratorial smile to touch his lips. "I spoke yesterday with a friend of yours."

Rickman looked puzzled. "Oh?"

"He claims you as a friend, anyway. Although, I don't think you would want anyone in military uniform to hear him do so."

The doctor's face went white. "He should know better," he said in a whisper.

"He did his best to be discreet," Ethan said. "I guessed that he referred to you, based on our conversations at Castle William."

Rickman exhaled through his teeth, calming himself with a visible effort. "Well, I suppose I ought to blame myself as much as Samuel."

"I didn't mean to trouble you so."

The doctor shook his head. "It doesn't matter. I've come about something far more important."

"Of course. What can I do for you?"

"I have questions for you first. Using your—" He glanced back toward the bar. "Your abilities," he said, whispering again, "could you bring a dead man back to life?"

Ethan shuddered, as if someone had dripped icy cold water down his spine. "No," he said, "I couldn't, and I don't know of any conjurer who could. I've seen conjurings used to take lives, but never to restore them."

"Well, could one of your kind use witchery to mimic death, to make himself appear dead, so that he might revive himself later?"

"Doctor, tell me what's happened."

"A second body is missing from among the dead of the *Graystone*. He was there when last I visited Castle William two nights ago, still in the vaults with the others. But by this morning he had vanished."

"Who?" Ethan asked. But of course he knew already.

"One of the conjurers you pointed out to me. Caleb Osborne."

id someone come to the island?" Ethan asked. "Is it possible that Simon Gant was there?"

"Who is—?"

"The man who was missing. The first one," Ethan added. "Was he there, perhaps with a group of regulars, so that no one would notice him?"

"I don't think so," the doctor said. "The regulars are all garrisoned in the city, at least for now."

"Has anyone else visited the island? Anyone at all?"

"Naval officers, the commissioners from the Customs Board, the governor and lieutenant governor. But really that's all."

"Assuming that Osborne could feign death as you suggest, could he have left the fort? Did any boats leave during the night?"

"Not that I know of. But if he was capable of the rest, surely he could have swum from the island. The distance to Boston is great, but it's less than a mile to Dorchester Point."

Ethan dragged a hand over his face. It hadn't occurred to him that a man might escape Castle William in that way, but of course the doctor was right. The air had turned cold, but the Atlantic waters held their warmth well into autumn, even this far north.

"Damn," he muttered. He had never heard of a conjurer faking his or her own death in this way, but he couldn't say for certain whether it was impossible. He could think of only one person in the city who knew spell-making well enough to tell him that. "I need you to come with me to the Neck," he said to the doctor.

"Why?"

"There's a woman there—another conjurer. She'll be able to tell us if any of this is possible. And she might have questions for you that I can't answer."

Rickman nodded. "Yes, all right."

Ethan stood and reached for his waistcoat and coat. They were still damp, though the fire had warmed them.

"Where are you going?" Kannice asked, coming out into the room from behind the bar.

"We have to get to Janna's," Ethan told her.

"What's happened?"

He shook his head. "Honestly, I don't know. That's why I need to speak with her."

Kannice glanced at Rickman, her expression wary, even hostile. "He's with the army?" she asked.

"He's a ship's surgeon in the navy. Do you remember who I went to see first thing yesterday morning?"

Kannice's brow creased. "You mean Mister A—"

"Yes," Ethan said. "The doctor is a friend of his, though few know it. Do you understand?"

She regarded Rickman again, considering him anew. "Yes, of course."

"I'll be back. If Diver comes in, tell him to wait for me."

"I will," Kannice said.

Ethan took her hand and raised it to his lips.

"I don't like the places this job is taking you," Kannice whispered. "Be careful."

He nodded, then led Rickman out of the tavern and into the cold rain.

They walked in silence for some distance, both with

heads bowed. Ethan hunched his shoulders against the elements, his hands buried in his pockets. Rickman held his black tricorn hat in place with one hand, and secured his collar with the other. The sky had darkened, and a chilling mist had settled over the city, shifting constantly, swept along streets and alleys by gusts of wind. The smell of wood fires mingled with the cool scent of rain and the mustiness of fallen leaves: autumn in Boston.

They passed the Manufactory, where all was now quiet. A few of the second-floor windows glowed with candlelight, and the building's brick exterior glistened with rain, so that the stone itself seemed to be bleeding. But most of the regulars had withdrawn and the crowd had dispersed. A small company of soldiers still stood nearby, eyeing the Manufactory, their uniforms sodden and their expressions sullen. Ethan wondered how long Brown could hold out before the British returned in greater numbers and resorted to more forceful means of taking the building.

They followed one of the side roads to Newbury Street and continued southward toward the Neck, stepping around filthy puddles in the cobblestone, and turning their shoulders when passing carriages and chaises splattered them.

"What is this woman's name?" Rickman asked at length, raising his voice to be heard over the rain and wind.

"Janna Windcatcher."

"Windcatcher? What manner of name is that?"

"One she made up." At Rickman's puzzled look, Ethan added, "She was a slave once, and managed to win and keep her freedom. She named herself."

"So she's a Negro?"

"Yes. Is that a problem?"

The doctor shook his head. "Not as long as she can be trusted. Can she?"

A thousand responses crossed his mind in the heartbeat that followed. Ethan had trusted her with his life in the past and would do so again without hesitation. On the other hand, he had no idea where her sympathies lay—Tory or Whig—and he didn't know how she would respond to seeing Rickman's uniform.

"I trust her," he said at last.

"That's not quite what I'm asking," Rickman said, sounding annoyed. "I want to know if she'll betray my confidence. Of course you trust her. She's your friend. But I'm—"

Ethan's laughter stopped the man short.

"You find this amusing?" Rickman asked.

"Forgive me, Doctor. You said that Janna's my friend. I don't know that Janna would agree with you. She's a . . . a difficult woman, regardless of how well one knows her."

The doctor scowled, reminding Ethan of Janna. Rainwater dripped from his hat and ran down the lines in his face. "Perhaps this is a bad idea," he said.

"We want to know if Osborne is still alive. I don't even know if it's possible. Janna knows more about conjuring than anyone in Boston, and I swear to you that no one will learn of our conversation from her. Not Osborne or Gant, and not Senhouse or Preston."

Rickman's frown lingered, but he walked on toward the Fat Spider, and he asked no more questions.

When they reached Janna's tavern, though, the doctor faltered, eyeing the building doubtfully. Ethan couldn't blame him. It appeared to sag under the onslaught of the storm, and as he did so often, Ethan wondered if this would be the day the structure gave way.

Still, he strode to the door and pulled on the handle. The door didn't open.

Ethan frowned. "It's locked," he said. "That's damned peculiar."

"Perhaps she closed early this evening," Rickman said.

"Janna never closes early." Ethan knocked on the weathered door. "Janna? Are you in there?"

After a few moments he knocked again. He didn't like this; not at all. Something wasn't right.

He knocked one last time and just as he started to consider breaking the lock with a spell, the door opened, although only a crack. Aromas of fresh bread and roasting meat seeped out into the cold night air. Janna peered out at him. "Kaille," she said, stretching out his name so that it sounded like a malediction.

"Are you closed, Janna?"

"Damn right I am," she said. "Soldiers came an' shut me down. Can you imagine that? Fifteen years I've been here, an' they just come in an' shut me down, just like that."

"When?"

"Just an hour or two ago. I was cookin' at the time, gettin' ready for the evenin' crowd." She shook her head. "They shut me down," she said again, disbelieving.

"Did they say why?" Ethan asked. But even as he asked the question he was thinking back on his conversation with Thomas Hutchinson two days before. He sensed that somehow this was directed at him, that it was a warning of more dire actions to come.

"Didn't tell me nothin'," Janna said. She glanced at Rickman, her expression guarded.

"Can we come in?"

"Why?" she asked in the same tone she had used to say his name.

"I need help with—"

"No!" she said. "No, no, no! Do you see that this is a business? D'you even understand what that means? I sell food. I sell ale. I sell all sorts of things. I don't care that I'm closed down. This is still a business; *my* business. I don't earn nothin' by helpin' you with whatever you're workin' on."

"I know that. But we've got—"

"No!" She leveled a bony finger at him. "I've done enough for you. And I'm tired—"

"That bread smells very good," Rickman said.

Ethan and Janna looked his way.

"What kind of meat is that you're cooking?"

"Venison," Janna told him, sounding suspicious and looking him up and down. "And some duck, too. Got it from a friend of mine who hunts just over near Roxbury."

"Well, Miss Windcatcher, I know that you're closed down, but it's cold out here and I'm feeling a bit peckish." The doctor dug into his pocket and pulled out a half crown—a good deal more than the cost of two meals and a few ales. He held it up so that it glinted with the candle-light from within the tavern. "I'd like some of that venison, please. And some bread." He looked at Ethan. "An ale for you?"

Janna kept her eyes fixed on the coin.

"Aye, thank you," Ethan said.

Janna still stood in the doorway, though she held the door open a bit wider now. She wore an odd expression on her wizened face. It took Ethan a moment to realize that she was trying not to laugh. At last she stepped back from the door and gestured them inside, all the while shaking her head. "Take a table by the fire," she said, not bothering to look their way. "I'll be right out."

Ethan motioned Rickman inside and then followed him into the smoky warmth and dim light. His eyes were slow to adjust to the darkness, but he wasted no time in shaking the rain off his coat and crossing to the fire to warm himself. After a few moments he joined Rickman at one of the tables.

"I don't think she likes you very much," Rickman said, keeping his voice low.

"I know. And she likes me more than she does anyone else in this city."

Janna emerged from the kitchen a short time later bearing a large trencher that held slices of steaming meat, and a small loaf of brown bread. She placed that in front of them and brought them a pair of ales. Even after she had put the tankards on the table, she continued to stand over them.

Rickman took a bite of meat and washed it down with a swig of ale. "Excellent!" he said, looking up at her.

Janna shifted her weight to her other foot, the corners of her mouth twitching. "Thank you."

"Why don't you sit, Miss Windcatcher?"

Her gaze slid toward Ethan. He nodded once and sipped his ale.

She pulled a chair over and lowered herself into it.

"Ask your questions," Rickman said to Ethan.

"A man has disappeared. Another one. I know he was a conjurer, but I don't know what he was capable of doing. When I saw him last, he was dead. Or he appeared to be. I need to know if a conjurer could feign his own death—make it appear to others that he wasn't breathing, that his heart had stopped, that his limbs were stiffening—and then come back to life later, when no one was nearby. Or is it possible for one conjurer to bring another back from death, assuming that the second man really had died?"

"Kaille," Janna said again, regarding him with the disappointment a mother might show for a wayward son. "All the time you ask me if spells can do this or spells can do that. Haven't you learned yet? Spells can do anythin' if the conjurer castin' them is strong enough."

Ethan felt the blood drain from his face, making his cheeks grow cold. "So—"

"So, a man who looked like he was dead, might not have been. Or a man who died, might be alive again."

"How?"

"Well, that's the thing," she said. Her eyes flicked toward Rickman, who watched her with interest and chewed another bite of meat. "Before I say more, who are you?"

"Forgive me," Ethan said. "Tarijanna Windcatcher, this is Doctor William Rickman. He's the ship's surgeon aboard the *Launceston*."

"British military shut me down," she said, an accusation in the words.

"I know. But Doctor Rickman can be trusted. You have my word on that."

Janna regarded him solemnly. She might have been mad at him for asking these questions of her again and again, but she knew what his word was worth. "And what's he doin' with you?" she asked, turning her gaze on the doctor once more.

"He's helping me with an inquiry. I'm still trying to figure out what was done with that powerful spell that woke us both up on Wednesday morn."

She turned his way. "It's not just that spell. There's been plenty of magick the past few days."

"I know," Ethan said. "Some of it has been mine, but not all. Not nearly."

She considered this, pursing her lips. "Thing about all those spells I mentioned—the ones that can revive a corpse, or make someone appear dead?—one man couldn't do them alone."

"Right," Ethan said. "Because a dead conjurer would need to be brought back by another. He couldn't raise himself."

"That's right. And neither could your man who's just pretendin' to be dead. If he looks dead enough to fool other people, he can't just come back later on his own. He'd need help."

Help. Simon Gant. Ethan closed his eyes and rubbed his temples with his thumb and forefinger. He could feel a headache building. "Aye," he said. "He has help." He looked at her. "You said there had been plenty of spells cast in the past few days. There will be even more if Osborne and Gant are working together."

"Simon Gant?" she asked.

Ethan straightened, his eyebrows going up. "Do you know him?"

She regarded him with manifest disdain. "Is there a conjurer in this city I don't know? I've known Gant longer than I've known you." She shook her head. "But he's not the one who's runnin' around Boston castin' all these spells."

"What makes you so certain?"

"He's weak," she said. "He can't do much more than illusion spells."

"Do you know that for certain?" Ethan asked, incredulous.

He saw doubt flicker in her dark eyes.

"Well, he couldn't before, when he used to live here."

"That was a long time ago, Janna. Seven years. I've learned a good deal about conjuring in that time."

"Yeah, you have," she agreed. "But it was more than him not knowin' spells. He didn't have the power."

"I've encountered him twice now," Ethan said. "And now that you say it, I think you might be right: He isn't very powerful. He doesn't like to rely on his conjuring abilities, either. But Osborne is alive again, or still. He and Gant are partners." He reached for the ale, but thought better of drinking any more of it. His head had started to pound. Two conjurers were roaming the city, working together, both of them looking for the pearls, no doubt. No wonder it had seemed for the past several days that he was always one step behind. He was fortunate to have kept up with the men as well as he had.

Rickman ate the last of his bread and meat, still watching Ethan and Janna. Ethan tried to overcome the feeling of helplessness that had settled over him with Janna's revelations about the spells. He felt addled; the worsening pain in his head had clouded his thoughts.

"You say Gant is too weak," he said, his voice sounding thick to his own ears. "Or at least that he was. What kind of spells would be required to do the things you spoke of—restoring life to the dead, or simulating death? Could a conjurer do these things with blood spells? Or . . . or would it take something stronger?"

"Depends," Janna said. "To fake a death and then wake a man. Yeah, that would be a blood spell. You could even maybe use an herb if it was powerful enough. Yew, maybe. Or linden. But to raise a man that was truly dead? That would take the death of someone or somethin' else."

Ethan had suspected as much. And, he realized, Janna was right in saying that a conjurer like Gant, whose abilities were limited, would be unable to cast such a spell. Any speller might choose to take a life in order to cast a spell, but that didn't mean that he had the skill to master and use the power drawn from the life of his victim. A conjurer with limited skill could murder again and again to fuel his spells, and none of them would ever work.

Rickman had stopped chewing and was staring at the two of them. "You're saying that the men who cast these spells might have . . . taken a life in order to work their witchery?"

"Aye," Ethan said. "Unfortunately, it happens more often than you might think."

The doctor swallowed, took a long pull of ale. "Have you—" Rickman shook his head. "Never mind. I would rather not know." He drained his cup and placed it on the table. "We should be on our way, Mister Kaille. I want to find these men."

"You a conjurer, too?" Janna asked him.

The doctor's cheeks went red. "Well, no."

"I didn't think so. You'd best let Kaille here do the findin'."

Ethan stood. "Let us be going, Doctor. Thank you," he said to Janna. "I'm in your debt."

She frowned. "You're always in my debt." She nodded toward Rickman. "Bring him next time you need somethin'. At least he buys my food and drink."

"And fine food it was," the doctor said.

Janna flashed a broad smile.

"I hope they let you open your place again soon, Janna," Ethan said. "As soon as they do, I'll come back and buy a meal and an ale."

"Yeah, I'll believe that when I see it."

She smiled again at the doctor and then returned to her kitchen. Ethan and Rickman pulled on their coats once more and left the Fat Spider. The rain continued to fall, and the air had grown colder still. Ethan wondered if nightfall would bring the first snow of the season.

The two men didn't say much as they walked back through the city toward Kannice's tavern. Ethan noticed regulars standing in pairs and small groups, or patrolling the soggy streets in larger companies. With the rainfall, and the fact that it was late on a Sunday, there were far more men in uniform on Boston's streets than there were workers or merchants.

"It has the feel of a garrisoned town, doesn't it?" Rickman said.

"I was thinking the same thing."

Rickman gave him a sidelong glance. "Do you work with Samuel Adams?"

Ethan laughed quietly. "Hardly."

The doctor recoiled. "Oh. Forgive me. I assumed, since you seemed to know so much about my dealings with him . . ."

"I'm sorry for laughing," Ethan said. "Up until recently—until this occupation began, to be honest—I had considered myself utterly opposed to all for which Adams and Otis have agitated these past few years."

"And now?"

Ethan shrugged. "I don't know. This . . ." He waved a hand at yet another cluster of soldiers. "This changes things."

The doctor eyed the regulars. "Yes, it did for me, as well."

As they neared the Dowser, Ethan said, "Janna was right, you know. There's not much you can do to help me find Gant and Osborne. I'm grateful to you for bringing Osborne's disappearance to my attention, but I'm afraid you're going to have to leave the rest of this to me."

"I'll leave the witchery—pardon me; the conjuring—to you. But I believe I can help in other ways."

Before Ethan could answer, they came around the slow bend in Sudbury Street to within sight of the Dowser. At least a dozen regulars stood outside the tavern, with Sheriff Greenleaf and a man who looked suspiciously like Captain Thomas Preston standing at the fore of the company.

Ethan slowed.

Rickman muttered, "Damn," under his breath.

"That's him!" Greenleaf said, pointing their way.

The sheriff and captain strode in their direction, the regulars in lockstep behind them. Ethan and the doctor halted; Ethan had to resist an urge to flee.

"Are they coming for you or for me?" Rickman asked in a whisper.

"I assume they're interested in me," Ethan said.

"Why? What have you done?"

Ethan shook his head. "It doesn't seem to matter."

Preston stopped a short distance from Ethan, his sword drawn. The regulars had leveled their muskets at Ethan's chest, rainwater dripping from their gleaming bayonets. Greenleaf didn't stop until he was nearly nose-to-nose with Ethan. He was grinning; Ethan thought he must be enjoying himself.

"Ethan Kaille?" Greenleaf said.

"What can I do for you, Sheriff?"

"You're to come with us to the city gaol."

At the sheriff's mention of the prison, Ethan's stomach began to knot like wet rope, but he kept his voice steady as he asked, "And why am I being arrested?"

"You're to be tried and hanged for murder."

"Murder!" Ethan repeated. "And who am I supposed to have killed?"

"Simon Gant, of course."

Ethan's legs nearly gave way beneath him. "Gant's dead?"

Greenleaf chuckled. "Dissemble all you like, Kaille. But this time you'll not wheedle your way to freedom. I have witnesses who heard you asking about him, talking about how he had beaten you." He reached out and grabbed Ethan roughly by the chin, turning his face so that he could see Ethan's cheek and jaw. "I can still see the bruises a bit, though not as much as I would have expected. I'd wager we both know why, don't we? If I can't hang you for a murderer, I'll hang you for a witch."

Ethan jerked his head out of the man's grasp. "Where did you find him?"

"Gant you mean?" the sheriff said. He shook his head. "I'm not going to play your games."

"I don't believe this man killed anyone, Sheriff," Rickman said. "He's been with me for some time now, and prior to that he was in that tavern there. When is this man, Gant, supposed to have died?"

Greenleaf's eyes narrowed and he looked the doctor up and down. "Never mind that. Who are you?"

"My name is William Rickman. I'm ship's surgeon aboard His Majesty's ship the *Launceston*."

"And what are you doing in the company of this man, Doctor?" Preston asked.

"You know as well as I do, Captain. Mister Kaille has been asked by agents of the Customs Board to look into a . . . a matter of some importance to the British fleet. I worked with him at Castle William, where you met with us. And I continue to work with him here in Boston."

"Well, you'd be best off keeping your distance from him," Greenleaf said. "I wouldn't expect a man of your position to be aware of this, but he's known to be a witch, not to mention a mutineer, a liar, and a cheat. Gant beat him to within an inch of his life, and he wanted his revenge."

"He came to the camp where my regiment is billeted," Preston said, taking up Greenleaf's story so smoothly that Ethan wondered if they had rehearsed it beforehand. "He asked one of my soldiers about where he might find Gant, and even offered to pay the man in treasure that he planned to recover once Gant was taken care of. His bruises were more obvious then. Thinking back on it now, we all should have known why he wanted to find Gant."

"Is any of this true?" Rickman asked.

"All of it," Ethan said. "And none of it. I did go looking for him, I did speak with a soldier, and I did offer to share some plunder with him. Gant was a smuggler, and this man knew it. It was the only way I could think of to learn whatever it was he knew. But I wanted to find Gant, not kill him."

"I think it's clear that you did both," Greenleaf said.

"Let me guess," Ethan said. "There wasn't a mark on the man. He just seemed to have dropped where he stood."

A cruel smile stretched across the sheriff's broad face. "Very good. It's almost like you were there."

"I don't understand," Rickman said.

"He was killed by a conjuring," Ethan told him, still gazing at the sheriff. "Just like the others."

Greenleaf's face fell. "What others?"

"You have to let me see him, Sheriff," Ethan said.

"See who?"

"Gant. You have to let me see the body."

Ethan might as well have said that Greenleaf had to give him the keys to the prison.

"Why in God's name would I let you do that?" the sheriff asked, a sneer twisting his face.

Because I can see the color of the power used to kill him. Because I can learn what kind of spell it was, and perhaps find the conjurer who cast it. But of course Ethan couldn't say any of these things. Greenleaf's threat to have him hanged as a witch was just that: a threat, empty and meaningless. But as soon as Ethan admitted to being a conjurer in front of the sheriff and Preston and all these men, his life would be forfeit.

"I can help you find the person who killed him," Ethan answered, not daring to say more, knowing that this wouldn't be enough to convince Greenleaf of anything.

"Tell me what you meant before," the sheriff said. "What others?"

Ethan glanced at Rickman, who stared at the ground, but gave one slight shake of his head.

"It was nothing," Ethan said. "I misspoke."

Greenleaf regarded the doctor. "Very well." He looked back at Preston. "Captain?"

Preston said something to his men that Ethan couldn't hear. One of the soldiers took Ethan's knife and two others grasped him firmly by each arm and started to march him back the way he and Rickman had come. The other regulars fell in around him. Preston and the sheriff followed.

"Is there someone I should tell?" the doctor called after Ethan.

Ethan craned his neck to look back. He stumbled, and the men beside him tightened their grips on his arms. "Kannice Lester, the woman who owns the tavern where you found me."

"I'll go to her right now! And I'll do everything in my power to win your freedom! I swear it!"

Ethan nodded once, and faced forward again. The soldiers' fingers dug into his flesh like manacles of steel. The wind blew, the rain pelted down on his bare head and drenched his coat. But these were nothing to him. Already Ethan could smell the fetor of the cell awaiting him in Boston's gaol.

*D*espite all his scrapes with Greenleaf and his encounters with representatives of the Crown, Ethan had not set foot in a prison since the night of his release from servitude in Barbados. Even then, the cell had only been a place where he could sleep until he set out the following morning for the Town of Saint Michael, whence he was to depart by ship for Charleston. He hadn't truly been a prisoner in a cell since the days of his trial for the *Ruby Blade* mutiny.

And yet as he neared the prison, memories of that old cell and of his captivity in Barbados flooded his mind like a rising storm tide. War had never frightened him, even in his youth. He had sailed through ocean storms that would have reduced some grown men to sobbing babes. He had been beaten and threatened; he had come close to dying more times than he could count. None of that scared him. But prison . . . He found himself choking back tears. His legs trembled as the regulars led him down the length of Queen Street that passed before the courthouse and gaol. One would have thought that he had just run up to the very top of Beacon Hill, his heart labored so. He could smell his own sweat, his own fear, and he hated himself. He recalled that feeling, as well.

The one small mercy was that neither Kannice nor Diver, nor any of the other people in his life, could see him at this moment. He was entirely alone and for now at least he was glad.

The gaol sat in the midst of one of Boston's finer neighborhoods, as out of place as a beggar—or perhaps a thieftaker—among men of society. It was a plain building, not particularly menacing and noteworthy only for its ancient, heavy oak door, which looked to Ethan as implacable as a mountain. A few small windows broke up the solid, ugly façade, but otherwise it was nothing more or less than a great stone box. And they were going to put him inside of it.

The soldiers halted. Greenleaf stepped past them, gesturing with a quick wave of his hand for the two who held Ethan to follow him. He led them through the prison entrance into the rank shadows within.

"Bring him this way," the sheriff said, his voice echoing in the cramped space.

The two regulars steered Ethan down a narrow corridor and through a second door nearly as ponderous as the one in front. As soon as they stepped into this second passageway, the smell hit Ethan, and he gagged. Sweat, urine, feces, vomit, fear, desperation, hopelessness. He was drowning in a noisome sea. The men holding him practically had to carry him along the stone corridor, his feet half walking, half dragging. The soldiers' fingers were like iron, gouging the muscles in his arm. And Ethan clung to that pain as a respite from his memories and his terror.

The last door on the left side of the corridor stood open. Greenleaf stopped beside it, smirking at Ethan as the men ushered him past and into the cell. It might as well have been the same cell in which he had been held during his trial. A shaft of silvery gray light shone through the small window high on the wall opposite the cell door. A pallet, tattered and leaking straw, lay along one wall with a single brown woolen blanket folded at the foot.

The foul smell from the privy hole in the far corner permeated the chamber, forcing Ethan to clamp his teeth against a wave of nausea.

But he made himself stand on his own two feet, and tried to wrest his arms from the hands of the soldiers. He had survived prison before; he would do so again.

"Chain him up," Greenleaf said from behind them.

Ethan tried to turn. "What?" he said, the word scraped from his throat.

The sheriff entered the cell and jangled a manacle that Ethan hadn't noticed before. It was bolted to the wall beside him. Several of them were.

"As I said before, Kaille, I know what you are. I may not be an expert in the ways of witchcraft, but I know better than to leave you in this cell and expect you to be here still come the morn. My thought is that if you can't speak your witchery, and if you can't wave your hands around in all manner and call demons to you in that way, you'll be powerless. And that's what I want." He gestured to the soldiers. "Chain him, lads. Don't worry about being too gentle with him, either."

The soldiers pushed Ethan against the wall, wrenched his arms up into an awkward position, and clamped the manacles around his wrists. The chains might have been set for a larger man, or Greenleaf might not have cared a whit for Ethan's comfort. In either case, the cuffs were so far apart that they stretched Ethan's arms and shoulders, leaving him in a great deal of discomfort and unable to move his hands at all. The iron carved into his skin, but only enough to bruise; not enough to make him bleed. The regulars attached two more manacles to his ankles. These were less restricting, though that hardly mattered given the positioning of the cuffs holding his wrists. At last, they put an iron collar around his neck and tied a gag in his mouth.

"There," Greenleaf said, a smug smile on his face as he examined the chains and tested the bolts that held them to the rough, cold stone. "I don't expect you'll be going anywhere. At least, not until we say so."

The sheriff reached into Ethan's pockets and removed a few coins—maybe five shillings and as many pence. He made a quick count and pocketed the money, smiling up at Ethan again. "My thanks."

Ethan glared at him, wanting nothing more than to speak a spell that would flay the sheriff's skin from his bones or perhaps crush his skull. But while Greenleaf had never given any indication that he knew the first thing about conjuring, on this day he had managed inadvertently to render Ethan powerless. He didn't need to say anything aloud to conjure, but in order to break free of the chains and the prison he did need blood. He didn't know if he could move his hands enough to cut or scrape himself. With the gag in his mouth, he couldn't even bite his cheek or tongue. Apparently, Greenleaf was as lucky as he was ignorant.

"Someone will come by later, I suppose," the sheriff told him, sounding calm and confident now that he had Ethan tamed. "You'll need some water and some food, such as it is." He stepped out of the cell, closed the door and threw the bolt, the metallic ring of the lock reverberating in the walls like a spell. "Enjoy yourself."

Greenleaf laughed as the click of his boots on stone retreated down the hallway. The two soldiers remained outside the cell. The sheriff wasn't taking any chances.

Ethan's arms and shoulders were already starting to grow sore, and the manacle around his neck held his head at an odd angle, making his neck and back ache, too. But like the pain of the soldiers' grips on his arms, the agony in his shoulders served to clear his thoughts, searing away those haunting memories of Charleston and Barbados, and concentrating his thoughts on his predicament.

Gant was dead. Osborne, it now seemed, never had been. All this time Ethan had assumed that Gant was the killer, the one who had killed every man on the *Graystone* and attacked Mariz. But Ethan would have bet the ten pounds Geoffrey had promised him that a *revela potestatem* spell would show that Gant had been killed by that same orange power Ethan had seen on Sephira's man and the dead soldiers aboard the ship. He wanted to believe that it had been Osborne all along, but how could he explain Osborne's presence among the dead soldiers aboard the *Graystone*? It was clear to him now that Osborne and Gant had been working together all this time, but how much conjuring had Gant done? How much had he been capable of doing? Rickman might have learned of Osborne's escape from Castle William today, but Ethan guessed that the thief had made his way back to Boston two days ago.

Too many questions still remained. And right now, there was nothing Ethan could do to answer any of them.

It occurred to him that he still had two leaves of mullein in the pouch in his pocket. Greenleaf hadn't thought to search for those. But while two leaves *might* allow him to break one cuff, he couldn't break all of them. And even if he could free himself of the chains, he still had to get through the door and past two armed regulars.

He turned and stared out the window. The sky was darkening; it would be night before long, at which point the only light would come from the single torch flickering in the corridor just outside his cell. He remembered the nights in the Charleston gaol—that had been the worst time.

No. He wasn't going to give in to those thoughts.

Rain still fell, driven by a cutting wind. Drops slapped against the side of the prison, chiming against the bars in that high window and splattering on the floor of his cell. Rain. Water.

Videre per mea imagine ex aqua evocata, he chanted silently to himself. Sight, through my illusion, conjured from water. Power hummed in the prison walls, tickling Ethan's back and legs. Uncle Reg appeared before him, gleaming like fire in the dim light of the cell. He stared at Ethan solemnly, with none of the mockery he some-times showed upon finding Ethan in dire straits.

The prison was no more than a stone's throw from King's Chapel. Ethan hoped that Pell was there. He closed his eyes and cast his awareness west to the chapel.

Candles burned in sconces that lined the main aisle of the sanctuary, and the high windows glowed with the last light of this dreary day. Henry Caner stood at the pulpit, reading the great leather-bound Bible by the light of candles in another iron sconce. He didn't look up, of course. Ethan's illusion made not a sound. More to the point, Pell was nowhere to be seen.

Ethan shifted his illusion downstairs to the crypts, which were also illuminated by candles. He could almost smell the spermaceti over the reek of his cell. A corpse lay on the stone table in the center of the corridor: an old woman, her white hair unbound and hanging loose nearly to the floor, her body looking frail and tiny be-neath a white cloth. Pell sat on a wooden chair near the table, his breathing heavy and slow, his eyes closed, his head lolling to the side. A sleeping vigil. Under other cir-cumstances, Ethan would have laughed at the sight.

"Mister Pell," he made his illusion say.

The young minister jerked awake, sitting up so quickly that he nearly overturned his chair.

"Ethan!" he said. "You startled me. I didn't hear you—"

He stopped, his mouth opening, his eyes growing wide. He shot to his feet, and this time the chair did topple over.

"What are you?" he asked, breathless, reaching for the wooden cross that he wore around his neck.

"Easy, Mister Pell," Ethan said through the image of himself. "This is a casting, an image that I've conjured so that I might speak with you. You have nothing to fear."

"How do I know that? How can I be sure that you're not some demon sent from hell?"

"You were a rascal as a youth. You once told me so yourself. And I once healed a bruise on your face, a bruise that I gave you when you surprised me outside my room. Do you remember that?"

The tension appeared to drain from the minister's body. "Yes, I remember," he said, still looking troubled. "Why have you come to me this way?"

"Because I can't come to you in the flesh. I'm a prisoner in the city gaol, chained to a wall and gagged."

Pell looked aghast. "Why?"

"Simon Gant is dead, killed by a conjuring if Sheriff Greenleaf is to be believed. A number of powerful men, including the sheriff, are convinced that I'm responsible."

"I assume you're not," Pell said, his tone dry.

In his cell, Ethan smiled. "No."

"And you believe I can help you."

"I hope you can. I didn't do this, Trevor. You know that I wouldn't. But I'm not going to be able to convince Greenleaf or anyone else of that so long as they have me trussed up like a pig waiting to be slaughtered. If they don't hang me as a killer, they'll burn me for a witch. I need your help, and Mister Caner's as well, I'm afraid."

Through the eyes of his illusion, Ethan saw the young minister frown. "I'll do whatever I can to help you, of course. But I can't speak for Mister Caner, except to say that he doesn't like you very much."

Ethan started to say that even so, Caner wouldn't want to see an innocent man hanged. But Caner knew for a fact that Ethan was a conjurer; so much for being innocent.

"There's a murderer loose in the streets of Boston," he said to Pell. "And he's every bit the conjurer I am. At least Cane—" He swallowed. "*Mister* Caner, knows me, and he knows that you trust me. That should count for something."

Pell didn't appear convinced. But he said, "Yes, perhaps it will."

"If you can, you should also ask Geoffrey Brower for

help," Ethan said. "It's because of him that I'm in this mess in the first place."

The agony in Ethan's shoulders and arms had worsened, and though this was a relatively simple conjuring, he felt his hold on the illusion spell slipping.

"I need to end this conversation. Come quickly, please. I don't know how soon they intend to carry out whatever sentence they've chosen for me. And I can't hang from these chains forever."

Pell glanced toward the dead woman, and Ethan knew what the minister was thinking. He had been directed to sit vigil with the body. He couldn't leave her.

But his friend fixed a brave smile on his youthful face. "I'll do whatever I can. God bless you, Ethan."

"And you, Mister Pell."

Ethan released the spell and slumped against the wall of his cell, the chains at his neck and legs jangling. He opened his eyes and saw that the last glimmer of daylight had almost faded. The rain still fell, and the prison air had grown colder. Uncle Reg stood in the middle of the cell, staring up at him like a man in mourning. At last, the ghost raised a hand in farewell—something he never did—and vanished. Was it possible that Reg thought they would not meet again in this world? Could he have foreseen Ethan's fate? Ethan had not felt so forsaken since his incarceration.

It promised to be a long, miserable night. Every muscle in his body burned. His jaw had grown stiff around the gag. He was chilled and damp and bone weary. And right now his bladder felt uncomfortably full—what he would have given to have skipped that ale in Janna's tavern. No doubt Greenleaf and his prison guards wanted him to soil himself, to soak in his humiliation. Ethan refused. Before the night was out he might well have no choice in the matter. But for now, he would cling to his dignity.

He stared out the small window at a sky that didn't

seem to change, and he waited for sleep to take him, welcoming the drooping of his eyelids, much as he remembered himself doing in Charleston and in Barbados, where sleep was his sole refuge from a wretched existence. He heard boots clicking in the stone corridor outside his cell, and instantly snapped awake once more, thinking that someone had come for him, for good or ill. Soon, though, he realized that it was two new guards taking the place of the men who had accompanied him to the prison.

Willing his pulse to slow once more, Ethan tried again to make himself sleep. Slumber, though, came grudgingly, and in fits. He careened from one strange, disturbing dream to the next. First, he was fleeing down an alley, pursued by the dead regulars he had seen in the vaults at Castle William, all of whom carried bayonets. The next thing he knew, he was on a lonely stretch of road near the Mill Pond, battling Osborne and Gant and Mariz, warding himself with spells that he knew would eventually fail. After that, he was at sea, alone on a fourteen-gun sloop, steering her through a howling storm, and then on a hangman's gallows, his hands bound, a crowd of onlookers shouting for his death.

He woke often to find the sky outside his window that same dull, starless black; it seemed that time itself had ground to a halt. But even after he grew leery of sleep and the dark dreams it brought, he could not manage to keep himself awake for very long. He would stare out the window, only to fall into yet another nightmare. Through it all, the pain remained, both blunt and piercing, overwhelming, pulsing through his body with every beat of his heart.

The last dream he remembered was of Kannice. She stood before him in his cell, naked to the waist, stretching out her arms to him. But when he tried to call her name, her hair darkened, curled. Her features shifted, her voice and laughter rang in the tiny chamber, lower than they should have been. Throatier. And before he could call Kannice's name Sephira Pryce stood before him, gloating.

He jerked awake, gasped at the anguish that shot through his limbs and back. An erection pressed painfully against the inside of his breeches and his bladder felt like it was about to burst. Ethan groaned. But looking toward the window, he knew a moment of profound relief. The sky was brightening. It remained gray; he could still hear raindrops pattering against the stone and steel. But it might as well have been a sunrise of dazzling yellows and pinks and purples. Never mind that he remained exactly as he had been the previous evening—chained and helpless; he had survived the night.

At least another hour passed before Ethan heard a set of footsteps approaching and the ringing of keys. The door to his cell creaked open and an army officer stepped in, regarded Ethan, and motioned the guards into the chamber.

Ethan stared at the man, knowing that he had seen him before, but unable to place him at first. The officer was barrel-chested and broad in the shoulders, but he appeared to be several inches shorter than Ethan. His face, open and square, might have been handsome had it not been so careworn. He had the look of a man who hadn't slept in days, and didn't expect to any time soon. He wore a powdered wig, and stood straight-backed despite the fatigue Ethan saw in his face.

"Unchain him," the man said, the command tinged with a subtle Scottish brogue.

One of the soldiers searched through the keys he held until he found the right one. He unlocked the manacles at Ethan's ankles, and then the one around Ethan's neck. Ethan tipped his head slowly, first to one side and then the other, wincing at the loud cracks that emanated from his neck joints. Within a few seconds, Ethan's arms were free as well, and as they fell to his sides, he staggered forward. Had the two regulars not caught him, he would have collapsed onto the filthy stone floor. His limbs trembled, and with every breath, pain coursed through his body.

While the soldiers held him up, the officer removed Ethan's gag and tossed it aside.

"Who are you?" Ethan asked, his voice sounding like steel scraped across stone.

"Lieutenant Colonel William Dalrymple," the man said. "Until General Gage arrives, I command the British army here in Boston."

Ethan nodded, though even that hurt. He remembered at last. The officer he had seen at the Manufactory the day before, the one who had spoken to Elisha Brown.

"I saw you yesterday," Ethan said. "You were trying to find quarters for your soldiers."

Dalrymple glowered. "I still am."

"And why are you here?"

"That's a fine question, Mister Kaille. I have no earthly idea. But it seems that you have more powerful friends than one might expect of a man who just spent the night in Boston's gaol."

"So, I'm free to go?"

Dalrymple shook his head. "Not yet you're not. The lieutenant governor would like a word with you."

Ethan knew that he should have been prepared for this, but still he sighed, closing his eyes against another wave of pain in his back and chest.

"Help him out, lads," Dalrymple said to the soldiers.

"No."

Ethan got his feet under him and straightened, gently trying to pull his arms from the soldiers' grasp. The men looked to the lieutenant colonel, who nodded once. They released him, and Ethan swayed, but remained upright. He staggered to the foul-smelling hole beneath the window and relieved himself at long last. When he had finished, he buttoned his breeches, turned, and walked out of the cell, the two soldiers ahead of him and Dalrymple behind.

The Town House stood less than a city block from the

prison. But to Ethan the walk seemed interminable. Every step was agony and though he had hoped that his muscles would loosen as he walked, they didn't. He hardly saw where he was going and took little note of those who watched him stumble past with his impressive escort. He entered the building in a haze of pain, and somehow managed to climb the marble stairs to the second floor.

Dalrymple and his men escorted him to Hutchinson's courtroom, pausing just outside the oaken door. The colonel slipped into the chambers, leaving Ethan and the soldiers in the corridor. Ethan said nothing, and the men avoided his gaze. Sooner than Ethan expected, Dalrymple opened the door once more.

"This way," he said, beckoning Ethan inside.

Ethan hobbled into the courtroom.

Hutchinson looked much as he had a few days earlier. He wrinkled his nose at Ethan's appearance and then waved Dalrymple toward the door.

The colonel hesitated, glancing toward Ethan before letting himself out of the chamber.

"You've been the subject of a good many conversations this morning, Mister Kaille," Hutchinson said, regarding Ethan over steepled fingers. "I've heard from Geoffrey Brower of the Customs Board, as well as Captain Preston, and one of his men—a Jonathan Fowler?—and the ship's surgeon from the *Launceston*. Doctor Ricker, I believe."

"Rickman, sir."

Annoyance flickered in the man's eyes. "Yes, that's right. Rickman. I've even had a written message championing your cause from no less a personage than the Reverend Henry Caner. Perhaps you'd care to tell me why all these people should be so interested in the arrest of one thieftaker."

"I think you can answer that question yourself, Your Honor. We've spoken of my inquiry; you know the work I've been doing on behalf of the Crown."

"Indeed. I also know that all this 'work' has yet to yield any results of consequence."

"That's not—"

"In fact," Hutchinson went on, "as I understand it, another man is dead. Is this true?"

Ethan knew in that moment that he hadn't been brought here as a precursor to his release. Hutchinson meant to follow through on the threats he had made a few days before. As far as he was concerned, Ethan had already failed.

"Well?" the lieutenant governor said.

"Aye, Your Honor. Simon Gant is dead."

"And do you know who killed him?"

"I believe he was killed by a man named Caleb Osborne, but I can't prove that yet."

"No," Hutchinson said, his tone dry. "Of course you can't. As I'm sure you know, Sheriff Greenleaf is quite certain that you are the guilty party."

"Sheriff Greenleaf is wrong."

"Sheriff Greenleaf gets results. He speaks of evidence, of motive." Hutchinson's glance fell to the fading bruises on Ethan's jaw. "You have nothing to show for the time I've given you. Nothing, that is, save for one more corpse. I'm afraid you're out of time."

"No!" Ethan said. "You gave me five days! I still have two in which to find Osborne!"

"Not anymore."

"You gave me your word!"

"This city is under occupation!" Hutchinson said, his voice echoing through the chamber. "I haven't the luxury of two days! Already soldiers are deserting, and the Lord knows what Samuel Adams and his mob have in store for us! I need to billet Gage's men and ruffians continue to occupy the Manufactory! And all the while men are dying, victims of all manner of devilry! You dare to speak of me keeping my word? Damn your two days!"

"And so your solution is to mete out punishment on a whim! To hang men and women who have done nothing wrong, and whose deaths will do nothing to end these killings!"

"What choice do I have? You're asking me to place my trust in a witch!"

"It is not witchcraft! It is spellmaking—I'm a conjurer—and the mere fact that you don't understand what I do doesn't make it wicked! Killing me would be foolhardy. Killing Janna and the others would be criminal!"

Hutchinson's face had turned crimson. No doubt he was unaccustomed to having people speak to him so. Ethan couldn't have cared less.

"Well, if not them, perhaps you can give me someone else," the man said, his voice tight.

"What do you mean?"

"Think, man. What else *would* I mean?"

Ethan was slow to understand, though once it dawned on him what the lieutenant governor was saying, he realized that he should have guessed right away. "You want Adams and Otis," he said, a sick feeling in his gut. "That's who you've wanted all along."

"Brower tells me that you met with Samuel Adams the morning the occupation began."

"That's right."

"You're in our employ. Agents of the Crown came to you seeking your help with this matter of the *Graystone*. And I would like to know why you felt it necessary to seek out the one man in Boston most likely to be behind it all."

"You've answered your own question, Your Honor. How could I not speak with Adams about this, knowing as I did how concerned he would have been about the presence of the fleet in Boston Harbor?"

Hutchinson frowned at this, but he didn't argue the point. Instead he asked, "And what did you learn from your conversation?"

"That he had nothing to do with what happened to your ship."

"I think you mean *our* ship. As I recall you were once

a navy man yourself, and we are all subjects of His Majesty King George the Third."

"Of course," Ethan said.

"So, Adams told you he had done nothing wrong and you took him at his word."

"Aye. I believe he told me the truth."

A bark of laughter escaped the lieutenant governor, scornful and dismissive. "Either you're a hopeless naif, or you're working with him."

"I'm neither, sir. I'm trying to find a conjurer. I don't care about your politics or Sephira Pryce's treasure hunt or anything else for that matter. I want to solve this mystery, preferably before I'm killed or arrested again. And then I want to be done with it."

"I'm sure you do. I would enjoy the same, but I can't relieve myself of responsibilities so easily. The Crown's enemies are real. They have killed nearly one hundred of the king's men! And we will have justice!" He pounded his fist on his desk as he said this last, spittle flying from his mouth.

"And your idea of justice includes false accusations against Samuel Adams? Or against Boston's conjurers, who have done you no harm? What a fine leader you are, Your Honor."

Hutchinson straightened, a menacing glint in his eyes. "What would you suggest I do?" he asked, biting off each word.

Ethan threw his hands wide, the motion rekindling the pain in his shoulders. "Allow me to my conduct my inquiry! Give me the time you promised me when last we spoke!"

Hutchinson glared at him, and Ethan knew that the lieutenant governor would refuse, that he would call Dalrymple and his soldiers back into the chamber and have Ethan returned to the prison. But Hutchinson surprised him.

"One day," he said. "No more than that. You have until dawn tomorrow. At that point I will send the king's men for you and for every witch in Boston."

"Yes, Your Honor."

Ethan didn't wait to be dismissed. He turned on his heel and strode toward the door, cursing the stiffness in his back and legs.

"Mister Kaille."

He had his hand on the door handle, and he considered leaving without hearing what Hutchinson had to say. But this was the second most powerful man in all of Massachusetts, and there was nothing to stop him from changing his mind. Ethan exhaled and turned.

"Witchcraft or spellmaking—whatever you call it, the power you wield still comes from Satan."

"That's your opinion, Your Honor."

"I suppose you would claim that it comes from God."

"No, sir. I know for a fact that my abilities come from my mother." He pulled the door open and walked out.

ne day.

Three days ago, Hutchinson hadn't given him enough time; not nearly. And now the lieutenant governor had cut his remaining time in half. He couldn't do this in a single day. But one day was all he had.

It took him several minutes to convince Dalrymple that the lieutenant governor had granted him leave to go, and several more to convince the colonel to return his knife to him. Once he felt the weight of the blade on his belt, he felt a bit more like himself. He was still sore all over, but there was little he could do about that without conjuring, and he didn't think it wise to start casting spells in the middle of the city after the conversation he had just concluded with Hutchinson.

If convincing Dalrymple to give him back his blade had been difficult, his next task bordered on the impossible. Ethan, though, had no choice but to try.

Stephen Greenleaf lived on West Street, near the Common, in a large stone mansion that was far more luxurious than the man deserved. The gardens surrounding his house were lush and had been tended to with such care over the years that they had become renowned throughout the city. Like the understated elegance of Sephira

Pryce's home, Ethan found the sheriff's gardens curiously at odds with all that he had gleaned about the man from their many encounters. In the past, he had admired the sheriff's home from afar, but on this morning, Ethan walked up to his door and rapped on it with the brass knocker.

An African man opened the door and stared out at him. He had white hair and wore a linen suit of pale blue. Pausing to look at Ethan's clothes, he frowned.

"Can I help you, sir?"

"Yes, I'm looking for the sheriff. Can you please tell him that Ethan Kaille is here?"

"Sheriff Greenleaf is busy just now. You'll have to come back later."

"Please tell him I'm here," Ethan said. "He'll be eager to see me. Again, my name is Kaille."

The man looked like he might argue, his eyes dropping once more to Ethan's grimy breeches, and coat. "Wait here," he said, and closed the door.

Ethan stood for several minutes, staring at the white door and its lion's-head knocker. After a while he began to stretch his arms and shoulders, and to walk in small circles to keep his legs from stiffening once more. He thought he could hear voices within, and footsteps, but still no one came to the door. He began to wonder if he had been foolish to come here, and as a precaution he pulled out his last two leaves of mullein, and held them concealed in the curl of his left hand.

When next he heard footsteps within the house, they were far clearer than they had been before. And so he wasn't completely caught off guard when the door was flung open, revealing Greenleaf with a flintlock pistol in hand, its barrel aimed at Ethan's forehead.

"If you so much as blink, I'll put a hole in your skull!" Greenleaf said, snarling like a cur.

"I'm just standing here, Sheriff." He tried to keep his voice level and calm, but he wouldn't have put it past the man to kill him. The hand holding the mullein was already slick with sweat. Ethan feared that at the first mutterings of a spell, Greenleaf would splatter his brains on the stone portico.

"What are you doing here? What sort of devilry did you use to escape my gaol?"

"No devilry at all. Colonel Dalrymple came for me at first light and took me to the Town House. Hutchinson has given me a day to find Gant's killer."

"Do you take me for a fool?"

"Not at all," Ethan said, his gaze flicking between the barrel of the pistol and the sheriff's face. "It's the truth. You have only to ask one of them."

"Thomas Hutchinson—the lieutenant governor. Do you really expect me to believe that he let you go free?"

"It's true. He threatened to have me hanged as a witch if I didn't find Gant's killer." When Greenleaf neither responded nor lowered the weapon, Ethan added, "Dalrymple didn't believe me at first when I told him that Hutchinson had granted my release. But I convinced him. He gave me back my blade. It's on my belt right now."

"So, the lieutenant governor sent you off to find the killer and thus save your skin, and you came here. Why? For revenge?"

"For help," Ethan said. "To ask you, as I did yesterday, to let me see Gant's body."

That seemed to reach the man. He regarded Ethan through narrowed eyes, and an instant later lowered the hand holding his pistol. Ethan closed his eyes and swallowed. He had seen more firearms in the past few days than he cared to recall.

"I remember you asking me," Greenleaf said. "Why are you so eager to see Gant?"

Ethan hesitated, unsure of how much he wished to reveal. "There are ways for me to determine what killed him," he said, trying to keep his answer as vague as possible. "And perhaps even who."

"More witchcraft," the sheriff said, his voice flat.

"Several times now, you've accused me of magicking, and yet you've never seen me do anything of the kind, have you?"

"I have a keen memory, Kaille. I recall the tales of what transpired aboard the *Ruby Blade*. There was talk then of you consorting with the devil himself and using witchery to bend men to your will. And since the day you returned to Boston, that talk has continued to dog your every step. This isn't rumor. You're a witch. And you won't convince me otherwise just because you've managed to confine your mischief to shadows and alleys beyond my sight."

They glowered at each other, Greenleaf still holding his pistol, Ethan with the mullein concealed in his hand.

Aware of precious minutes ticking away, Ethan asked, "Will you allow me to see Gant?"

"I shouldn't," Greenleaf said, smirking. "You say Hutchinson gave you a day. If you fail, I'm rid of you for good."

"If I fail, you'll still have a conjurer roaming your city, one who's not afraid to use his powers to murder."

The sheriff's smile melted away. "You can find him?"

"Maybe."

"And what do I gain if you succeed?"

Ethan knew he should have expected this. "What do you want?" he asked, feeling too weary to play games with him.

"How much are the customs men paying you to do this work you were talking about yesterday?"

"Ten pounds."

Greenleaf's face fell. "Ten pounds? You're doing all of this for ten pounds?"

"Remarkable, isn't it?"

"You're even more of a fool than I thought."

"Take me to see Gant. I can't offer you much money, but you don't want the man's killer getting away any more than I do."

Greenleaf eyed him for several moments longer. Ethan

could see that the sheriff still didn't believe him, but he hoped that he would hear enough truth in what Ethan had said to know that he couldn't risk refusing. "Yes, all right," he said, surrender in the words.

He didn't put his pistol away, but he pulled the door to his house shut, muttering to himself about stupid thieftakers and stingy agents of the Crown. Ethan did his best to keep his expression neutral. And while the sheriff wasn't looking, he slipped the mullein leaves back into his pocket.

They walked up Common Street to the old Workhouse, a large two-story brick building where petty thieves and vagrants were housed. Greenleaf led Ethan through the house to a small back chamber. There on the dirt floor, in the center of the small room, was a bulky form covered with a dingy, stained sheet. Greenleaf halted just inside the narrow portal, but he gestured with an open hand at the shrouded body.

Ethan glanced at him before stepping past and pulling back the sheet.

Simon Gant's mismatched eyes were still open, staring sightlessly at the low ceiling. His mouth was slack, his red hair unkempt, his face white as a winter moon. He still wore the clothes he had been wearing when Ethan chased him from the Manufactory—brown breeches, a stained white linen shirt, and a heavy black coat, threadbare in spots.

Ethan began by examining his head and neck and the upper part of his chest. All were unmarked. There was no blood on Gant's clothing, but still Ethan struggled to pull the big man's stiff arms free of his coat so that he might make a more thorough examination. After a few minutes of this he looked at Greenleaf, hoping that the sheriff would offer to help. But though he sensed that the sheriff had been watching his every move, Greenleaf refused to meet his gaze, and Ethan went back to working the dead man's arms free on his own. When at last he had Gant's limbs out of the coat, he looked for wounds on the man's chest and back. Nothing.

"There's no obvious sign of what killed him," Ethan said.

"I could have told you that."

Ethan ignored the remark. "Was there blood on the ground where he was found?"

"Not that I know of."

He looked over the corpse one last time, making certain that he hadn't missed anything. Standing once more, he walked back to where the sheriff stood.

"Thank you," he said. "I'm grateful to you for bringing me here."

Greenleaf had been leaning against the wall, but now he straightened, alert and suspicious. "What? You mean you're done already?"

"Yes," Ethan said. "I've looked at him. I see no indication of what killed him. I had hoped I would but . . ." He shrugged and looked back at Gant.

"But what about your witchery?" the sheriff asked, looking both fearful and excited.

Ethan kept his expression neutral. "I don't know what you're talking about."

"Don't talk to me like I'm a fool! You came here expecting to use your witchery in some manner. I know you did!"

Ethan stepped past him and walked out of the building. Greenleaf hurried after him.

"Kaille! Tell me what you were going to do to him!"

He shouldn't have said a word, but Ethan found the man so tiresome that he couldn't resist.

He halted and turned abruptly so that Greenleaf had to stop short to avoid walking into him. "Nothing with you there," he said, dropping his voice. "I wouldn't want anything to . . . happen to you."

Greenleaf's eyes went wide. "Happen to . . . What do you mean?" He licked his lips. "What could . . . ? You mean it could . . . it could *affect* me?" He took a step backward.

"Not permanently," Ethan said, resisting the urge to laugh. "At least probably not. But I didn't wish to take the chance. These things can be unpredictable. Something might get out of hand and I wouldn't even realize it until it was too late."

"But this witchcraft—what was it going to do?"

Ethan shook his head and started away again. "It doesn't matter. Good day, Sheriff."

"Kaille!" Greenleaf shouted again. This time, though, Ethan didn't halt. At least not until he had turned two corners and was certain that the sheriff couldn't see him anymore. At that point, he made sure that no one else was watching and ducked onto a small lane near King's Chapel. He drew his knife and cut himself.

"*Velamentum ex cruore evocatum.*" Concealment, conjured from blood. With the hum of power, and the sudden appearance of Uncle Reg, came the odd, familiar sensation of the concealment spell—like a sprinkle of cold water washing down over him from head to toe.

He stepped out of the small lane, but paused to look at the old ghost.

"I don't know who might be watching for me," he said. "You can't come along."

Reg's expression soured, if that was possible for such a dour figure, and he winked out of sight.

Greenleaf had planted himself outside the Workhouse, daring Ethan to return, just as Ethan had assumed he would. The sheriff swept his gaze back and forth over the street, his arms crossed over his broad chest, a fearsome look on his face. But he stared right through Ethan, as did everyone else on Common Street. Ethan crept past him, taking care to make no noise, and entered the building. Once inside, he returned to the small room where lay Gant's corpse. Greenleaf hadn't bothered to put the covering sheet back in place over the body, which made things a bit easier for Ethan.

He cut himself once more, and marked Gant's body with blood. "*Revela potestatem ex cruore evocatam,*" he whispered. Reveal power, conjured from blood.

Feeling the thrum of his spell, he glanced back toward the doorway, though he knew that Greenleaf wouldn't have sensed anything. Reg, who had reappeared with the casting of the spell, glared at him from the far side of Gant's body, but Ethan ignored the ghost and stared down at the corpse.

He had known what he would see, had guessed the instant he heard from Greenleaf that Gant was dead. Still, the sight of that bright orange glow spreading from the center of Gant's chest over the rest of his body made him wince, as from a physical blow. It was the same color he had seen on the dead sailor aboard the *Graystone*, and also on Mariz after the attack that left him unconscious. Ethan had been following the wrong person all this time. It had never been Gant.

What else had he gotten wrong? What other assumptions had he embraced without thought, without question?

He considered leaving the spell's glow on the dead man's body. He could imagine Greenleaf walking back into the chamber and shrieking like a little girl at the sight. But he didn't wish to frighten anyone else, nor did he want to give the sheriff any new excuse to pay him another visit.

"*Vela potestatem ex cruore evocatam.*" Conceal power, conjured from blood. Reg looked disappointed.

Ethan exited the Workhouse, and snuck past Greenleaf once more. A part of him—perhaps not the wisest part—wanted to remain on the street and, while still concealed, toy with the sheriff for a while. But his better instincts prevailed. Instead, he made his way to Sephira's house.

Several times now—during the night, again as he argued with Hutchinson in the Town House, and once more just now as he saw that orange glow on Gant—it had occurred to him that there was one other conjurer in Boston whom he had yet to factor into all that had happened in the past day. If Gant was dead and Osborne alive, where did that leave Mariz, who had seemingly hovered in between life and death the last time Ethan saw him? If death could be feigned, so could unconsciousness. It seemed too convenient that Mariz should be incapacitated all this time.

Afton stood by Sephira's doorway as Ethan neared the house. Ethan had not yet removed the concealment spell, but he made no attempt to mask the sound of his footsteps. Hearing him approach, Afton stepped away from the door and planted his feet at the top of the small stairway leading up from the stone path. He scanned the street, frowning, cocking an ear toward the path, trying to figure out where Ethan was.

Ethan didn't give him the chance. Without breaking stride he said, "*Dormite ex gramine evocatum.*" Slumber, conjured from grass. Power flowed through the ground and the stone, and Reg fell in step beside Ethan, ethereal in the silvery light.

Perhaps recognizing the cadence of a spell from the time he had spent with Mariz, Afton threw up a hand to ward himself. A second later he staggered back against one of the grand marble columns outside Sephira's door. As the spell began to take effect, he slipped down to the ground, his eyes closing, a contented smile touching his lips. By the time he tipped over onto his side, he was slumbering deeply.

Before pushing the door open and entering Sephira's house, Ethan reached for his knife, rolled up his sleeve, and cut his arm yet again. Yellow-hair and Nap were in the common room, and they leaped to their feet at the same time. Nigel brandished his pistol, Nap his blade. Both of them gaped at the doorway, waiting to see who had come. Seeing no one, Yellow-hair opened his mouth, no doubt to call for Sephira.

The words of Ethan's spell were on his lips before the

big man could get out a word. "*Dormite ambo ex cruore evocatum!*" Slumber, both of them, conjured from blood.

The men swayed, dropped their weapons, and toppled to the floor, Nigel smacking his head on the wood boards with a satisfying thud, Nap—appropriately named— landing on a colorful rug.

"Nigel?" Sephira's voice.

Ethan dragged the blade over his forearm again. "*Fini velamentum ex cruore evocatum.*" End concealment, conjured from blood.

The reverberation of this spell was still dying away as Ethan strolled into Sephira's dining room. She sat at her long table before a sumptuous breakfast. Her hair was down, and he could smell her perfume from the opposite end of the table.

Her eyes blazing, Sephira started to rise. But Ethan had cut himself once more, and he shook his head, his blade pointing at the welling blood. "Don't," he said.

"Where are Nigel and Nap?" she demanded, her voice higher than usual.

"Sleeping in your common room. I expect Nigel will have a bit of a headache when he wakes."

She sat back in her chair, glaring at him, no doubt biding her time. "And Afton?"

"Napping outside. Where are Gordon and Mariz?"

Her smile didn't reach her eyes. "No idea."

"*Ignis ex cruore evocatus.*" Fire, conjured from blood.

The spell thrummed, and the eggs, bacon, and bread on her plate burst into flames.

"I'm not playing games. Where are they?"

"What are you doing here, Ethan? You must know that I would be justified in killing you for this. Not now perhaps, not while you have your knife out and blood on your arm. But eventually. So, what could possibly lead you to do something this stupid?"

"Desperation. Fear of something more dangerous than you."

Oddly, that seemed to set her at ease. She nodded and

reached with a steady hand for the wineglass next to her blazing platter of food.

"Is this going to burn out on its own, or do you have to magick the flames away?"

"It will burn away, just like any other fire."

"What a shame. It was a fine breakfast. I could have offered you some." She sat back and regarded him through narrowed eyes. "You don't look well. The past few days haven't been kind to you."

"Where are Gordon and Mariz?" he asked again.

"Gordon is away on an errand. Mariz is upstairs."

"Take me to him."

She sipped her wine. Then, "No."

"Humor me, Sephira," he said, his knife still poised over his bloodied arm. "Pretend for a moment that I'm not myself, that I'm so exhausted and frightened and frantic I might do something crazy, beyond conjuring my way into your house. Pretend that I'm just foolish enough to shatter every bone in your hand or use my 'witchery' to squeeze your heart until it stops beating."

She considered him for another few seconds, drained her cup, and stood. "This way," she said.

He followed her into the common room. She paused, looking down at her men and giving a small shake of her head. Stepping over them, she walked to the broad, curving stairway they had used the other day, when he and her men brought Mariz back to her house from New Boston. Reaching the top of the stairs she led him down the same corridor, and into that same small bedchamber.

Mariz lay in the bed; as far as Ethan could tell, he hadn't moved at all since the last time he had been there. His color was better, but in all other ways he was unchanged.

"He still hasn't woken," Ethan said in a whisper.

"No. The doctor seems confident that he will, but he doesn't know when. It could be any day now."

Blood continued to flow from the fresh cut on Ethan's

arm, but he barely noticed. He sat in a chair near the bed and stared at Mariz.

"Perhaps you should leave now, Ethan. Like the fire on my food, your sleeping spells won't last forever, and when Nigel and the others wake, they're not going to be very happy with you."

"Tell me about Gant and Osborne," he said.

She laughed. "I've told you before—"

"Please," he said, turning to look up at her.

The first quirk of her mouth he recognized—the beginning of her usual mocking smile. But she didn't answer him right away, and when at last she did it was with a question rather than another refusal.

"Who's after you?"

"Thomas Hutchinson," Ethan said. "He's threatened to put to death every conjurer in the city if I can't give him the information he wants by tomorrow morning."

She blinked. "You're serious."

"Yes. I don't expect you to tell me everything. I know better, and I won't believe half of what you do tell me." He held up his bloodied forearm again. "But I need answers, and I'm not feeling particularly patient."

Sephira stood unmoving; once more, as the last time he had spoken with her, he could almost see her weighing the risks and rewards of helping him. At last, though, she gave a small shake of her head and a breathless laugh. "You're mad," she muttered. "There'll be a price for this. You understand that, don't you? I can strike at you any time I want, and I don't have to come near you to do it. You have friends, and I know who they are."

He didn't say a word, although the Latin for several painful spells leaped to mind.

"Fine," she said. "Have your fun. Gant and Osborne worked together for years. They were with me for a time, as inseparable as Nigel and Nap. But they both claimed to be conjurers. As you know, I'm not an expert in such things, but it seemed to me that Osborne was the more talented of the two. I'm sure he was the more clever."

"At some point they turned on you?" Ethan asked.

"That was Gant's idea, or so I'm told. They secreted away a few items for themselves. Small things at first—worth a few pounds; no more. But with time they grew more ambitious."

"And that's when they stole the pearls?"

He knew from Sephira's tight smile that whatever impulse led to her candor had passed.

"I won't discuss that with you," she said.

"I understand. Tell me this, though: Did you or your men kill Simon Gant?"

This time he didn't expect her to answer. He merely wanted to see how she reacted to the question. But even looking for her response, he was surprised by what he saw in the scintilla of time before she managed to fix another defiant smile on her lovely face.

"Of course we didn't," she told him.

But her expression had said, *Gant is dead?* Not only had she not ordered the man killed, she hadn't yet known of his murder.

Ethan stood, his knife still in hand, the blood on his arm beginning to dry. Reg hovered in the corner by Mariz, unseen by Sephira.

"I think it's time I was leaving," Ethan said.

"Yes, I agree. I'll be waking my men, and I don't think you want to be near here when I do."

Still, neither of them moved.

"Thank you for telling me what you did," Ethan said. "Why did you answer at all?"

"You mean aside from the fact that you were threatening me with your damned witchcraft?"

"Yes, aside from that."

"A moment of weakness," she said, sounding far more like herself. "Not one I'm likely to repeat."

"Why, Sephira?"

She shrugged. "You said that Hutchinson intends to

put you and the rest of your kind to death. I want that pleasure for myself. Now, go."

Ethan grinned; so did she.

He descended the stairs and let himself out of the house, cutting over to the waterfront and winding through the heart of the South End, where he would be harder to find. Ethan knew that Sephira would send her men after him at the earliest opportunity. A few seconds of honesty and a shared grin couldn't unmake years of hostility. He had forced his way into her home; she would have to punish him for that. He doubted that she would allow her men to kill him—she had told him in the past that she needed him around to conduct inquiries that lay beyond her talents—but Nigel, Nap, and the others would be none too gentle in conveying Sephira's displeasure.

Chapter
TWENTY

*E*than expected Sephira and her men to begin their search for him at Henry's cooperage; he would have been well advised to stay as far from Cooper's Alley as possible. But the rank smell of Boston's prison clung to his clothes and hair, like the stink of ale on a drunkard, and Ethan had no desire to have it following him around the city all day. He hurried up to his room, retrieved a pitcher, and took it down to the nearby street pump. Returning to his room with the icy water, he stripped down to his undergarments and put on a fresh pair of breeches. He didn't dare take the time to pour the water into a cooking pot and start a fire, nor did he think it wise to conjure. Instead, before putting on a shirt, he stepped outside onto the landing at the top of the old wooden stairway and scrubbed his scalp and torso with the frigid water, his teeth chattering in the cold air. It was bracing to say the least, and it left him feeling more alert and ready to face what remained of the day.

He put on a fresh linen shirt and his other waistcoat. He didn't have a second coat, but with everything else clean, including himself, the outer garment didn't feel as grimy or smell quite so bad.

Taking care to see that his knife was on his belt and that the two remaining mullein leaves were in his pocket, Ethan left the room and started to pull the door shut. It was then he noticed the folded piece of parchment on the floor just inside the doorway. He stooped, snatched it up, and unfolded it. He recognized Diver's hand right away, but it took him longer to decipher the scrawled words.

> *Have been contacted by buyer. Wants to meet. Need more instructions. Staying with D. Find me at Dowser.*
> —Derrey

Ethan crumpled the note in his hand and tossed it into the room, where it skittered across his table and fell to the floor. With all that had happened in the past day—Gant's murder, his own arrest, his encounters with Hutchinson and Greenleaf and Sephira—he had forgotten about Diver and the task he had left to his friend. And he had failed to tell him that the pearls might not be in New Boston after all. He was glad to see that Diver had taken his warnings to heart and had chosen to stay with Deborah, and he couldn't deny that he was excited to hear that their ruse had worked, that someone had contacted Diver. But he had wanted to keep a closer watch on his friend, and he feared that his negligence might have placed Diver in greater danger. For all he knew, this "buyer" was the conjurer who had killed Gant and the king's soldiers.

He locked his door and headed toward the Dowsing Rod, walking as swiftly as his bad leg would allow, but keeping to side streets, and watching for any sign of Sephira's toughs. He didn't see any of them and soon reached the tavern. Entering the Dowser, he scanned the tables for Diver. The young man wasn't there. Kannice was, though, and seeing him she rushed out from behind the bar and threw her arms around him.

"I've been worried sick," she said, her lips brushing his neck.

"I'm all right."

She pulled back and looked into his eyes. "That man—the doctor—he said you'd been arrested."

"I was. I spent last night in the gaol as a guest of Sheriff Greenleaf."

"How did you get away?"

"I haven't yet," Ethan said, keeping his voice down. "Thomas Hutchinson wants me to find Gant's killer by morning. If I don't, he's threatened to hang every conjurer in the city."

Kannice's expression turned stony. "Well, that seems reasonable."

"Where's Diver?" Ethan asked.

She shrugged. "I haven't seen him since last night."

He swore under his breath. "I was afraid of that."

"He was looking for you," Kannice told him. "He was acting strangely, even for Derrey. Like he was scared."

"He probably was. I'm afraid I might have gotten him in trouble."

"This is Derrey: He's perfectly capable of getting himself in trouble."

"I know," Ethan said. "But this time I did it for him. He's trying to sell some pearls he doesn't actually have, and he's doing it because I asked him to. How long did he wait for me?"

"Most of the night," she said. "I told him that you had been arrested, and that the doctor was trying to get you released. I tried to send him home, but he kept insisting that you would show up eventually and that he just had to wait. 'Ethan'll know what to do.' That was what he kept saying. I sent him away when we closed."

"I'm hoping he didn't go to his room," Ethan said. "Did he have a girl with him?"

"No, he was sitting alone, at the usual table."

Ethan rubbed a hand over his face. "Damn. Have you seen him with a girl recently—red-haired, pretty?"

"I haven't noticed. The way Derrey is, there's always

a new one, isn't there? Even if I had seen her, I wouldn't think much of it."

"You're sure?" Ethan asked. "Her name is Deborah."

"Deborah Crane?"

Both of them turned. Kelf had stepped out of the kitchen, a cask of ale balanced on his massive shoulder.

"You know her?" Ethan asked, crossing to the bar.

"Diver's friend, you mean," the barkeep said, the words running together.

"Yes."

"Right. That's her. Deborah Crane."

"Do you know where she lives?" Ethan asked.

The big man put down the cask and thought for a moment. "Cornhill, I think. On one of them little streets off of King." He frowned. "Pierce's Alley!" he said suddenly, his face brightening. "That's it. Can't remember the number, but I know it's on the alley."

"How do you know so much about her?" Kannice asked.

The barkeep blushed to the tips of his ears. "Well, I might have been with her once or twice a while back. Before Derrey, of course."

Kannice eyed him, looking doubtful. But Ethan reached across the bar and patted the big man's shoulder.

"I'm grateful to you, Kelf," Ethan said, and started toward the door.

"What if he comes back while you're gone?" Kannice asked.

"Keep him here, no matter what he says. And put him upstairs, in one of the back rooms, where no one will think to look for him."

Ethan ran from the Dowser to Cornhill. By the time he turned onto the narrow byway known as Pierce's Alley, both his bad leg and his newly injured knee throbbed, and his lungs were burning. The lane was but a single block long, running between King Street and Dock Square, but Ethan didn't have time to check every door on the street. He stopped in at a small grocery, assuming that it was the one shop on the lane most likely to see business from everyone in the neighborhood.

As he entered the store, an old woman behind the counter eyed him with manifest distrust. When he asked where he might find Deborah's home, she scowled at him and called for her husband.

The man who emerged from the storeroom looked even more ancient than his wife. But he smiled at Ethan's question and nodded with more exuberance than might have been wise.

"Oh, I know her," he said. "Pretty thing; sweet as can be. I make a point of calling her 'Miss Crane.' She seems to like that. Makes her feel like a proper lady, I think."

"Just give him the number, Walter," the woman said. Something in her voice made the man flinch.

"Twenty-seven," he said, with considerably less enthusiasm. "It's three buildings down toward King, on the other side of the lane. She lives upstairs with her sister."

"Thank you." Ethan nodded to the man and then to his wife, who scowled again. Back out on the street he limped to the building the man had described. At street level, it was a milliner's shop. But a stairway at the side of the building led to a wooden door. Like Diver's building this one was brick, the original structure no doubt having been burned in the fire of 1760. Ethan climbed the stairs and knocked on the door. When no one answered, he tried again.

He heard no sound from within. He tried the door handle, but it was locked. Glancing down at the street to make sure that no one was watching, he drew his knife and pushed up his sleeve. To his surprise, there was still dried blood there. He had never conjured after cutting himself that last time at Sephira's house. "*Resera portam ex cruore evocatum*," he whispered, not bothering to cut himself again. Unlock door, conjured from blood. The latch clicked as Uncle Reg appeared at his side. Ethan pushed the door open and peered into the dark room. He hesitated before stepping inside.

A pale blue waistcoat that Ethan recognized as Diver's lay over the arm of a chair, and a Monmouth cap that might well have been his, too, sat on the table beside it. But he saw nothing to indicate where Diver might have gone, or who he intended to meet. After looking around for another minute or two, he left the room, locked the door, and descended the stairs.

As he reached the street, he heard someone call out, "Mister Kaille!"

He spun, drew his knife, and dropped into a fighter's crouch, all in one motion, all without thinking. Seeing the red-haired woman walking toward him, he straightened and slipped his blade back into its sheath.

"Miss Crane," he said.

"Thank goodness you're here," she said, halting in front of him. She sounded winded, and her cheeks were flushed. "I was just at the Dowsing Rod. The woman there told me that you had gone to my home to find Derrey. I'm glad I caught you before you left."

"Do you know where he is?" he asked.

She shook her head and swallowed, still trying to catch her breath. Ethan wasn't certain that he would have remembered the woman from their first brief meeting at Diver's room; he'd had other matters on his mind, and she had left quickly. She was both taller and prettier than Ethan recalled. She stood an inch or two shorter than he. Her eyes were bright blue and she had a generous sprinkling of freckles across the bridge of her straight nose. She wore a simple green gown and quilted petticoats beneath a scarlet woolen cape.

"I haven't seen him since last night," she said. "He said he was going to the Dowsing Rod to find you and that he'd be back later."

It seemed to Ethan that the temperature around them dropped like a stone. "And he never came back?"

"No. I finally fell asleep and when I woke this morning, I was still alone."

"Did he tell you anything else? Anything at all?"

She shook her head, her expression pained. "Very little."

Of course. He had insisted on Diver's discretion, and this one time his friend had done as he instructed.

"Did he say anything about someone he was supposed to meet? Aside from me, I mean."

"He did say he had to meet someone—that he was doing it for you—but he told me nothing about her, either."

Ethan felt a sudden tightness in his chest. "Her? It was a woman?"

"Yes, I think so."

He had to resist the impulse to go back to Sephira's home and smash it to pieces. What had she said to him just a short while before? *You have friends, and I know who they are.* Had she taken Diver as a prisoner before he even got there? Had she already killed him?

"Did he say it was Sephira Pryce?" Ethan asked, afraid to hear the woman's answer.

"Miss Pryce?" Deborah repeated, sounding like that had been the last name she expected to hear. "Oh, no. He didn't mention her at all."

That stopped him short. "You're sure?"

"I would have remembered if he had mentioned her. She's a very important lady."

How could he argue? "But who—?"

It came to him in a rush, stealing his breath. He had been staggeringly stupid for so long. And it was possible that his foolishness had cost Diver his life. *I'll be keeping an eye on you,* he had told him. *I won't let anything happen to you.* How could he have failed his friend so miserably?

"Mister Kaille?" Deborah said, leaning toward him, her forehead creasing with concern. "Are you all right?"

"Go upstairs," Ethan said. "Don't open your door for anyone other than Diver or me."

"All right," she said, wide-eyed and puzzled. "Do you know where he's gone?"

"I have an idea, yes."

He started away, heading toward Dock Square and the North End.

"Do you think he's all right?" the woman called after him.

"I hope so," he said without breaking stride.

❦

The home of the sisters Osborne wasn't far from Pierce's Alley, but even running, his leg and knee aching, Ethan felt like it took hours to cover the distance. If Caleb Osborne was still alive, his daughters would know. They might well have been sheltering him. From the first day Ethan spoke to them, they had struck him as odd. Perhaps they had been hiding the truth from him all this time. Perhaps they had been working with their father to gain the riches he stole from Sephira. That would explain why they had been so reluctant to speak of Simon Gant. Not only did they fear the man, they also knew that their father intended to steal the pearls from him. They might even have known that he intended to kill his old associate.

As he approached the worn wheelwright's shop on Wood Lane, Ethan pulled his knife free and pushed up the sleeve of his coat. He wanted to be ready if Osborne was there. Pausing at the base of the dilapidated stairway, he cut himself, then faltered once more. He wanted to try a listening spell, but any conjurer in the North End would sense the power of it. A conjurer in the room above him might well determine from the casting just how close Ethan was. He started up the stairs, taking each step with painstaking care and wincing at every creak and crack of the ancient wood. When at last he reached the door, he half expected to see it crash open, revealing Caleb Osborne, knife in hand, blood welling from a fresh wound.

But nothing happened, and when Ethan pressed his ear to the side of the building, he heard not a sound within.

He tried the door handle. Locked. Knowing that he was taking a risk, he spoke the unlocking spell again, and at the sound of the lock tumbling, let himself into the Osborne sisters' room. As before, the floor and furniture were littered with colorful cushions. Molly Osborne had been working her fingers to the bone. The faint aroma of cooked meat hung in the air, but otherwise Ethan saw nothing to suggest that anyone had been there for hours.

He would have liked to search the place—for the pearls, for any sign that Diver had been there, for evidence proving that Caleb Osborne was still alive. But he didn't dare take the time. Now heedless of whatever noise he made, he slammed the door shut and charged back down the stairs, stumbling halfway down. He stopped in the middle of Wood Lane, unsure where he should go next, panic rising in his chest like a river in flood.

And in that instant it came to him. Hull Street. Gant's old house. If Osborne had worked with Gant, he would know of the place, and so might his daughters.

He broke into a run once more, ignoring the pain in his leg and the cold sweat on his back. Cutting across the heart of the North End, he dodged carriages and chaises and sprinted past clusters of British regulars, on one occasion ignoring their calls for him to stop, and wondering if he was about to be shot in the back.

When at last he reached the coppersmith's shop, he slowed and readied himself: knife out; sleeve up. He wanted to summon Uncle Reg, but even that small spell would attract notice. He stole around the building into the enclosure in back, and upon seeing the run-down house, knew that at last he had guessed correctly. The tall grass surrounding the old shack had been trampled down, and the building's lone window glowed with the warm light of a candle or oil lamp. The broken shutter had been repaired since the last time he had been here. He saw as well that the cart standing near the house had also been fixed. Had the repairs been done with conjurings?

Ethan slipped through the grass until he reached the pair of worn wooden steps that led to the door, which had been repaired as well. It hung straighter on its hinges, and something told Ethan that it would swing open easily, without scraping the floor.

He put his foot on the first step, and as soon as he did he felt the weblike touch of yet another detection spell. A keening sound, like an ocean wind whistling in a seawall, pierced the silence.

Ethan cut himself. "*Teqimen! Ex cruore evocatum!*" Warding, conjured from blood! Power from his spell pulsed, and was answered an instant later by a second pulse that emanated from within the house. He had time to think, *Fire spell!*

And then he was on his back, lying in the grass. The warding had held against the flames, but the sheer power of the attack had been like the kick of a mule. Reg, who had materialized as soon as he conjured, looked down at him, disapproval twisting his mouth.

The door flew open—as smoothly as Ethan had imagined—and Hester Osborne stepped onto the front porch, her mouth set in a thin hard line, her hair down. Seeing Ethan and the glowing ghost, she narrowed her eyes.

"Mister Kaille! What are you doing here?"

Ethan climbed to his feet.

"I could ask you the same thing," he said. He had managed to hold on to his knife and he tightened his grip on it, weighing whether or not to cut himself again.

"This was Simon Gant's home," she said. "But I assume you knew that. My sister and I didn't feel safe in our home, so we came here."

"And where's your father?" Ethan asked.

Her face seemed to turn to stone. "That's not funny."

"It wasn't intended to be. I know that his body vanished from Castle William. For the the past day I've assumed that it was Gant who awoke him from whatever spell took his life. But I realize now that I should have known better. You're a conjurer. I'd wager that your sister is, too, and that you're both more skilled with your castings than Simon Gant. One of you woke your father, didn't you?"

"You should leave."

He shook his head. "I don't think so. I need to know where your father is. I believe he has a friend of mine with him."

She regarded him, a shrewd look in her eyes. "What friend?"

"Where is he?"

Hester stared at him for another moment before shaking her head. "You should leave now," she said, her voice wavering. "It's not safe for you here, and . . . you should just go. Quickly."

Ethan stepped closer to the house, and even put one foot on the bottom stair. "He's here, isn't he? Your father is inside."

"Please—"

"Hester?"

The woman turned, and Ethan looked past her. Molly Osborne stood in the doorway, the candlelight within the house shrouding her in shadow.

"It's all right, Molly. Go back inside."

"But it's not all right."

The two women gazed at each other for several seconds. Ethan couldn't see either of their faces, but he sensed their tension, their fear.

Hester looked down at him again. "Go, Mister Kaille! Now!"

He shook his head with grim purpose and stepped up onto the front porch of the shack. "I can't."

Before he could shoulder his way past her, a knife flashed in her hand and she cut the back of her own wrist.

"*Corpus alligare! Ex cruore evocatum!*" Bind body! Conjured from blood!

The thrum of her conjuring seemed to rattle the house, and the glowing red ghost of a young man appeared beside her. Ethan had warded himself, but hers was a powerful casting. Without the warding it would have incapacitated him; as it was, he had to struggle to move his limbs, as though he had been snared in a heavy net. He lurched forward, but managed not to fall on his face.

"You can't go in there," she said.

"What the hell was that?" a man bellowed from the back of the house. He sounded drunk or sleepy, or both.

Ethan glared at Hester before pushing past her again. This time she let him go.

Molly stood just inside the door, her fists clenched, her jaw set in defiance. "You should have listened to her!" she said.

But he stepped around her as well, starting toward the small back room of the ramshackle house.

Before he reached it, though, a man blocked his way. The boyish face and round cheeks were familiar, as were the flecks of gray in his straight brown hair. Unlike the last time Ethan had seen him, though, Caleb Osborne now looked very much alive.

He held a pistol in one hand and in the other he grasped the arm of a second man, whom he had dragged from the back room. Giving this figure a hard yank, he pulled the man into view and then let the slack arm drop to the floor.

Ethan needed no more than a cursory look to know who this second man was. The black curls, the square handsome face, marred now by dark bruises around both eyes, and a good deal of dried blood around his nose and mouth. Diver. There was a deep gash under one of his friend's eyes and another high on the side of his head. His hair was matted with blood. He appeared still to be alive, but Ethan didn't know how long he could keep his friend that way.

Osborne laughed at what he saw on Ethan's face. He shoved the toe of his shoe under Diver's shoulder and pushed hard, rolling the young man onto his back, so that his head lolled to the side and struck the doorframe with a dull thud.

"This who you're lookin' for?" Osborne asked.

Chapter

TWENTY-ONE

sborne planted his foot on Diver's chest and aimed his pistol, full-cocked and ready to fire, at the center of the unconscious man's forehead. Looking over at Ethan, he grinned, revealing a large gap where his bottom front teeth should have been.

"I see by your glowin' friend there"—he tipped his head in Reg's direction—"that you know somethin' of conjurin'. And you obviously care 'bout this one. So I'm gonna keep my flintlock just like this, and you're gonna answer some questions for me. Get it?"

"What do you want to know?" Ethan asked.

"Let's start with your name."

"I'm Ethan Kaille."

"And what the hell are you doin' in my house, talkin' to my girls, and pokin' your nose in my business?"

Ethan glanced at Hester, who had closed the door and was watching him and her father.

"Don't look at her!" Osborne said, his voice suddenly so loud that both women started. "It's me as asked you the question!"

"I'm a thieftaker," Ethan said.

"Ah," the man said, nodding. "I figured as much, or somethin' like it. You're after what's mine."

"I'm not the only one. You're playing a dangerous game with Sephira Pryce."

"You let me worry 'bout her. The Empress of the South End don't scare me." He looked Ethan up and down, seeming to take stock of what he saw. "You know what you're chasin' or are you just lookin' for the first coin that comes your way?"

"I'm looking for the pearls that you and Simon Gant stole from Sephira."

Osborne had been grinning all this time, but now the grin faded. He waved the pistol at Diver. "So that's where this one comes in, eh? He's workin' with you, or for you."

"He's no one: a lad I hired to do a little work. That's all. Let him go. You have me now. I'm a lot more important than he is."

"I don't think so. He's important to *you*, and that makes him valuable to me." He narrowed his eyes, much as Hester had done. Up until that moment, Ethan hadn't noticed the resemblance between Osborne and his daughters. But it struck him as obvious now that he was looking for it. "But tell me, Kaille. What makes a thief-taker so important?"

When Ethan didn't answer, Osborne pressed the barrel of his pistol against Diver's forehead and looked Ethan's way.

What could he do but answer? "I'm working for the Crown."

"The Crown?"

Ethan laughed, breathless and desperate. "You didn't think you could attack a British ship that way and not attract the notice of the king's men, did you? Are you that much a fool?"

The muscles in Osborne's jaw bunched. "Have a care, man," he said. "I'll kill him, and then I'll kill you, and I'll sleep fine tonight havin' done it."

Ethan swallowed the retort that leaped to mind.

"What is it the Crown has you doin'?" he asked, his

tone mocking, his pronunciation of the word "Crown" exaggerated.

"Looking for you, as it turns out."

"Well, that's too bad for you, Kaille. 'Cause they'll never know that you found me." Osborne looked past Ethan. "I want him bound, girls."

Neither Hester nor Molly moved.

"Now!" their father said, sounding like he was speaking to ten-year-olds.

"He warded himself," Hester said, her voice shaking. "I tried a spell against him before. It didn't work."

Osborne grinned. "Do it the way I taught you. Together."

Molly made a small sound in her throat, like a trapped animal. Hester laid a hand on her sister's arm and looked to her father once more.

"Do it!" Osborne's words seemed to lash at the women.

Hester continued to glare at him. He stared back at her, daring her to defy him. And in the end, she looked away.

"It's all right, Molly," she said, her tone gentle. "It's just a binding."

Ethan watched them all, looking back and forth between the young women and their father. He knew better than to reach for his knife, but he remembered the two mullein leaves he still carried with him. They weren't enough for a powerful casting, but perhaps a simpler spell would be enough. He had a feeling that if he could overpower Caleb, the women would let him take Diver and go.

He began to speak a spell to himself. "*Conflare ex verbasco*—" It would have been a heat spell, one that would force the man to drop his pistol. But as soon as Ethan began to recite the Latin, Uncle Reg's bright eyes snapped to his face.

Osborne saw this. "Stop it!" he shouted, turning the pistol on Ethan.

Ethan faltered—only for an instant, but that was enough. With one quick stride, Osborne covered the distance between them. He slammed the butt of his weapon into the side of Ethan's head.

Pain exploded in Ethan's temple and white light flared behind his eyes. He staggered, fell to the floor.

"Now!" Osborne said, his voice like a hammer. "The spell! Cast it!"

A heavy silence fell over the room and Ethan tried to rouse himself. Before he could, he heard the women say in unison, "*Corpus alligare ex cruore evocatum.*" Bind body, conjured from blood.

The spell that rumbled like thunder in the floor beneath him, that pulsed through his body with such force it seemed to make his teeth clatter, dwarfed any spell Ethan himself had ever cast, save the one that he had sourced in the life of Shelly's mate, Pitch. Whatever Hester and her sister had done rivaled a killing spell, something Ethan had never thought possible.

That the spell worked just as the women had intended, carving through his warding as if it were paper, came as no surprise. He couldn't move. He had lost all control over his limbs, his neck, his mouth. His gaze could roam, but beyond that, he was helpless. On the other hand, he still felt everything. His head ached where Osborne had hit him; the rough floor pressed against his cheek, his arm, his side. He was growing more uncomfortable with every breath. But he couldn't do anything about it.

He heard footfalls by his head and back and felt himself hoisted up into a chair. He started to tip over to one side, but Osborne braced him before he fell back to the floor.

"Rope," the man said.

Hester nodded to Molly, who hastened to the back room and returned with a long piece of ship's rope.

"Tie him up," Osborne told her. "Just enough that he won't fall over." He smiled. "Spell'll take care of the rest. But just in case, take his blade."

Ethan hardly heard him. His mind was reeling from what he saw, and with the implications for all that had happened over the past several days. Hester's red ghost had appeared again with the binding spell. It stood beside her. And a second ghost followed Molly everywhere she went. This one was a young woman who looked very much like the young man glowing at Hester's shoulder. Both of the ghosts had large dark eyes, aquiline noses, and full, sensuous mouths. These features seemed odd, almost womanly, on the red figure of the young man; they were far more attractive on the glowing girl. Still the ghosts resembled each other; they were related, perhaps even brother and sister. This was not surprising, since Hester and Molly were sisters.

What had sent Ethan's mind careening down a dark and troubling path was the color of Molly's ghost. She was yellow. Bright golden yellow.

He stared at the shade for several moments, then shifted his stare back to Hester's bloodred ghost. Yellow and red. He hadn't seen either color before this day. But he would have wagered all he owned that when blended together, the yellow and red of their spells would leave a residue of brilliant orange. The same orange he had seen aboard the *Graystone*, on Mariz, and on Gant.

Osborne hadn't killed anyone. His daughters had done it all. Together, their separate conjurings working as one.

He felt light-headed, sick to his stomach. The truth had been right there in front of him for so long, since that first day when he went to speak with them. Still, even knowing this, he couldn't reconcile those yellow and red ghosts with what he had observed of the two women. They weren't killers. They couldn't be. And yet, ninety-seven men were dead; ninety-eight if he counted Gant. Killed by power that glowed orange.

He stared at them, at their ghosts, yellow and red. He wanted to ask them why, whether their father had forced them. But he could no more speak than he could stand up and walk out of the shack.

"What now?" Hester asked, looking to her father.

Osborne put on an old begrimed coat. "Now, I go out and look for some pearls. I might even be able to sell them."

"But you don't know where they are," Hester said. "You told us that before."

"Well, I've more of an idea than I let on. Gant told me some before he died. And Sephira don't need to know I ain't got them yet. Just as long as we agree on a price. The rest'll take care of itself."

Hester didn't appear convinced, but she also didn't seem concerned. She eyed her father a moment longer and turned her attention back to Molly, who was staring at Ethan, looking both frightened and contrite. Osborne retreated to the back room and soon returned with a second pistol. One he placed in his coat pocket. The other he handed to Hester.

"You girls watch him," Osborne said. "And keep a good eye on his friend, too. If he wakes, bind him up like Kaille. You can shoot them if you have to. One or both."

"We can't keep them like this forever," Hester said.

"Don't need to. I'll talk to Sephira, come back here and learn what I can from these two. And then we'll ... well, we'll deal with them." He looked at Diver once more and pursed his lips. "One of you girls ought to clean that blood ... Or better yet." He swung his gaze Ethan's way, the cruel smile on his lips Ethan's only warning of what was coming.

He heard the man whisper his spell, felt the pulse of power, and saw the glowing blue ghost of an ancient soldier, much like Reg, appear beside Osborne. Flames erupted from Ethan's sleeve. They licked at his neck and face, the heat sudden and intense. Terror stole his breath. He couldn't bat at the flames or rip off his shirt or drop to the floor and roll over the burning clothes to smother the blaze. He felt his skin blistering and he couldn't even scream.

It took the two women several seconds—which might as well have been hours—to understand what was happening. Ethan could smell burning cloth, hair, flesh, and perhaps they finally did, too. Molly gave a small yelp and both women rushed forward to put out the fire.

They managed to extinguish the flames in mere moments, though it seemed to Ethan that they took far longer. His arm throbbed, and he could feel burns on his neck, as well.

No one in the room spoke. Osborne's smile had vanished, and he was staring hard at his daughters.

"You were awfully quick to save him," the man said. "Like you was worried 'bout him."

Neither woman spoke at first.

"Well?" Osborne said.

"You would have preferred we let the house burn down?" Hester said at last. "It wasn't him we were saving; it was us."

"Well, that's good. 'Cause when I come back, he's a dead man. You understand that, don't you?"

Molly blanched. Hester nodded.

"Why did you do it?" Molly asked, her eyes brimming with tears. She wiped at them, leaving a dark, sooty smear on her cheek. "You didn't have to burn him."

Osborne pointed back to Diver. "There was blood on his face. Kaille coulda used it to conjure. So, I did instead."

The women looked down at Diver, as did Ethan. The blood on his friend's face and hair was gone, washed away by Osborne's conjuring.

"All right, I'm goin'. Watch him. Even without that blood, he's dangerous." Osborne turned to Ethan once more. "I shoulda asked you 'bout them pearls before Hes's spell shut your mouth. But we can deal with that later."

He left the shack, his boots scraping first on the porch and then the stairs. Still the women said nothing. They seemed to be listening, and Ethan did the same, until he could no longer hear the man tromping through the tall grass.

Ethan's one hope was that Hester and Molly might help him once their father was gone. That hope evaporated as soon as Osborne was out of earshot.

"You're a fool!" Hester said, rounding on him, her hands on her hips. "You wouldn't listen to me. You couldn't just leave when I told you to."

Ethan flicked his gaze to Diver and back to her.

"Yes, I know. Your friend. He's as stupid as you are. You can't save him. So you're both dead, and Molly and I will have two more souls to worry about."

"I don't want to do any more conjuring, Hes," Molly said.

Hester took her hand. "I know, love. Neither do I. Why don't you sew some more? That always helps."

Molly cast a furtive glance Ethan's way one last time and crossed to a chair at the far end of the room. One of her bright, patterned cushions lay on the floor, and several more scraps of matching material rested on the arm of the chair. Molly sat, took up the material, and soon was absorbed in her craft. She didn't look happy, but the sewing did seem to calm her.

Hester, on the other hand, remained where she was, watching Ethan, the pistol still in her hand.

Ethan thought once more of the mullein in his pocket. He thought he could make a spell work without speaking it aloud. The problem was, two leaves weren't enough for any casting that could overcome the combined might of the sisters Osborne. He couldn't defeat their binding spell. He might be able to heal the worst of Diver's injuries, but the women would use a conjuring to bind his friend, or worse. He could light a fire, or bring the roof of the shack down on them all, but he and Diver were both helpless to escape. He was more comfortable than he had been in the gaol, but the invisible shackles conjured by Hester and Molly were no less effective than Greenleaf's chains.

The wood of the shack was too old and lifeless to provide much power for a spell. On the other hand, there was more than enough grass outside for several castings. But bound as he was, by both conjuring and rope, he would have to give much thought to which spell he chose to cast. Hester had the pistol, both women could conjure, and Ethan had Diver to worry about as well as himself.

He considered an illusion spell. Though the rain had stopped, leaving him with little water for an elemental spell, there was no reason he couldn't use grass to send for help using an image of himself as he had at the prison. But as soon as he cast the spell, and sent such an image to Kannice or Pell or anyone else who might have been able to come to his aid, Hester would feel the spell and know that Ethan was conjuring.

Which left him back where he had been before he started thinking in circles: helpless, a captive.

He again glanced at Hester, but then looked away, and let his gaze settle on Molly instead. At first she took no notice of him, so intent was she on her sewing. After some time, though, she happened to look up and catch sight of him watching her. She dropped her gaze, but a few seconds later her eyes flicked his way a second time.

Looking down once more, she shifted in her seat, bent lower over her work, and stared hard at the thread and cloth, seeming to will herself not to glance his way anymore. And yet, seconds later she did.

A small whine escaped her and she looked over at her sister.

"Hester?" she said.

"Stop it, Kaille."

Ethan didn't look away.

Hester stepped forward, planting herself directly in front of him so that he could no longer see Molly. He raised his eyes and she slapped him hard on the cheek. Not only did it sting, but it also turned his head enough that he could no longer see Molly. Hester smiled with grim satisfaction and took a seat near her sister, in a chair that was also outside of Ethan's line of sight.

After that, time slowed to a crawl. Hester remained where she was, Molly sewed, and Ethan sat doing nothing, waiting to be killed.

He must have dozed off, because the next sound that reached him was a low groan that cut through his slumber. He woke with a start, his neck and arms and legs feeling stiff. Someone—Hester—walked to his chair and roughly turned his head so that he could see Molly again, and, more important, so that he could see Diver.

His friend groaned a second time, and his eyes fluttered open. He started to sit up, but stopped when he saw Hester standing over him, the pistol trained on his heart.

"Stay right where you are," she said.

Diver nodded, groaned again, and raised a hand to the gash on the side of his head. "Where are—?" he started to ask, looking around the shack. But when he spotted Ethan, he stopped, his mouth falling open, astonishment and despair in his gray eyes.

"Ethan! What are you doing here?"

"He can't answer you," Hester said.

"Why not? What have you done to him?"

"It's called a binding spell. He can't move at all, not to speak, not to conjure, not to help you in any way. It's just you against the two of us, and we're both capable of doing to you what we've done to him. So sit still, and keep quiet."

Diver faced Ethan again, a question on his youthful face. All Ethan could do was stare back at him. After a moment or two of this, Diver seemed to realize that the woman had spoken the truth.

"What happened to his arm?" Diver asked. "And that bruise on his face—where did that come from?"

"My father," Hester said, as if the words tasted bitter in her mouth.

Diver slumped against the wall and reached up once more to the gash on his head. "Your father," he repeated. "A fine man. He's the one who did this to me, too."

"Keep quiet," Hester said, taking her seat once more, the pistol still held ready.

Diver fell silent, but not for long. "He wasn't happy when he found out I didn't have the pearls. The first time we met, I was able to put him off, but not the second. When I didn't have them, he got angry, pulled out a gun. I tried to run, but he must have used a spell on me, brought me back here." He gestured at the bruises on his face. "The rest you can see."

Hester leaned forward in her chair. "Stop talking! We don't want to hear this."

But of course, Diver was saying it for Ethan's benefit, not hers.

"The first time we spoke, he offered me twenty pounds— not a lot for pearls, but enough to make me think that he must think he can get a lot for them. He wanted to know where in New Boston I found them. He asked if they had been near the church. And I told him that they had. That seemed to be the right—"

Hester was on her feet again, standing over Diver, the pistol pressed against his chest.

"Another word, and I swear I'll kill you!"

Diver stared up at her, his mouth clamped shut.

"Don't you think I understand what you're doing?" She gestured back at Ethan, waving the pistol. "You're telling him all of this. And I want you to stop!"

"Hester, it's all right," Molly said, meek and scared.

"No, Molly, it's not! So just shut your mouth. All of you, keep quiet!"

Molly's face crumbled and tears slipped from her eyes.

"You see?" Hester cried, glaring down at Diver, looking and sounding more like her father with every word. "If you would just keep silent—"

The report of the pistol was deafening, and for the span of a heartbeat or two, no one moved or said a word. Gray smoke filled the room, along with the acrid scent of gunpowder. At last, Hester looked down at the pistol, which she still held, a look of stunned incredulity on her face.

Molly screamed and pointed at Diver with a trembling hand.

Blood had begun to spread over his chest, staining his shirt and waistcoat. He looked toward Ethan for an instant before his eyes rolled back in his head.

Ethan struggled with all his strength to break free of the binding spell, to bolt from his chair to Diver's side, to roar his friend's name. But the binding spell held him fast. He could do nothing but watch as his friend's life bled away.

"Molly, quickly!" Hester said.

Their eyes met. Molly nodded, pale, her lips trembling.

"*Extrica ex alligatione!*" the two women said as one. "*Ex cruore evocatum!*" Release binding! Conjured from blood!

The two ghosts appeared again—red and yellow—and at the same time the blood on Diver's clothes vanished. The shack was electric with their conjuring. And Ethan felt life flow back into his limbs.

"Get this rope off me!" he said.

Hester rushed to him and cut the rope.

Once free, Ethan flung himself out of the chair to the floor by Diver's side. His friend's skin had turned cold and gray. He was breathing still, but already each breath sounded labored, and as thin as parchment. Blood had started to soak the front of his shirt again, but much less this time. He had lost too much already.

Hester hovered at his shoulder. "Do you know how to . . . how to get it out of him?"

"There's no time for that! He's dying!"

"So what do we do?"

"A healing spell," Ethan said. "All three of us."

"Have you ever cast a spell with another conjurer, Mister Kaille?" Hester asked him, her expression grave.

His mouth twitched. "No."

"Then you aren't ready. It's not just a matter of casting at the same time. It's . . . I haven't time to explain it. Molly and I will do this. We owe him that." She grimaced; Ethan thought she might have meant to smile.

"Your knife, Molly," Hester said to her sister. "He hasn't enough blood for another casting."

Molly stood beside her sister, a blade in her hand. The two ghosts joined them, holding hands, so that where their fingers met, the light turned to that familiar orange Ethan had seen so many times in the past few days. He stood and backed away, allowing Hester and Molly to kneel on either side of Diver. The two women cut themselves, dragging the blades over the backs of their wrists in unison, performing a ritual he was sure they had practiced for years. Dropping their blades, they both touched their free hands to the cuts they had made, covering their palms and fingers with blood. Then each laid a crimson hand on Diver's wound, Molly's beneath Hester's.

"*Remedium ex cruore evocatum,*" they said together, their eyes closed. Healing, conjured from blood.

The surge of power felt different this time. It wasn't a single pulse that came and went. It growled in the wood of the house, like some mammoth beast. Ethan said nothing. He watched, tight-lipped, his heart pounding, racing.

Hester and Molly looked like marble statues, their bodies rigid, their faces as pale as bone. Had it not been for the sweat on their faces, Ethan might have wondered if they had reached too deep with their casting.

Ethan couldn't see Diver's wound, so he didn't know if it had closed up. The bloodstain on his shirt hadn't spread further, but that could mean that he had died. The gray pallor—the color of death—clung to his face, his hands, and with the women's hands on his chest it was hard to see if he still breathed. But neither Hester nor Molly paused in their efforts, so he refused to give up hope.

So intent were all three of them on Diver that they heard nothing from outside until a boot thudded on the wooden stairs and porch, and the door swung open once more.

The women turned as one toward the door, their faces like those of children caught playing some forbidden game. Ethan turned, too, a whispered curse on his lips.

Caleb Osborne stood in the doorway, his pistol aimed at Ethan, his dark, angry glare fixed on his daughters.

Chapter TWENTY-TWO

W hat, in the name of all that's holy, do you think you're doin'?" Osborne demanded. He stormed into the house and kicked the door closed.

Ethan kept quiet and watched Hester and Molly. They stared back at their father, also saying nothing. Hester raised her chin, defiance in her hazel eyes. Molly gaped at Osborne, terror etched on her face.

"I asked you a question, girls! I want an answer!"

"The pistol went off," Hester said at last, stooping to retrieve the weapon. "He was talking and I wanted him to stop. And I yelled at him, and I must have . . . I don't know. But it went off and— The bullet hit him in the chest. There was blood and— We released Kaille so that he could help us heal him. He would have died."

Osborne rubbed a hand over his mouth, his face reddening. "I see. And you never gave a thought to what I said before I left? That he was gonna die anyway?" His voice grew louder with every question. "That I intended to kill him? Did you forget everythin' I said?"

Molly had covered her ears. Hester's cheeks burned bright red.

"Didn't I tell you to bind him if he woke? Do you remember me sayin' as much? He's dangerous, I said. Just like Kaille. And still you didn't bind the one, and you released the other. It's like I raised simpletons." He looked down at Diver, squinting. "Doesn't even look like you saved him."

"Yes, we did!" Molly said through tears.

"Looks dead to me. But if you say so, I'll believe you." Osborne still had his pistol aimed at Ethan, and now he turned his full attention to the thieftaker. "I want you t' tell me how you heard about the pearls."

"I'm sure you do," Ethan said. "Just as I'm sure you'll kill me—and Diver, too—as soon as I tell you what I know."

"Maybe not. But I will if you don't tell me what I want to know. And I'll start with him."

"Fowler," Ethan said.

Osborne stared back at him. Ethan sensed that this was the last name he had expected to hear. "Jon Fowler?"

"That's right. He made it sound as though Gant talked about them day and night. I wouldn't be surprised if half the British army is out there looking for them."

"You're lyin'."

Ethan shrugged. "I knew about them. And I promise you that Fowler's the one who told me."

Osborne indicated Diver with a lifted chin. "And why'd you send this one out into the streets with that fool story about havin' them to sell?"

"Because I knew that would be the quickest way to find you and Gant. It was clear to me that Gant had no idea where they were. Just yesterday I saw him at the Manufactory. He was probably looking for them there."

Osborne's face went white.

"He *was* looking for them there," Ethan said. "Wasn't he? What's more, I'd wager that he found them."

"You can believe that if you want," Osborne said. But his tone told Ethan that he had hit too close to the truth for the man's comfort.

"No, he didn't find them," Ethan said, guessing now, and eager to keep Osborne talking. "But he told you they were still there, and that's when you killed him. Or had your daughters do it for you."

"Shut your mouth, Kaille."

"Do you have them?" Hester asked her father.

"We'll talk about it later."

"Why wait?" she said. "He knows what happened, and you're going to kill him anyway. So answer me. Did you get them yet?"

"Aye, I've got them," Osborne said. "But not here. They're in a safe spot. That's all you need to know."

"But he hasn't sold them yet," Ethan said. Another guess.

"I told you to be quiet."

"Sephira wouldn't agree to a price, would she? That's not her way. She'd demand to see them first, and you, knowing her as you do, would understand that bringing her the pearls, even if it was just for her to look at, would be like putting that pistol to your head and pulling the trigger. Which means that you have the pearls, but you have no agreement, and you don't know what to do next. She's probably got her men watching you, and so she'll know if you try to sell them to anyone else."

"That's enough!"

"She knows about this place," Ethan went on. "Nigel and Nap were here just a couple of days ago. She's going to come looking for you. And then you'll really be in trouble."

"How do you know so much about it?" Hester asked.

Ethan laughed, his gaze still on Osborne. "There's no one in this city who knows Sephira Pryce better than I do. If your father was smart, he'd let me help him. But that would mean splitting his share of the sale, and we know how he feels about that. Certainly Simon Gant does."

"I said that's enough!"

Ethan knew what was coming, but he held his ground

and braced himself. Osborne took two quick steps in his direction and hit him again with his pistol, this time connecting just above Ethan's left eye. Ethan staggered but stayed on his feet. Osborne struck him again in the same spot and Ethan collapsed, pain clouding his vision, and blood running down his face.

But if there had been any doubt in Ethan's mind, Osborne's assault erased it. For all his bluster, the man had no intention of shooting him or Diver. He had let his daughters do all the killing up until now, and he would be content to let them do the rest. That was Ethan's best hope.

The man dragged Ethan back to the center of the room.

"Help me, Hes," he said.

Osborne's daughter joined him at Ethan's side, and together they lifted him into the same chair he had been trapped in earlier.

"Now, bind him like you did before. Both of you."

"How much do you think you'll get for the pearls, Osborne?" Ethan asked through the throbbing pain. "Were they worth the lives of all those men on the *Graystone*?"

This blow Ethan hadn't anticipated. Osborne hit him in the jaw with what felt like a cobble from King Street. He flew off the chair, landing hard on his side and smacking his head against the floor.

"*Shut your mouth!*" the man hollered at him.

Ethan tried to push himself up off the floor, but he couldn't seem to make his arms or legs work. He lay there, trying to clear his head and waiting for the pain in his jaw and teeth to subside.

"What did he mean by that?" Hester asked after a brief, tense silence.

"He's talkin' nonsense, Hes. Don't worry about it. Just help me get him up."

Ethan felt someone grab one of his arms, but not the other.

"Molly, grab his other arm," Osborne said. "Let's put him back in that chair."

"What did he mean, Father?"

"Now, Molly!"

A moment later, someone took hold of Ethan's other arm, and once more he was lifted into the chair. He started to topple back onto the floor, but strong hands held him up.

"Gimme that rope."

With some effort, Ethan managed to open his eyes. Osborne stood over him, tying him to the chair once more.

"Now, bind him," the man said, when he had finished with the rope.

Molly turned to look at her sister, but Hester didn't seem to have moved. She still held the pistol, though she appeared to have forgotten about it. She stared hard at her father, fear and disgust and rage chasing across her features.

"You told us it was nothing," she said, her voice so low that Ethan had to resist the urge to lean forward to hear her better. She pointed at Ethan. "The first time he came to us, he said something about an attack on the *Graystone*, and you told us later it was nothing to worry about. Just something that the fleet commanders had made up to cover your escape."

"He lied," Ethan said.

Osborne had turned to face his daughter, but at this he whirled on Ethan again. He pressed the barrel of his gun against Ethan's face, just below his bleeding eye, pushing so hard with it that he tipped Ethan's head back.

"I swear to God, Kaille! Another word and I'll blow a hole in your face!"

"I want to know what he meant, Father!"

"First you bind him, like I told you. We'll talk when you're done."

Hester still didn't move. At last Osborne dismissed her with a wave of his hand and turned to Molly.

"You'll have to do it," he said. "Quickly girl, before he tries more of his magick. Use the blood on his face."

Molly gave Ethan a pained look, but nodded to her father. Ethan watched her, waiting. And as soon as she opened her mouth to speak the spell again—"*Corpus alligare ex cruore evocatum.*" Bind body, conjured from blood—he chanted a spell to himself, hoping that this once Reg would do what Ethan needed him to. "*Tegimen ex cruore evocatum,*" Ethan said in his mind. Warding, conjured from blood. He finished reciting his spell to himself just an instant before Molly finished speaking hers.

He felt the blood vanish from his face, sensed conjurings humming in the old worn wood of the shack. They felt powerful, but not so much so that anyone would guess that there had been two spells cast instead of one. And just as Molly's bright yellow ghost appeared beside her, Reg materialized as well. He was behind both Osborne and Molly. Neither of them could have seen him. A smile flashed on his glowing face and he vanished again.

Ethan couldn't be certain that Hester hadn't seen the ghost, and he dared not look at her. He would have to trust that Hester was angry enough with her father, and suspicious enough of what he had done in recent days, to keep Ethan's secret. He was supposed to be bound, and so he held himself still. But though he felt the leaden weight of Molly's spell on his body—that same feeling of a heavy net that had come when Hester tried the binding spell outside—he knew that his warding had worked.

For several seconds no one spoke. Ethan could almost feel Hester weighing her choices, and he feared that despite the tension in the room, she would remain loyal to her father. But at last she said, "All right, he's bound. Now tell us what happened to the *Graystone.*"

"Nothin' happened to it," Osborne said, turning away from her and walking to where Diver lay, still pale and unmoving. The man let out a small laugh and looked back at his daughters. "Looks like you saved this one after all. What a waste."

"Why did Kaille ask you about the lives of those men?" Hester asked. "What did he mean by that?"

"Stupid girl! He's tryin' to confuse you, t' turn you against me! Can't you see that?"

Hester raised her pistol. "Don't you dare call me stupid! And don't lie to me anymore! I want to know the truth!"

Osborne stared at her, dropped his gaze to the weapon in her hand. Ethan thought he might strike her. Instead he began to laugh, which might have been worse. "No, Hes, you're not stupid. But you don't know a thing about pistols. That's a single-shot flintlock you've got in your hand. And there's nothin' in it." He gestured vaguely back at Diver. "The lead's in him, isn't it?"

Her face blanched, perhaps with the realization of what she had done in pointing the weapon at her father. She looked down at the pistol and sagged into the nearest chair.

"But fine," Osborne went on, his voice eerily calm. "You want the truth. I'll give you the truth. That spell you both did, the one that was supposed to make me look and feel like I was dead. It worked fine." He laughed again. "It worked more than fine. It was remarkable. A thing of beauty. It made me look dead all right." His laughter bubbled over once more, but he talked through it. "It made every man on the ship look dead. Imagine what it was like. The officers from those other ships come to the *Graystone*, and every man on board is lyin' there, lookin' like someone came along and poisoned the food or somethin' of the sort." He wiped away the tears of mirth that were now streaming from his eyes.

"My God," Hester whispered, covering her face.

"You girls forgot what I told you 'bout the way spells work on water as opposed t' on land. They're stronger on water, remember? So your spell for me worked on every man on that ship." Osborne laughed again, and shook his head. "Wish I'd seen their faces—all those officers."

Ethan remembered his own revealing spell aboard the *Graystone* and how it worked on several of the soldiers instead of just the one. It seemed the same thing had happened to the sisters' spell.

Molly stood by her father, gaping at him, her mouth open, a stricken look in her large, dark eyes. "I don't understand," she said. "The spell we used to wake you—"

With a visible effort, Osborne managed to control his laughter. Still, a grin lingered on his face. "Oh, that one worked just the way it was supposed to. We was on land by then, at Castle William. That one worked just fine."

"Do you mean to say that we killed every man on that ship?" Hester said, her voice breaking on the last word.

The question appeared to sober her father. "No," he said, sounding earnest. "Hes, no! Don't you see? That's the beauty of it all! Neither of you killed a soul. You cast your spell and did just what you was supposed t' do. The king's men are the ones what killed all those others!" He opened his hands, a smile on his face now, a look of wonder, like that of a man explaining to his children how caterpillars became butterflies. "I'm proof that you killed no one. They did it all! They burned them, or buried them, or dumped them in the sea! It was perfect! And it's all on account of the two—"

"Shut up!" Hester screamed at him, clutching at her belly and doubling over. She stumbled to the door and yanked it open. An instant later Ethan heard her retching.

Molly cast a furtive look at her father, but the sound of her sister being ill seemed to overmaster her fear of Osborne. She ran out of the house. Ethan could hear her speaking in soothing tones to Hester, but after a few seconds of this, the other woman cut her off.

Osborne stared at the door. Ethan could see that he

was bewildered by his daughters' response to what he had told them. He thought that this might be his best chance to surprise the man, but before he could even decide what spell to cast, Osborne seemed to remember that he was there.

He raised his pistol again, his eyes narrowing. "You think this is your big chance, don't you? You think my girls will help you now." He shook his head. "They won't. They'll understand soon enough. It's better this way. There's riches waitin' for us. You'll see." He put the barrel to Ethan's brow. "Or you won't."

Ethan closed his eyes, and was about to speak a spell that would shatter the man's hand. But before he could cast, the two women entered the house once more, their footsteps heavy. Neither of them spoke.

"I'm sorry, Hes," Osborne said. "I won't laugh about it no more. I know you're upset. I understand. Really."

Ethan could see the women now without having to turn and give away his one advantage over Osborne.

"What were you going to do?" Hester asked, nodding toward Ethan. "Kill him here?"

"No," her father said. He lowered the pistol once more. "That wouldn't be smart. We need t' do it somewhere else, far from here."

Hester straightened. "Of course. We shouldn't use that pistol, either. Someone might hear. It's best done with a conjuring."

Osborne beamed. "That's my girl. You was always so clever, Hes. Like your ma."

"And you'll want us to do it—Molly and me—because our spells are stronger than yours. And we need to be sure. Kaille being a conjurer and all."

"I suspect you're right," he said. "That'd be the best way. There's the other one, too—Kaille's friend. We should take care of both of them."

Hester considered Diver. "Maybe we can put them in the cart, take them down to the Neck, or over to Mill Pond."

"The pond'll be better," Osborne said. "That's good thinkin', Hes."

"You'll have to carry them for us. Molly and I aren't strong enough." She held out her hand to him, palm up.

Osborne frowned, unsure of what she was doing.

"The pistol," Hester said. "I'll hold it for you."

He gave it to her without hesitation. Perhaps he had forgotten that a short time before she had turned the other weapon on him. Or maybe she had sounded so reasonable in these last few moments that he assumed her rage had spent itself.

It hadn't. As soon as she closed her fingers around the wooden stock of the pistol, she leveled it at her father. Osborne tried to grab it back from her, but Hester jumped back beyond his reach. Molly screamed and threw herself at her sister just as the firearm went off with another flash of light and a deafening report.

Osborne dropped to one knee in front of Ethan, clutching his left arm. Blood flowed over his fingers and dripped to the floor.

"You stupid, ungrateful—!" He broke off, his teeth gritted, a snarl on his lips as he glared up at her.

Hester dropped the pistol and backed up to the wall, her eyes wide and fearful like those of a horse in a lightning storm, her cheeks bloodless. Osborne got to his feet, glanced down at his bleeding arm, and took a menacing step in Hester's direction.

Ethan lashed out with his foot, catching Osborne just below the knee and sending him sprawling to the floor. Molly screamed. Ethan launched himself out of the chair and onto Osborne. He hadn't noticed, though, that the man had pulled a knife from his belt. At the last instant Ethan had to twist to the side to avoid impaling himself on Osborne's blade.

Osborne slashed at him with the knife, but Ethan managed to block the man's arm with his own. He dug his fist into the bullet wound in Osborne's arm and the man howled in pain.

"*Remedium! Ex cruore evocatum!*" Healing, conjured from blood!

"Molly, no!" Hester's voice, piercing and frantic.

But it was too late. Ethan felt the spell, the pressure building in his leg. It was unfocused—she had put no blood on him. But she had conjured out of rage and fear and hatred, using a healing spell not as a balm, but as a weapon. And her casting was strong. He heard the bone in his leg snap. He roared, rolling off of Osborne and clutching at his thigh. He couldn't breathe for the pain, and he barely noticed when Osborne got to his feet again. The thief kicked him in the head and Ethan pitched over onto his side.

"Good girl, Molly!" Osborne said. "That spell saved me."

Looking down at Ethan once more, he reared back and dug the toe of his boot into Ethan's gut. Ethan folded in on himself, retching, gasping for air.

He assumed that Osborne would slit his throat and turn his rage on Hester for shooting him. But it was Molly who rounded on her sister, eyes blazing, fists raised.

"*Why did you do that?*" she shrieked. "Why did you shoot him? He's our father! You don't shoot your father! You don't! You just don't!"

Hester cowered away from her sister, pressing herself against the wall. Her face was streaked with tears, and her chest heaved with every breath she took.

"I won't kill for him again! Don't you see what he's turned us into? We're his knife! His pistol! That's all! *And we killed every man on that ship!*"

"No!" Molly said, shaking her head. "That wasn't us! Father said so!"

Hester shook her head, swallowed. "He lied, Molly."

"That's enough outta both of you." Osborne loomed over Ethan, his blade in hand. "I want him dead. Now." He turned to his daughters. "Cast your spell."

"No," Hester said. "Kill him yourself."

Blood had started to flow from Osborne's arm again, replacing the blood Molly had used for her spell.

"*Discuti!*" Ethan muttered. "*Ex verbasc—*" The spell would have shattered Osborne's leg, using the mullein leaves in his pocket as its source. But before he could finish it Osborne kicked him again, once in the head, and a second time in the gut.

Ethan vomited onto the floor.

"So you've got mullein in your pocket, do you, Kaille?"

He couldn't answer and he couldn't fight back when Osborne knelt beside him and began to fish through his pockets for the small pouch containing his precious leaves.

"Not much," the man said. "But more than I had b'fore." He grinned, turned back to the two women. "Like I said, I want him dead now. And his friend, too. No more games. No more of your foolishness, Hes. Do it, and let's end this."

Ethan tried to rouse himself, but Osborne placed his foot on Ethan's throat, pressing down hard enough to cut off his breathing, but not enough to crush his windpipe. Ethan thrashed at the man, but he was too hurt, too addled. He hadn't the strength to stop them.

Molly pulled out her knife. Hester flinched at the sight of her sister's blade, but then drew hers as well. Her face was ashen. Molly's outburst seemed to have snuffed out the fire within her. She cut herself. Molly did the same. Locking their gazes on each other, the women began to chant.

"*Fini pulsum,*" they said in unison. "*Ex cruore evocatum.*" Stop heartbeat, conjured from blood.

Power surged through the floor, the walls, Ethan's body. He shut his eyes, waiting for the spell to take him. He didn't realize what the women had done until Osborne made a small strangled noise in his throat. An instant later he gave a faint grunt.

"Father?" Molly's voice. "*Papa? Hester, what did you do?*"

The pressure on Ethan's neck eased, and the man fell backward to the floor, landing in a sitting position. Molly screamed again. Osborne looked up at the two women, his eyes bulging, his mouth open. He jerked once, twice, struggling to inhale. His lips had turned blue. He dropped his knife and clawed at his chest, then lifted his gaze to Hester and Molly once more as his hands stilled. Molly reached out to him, but Hester snatched her sister's hand back, staring hard at her father. Osborne swayed, tipped over onto his side, and lay motionless, his dead eyes fixed on the floor at his daughters' feet.

TWENTY-THREE

olly dropped to her father's side, crying "Papa! Papa!" again and again. She struggled to pull him upright, but he was too heavy for her and at last she fell over him, sobbing and clutching at his shirt.

Ethan pushed himself up into a sitting position. His head spun, and his stomach ached where Osborne had kicked him. But all of that was nothing compared to the agony in his broken leg.

At his first movement, though, Molly's head jerked up. She glared at him for an instant, scrambled to her feet, and huddled by her sister.

"What do we do with him?"

"We let him go," Hester said, her tone firm. "He's here because of what we did to the *Graystone*. None of this is his fault."

"But Father—"

"Don't, Molly. You know what kind of man he was. Just as Mother knew. We should never have read that last letter he sent. We should have burned it with the others."

"I wanted him back," Molly said in a small voice. "I missed Mama, and I wanted him back."

"I know."

Molly began to cry again, and Hester put her arms around her sister and gathered her close.

Watching them, Ethan leaned forward and picked up Osborne's knife from where it lay on the floor. He cut himself, glancing up at the sisters once more. Seeing that Hester was watching him, he faltered. But she closed her eyes and stroked her sister's hair. Ethan took this as a sign that she wouldn't try to stop him.

He put blood on his leg and spoke his spell. "*Remedium ex cruore evocatum.*" Healing, conjured from blood.

Molly started at the hum of power and turned to face him. But her tears still flowed and he could tell that she hadn't the strength or inclination to stop him. He let his conjuring flow into his leg, sucking his breath through his teeth at the first painful touch of the healing spell, but breathing easier as it began to knit the bone back together.

He had to cut himself twice more to complete the healing, and by the time he had finished, he was sweating and his hands shook. At last he released the spell and struggled to his feet. Once more he turned to Hester, wondering whether she would try to keep him there.

But she was already watching him. "Go, Mister Kaille. Your friend is alive still, but he needs more than we were able to give him. Take the cart if you need it."

"Thank you," he said. "For letting us go, and also for saving our lives."

She flinched at the words.

"You understand—" he began.

"Do what you have to do. You were hired to learn the truth about the *Graystone*. You and I both know what that means."

He nodded, holding her gaze. At last he turned away and crossed to where Diver still lay. His skin felt warmer than it had earlier, but his face remained pallid, his breathing shallow.

Ethan lifted the younger man and slung him over his shoulders. Both of his legs ached, and they nearly gave out beneath the added weight. But he staggered to the door and out into the cool, damp night. When he left the Osborne sisters, they had sunk to the floor beside their dead father. But they were still holding each other and seemed as much at peace as Ethan could expect under the circumstances.

The old cart stood near the shack, its wheels both whole, but Ethan saw little advantage to pushing it through the streets of Boston. He kept Diver on his shoulders and made his way from Hull Street back through the North End and on toward the Dowsing Rod. His legs trembled with every step and his back and shoulders soon were screaming with exhaustion and the remembered pain of his stay in the gaol. But he didn't stop.

When regulars tried to stop him, asking what had happened to his friend, Ethan forced a smile and told them Diver was too drunk to walk on his own. The soldiers found that amusing, said something about Diver being typical of American colonists, and let them go. He used the same story three more times before reaching Kannice's tavern.

The crowd he found in the Dowser was typical for a Monday night. There were enough people there to keep Kannice and Kelf busy, but there were also a few empty tables. When Ethan staggered inside, the warm air and din of conversations and laughter were like a slap in the face. After his seemingly endless journey through the city streets, his legs buckled beneath him just within the door. He fell to his knees and allowed Diver to slide off his shoulders to the floor.

The conversations of those nearest to him died away, and the silence crept back through the rest of the tavern, like a slow-moving fire.

"I need help," Ethan panted.

A man called for Kannice. And another.

A moment later she was there by Ethan's side, also on her knees. Kelf stood over them.

"What happened?" Kannice asked, concern etched in the lines around her eyes and mouth as she looked at Ethan's bruises, the burn marks on his clothes, the gash at his eye. "Who did this?"

"I haven't time to explain it all," Ethan told her. "There's more I have to do. But Diver was shot."

She had been examining the wound on Ethan's temple, but now she pulled back with a start. "Shot!"

"Yes. In the chest."

He looked down as she did. There was a hole in Diver's shirt and waistcoat, but very little blood.

She shook her head. "It doesn't look—"

"Listen to me." He touched her chin gently, forcing her to meet his gaze. "He was shot in the chest. By all rights, he should be dead. You understand why he's not?"

She nodded.

"He needs more attention, and I haven't the skill or the time to help him. The bullet is still in him; I think he needs to see a surgeon."

"The one who was here," Kannice said, one step ahead of him.

"Yes. William Rickman. He's probably back on board the *Launceston*. You'll need to get word—"

"I know." Her eyes held his for the length of a single breath. "He'll be all right. I'll see to it. Go do whatever you have to."

Ethan forced himself back to his feet, his gut hurting , where Osborne had kicked him. He staggered, and might well have fallen to the floor had Kelf not caught hold of his shoulder with a massive hand.

"You sure you don't want t' sit awhile and eat somethin', Ethan?" Kelf asked, the words running together as always.

"I'm sure. But thank you anyway."

"Come back as soon as you can," Kannice said, giving his hand a squeeze.

Ethan turned and pulled the door open, taking one last look back at Diver. Kelf had bent over and taken the young man in his arms. He straightened, lifting Diver with such ease, one might have thought the young man weighed nothing at all. Ethan knew all too well that he didn't. Confident that his friend would be cared for, he stepped once more into the night air and started back the way he had just come. His first choice would have been to go to Thomas Hutchinson's chambers, but this late in the evening the lieutenant governor would already be back at his estate in Milton. Greenleaf's house was some distance to the south, and he wasn't certain that he wanted to show up at the man's door after dark, lest it give the sheriff just the excuse he needed to shoot him.

This had all started with Geoffrey Brower coming to his room. It seemed to Ethan that it should end with him going back to Brower's door. He followed Middle Street into the heart of the North End, passing many of the same groups of regulars he had seen not long before. Most showed no sign of recognizing him, but one soldier shouted to him as he hurried past, "Where's your drunk friend?"

"Sleeping it off!" Ethan called back, not breaking stride.

The soldier and his companions laughed. Ethan was surprised to realize that he had come to hate them.

He reached the Brower house a short time later, his legs sore and weak. This time it was an African servant who answered the door at Geoffrey and Bett's house. He had Ethan wait at the door until Bett came to greet him.

She said nothing at first except to send the servant for Geoffrey, but she flinched as she took in his various wounds, the state of his clothes, perhaps even the weariness in his eyes.

"You should see a doctor," she said.

"I will," he said. "But these matters can't wait."

"Do you enjoy it?"

Ethan surprised himself by managing to smile. "Enjoy what? Being beaten, burned, shot at?"

"Your work? I was asking if you enjoy it enough to deal with . . ." She indicated his clothes and face with a vague wave of her hand. "With all of this."

He wanted to tell her that he did; saying anything other than "yes" felt like a surrender in their years-long feud. But he was too sore, too weary, and her question cut too close to the bone. "Ask me tomorrow, Bett," he said at last. "I'll be able to answer you then."

"Ethan!"

Geoffrey strode into view, dressed impeccably as always. His face fell when he saw Ethan's state.

"Good God! What happened?"

"I'll tell you everything I can," Ethan said. "But you need to get messages to Sheriff Greenleaf, Lieutenant Colonel Dalrymple, and, if possible, the lieutenant governor. I know who's responsible for the deaths of all those soldiers as well as for the murder of Simon Gant. I also know where they live."

"They?" Geoffrey repeated. "There's more than one of them?"

"They're the daughters of Caleb Osborne, who was one of the men we thought had died aboard the *Graystone*."

Geoffrey frowned. "*Thought* had . . ." He shook his head. "I'm afraid I don't follow."

"I know. As I said, I'll explain everything. But I don't know how much time we have. They may try to leave the city, and believe me when I tell you that my life depends on them not getting away."

"Of course," Brower said. "I'll send word immediately to the sheriff and Colonel Dalrymple. The lieutenant governor will be a more difficult matter, but we'll inform him as soon as possible." He started back into the house. "I'll pen messages right away."

"Thank you, Geoffrey."

Brower raised a hand as he walked off. Ethan looked at Bett again and took a long breath. Their interaction had always been strained, and tonight he was too exhausted to make any effort at civility. "I can wait out here," he said, leaning back against one of the marble columns.

"No," she said. "Come inside. Sit. When was the last time you ate something?"

Ethan's laugh surprised even him. "I couldn't tell you. It feels like days."

Bett took his hand, something she hadn't done since they were children, and led him into the dining room. She spoke in a low voice to another of their servants, a young woman with brown curls that framed a plain, pale face. As the girl hurried off, Bett poured Ethan a glass of Madeira.

She placed it in front of him and sat at the end of the table, watching him as he took a sip. "Should I call a doctor for you? You really do look terrible."

"I'll be all right. Thank you, though."

He took another sip, feeling self-conscious under his sister's gaze. Neither said anything more. Eventually the servant returned with a platter of bread, cheese, and apples. Ethan took some bread and cheese, but ate slowly. He wasn't as hungry as he should have been given how much time had passed since his last meal.

From the back of the house he heard the opening and closing of a door, and a minute later Geoffrey joined them in the dining room.

"The messages are off," he said. "There's nothing to do now but wait." He sat, looking hard at Ethan. "I need you to explain all of this to me. I know I don't understand much about—" He paused, his gaze flicking toward Bett. "About conjuring," he said at last, stumbling over the word. "But I want to understand what I saw on the ship."

"Of course." But Ethan hesitated, his eyes fixed on the food in front of him. Speaking of spellmaking in front of Bett was never easy, and he wondered how she would react to hearing of the conjurings worked by the Osborne sisters.

She seemed to read his thoughts. She stood and stepped away from the table. "I'm going to check on George. I think I would prefer that he didn't walk in on the middle of this conversation." She paused at the door. "Take care of yourself, Ethan."

"Thank you, Bett."

Once she had left, Ethan began to tell Geoffrey all that he had learned in the past few days. He had mentioned the pearls the last time they spoke, but at that time he hadn't known that Osborne still lived. So he explained all of it again, describing as best he could all the spells that had been cast, answering questions whenever Geoffrey interrupted him, and telling him all that he remembered of those frenzied moments in the shack on Hull Street.

For some time after he finished his tale, Geoffrey sat unmoving, watching Ethan.

"I don't know whether to thank you for all you've done, or to ban you from this house and demand that you never return," he said, his glare smoldering in the candlelight.

Ethan stared back at him, unsure of what he had done to earn such a response. "I don't understand. I didn't—"

"It's not a matter of what you did or didn't do," Geoffrey said. "But if this power you wield can give and take life with such ease . . ." He shook his head. "How can such a thing not be evil?"

"I carry a knife on my belt," Ethan said. "I can take a life with it. Does that make the knife evil? Or does the question of good or evil fall to the man holding the blade?"

Geoffrey sat back, his eyebrows raised. Before he could answer, there came a knock at his door. He pushed his chair back and stood. "Excuse me."

He left the room, only to return seconds later with Stephen Greenleaf in tow.

"Kaille," the sheriff said, his lip curling. "I figured you had to be behind this."

"You should be happy, Sheriff," Ethan said, taking another bite of bread and cheese. "Caleb Osborne is dead."

"I don't even know who Caleb Osborne is. Unless you mean the Osborne who worked for Miss Pryce all those years ago."

"One and the same." Ethan stood. "We should go back and talk to his daughters."

"Talk to them?" Geoffrey asked.

"You heard what I told you," Ethan said. "They didn't know they had killed anyone. We need to place them in the colonel's custody, but I believe they should be shown mercy. They were ruled by a tyrant, a cruel and violent man who threatened and abused them. They intended only to help him get away from the army."

"Hardly admirable," Greenleaf said, glancing at Geoffrey.

"I agree. But I'm not sure theirs was a hanging offense."

Another knock sounded at the door.

"That will be Colonel Dalrymple," Geoffrey said, and left the room once more.

"You look like you took a beating," Greenleaf said, sounding far too pleased. "All this for ten pounds. Are you sure it's worth it?"

Ethan took one last sip of wine, stood, and left the room without bothering to answer. Geoffrey stood at the door talking to Dalrymple. They both turned at Ethan's approach.

"Where is it we're going, Mister Kaille?" the colonel asked.

"Hull Street," Ethan said. "That's where Osborne and his daughters held me earlier today."

Dalrymple's brow furrowed. "Osborne. Why do I know that name?"

"He was on the *Graystone*, sir," Ethan said. "A member of the Twenty-ninth Regiment."

"I thought Gant was the only man who deserted in time."

Geoffrey and Ethan shared a quick look.

"Apparently Osborne got away, too," Ethan said.

"Yes, all right," Dalrymple said, sounding impatient. "Let's be on our way, then."

The colonel had a dozen men with him, and as it turned out the sheriff had brought two of his ruffians as well, both of whom carried torches. No doubt every man there would have been shocked to learn that if Hester and Molly Osborne decided to fight them, a contingent of men twice as large wouldn't be enough to overpower them. But Ethan kept this to himself.

They set out northward toward Hull Street, Ethan walking with Geoffrey, the sheriff, and Dalrymple. The soldiers and Greenleaf's men followed. It was a cold, still night and clouds still blanketed the sky. The streets were mostly empty, but those people they did encounter gave the company a wide berth.

They walked at a brisk pace and soon reached the coppersmith's shop. Resisting an urge to draw his knife and push up his sleeve, Ethan led the men around to the grassy clearing behind the shop. Seeing the shack, his heart sank. The window was dark.

"It doesn't look like anyone's here, Kaille," the sheriff said, a smug grin on his face.

Ethan didn't answer, but he held out a hand to one of Greenleaf's men. "Give me your torch."

The man glanced at the sheriff, who hesitated before nodding.

Ethan walked to the shack and pulled the door open. The room remained much as he had left it. Osborne lay in the center of the floor, drying blood pooling beneath his wounded arm, his eyes still wide, his mouth still hanging open.

Greenleaf joined him in the doorway. "That's Osborne?"

"Aye," Ethan said.

"And he killed Gant?"

"His daughters did. But they did so because he made them, because they were terrified of him."

"And who killed him?"

"They did."

Greenleaf glanced at him, narrowing his eyes. "Are you sure of that?"

"I was there when they did it. If they hadn't, I'd be dead."

The sheriff twisted his mouth. "Remind me to thank them," he said, the words dripping with irony. "What now? Where else could they be?"

"They live on Wood Lane. Perhaps they've gone back there."

"This place isn't theirs?"

"No," Ethan said. He descended the steps and trudged through the trampled grass. "This was Simon Gant's house," he said over his shoulder.

Ethan led the men back through the streets of the North End, to the wheelwright's shop at fourteen Wood Lane. They went around to the side of the building and Ethan looked up the stairs. To his relief, the small window of the Osborne sisters' room glowed with candlelight.

"This way," he said, starting up the stairs. This time he did pull out his knife, but he kept it out of sight. He knew better than to think that he could conjure without drawing attention to himself and his spellmaking abilities. But after seeing what these women could do with their conjuring powers, he refused to meet them without a blade in hand.

Dalrymple, Greenleaf, and Brower followed him up the stairs. The others remained on the street.

Reaching the door, Ethan knocked once. When no one answered, he tried the door handle. The door swung open, and Ethan swore at the sight and stench that greeted him.

The two women dangled from the rafters of the room, nooses at their necks, chairs overturned beneath their feet, their dresses soiled where their bladders and bowels had released.

"Good Lord!" Geoffrey said, breathing the words.

Hester stared straight ahead, her mouth open much as her father's had been. But Molly's eyes were closed, and she appeared almost to be smiling. In the short time Ethan had known her he had never seen her look more at peace.

He stepped into the room, his throat tight. There were cushions everywhere; a half-completed pillow sat on the floor by one of the beds along with several spools of thread.

On the table in the center of the room, he found a piece of parchment and, beside it, a pen and an inkwell. He picked up the note and looked at the others.

"What does it say?" the colonel asked.

"'We're sorry.'"

"That's all?" Greenleaf said.

Ethan held the note out to him.

The sheriff didn't bother to reach for it. "Well, that's very convenient for you, isn't it?" But Ethan could tell that the man's heart wasn't in the accusation.

"He was with me at my house for some time before you arrived, Sheriff," Geoffrey said.

"Aye," Ethan said. "And before that I brought Derrey Jervis to the Dowsing Rod. He had been with me at the shack on Hull Street. He was wounded there."

Dalrymple crossed to where Ethan stood and took the note from him. He examined it briefly before turning to Greenleaf. "Sheriff, do you honestly believe that Kaille had a hand in the deaths of these women? It looks a good deal like suicide to me."

For just a second Ethan thought that the sheriff might try to blame him for everything. But the man's shoulders slumped and he shook his head. "I agree," he said. "They killed themselves. As to the rest . . ." He shrugged. "I suppose their note is proof enough of their guilt."

He walked out of the room, making no effort to hide his disappointment. Ethan glanced at the colonel, who raised an eyebrow.

"He doesn't like you very much."

"No, sir," Ethan said. "There are few people in positions of power in this city who do."

Dalrymple grinned. Ethan hadn't seen him smile before; it made him look ten years younger.

"You seem proud of that," the colonel said.

"Not proud exactly. But I have gotten used to it."

The colonel looked up again at the corpses of the two women, his grin turning to a grimace. "Did they really kill every man on the *Graystone?*" he asked.

Ethan considered this. He could still hear Osborne bullying them both with one breath and with the next assuring them that the army had done the actual killing. And he could hear as well what Hester had said. *He lied.*

"Yes," Ethan said at last. "They killed them. They were trying to help their father, and did far more damage than they ever thought possible."

"You sound like you almost feel sorry for them," Dalrymple said.

"I do. If you had met their father, you would, too."

With the colonel convinced of the guilt of the Osborne women, and Greenleaf resigned to the fact that he wouldn't be able to blame Ethan for any of what had transpired in the past week, Ethan was free to leave Wood Lane.

He made his way back to the Dowsing Rod as quickly as he could. Kannice must have been watching for him, because she met him at the door with assurances that Diver was all right.

"I gave him a room upstairs," she said. "He's resting. And Doctor Rickman is waiting for you at a table in back."

"Good," he said, exhaling the word. He put his arms around her and held her for a long time.

"Is it over?" she asked at length.

"Almost," Ethan said. "The worst of it is."

"I'm glad. Go find the doctor. I'll get Kelf to bring you something."

Ethan found Rickman sitting alone near the back of the great room. The surgeon regarded him with genuine alarm and was on his feet before Ethan reached the table.

"You look like you've been through a war."

"Close to it," Ethan said.

"I know that you can heal your own wounds if you have to," he said, dropping his voice. "But at least let me see to the burns and cuts."

The truth was, too many people had seen his injuries for him to heal them with spells, and so he welcomed Rickman's ministrations. "I'd be grateful, Doctor," he said, lowering himself into a chair. "But first tell me about Diver."

Rickman shrugged. "There's not much to tell," he said, still whispering. "The wound is closed, and it appears to have been healed internally, as well as externally. He's breathing easily, his pulse is steady. I wouldn't call it strong yet, but if there was lingering damage to his heart I'd know it."

"The people who healed him never got the bullet out. There wasn't time."

Rickman blinked, but kept silent as Kelf came to the table and set a cup of ale, some bread, and a bowl of chowder in front of Ethan.

"My thanks, Kelf."

"Anythin' for you, Doctor?" the barkeep asked.

Rickman shook his head. Once Kelf had gone, he leaned toward Ethan. "I assumed that you had healed him."

"No."

"I'd like to speak to the people who did."

"That isn't possible," Ethan said.

The doctor seemed to hear the finality of this. He nodded, his expression grave. "I see."

"The bullet, Doctor?"

"It shouldn't prevent a complete recovery," Rickman told him. "I don't think it's still in his heart—I can't imagine that he'd be doing as well as he is if that were the case. Which means it's probably lodged in the muscles or flesh surrounding his heart, nearer to his back, I would assume. It might cause him some discomfort, or it might not. But I doubt it poses any real danger to him."

Ethan closed his eyes, knowing a moment of blessed

relief. Swallowing the lump in his throat, he reached for his ale and nearly drained the tankard.

"The people who healed him saved his life," Rickman said. "You understand that."

"Yes, I do. They were also the people who killed the men aboard the *Graystone*."

Rickman didn't appear to know how to respond to that. He stared at his hands for a long time. After several moments, he looked up at Ethan and said, "Let's see to that burn, shall we?"

For the next hour or so, Rickman swabbed and bandaged the burns on Ethan's neck and arm, cleaned the cuts on his head, and probed his side for broken ribs. By the time he finished, Ethan felt marginally better. He promised himself, though, that once the doctor was gone and he was alone with Kannice, he would use spells on the burns. They hurt far more than his other injuries, and as long as they were bandaged no one would ever know that he had healed himself.

Rickman left not long after. He needed to return to the *Launceston*, but he promised Ethan that he would check on Diver again in the next day or two.

Ethan sipped a second ale by himself for a short while, but when Kannice came by to ask if he planned to wait up for her, he shook his head.

"I'm about to fall asleep right here," he said.

"Go to bed," she said, kissing him gently on the lips. "I'll try not to wake you when I come up."

"All right. What room is Diver in?"

"First one on the right."

"Thank you, Kannice." He climbed to his feet, and waded through the crowd to the stairs.

At the top of the stairway he let himself into Diver's room, trying not to make a sound. A single candle burned atop a bureau by the door, and a chair had been set beside the bed. Diver lay beneath a pair of woolen blankets, looking pale and very young. Ethan walked to the bed and laid a hand on his friend's brow. It felt warm, though not fevered.

"I thought I'd gotten you killed," Ethan murmured.

He watched Diver sleep for a few moments before letting himself out of the chamber and going to Kannice's room.

He slept like a dead man—he didn't notice when Kannice came to bed, or when she got up and dressed the next morning—and only woke when she returned to the room to tell him that a soldier was waiting for him down in the tavern. He rolled out of bed, stiff and sore, wincing with every movement, and he donned the last set of clean clothes he had put aside in Kannice's wardrobe. If his next job was anything like this one, he would have to remember to buy himself more shirts and bring half of them over here.

The soldier snapped to attention as Ethan came down the stairs.

"I'm Ethan Kaille," he said to the man.

"Yes, sir. I'm here to escort you to the lieutenant governor."

This Ethan had expected. "Lead the way," he said.

Ethan took it as a good sign that Hutchinson had sent one man for him, rather than a detachment. But he couldn't deny that with every step that took him closer to the Town House, his trepidation grew.

Upon arriving at the Town House, he didn't have to wait long before being ushered into Hutchinson's chambers.

The lieutenant governor eyed him as he walked in, the look on his face so grim that Ethan wondered if the man had hoped he would fail, so that he could rid himself of Boston's conjurers.

He still can, said a small voice in the back of his mind.

"It seems one day was more than enough time for you, Mister Kaille."

"Yes, Your Honor."

"You were hurt, I see."

"Not badly, sir."

Hutchinson's smile was perfunctory and cold. "Yes, well, you have our gratitude," he said, sounding none too grateful. He tossed a leather pouch onto the desk. It landed with the clink of coins. "Mister Brower tells me you were promised ten pounds."

Ethan picked up the pouch and placed it in his coat pocket. "Is there anything else, Your Honor?"

"Yes. Be careful how you use that . . . that witchery of yours. I'll go to my grave believing that it's an abomination, and I know that I am not alone in my belief. We'll be watching you and your kind, and we won't look kindly on any association you might have with Samuel Adams and James Otis."

"Yes, sir," Ethan said, and left. He should have been angry; Kannice would have been livid on his behalf. But with all that conjurings had wrought in the past several days, he could not bring himself to blame the lieutenant governor for fearing his spellmaking abilities.

From the Town House, Ethan walked out to Sephira's house on Summer Street. It was a clear, cool day, with a sky so blue Ethan could barely look at it. Leaves of orange and yellow and bronze clung to the trees lining Rowe's Field and d'Acosta's pasture. He knew that he was being foolish and reckless paying a visit to Sephira so soon after forcing his way into her home. But one part of the *Graystone* mystery remained, and he suspected that she was as aware of this as he.

Gordon saw him approaching and this time, rather than standing on the portico to face him, the big man retreated into the house. When he came out again, he was accompanied by Nigel, Nap, Afton, and even Mariz, who looked tiny next to the others.

"You got some nerve comin' here," said Nigel, toying with his pistol.

"I need to speak with Sephira," Ethan said in an even voice. He hadn't drawn his knife, but there was enough grass around him for a dozen conjurings.

He thought that Nigel would refuse to call for her, but he leaned toward Mariz and whispered something. The conjurer glanced at Ethan and slipped into the house.

"You shouldn't have put us to sleep like that," Nap said.

Ethan raised his eyebrows. "You'd have preferred it if I broke your neck or lit your clothes on fire or just crushed the life out of your heart?"

None of them offered any response.

The door opened and Sephira came out, followed by Mariz.

"Ethan," she said. "You're alive. What a surprise."

"I'd like a word with you, if I may."

She gave a guileless smile, which looked out of place on her features. "All right. Leave us," she said to Nigel and the others. "There will be other chances for you to take your revenge." This last she said with a glance at Ethan.

The men filed back inside. Sephira leaned back against one of the marble columns and looked down at him, beguiling and lovely as ever. "What shall we talk about?"

"The pearls," Ethan said.

"I've told you, Ethan—"

He raised a hand, stopping her. "I've been paid by the Crown. Ten pounds. I don't want anything else. Besides, I never had any claim to whatever treasures were stolen from you. Gant and Osborne are both dead now, as are Osborne's daughters. And I've come to realize that I don't want to see the customs boys get their hands on the pearls."

Sephira had straightened and her smile had vanished. "Do you know where they are?"

"I have an idea," Ethan said. "This would level things between us. It would more than make up for my unannounced visit the other day, as well as anything I did to your men."

"We'll see about that," she said, purring.

"No. Those are my conditions. I tell you where they are, and you call off your dogs."

"What if you're wrong?"

"I'm not."

She took all of two seconds to consider his offer. "Done. Where are they?"

"There's a house on Green Lane, near West Church. The structure itself is unimportant—it's the plot of land on which it sits. There should be a small gravesite there, somewhere in the yard. And if I'm right, the earth at the grave site has been disturbed recently. You'll find the pearls there."

"Osborne's wife," Sephira said in a breathy whisper.

"That's right."

"That's well done, Ethan. Not surprising, though. Of the two of us, you've always been the more sentimental."

Ethan grinned, refusing to let her goad him. "Good day, Sephira," he said, turning to go. "Remember, we have a deal."

"Of course we do. But sooner or later you'll give me another excuse to send Nigel and Nap after you. You always do."

He couldn't argue.

He headed back into the South End, but hadn't gone far when he heard someone calling his name. Turning, he saw Mariz hurrying after him. This time Ethan did pull his knife.

Mariz slowed, holding up his hands so that Ethan could see that he carried no weapon. He was breathing hard and sweating. Ethan wondered how recently he had awakened and risen from the bed in Sephira's house.

"Sephira and I reached an agreement," Ethan said, watching the man's every move.

"I came for myself, not for her," Mariz told him, his accent thicker than Ethan remembered.

Ethan lowered his blade. Mariz stepped closer.

"You healed me. You got me back to Miss Pryce's home. I owe you my life."

"I'm not sure Sephira would want you thinking that way," Ethan said.

"No, I imagine she would not. But still, it is true."

"You'd have done the same for me," Ethan said.

Mariz laughed, and after a moment Ethan joined in.

"I think we both know that I would not have." Mariz grew serious. "But if you have need of my aid in the future, you shall have it." Before Ethan could say anything, he added, "I still work for Miss Pryce, and I will follow what orders she gives me. But when I am not acting on her behalf, I am free to honor whatever friendships I choose. And like it or not, Kaille, you and I are now friends."

Ethan didn't know what to say. At last he nodded. Mariz flashed a smile and started back toward Sephira's house. As he walked away, a memory stirred in Ethan's mind. He reached into his coat pocket and grinned at what he found there.

"Mariz!"

The conjurer stopped, turned. Ethan walked to where he waited and handed him his glasses.

"I forgot to give these to Sephira the other day."

Mariz grinned again and put them on.

"What do you remember from the day you were attacked?" Ethan asked.

"Very little," Mariz said, his expression sobering. "I was in New Boston, looking for Gant. I cast a finding spell, one of several I cast that day, and sensed a conjurer just behind me. I tried to turn and ward myself, but the spell hit me before I could."

"A warding wouldn't have helped you. Osborne's daughters cast together, and their spells were very powerful."

"Do you know why they attacked me?"

"Not for certain, no. But I believe they were checking on their intended hiding place for the pearls, and when they felt your spell, they panicked. You're lucky it was just them. If their father had been there, he would have insisted that they kill you."

"I was lucky because you found me, Kaille. And I will not forget that." He smiled once more and started away again.

Ethan watched him go, unsure of whether he could trust the man, even now. Once Mariz was out of sight, he walked to Henry's shop and up to his room. He remained there long enough to bundle up a change of clothes to take back to the Dowsing Rod. Crossing the city, Ethan pondered what Mariz had said to him. He didn't know how the man could work for Sephira while also being a friend to him. But he hadn't sensed that Mariz was lying to him, and he couldn't imagine that Sephira would have been pleased by their conversation. For now, that was enough to satisfy him.

On his way to the Dowser, he stopped at King's Chapel, where he found Mr. Pell tending to the chapel gardens.

Seeing Ethan, Pell stood and shook his head. "You look terrible."

"Why does everyone insist on telling me that?"

"Simple courtesy," the young minister said, mischief in his eyes. "I didn't want you to think I hadn't noticed."

Ethan smiled. "I came to thank you for helping to win my release from the gaol. And I'd like a word with Reverend Caner. I owe him my thanks, as well."

Pell averted his gaze, though his smile remained. It might even have deepened. "I was glad to help," he said. "But I'd prefer you didn't say anything to Mister Caner."

"But he sent a message on my behalf to the lieutenant governor."

"Have I mentioned to you," Pell asked, still not looking Ethan's way, "that over the years I've learned to write in a fair approximation of the rector's hand?"

Ethan's jaw dropped. "Trevor!" he whispered.

"You needed help," the minister said, looking Ethan in the eye. "And I didn't think you could afford to wait while I convinced Mister Caner that you were worth saving."

"But still—"

"It's done," Pell said. "Best we not speak of it again."

Ethan nodded. After a moment's pause he laughed and gave a small shake of his head. "You are still a rascal, aren't you? And because you are, I'm still alive."

His friend beamed.

"Thank you, Pell," Ethan said, proffering a hand.

Pell gripped it. "My pleasure."

Ethan left the young minister, and continued up Treamount toward Sudbury Street. When he reached the Dowsing Rod, Kannice told him that Diver was awake and eager to talk to him. Ethan hurried upstairs to his friend's room. At his knock, Diver called him inside.

"How are you feeling?" Ethan asked, closing the door and crossing to the chair by Diver's bed.

"Sore," Diver said. "Tired."

"You look good."

It was true. His cheeks had color again and though his face was still bruised from the beating Osborne had given him, he seemed to have come through his ordeal mercifully well.

"Kannice says I got shot."

"You don't remember?" Ethan said.

"No. She also says that a healing spell saved me. Thank you."

Ethan took a long breath. "It wasn't me, Diver. Osborne's daughters saved you. All I did was get you back here. And if it wasn't for me, you wouldn't have been hurt in the first place. You very nearly died because of me and my foolish idea."

Diver shook his head. "You asked me to do some work for you. I knew the risks." He grinned, winced, and lifted a hand to his black and blue jaw. "Anyway, it was fun until Osborne started using me as an anvil."

"Well, speaking of working for me," Ethan said, pulling out Hutchinson's pouch of gold. "This is the ten pounds I earned for finding the Osborne sisters.

Hutchinson gave it to me today. I believe half of it is yours."

"Half?" Diver said, looking like he might argue. Instead he shrugged. "All right. Half it is."

Ethan laughed and placed a pile of coins in his friend's outstretched palm. Diver wrapped his fingers around the money, a contented smile on his face. Even five pounds, though, wasn't enough to overcome the young man's weariness. He lay back against his pillow and closed his eyes.

"I'll let you rest," Ethan said.

"Aye, all right." Before Ethan could leave, though, Diver looked at him again. "Say, Ethan, can you do me a favor?"

"Of course."

Diver's face reddened and he wouldn't quite look Ethan in the eye. "I haven't gotten word to Deborah that I'm all right. And I think she might be worried about me. Could you let her know that I'm here?"

"I'll go to her right away."

"Thank you," Diver said. He lay back once more, still clutching the coins in his hand.

Ethan went back down to the tavern, where Kannice waited for him.

"Is he all right?" she asked.

"I think he's fine," Ethan told her. "He wants me to go find his girl and tell her where he is."

Kannice's expression soured. "I might have to start charging him for that room."

"You should," Ethan said, striding to the door. "He's got some money now."

"And what about you, Mister Kaille," she asked. "Will you be staying here tonight as well?"

"That was my plan."

"Well, go on then," she said, smiling once more and shooing him from the tavern. "They sooner you're gone, the sooner you're back."

Ethan held her gaze, lingering in the doorway.

"Go," she said, mouthing the word, her cheeks flushed, the blue of her eyes as deep as an autumn sky.

Ethan nodded, grinned. And buttoning his coat, he stepped out once more into the cool New England air.

Historical Note

Writing historical urban fantasy demands that an author strike a balance between fictional elements and known history. The central premises of the Thieftaker books, that thieftakers and conjurers were active in the American colonies, are not true. Thieftakers were known in England at this time, and they made a brief appearance in the fledgling United States in the early nineteenth century. But there were no thieftakers in Boston in the 1760s. Sephira Pryce and Ethan Kaille have no direct, real-world counterparts. As for the magic . . . well, you can make up your own mind about that.

The other historical elements of the novel, however, are largely accurate. The occupation of Boston by British troops began at the end of September in 1768, after a summer of unrest, precipitated by the seizure in June of John Hancock's ship, *Liberty*. The search for quarters for General Gage's soldiers provoked a good deal of controversy and concern throughout the city. The fleet that carried the troops to Boston from Halifax did include HMS *Launceston*, HMS *Bonetta*, and HMS *Senegal*. I added the *Graystone* for the purposes of this book.

In writing this novel and others in the Thieftaker series, and interweaving my fictional characters and storylines with actual events, I have consulted a number of scholarly sources, as well as documents from the pre-Revolutionary period. A partial list of my sources for this and other Thieftaker books and stories—along with a good deal of other information—can be found at my website: www .dbjackson-author.com.

Acknowledgments

I have a good many people to thank for their help on this novel.

John C. Willis, Ph.D., Professor of United States History at Sewanee, the University of the South, again proved an invaluable resource as I delved into Colonial history, answering questions and steering me toward sources.

Christopher M. McDonough, Ph.D., Professor of Classical Languages at Sewanee, served once more as my Latin translator, turning my odd incantations into spells that sound truly magical. He also shared with me his vast knowledge of Boston and its environs.

Dr. Robert D. Hughes, Professor of Systematic Theology at the School of Theology of the University of the South, has taught me more than I ever thought I might need to know about Anglican clergy in the eighteenth century.

Dr. Richard Archer generously responded to my written questions about the 1768 occupation with an email that was friendly and deeply detailed.

Also a word of thanks to the Norman B. Leventhal Map Center at the Boston Public Library for allowing us to use the map of Boston that appears at the front of the book. I am especially grateful to Catherine T. Wood, the Center's office manager, for locating the map.

As always, any mistakes that remain despite their efforts on my behalf are entirely my own.

My wonderful agent, Lucienne Diver, not only sold the Thieftaker books, she also offered enormously helpful editorial feedback on this novel. The dedication is small thanks for all that she has done for me over our years together. I'm grateful as well to Deirdre Knight, Jia Giles, and the other great people at the Knight Agency.

James Frenkel, my editor at Tor, has edited every book I've ever published. He is not only an insightful and perceptive reader, he is also a terrific friend. Thanks as well to his assistants, Kayla Schwalbe and Gayle Cottrill, each of whom in her turn helped shepherd the project, and his intern, Katherine Busalacchi, for her help.

I'm also deeply grateful to publisher Tom Doherty, Patrick Nielsen Hayden, art director Irene Gallo and her staff, Cassie Ammerman, Leah Withers, Diana Pho, and all the other great people at Tor Books. And I want to thank Terry McGarry; who again did an excellent job copyediting the book.

Deepest thanks to my colleagues at the Magical Words blogsite (magicalwords.net): Faith Hunter, Misty Massey, C. E. Murphy, A. J. Hartley, Carrie Ryan, Kalayna Price, John Hartness, Mindy Klasky, and Diana Pharaoh Francis, and also to Charles Coleman Finlay, Kat Richardson, Blake Charlton, Kate Elliott, Eric Flint, Mary Robinette Kowal, Alethea Kontis, Stephen Leigh, Lynn Flewelling, Joshua Palmatier, Stuart Jaffe, Edmund Schubert, and Patricia Bray, all of whom have helped to shape this series in one way or another through emails, online exchanges, and the occasional conversation over beer.

Finally, I want to thank my wife and daughters, who are the most important people in my life. Their love and laughter are more powerful than any conjuring I've ever written into a book.

About the Author

D. B. JACKSON is the award-winning author of fifteen fantasy novels, many short stories, and the occasional media tie-in. His books have been translated into more than a dozen languages. He has a master's degree and Ph.D. in U.S. history, which have come in handy as he has written the Thieftaker novels and short stories. He and his family live in the mountains of Appalachia.

Visit him at www.dbjackson-author.com.

Turn the page for a preview!

A PLUNDER
OF SOULS

by D. B. Jackson

Available in July 2014
from Tom Doherty Associates

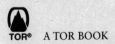

TOR® A TOR BOOK

Chapter
ONE

Boston, Province of Massachusetts Bay,
July 13, 1769

*E*than Kaille knew that he was followed. Like a
fox running before hounds, he sensed Sephira
Pryce's toughs bearing down on him, snarling
like curs, determined to rob him of spoils he had claimed
as his own.

Even as the men closed on him, he himself pursued a
thief who had stolen a pair of ivory-handled dueling pistols from a wealthy attorney in the South End. His quarry,
Peter Salter, led him out along Boston's Neck, the narrow
strip of land that connected the city to the causeway
across Roxbury Flats. British regulars had established a
guard post at the town gate, and so before reaching the
end of the Neck the young thief turned off of Orange
Street to cut across the barren leas that fronted the flats.
Ethan could see the pup ahead of him, wading through
the grasses.

The western horizon still glowed with the dying light
of another sweltering summer day, and a thin haze
shrouded the quarter moon and obscured all but the
brightest stars in a darkening sky. Not a breath of wind
stirred the humid air, heavy with the sour stink of tidal
mud; even with the sun down, the heat remained un-
abated. The city itself seemed to be in the throes of ague.

Ethan's sweat-soaked linen shirt clung to his skin, and his waistcoat, also darkened with sweat, felt leaden. His usual limp grew more pronounced with each step he took, the pain radiating up his leg into his groin. He hoped that the sound of his uneven gait wouldn't alert Salter to his pursuit, or allow Sephira's men to locate him too soon.

If not for the concealment spell Ethan had cast, making himself invisible to all, Sephira's toughs might have spotted him from a distance, and Salter would have needed only to glance back to see him. Still, Pryce's men dogged him, whether directed by his tracks or by Sephira's uncanny knowledge of all that he did, Ethan could not say.

Ahead, the young thief slowed, then halted. He surveyed the ground before him, turning a slow circle. After a few seconds of this he let out a soft cry and strode forward with greater certainty, taking three or four steps before stopping again and dropping to his knees.

Ethan crept after him, placing his feet with the care of a deer hunter, and drawing his blade with a whisper of steel against leather. He could barely see Salter, who was hunched over, no doubt digging up the goods he had stolen. The pup was of average height and build—much like Ethan—but he had a reputation as an accomplished street fighter. If Ethan could avoid a fight he would. He knew, though, that the chances of this were slim.

He continued to ease toward the man, but as he drew within a few yards, his bad foot caught on a clump of grass and he stumbled. He managed not to fall, but at the sound Salter leapt to his feet.

"Who's there?" he called, brandishing a flint-lock pistol.

Ethan cursed under his breath. Since the beginning of the city's occupation by British troops the previous autumn, it seemed that every man in Boston had taken to carrying a firearm. Every man but him. He scanned the ground at his feet and thought he could see a rock or clump of dirt just in front of him. He squatted, wrapped his fist around what turned out to be a stone, and tossed it a few feet to his left.

It rustled the grass and landed with a low *thump*. Salter pivoted with lightning speed and fired off a blind shot. The report of the pistol echoed across the Neck.

Seeing no one there, the pup blinked once and let the hand holding his weapon drop to his side. Before the thief could do more, Ethan launched himself at him, covering the distance between them in three quick strides and driving his shoulder into Salter's gut. As they toppled to the ground, the pup flailed at him, using the butt of his pistol as a cudgel against Ethan's back. But Ethan had the advantage. With Salter pinned to the ground beneath him, he hammered his fist into the man's jaw once, and a second time. A third blow left the pup addled and unable to fight back.

Ethan rolled off of him and flexed his right hand. His knuckles ached. He took Salter's pistol, which lay on the ground beside them, and tossed it beyond the lad's reach. The weapon would have to be reloaded before it could be fired a second time, but Ethan didn't wish to be hit with it again. He picked up his tricorn hat, brushed a bit of dirt off of it and set it back on his head. Seeing that a thin trickle of blood ran from Salter's mouth over his chin, Ethan whispered a spell.

"*Fini velamentum ex cruore evocatum.*" End concealment, conjured from blood.

His spell thrummed in the ground beneath him, deep and resonant, and the air around them sang with power. A ghost appeared beside him, like a flame suddenly igniting atop a candle. The spirit, which glowed with the deep russet hue of a newly risen moon, was the shade of an old warrior, dressed in chain mail, his tabard emblazoned with the leopards of the ancient Plantagenet kings, his expression as hard and cold as a sword blade. Ethan called the ghost Uncle Reg, after his mother's waspish brother, though he didn't know for certain where in his family tree the man would have been located when he lived. So far as Ethan knew, his name wasn't actually Reg, either.

The ghost was a guardian of the power-laden realm be-
tween the world of the living and the domain of the dead.
Without him, Ethan could not conjure. Reg regarded
Ethan with bright, gleaming eyes, appearing annoyed at
having been disturbed from whatever it was he did when
Ethan did not conjure. Seconds later, he faded from view.

As the concealment spell Ethan had cast wore off, Salter
stirred. He squeezed his eyes shut, opened them again. After a few seconds he tried to push himself up, but Ethan
laid the edge of his blade against the pup's throat. Salter
stiffened, his eyes going wide.

"Easy, lad. You wouldn't want my hand to slip."

"Who are you?" the pup asked, staring up at him.

"My name is Ethan Kaille. I was hired by Andrew Ellis
to retrieve the dueling pistols you pinched from his home."

"I didn't—"

Ethan pressed the knife against Salter's neck and
shook his head. "Don't lie to me, lad. I haven't much
time, and I've even less patience."

Salter swallowed.

"You've buried the pistols here, isn't that right?"

The pup hesitated before nodding.

"You intended to sell them tonight? At the Crow's
Nest, perhaps?"

"How did you—?"

"It's not exactly a new approach to thieving."

Salter scowled. "Well, it works for me."

"You mean it has worked, up until now."

The scowl remained on the pup's face, but he said
nothing.

"You're in a bit of trouble, Peter."

"From you?" Salter asked, sounding incredulous despite the knife at his throat.

"Aye, from me. And also from Sephira Pryce. She and
her men are on their way here now."

At that, the thief tried to sit up once more. Ethan
pushed him back down and tapped the edge of his blade
against Salter's throat.

"For now at least," he said, "you still have more to fear from me than from her."

"But if she finds me, she'll kill me."

"She might. I can protect you, but I'll need some help in return."

Salter laughed, high and desperate. "How can you protect me from Pryce? I've yet to meet anyone who's a match for her and her men."

"You'd be surprised," Ethan said. "I've dealt with Sephira for many years, and she hasn't killed me yet." He didn't bother to mention that several years before she had killed one thief Ethan tried to protect, or that just the previous fall, one of her men had slit the throat of another, though Ethan managed to save this second man's life. "Now, listen to me. If we work together, you'll survive the night, and I'll be paid what I'm owed by Mr. Ellis."

"And what about the pistols I pinched?" Salter asked.

"Those have been forfeit from the moment I learned your name."

The pup's mouth twisted sourly. "So, you're a thief-taker, too."

"Aye."

Salter narrowed his eyes. "Where did you come from, Kaille? Tonight, I mean. I didn't see you before; not until I came to."

Ethan glanced toward the spot where Salter had been digging. "What are the pistols in?" he asked. "A box?"

Salter continued to stare at him. "I've heard of your kind," he said, his voice hushed. "You're a witch, aren't you? That's how you crept up on me, and how you managed to knock me down without getting yourself shot."

Conjurers didn't think of themselves as witches. Witch-craft was the stuff of myth and nightmare, a term used by those who possessed no spellmaking abilities to explain powers they didn't understand. Conjuring, on the other hand, was real. Nevertheless, the better part of a century after the tragic executions of twenty men and women in

nearby Salem, so-called witches were still put to death
in the Province of Massachusetts Bay. Ethan had hoped
to finish this encounter without having to admit to
Salter that he was a conjurer—a speller, as his kind were
known in the streets of Boston.

"What are the pistols in, Peter?" he asked, hoping to
change the subject. He should have known that wouldn't
work.

"I'd wager Miss Pryce would be interested to know
that about you. It might be worth some money . . ." He
trailed off, his new-found confidence wilting in the face
of Ethan's laughter.

"She knows, lad. How do you think I've survived as
her rival all these years? How do you think you're going
to survive the night?" He paused, allowing the words to
sink in. "Now, the pistols?"

Salter didn't respond at first, and Ethan had to bite
down on his tongue to keep from hurrying him. A year
ago he wouldn't have feared a confrontation with Sephira.
Yes, she was deadly, not to mention brilliant and beautiful. But he was far from defenseless. He could cut his arm
to draw blood for conjurings, or he could use the grass
growing around them to fuel spell after spell. Sephira's
men were as dangerous with their fists as they were with
blades and pistols, but Ethan's spellmaking was more than
a match for them.

In the past year, however, Sephira had added a conjurer to her retinue of toughs. The man, a Portuguese
spellmaker named Gaspar Mariz, had claimed Ethan as
a friend after Ethan saved his life. But he still worked
for Sephira, and Ethan had no doubt that he would follow any orders she gave him. With a conjurer in Sephira's employ, Ethan's one advantage over the Empress of
the South End was gone.

Ethan heard voices coming from the direction of Orange Street. He gazed into the darkness for a second before facing Salter again. "Now, Peter. The pistols."

"They're in a sack," the thief finally said. "Burlap."

Ethan nodded. "Good. Quickly then, here's what we have to do."

He explained his plan, making every effort to be succinct.

For several moments after he had finished, Salter gaped at him. "That might be the most idiotic thing I've ever heard," the lad said.

"Aye, but it will work."

"All right," Salter said. "Let me up and I'll retrieve the pistols."

Ethan read a different intent in the pup's eyes and tone of voice.

"You do that, lad. And remember as you dig that with my . . . my witchery, I can turn you into a human torch with no more than a thought."

Salter licked his lips and nodded, the defiance Ethan had seen in his eyes vanishing as quickly as it had come.

Ethan removed his knife from the lad's throat and watched, wary and alert, as Salter resumed his digging and retrieved the burlap sack.

Sooner than Ethan would have thought possible, Sephira and her men emerged from the gloaming. She led them, and notwithstanding the dim light, Ethan could see that she looked as lovely as ever. Black curls cascaded down her back and framed a face that was as flawless as it was deceitful. She wore her usual attire: black breeches, a white silk shirt opened at the neck, and a waistcoat that hugged her curves like a zealous lover. Behind her strode Nigel, yellow-haired with a long, horselike face; Nap, dark-eyed, lithe, watchful; Gordon, hulking, ginger-haired, and homely; and Afton, as huge and ugly as Gordon. Mariz brought up the rear, appearing tiny beside the others, a knife poised over his bared forearm should he need to cut himself for a conjuring.

Nigel and Nap held pistols and kept them aimed at Ethan.

"Whatever you're doing, stop it," Sephira said, a note of command in her throaty voice.

Salter darted a nervous gaze Ethan's way.

Sephira halted a few paces short of the hole Salter had managed to dig. "So good to see you again, Ethan."

"I wish I could say the same."

She pouted. "I would have thought you were expecting me. You know how I feel about you working for men as wealthy as Ellis."

"Aye, and you know how little I care."

Her expression hardened and she turned to Salter. "I take it this is our thief?"

The pup said nothing.

"Peter Salter," Ethan said. "He was just digging up the pistols for me."

Sephira's smile was dazzling. "I think you mean to say he was digging them up for me."

Ethan glared at her. "Ellis hired me, Sephira. That may nettle, but it's the truth."

"Yes, and you know as well as I how little that truth is worth. When I return the pistols to him, he won't care who he hired. He'll pay me the balance of your fee—no doubt less than my services would have commanded, but I'm sure a substantial amount nevertheless—and he won't give you a second thought." She reached out her hand toward Salter and nodded toward the mud-stained sack he held. "Give me that."

Salter looked at Ethan again.

Ethan grabbed the sack from him. "These are mine to give to Ellis. And that payment will be mine as well."

"I don't think so," Sephira said, her tone glacial. "Nigel."

Nigel and Nap turned their weapons on Salter. The thief stumbled back a step.

"Give me the pistols, Ethan, or he dies."

Ethan drew his knife once more. Mariz shook his head, his own blade still hovering over his arm.

"Do not try it, Kaille," the conjurer said, the words thick with his accent.

Sephira smiled again. "You see, Ethan? Even your witchery isn't enough to save you anymore." Her expression turned stony. "My patience has limits. Give them to me."

Reluctantly, Ethan stepped forward and handed her the sack, her cool hand brushing his.

"Very good," she purred.

"There's enough grass around us for me to kill every one of you, Sephira," Ethan said, his voice tight. "You've got what you wanted. Now leave."

"Salter—"

Ethan shook his head. "You're not to touch him."

"Ellis won't be happy."

"I don't give a damn."

She smirked. "You're too tenderhearted for your own good. You know that, don't you?"

"Just go," he said.

She continued to eye him, and Ethan wondered if she would make an attempt on the pup's life, or on Ethan's. But at last she nodded once to her men, and started to lead them away.

"My thanks, Ethan," she said, holding up the burlap sack, but not bothering to look back at him. "It's always a pleasure to do business with you."

Ethan didn't deign to answer. He and Salter watched as she and the toughs receded into the darkness. Only when they were beyond hearing did Ethan say, "That was well done, lad."

"What do we do now?" Salter asked. "Before long, she'll look in that sack and realize what you've done."

Ethan retrieved Mr. Ellis's dueling pistols from where they lay in the hole, brushing off the dirt and grass with which he and Salter had covered them in their haste. As an afterthought, he also retrieved Salter's weapon.

"That's mine," the pup said.

"It was." Ethan glanced back to make certain Sephira hadn't decided to come back and kill them both after all. "Sephira is my problem, Peter. You're to leave Boston, never to return."

"But Boston is—"

"Your home," Ethan finished for him. He had heard similar protests from thieves in the past. He preferred to

let them go free when he could. He had spent too many
years as a convict to take lightly the notion of sending a
young man to prison over a few baubles. "Aye, I'm sure
it is," he said. "But you forfeited your right to remain
here when you decided to do your thieving in the home
of a wealthy man. Either you leave, or I'll place you in
the custody of Sheriff Greenleaf. He's likely to be far less
gentle with you than I've been. Or, if you like, I can
leave you to Sephira and her men. As you say, it won't
be long before she realizes that she's carrying your dirt-
filled shoes instead of these ivory-handled pistols."

"Can I go back to my room and gather my things?"
the pup asked. "Can I try to find another pair of shoes?"

"You can. But I assure you, Sephira knows where you
live."

"How? Why? She doesn't know anything about me,
at least she didn't before tonight."

Ethan sympathized with the pup. How many times
had Sephira bested him by somehow knowing his every
movement, his constant whereabouts? "Believe me, I
understand. But she knows now who you are, and your
room will be the first place she looks for you."

Salter's expression curdled. "So, I'm supposed to walk
out of the city and across the causeway wearing nothing
on my feet?"

Ethan grinned. "Be glad I caught you in July rather
than January."

The pup didn't appear to find much humor in this.
nodded toward the pistols. "How much is he payi
you to retrieve those?"

"Three pounds," Ethan said.

"I could have sold them for twice as much. May
more."

"Aye," Ethan said. "I'm sure you could have." Afte
moment's consideration, he tossed Salter's pistol to
lad before turning away and starting the long walk ba
to the home of Andrew Ellis. "But," he called over
shoulder, "they're not yours to sell."